AMISH COZY MYSTERIES: 5 BOOKS-IN-1

THE AMISH WIDOW, HIDDEN, ACCUSED, AMISH REGRETS, AMISH HOUSE OF SECRETS

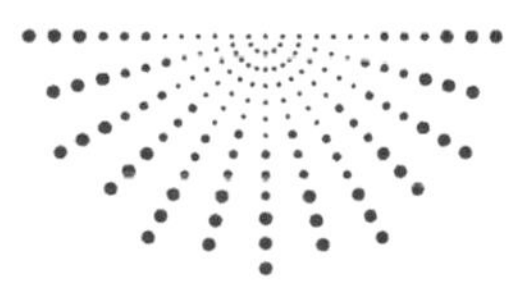

SAMANTHA PRICE

THE AMISH WIDOW

CHAPTER ONE

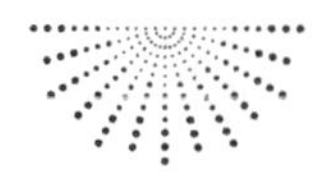

To every thing there is a season, and a time to
every purpose under the heaven:
A time to be born, and a time to die; a time to plant, and a time to
pluck up that which is planted;
Ecclesiastes 3:1-2

"Why did you leave me?"

Emma Kurtzler stared at the body of her late husband. Of course, she didn't expect him to respond, but she felt as if she deserved some kind of answer. Why did he have to die when everything in her life was just the way she had always dreamed it would be?

The rumbling of muffled conversations from the crowd in the next room made Emma aware that her time with Levi was drawing to a close. As was custom in Emma's Amish community, the body laid in the *familye haus* before being taken to the cemetery.

Emma smoothed Levi's hair back with two fingers and touched his hands, which were placed across his chest. "Oh, Levi, you don't even look like you anymore." It was true, the body that lay before her was Levi, but there was a different feeling about him, as if he were someone else. In a way, she wanted to keep him there, right in the house with her forever, but she couldn't – that would be weird.

The noises from the other room distracted her once more. Levi would soon have to go to the cemetery, his body's final resting place. She touched her stomach lightly, knowing there was a chance that there might be a little *boppli* inside. If there were, then she would have a piece of Levi with her forever; she would have someone to love and wouldn't be alone.

"Emma, are you ready for everyone to come in now?"

Emma looked up to see the solidly built, dark-haired Wil, who had been Levi's best friend and constant companion. Levi and Wil were complete opposites, which was most likely the very thing that had drawn them together. Levi had been stable and dependable, whereas Wil was flighty, full of fancy notions and always thinking of grand ideas for new gadgets. Sometimes Emma found Wil funny, at other times tiresome, but on this day she didn't know what she would have done without him.

"Just one more minute, Wil. Just one more minute."

Wil bowed his head and left the room. Emma heard him say something to the crowd in the living room and a hush fell.

"I have to go now. I guess *Gott* wanted you home for some reason." A tear trickled down her cheek and dropped onto the black fabric of Levi's suit. She had made sure that he was dressed in the same suit that he had worn on their wedding day.

With the back of her hand, she wiped the damp from her cheek. "I guess I won't be far behind you. We all have to go sometime, don't we?" At that moment, Emma wished that she had been the one to die. If *Gott* wanted one of them home, couldn't it have been her? Why did He have to take Levi?

Emma put her fingers to her lips and then placed them on Levi's forehead before turning and opening the door for the waiting group of relatives and friends. Some folk smiled at Emma as they filed past to see Levi, while others offered their condolences. After a few minutes in the crowded room her head began to swim.

"You okay, Emma?"

Emma knew it was Wil's voice beside her. "I need some air."

He ushered her through the crowd and out into the open for some fresh air. Once outside, Emma felt much better. She took a little walk along the row of buggies and drew in a deep breath. As she exhaled, she caught sight of her reflection in the window of a buggy. At first, she hardly recognized herself; she seemed much smaller and thinner, her cheeks sunken from too much crying. She studied her reflection and adjusted her white starched prayer *kapp,* reminding herself to put on her black over-bonnet before she headed to the cemetery.

Emma swung around to talk to Wil, who was still standing close by. "*Denke,* Wil, for helping me these last few days. I really don't know what I would've done without you, with my parents not being able to make it here and everything."

"Emma, you don't have to thank me. Levi and I were like *bruders,* so I guess that makes you like my *schweschder.*"

He laughed as he tried to make light of the situation. When Emma remained silent, with no hint of a smile on her face, he added, "I'd do anything for you, Emma, remember that. If you need anything, please ask me, whatever it is."

"Okay, *denke."*

"I mean it, Emma. Look at me."

Emma looked into his deep brown eyes and noticed for the first time how beautiful they were. Not that she would ever – or could ever – be interested in another *mann;* certainly not the very flighty and unstable Wil. She continued to look at him, but he didn't speak. *"Jah,* Wil?"

"I want you to know you can rely on me for anything. House repairs, buggy repairs, anything at all – I'll be there."

Emma dragged her eyes away from him. *"Denke.* I will remember that." It warmed her heart that she lived within such a close-knit community of caring people and wouldn't have to be alone.

Wil looked over her shoulder. "Don't look now, but Elsa-May and Ettie are headed this way."

Elsa-May and Ettie were two elderly sisters, both widows. Up until a few days ago, Emma had not had anything in common with the funny old ladies. Now, she knew the heartache they must have gone through when they lost their husbands. The bonds of loss united them.

"There you are, dear. How are you feeling?" Ettie was the more gentle, soft-spoken of the two, whereas her *schweschder,* Elsa-May, was loud and to the point.

Before Emma had a chance to open her mouth, Elsa-May said, "Oh, Ettie, how do you think she'd be feeling?"

Ettie wrung her hands. "Oh dear – I'm sorry, Emma. I'm always saying the wrong thing."

Emma smiled at Ettie and put a comforting hand on her shoulder. *"Nee.* That's fine. I appreciate your kindness." Emma guessed the two of them to be in their seventies, or perhaps even their eighties.

There were two other widows in the community, Silvie and Maureen, who were much younger. Even though she wasn't close to many people, Maureen was Emma's dearest friend. She was the kind of person that people liked instantly from the moment they saw her. A large woman with a most generous smile, one couldn't help but smile back at her. Her face was round and glowed with an inner radiance, and she had a delightful small gap between her two front teeth. Maureen had been a widow for some time, but her husband had been unwell for many years so his death had not been unexpected.

Like Maureen and Silvie, Emma was childless unless *Gott* showed His kindness – she wouldn't be sure for another couple of weeks.

Emma couldn't even count all the buggies that made up the procession to the cemetery.

Standing by the graveside, Emma looked around her. Everyone was dressed in black. Never in her wildest dreams did she think she would have been widowed so young. She and Levi had barely started their lives together.

The bishop walked forward and cleared his throat. Emma had respectfully asked him to be brief in what he said at the graveside. She didn't think she could take a long, drawn-out sermon and the bishop was extremely fond of long, drawn-out sermons. He had agreed to keep it short.

He preached the usual funeral jargon that Emma had heard so many times before. We all return to the dust of the ground – not very cheerful. Neither was life being likened to a vapor that is here one minute and gone the next. Emma closed her eyes and replaced the bishop's words with Levi's smiling face, happy to be home with the Lord at last; that made Emma feel better. She mentally blocked out the words about the 'dust of the fields' and the 'vapor.'

It was after Levi had been placed in the ground and everyone was returning to their buggies that Wil whispered to Emma, "Who is that *Englischer* standing over there? Do you know him?"

She followed Wil's gaze. Emma had not even noticed the *Englischer.* She stared at the stranger and he stared back before walking toward her. "I don't know him at all, but he's coming this way."

"Looks like you'll soon find out," Wil said.

"Good morning, Mrs. Kurtzler."

Emma nodded hello to the stout man with thinning gray hair. By the look of his suit and the shine on his fine leather shoes, Emma presumed him to be quite wealthy.

"It's likely not a good time, but I'm here to make you an offer for your land," the stranger said.

Wil put his strong arm between the two of them and turned Emma away from the man. "She'll not talk of business today, or of anything like that. Good day to you." Wil steered Emma away.

She glanced over her shoulder at the man to see that he was still looking at her with desperation written all over his face. Emma had just inherited Levi's prime parcel of farming land.

Levi had leased it out to Henry Pluver, an Amish man who also leased other Amish farms, including Wil's.

Once they were a distance away, Wil moved his arm from Emma's back.

"I wonder why he wants the land," Emma mused as she looked around for the Pluver family. Surely they would be at the funeral. She caught sight of the three of them standing together – Mr. and Mrs. Pluver and their only son, Bob. The Pluver family kept to themselves, but Mrs. Pluver seemed a most unhappy woman and their son never spoke to anyone. Bob worked with his father and, as far as Emma knew, he had no friends.

Wil shook his head. "Vultures, nothing but vultures. I'm sorry, Emma. I should have gone over and asked him what he was doing here or who he was."

"You weren't to know. It's not unusual to have *Englischers* at one of our funerals. Levi's boss and the men he worked with are all here; for all you knew, he could've been one of them." Levi had worked for one of the new high-rise building construction companies. Emma had been told that Levi had refused the mandatory safety harness, and a sudden downpour of rain caused him to slip on his footings. Emma was shocked when she'd learned that he had refused the safety harness, as Levi was normally such a stickler for rules.

Wil whispered to Emma, "Is that Levi's boss walking over now?"

Emma turned to face Mr. Weeks.

"I'm so sorry, Emma. Is there anything at all I can do?"

Emma shook her head and Wil butted in, saying, "The community looks after its own."

Emma frowned at Wil, which caused him to look at the ground and take a slight step back. Emma knew that he was only being protective, but Mr. Weeks was just being nice and she considered Wil's actions to be quite rude.

"Do you mind if I visit you at some point in the future?" Mr. Weeks' eyes flickered nervously toward Wil. "To make sure you're okay?"

Normally Emma would have laughed and said she would be fine, but with Wil's outburst just moments before, she felt she had to be extra polite to make up for his rudeness. "That would be lovely. I'll look forward to it."

Mr. Weeks was an older man and Emma guessed that he would have been dashingly handsome in his day. He had good bone structure with dark hair that was graying slightly at the temples. He reached into the breast pocket of his black suit and pulled out a business card. "Here's my number if you should have need of anything before then."

Emma took his card and watched Mr. Weeks walk away. There was something nice and old-worldly about the man.

"It appears I have my work cut out for me."

Emma had forgotten that Wil was standing behind her. She turned and looked into his face. "What?"

"Watching out for you. You haven't even left the graveside and already you have vultures after your farm and elderly men out to capture your heart."

By the way his jaw clenched, Emma knew that Wil was being serious for once. "Wil, you don't have to watch out for me. I'm a grown woman. Besides, I don't think that Mr. Weeks is that old, and he's rather charming." Emma loved to tease Wil whenever she could.

"Emma, Levi's only been gone five minutes – how could you even look at another man?"

Her light-hearted moment was gone, replaced with anger at Wil's response. Surely he should have known she was joking. She wanted to yell at him or tell him to mind his business. Of course she was not entertaining the slightest notion of another man in her life, but she was far too tired to explain herself; besides, why should she? "Wil, I love you like a *bruder*, but today I just can't deal with your nonsense." Emma looked at Wil's waiting buggy and then glanced back at Levi's grave. "Just take me home."

As Wil pulled the buggy away from the cemetery, the man who had asked to buy her land leaped toward the horse and grabbed the reins. The horse had no choice but to come to a complete halt.

"Get away from there, man! What the devil are you doing?" Wil leaped out of the buggy and towered over the man, who meekly offered up his calling card.

"I forgot to give this to the lady. My phone number, in case she changes her mind about selling." He looked directly at Emma. "I'm offering top dollar – I'll pay more than anyone else."

Wil snatched the card from his hands. "Don't ever jump out at another buggy like that again. Do you hear me?"

The man nodded, but it didn't stop him from repeating, "I'll pay more than anyone else." The man backed away, stepping in front of another buggy before scampering off the road.

Emma put her hand over her mouth and stifled a giggle at the man's antics.

"That man is a vulture." Wil threw himself back heavily into the buggy seat and handed her the man's card. "Here, not that you'll ever need it."

"Why not?" She took the card and ran her eyes over the gold script writing.

Wil drove the horse forward and shot a glance at Emma. "You'd never sell, would you?"

"I haven't thought about it." It was true; she hadn't thought about it. There didn't seem to be any reason to sell. Even without Levi's weekly wage coming in, the monthly lease from Henry Pluver was enough to live on. She wouldn't have to go out and work. *Gott* had blessed her in that way – she knew that both Silvie and Maureen had been forced to find work when they lost their husbands.

"I don't want you to leave Levi's farm, but let me know if you ever want to sell and I'll buy it from you."

Emma smiled politely as she mumbled, *"Jah."* She didn't know if Wil could raise enough money to buy the farm. Wil fancied himself as an entrepreneur, with his hands in lots of businesses, but Levi had told her in confidence that they never made him any money. Wil owned the farm next to Emma, but just like Levi had, he leased it out to Henry Pluver to raise wheat crops while he chased income from other sources.

CHAPTER TWO

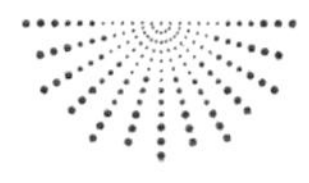

Wealth gotten by vanity shall be diminished:
but he that gathereth by labour shall increase.
Proverbs 13:11

It had been one week since the funeral, and that was all it took – one week for Emma to find out that she was not having a *boppli*. She wondered if her life would get better; if not, she'd rather go home to be with the Lord now than carry on. She was all alone in the big *haus* that Levi had built for them; alone with memories of him and thoughts of what their life might have been.

Still in bed, Emma pulled her robe over her shoulders and watched the rain beat against the window. If Levi were alive, she'd be sipping hot coffee right now instead of trying to keep warm, alone. Levi had brought her coffee in bed every day, as she wasn't a morning person.

Levi was such a dear husband; he was one of a kind. She knew of no other Amish *mann* who looked after their *fraa* as well as Levi had. What other Amish *mann* would cook breakfast for their wife before they left for work? A smile crossed Emma's face. Mostly, it was the women who got up early to look after their men-folk.

Emma had never told anyone how good Levi was to her, just in case she was thought of as a lazy and hopeless *fraa*. She was sure he liked doing things for her – it seemed to make him happy.

What reason did Emma have to get out of bed? She could think of a few – the chickens, along with the other animals, needed feeding. If it weren't for the animals relying on her, she would surely stay in bed all day. As it was, she would stay in bed as long as she possibly could. Surely the animals wouldn't mind getting fed a little later today, seeing that it was raining. She pulled the warmth of her robe tighter around her shoulders and sank back under the covers while she listened to the rain drumming against the windowpane.

The next thing that Emma was aware of was a steady rhythmical pulse. At first she thought it was her heart beating, but quickly realized that someone was pounding on her front door.

"Emma! Emma!"

The voice was Wil's, but what was the urgency? Pulling the robe around her, she made her way down the stairs and opened the door just slightly, so he wouldn't see her in her state of undress. "Wil?"

"Emma, it's Sunday."

Wil's thick, dark hair was windswept and fell about his face. Emma had to stop herself from reaching out to straighten it.

"Oh, is it the second Sunday already?" She hoped she didn't look too much of a fright since she'd just gotten out of bed.

"Jah, it is. Are you coming to the gathering? I don't see your buggy out front."

"Nee – I mean, I want to. Am I late?"

"I'll take you there, to save you hitching your buggy." He glanced at the bathrobe that she was doing her best to hide behind the door. "How long will it take you to get ready?"

"Nee, I don't think I can go – I haven't fed the animals yet." Emma shut her eyes tightly. Why was it so hard to carry on with simple daily chores? Well, it was morning, and she was never *gut* at mornings; maybe she'd be better later in the day.

"You get ready and I'll feed them," Wil offered.

Emma looked up into his face, groggy from still being half-asleep.

"Well? Go on," Wil told her before he turned and strode toward the barn, leaving her staring after him.

She closed the front door and headed up the stairs. Maybe the meeting would take her mind off things. *Jah,* getting out of the *haus* and talking to people would be just what she needed.

~

THE FIRST PERSON who approached her as she got out of the buggy was Maureen. After they exchanged greetings, Maureen said, "Emma, it might be too soon for you, but Silvie and I get together with Ettie and Elsa-May and we have – sort of have – a little group." Maureen's voice lowered. "A widows' group. We don't talk about morbid things, it's not like that. We just get together as a group of friends. Do you think you'd like that?"

"I'd really love to come, *denke.*" Emma wondered why this was the first time she'd heard of Maureen meeting with the other widows. Emma had thought she knew everything about Maureen – apparently she'd been wrong.

"Wednesday night at Elsa-May and Ettie's *haus* then. That's the next time we're meeting."

"Okay, I'll be there."

Wil had already gone ahead toward the crowd, which Emma was thankful for. No doubt he would have something to say about her meeting with the group of widows. *Now, he'd never have to know. It's none of his concern anyway,* Emma thought. Wil had become overprotective of her in the last week, calling in every day and trying to fix things around the *haus,* things that didn't even need fixing. He was like an overbearing older *bruder.*

As was usual at the meetings, Emma sat next to Maureen. The men and women never sat together – it was always men on one side and women on the other. Emma knew now how Maureen must have felt when she'd lost her husband. She had thought she'd understood at the time, but now she really knew what it meant. It was like having part of one's heart ripped out, leaving it bare and exposed. Emma glanced sideways at Maureen and marveled at the fact that she was always smiling.

Maureen caught her eye. "You okay?"

Emma managed a smile and a nod. The right thing to do was to carry on with life and manage the best that she could; there was no other choice.

As if reading Emma's thoughts, Maureen said, "It takes time."

"Jah, that's what everyone keeps telling me." Emma would have to wait and see if they were right. In a way, she didn't want to feel better. Maybe then it would seem like Levi's absence didn't affect her, and it did.

Emma found comfort in the bishop's words as he gave the talk. *Gott's* words always comforted her. Levi and she used to read the Bible together every night after dinner, even if it were just one or two verses. Since Levi had gone, she had not picked up the Bible once.

That night was the first time she'd arrived back home from a gathering without Levi. As if sensing her dread of entering an empty home, Wil said, "Are you going to be all right? Do you want me to stay for a while?"

"Nee, of course not. I'll be fine." Emma pursed her lips together as she realized that had become her stock standard answer for everything – 'I'll be fine.' Maybe if she said it enough times, she might even come to believe it. Emma wanted Wil to stay – she wanted someone to be with her – but she would have to face being alone eventually, and the sooner she got used to it the better off she'd be. She'd already had Wil stay with her through the young peoples' singing rather than go home earlier.

"All right. You know where I am if you need me."

Emma nodded and got out of the buggy. Wil waited until she opened the front door before he turned the buggy around and drove away.

It was dark inside the empty home. Emma promptly turned on the overhead gaslight, which was the one that gave the most illumination.

It had been a nice day and hearing the young people singing had brightened her mood, as had Maureen's invitation.

Emma had grown too used to just having Levi's companionship and had distanced herself somewhat from the women of the community. Now, she knew that had to change.

If she was going to adapt to her new life, she needed to be more outgoing and friendly. She should have more friends, she told herself, rather than just Maureen. Maybe she would find some new friends amongst the widows.

Emma pulled her prayer *kapp* off and sat down on the couch. She unpinned her braid and unraveled it so her hair warmed up her bare neck. Without Levi's companionship, Emma would have to find something else to occupy her days. She needed something to do or she would surely go mad.

Emma's thoughts turned to Wil. He'd been good to her, and she wondered why someone so thoughtful and caring had never married. Casting her mind back, she tried to recall if he had ever courted anyone. She couldn't remember him courting, which she considered odd. He was handsome and had his own farm. Why wouldn't he have a wife by now?

At one time, Levi had mentioned that Wil was waiting until he was financially secure – whatever that meant.

Well, maybe that's it. He's waiting for some reason that only he knows. Emma smiled. *That would be typical of Wil. Sometimes he's in his own little world.*

Emma put the kettle on the stove, deciding that she would have a hot cup of chamomile tea to help her sleep. Maureen had told her that she didn't have a full night's sleep for two months after her husband died.

Would she be better off away from this farm and this house

with all the memories? But the house would still be there, and to have someone else living in the home that she'd once shared with Levi might be worse than staying in it. Maureen had also advised her not to make any major decisions for some time.

She spooned the chopped chamomile flower heads into the muslin pouch and poured the hot water over. As she let the tea steep, she thought of the bishop's words that day.

He spoke on being grateful for everything and giving thanks. Maybe in a few weeks' time she could think of things to be grateful for, but right now it was a little difficult.

Maureen had told her that time would help to heal her heart. Why couldn't she go to sleep and wake up a year later? Maybe by then she would have some happy thoughts.

It was hard not to think of Levi when everything reminded her of him. The very table and chairs where she sat had been made by Levi's *daed*. The china teacup from which she drank was part of a tea set given to her by Levi when she'd agreed to marry him.

At some point, she would have to do something with Levi's clothes. His black Bible was his only possession she would keep. After removing the muslin package from the hot water, she sipped the tea while thinking peaceful thoughts to encourage a *gut* sleep; that's what Maureen had advised her to do.

Half a cup of tea was all that she could manage. As she walked over to the sink to rinse out the teacup, she noticed the two cards that were handed to her on the day of the funeral. She placed the cup in the sink, picked up the cards and sat down.

The first card was Mr. Weeks', and it reminded Emma that

he had said he would visit. The other card was from 'The Vulture,' and she hoped that she would never see him again.

It was rude of him to come to the funeral to ask her to sell her farm. According to the card, the man's name was 'Wiley McAllister.' He had to be the same man who had spoken to Levi about selling the land some time ago – Levi had given him a flat 'no', but that didn't stop the man from asking him again another two times.

Levi had told her that farming land was growing scarce, but he never wanted to sell. She would make sure that she held on to the land for him.

Besides, she reminded herself, it gave her an income. She stretched her hands over her head and yawned.

Hmm, perhaps I might sleep tonight.

With that, she rose from the table, popped the two cards into the top drawer of the kitchen cabinet, and headed up the stairs to her bedroom.

~

THE VERY NEXT DAY, Emma decided it best to pack Levi's things and drive them to Bessy's *haus.* Bessy took the community's unwanted items and distributed them to the various charities about the place.

Emma had five large cardboard boxes that she had collected from the produce store. That ought to fit it all, she thought, fighting back tears as she folded his clothing into the boxes. They might help someone else. She knew she wouldn't feel better with his clothing gone from the bedroom, but it had to be done. She may as well do it now rather than later; she'd only be delaying the heartache for another day.

As she folded clothes, she heard a car outside. Looking out from her bedroom window, she saw Mr. Weeks step out of the vehicle. She threw the black suit jacket that she was holding onto the bed and hurried downstairs.

"Good morning, Mr. Weeks," she said as he stepped onto the porch.

"Good morning. I hope you don't mind me paying you a visit."

"Not at all. Please do come in." Emma stepped aside to let him into the *haus.* "Would you like a cup of tea or coffee?"

"That would be lovely, thank you."

"Sit down, please."

Mr. Weeks took a seat at the kitchen table. "The reason I'm here, besides checking that you're okay, is to tell you that I've put in an insurance claim for your husband's accident."

"I see." Emma busied herself getting the tea and cookies. She knew that *Englischers* drank black tea and she was sure that she had some hiding in the kitchen somewhere.

He continued. "So that means you might get quite a sum of money."

"Oh, that will come in handy." Emma looked across at him.

"Maybe I shouldn't have mentioned it at all." He looked down at his hands, which were clasped on the tabletop.

"Why do you say that?"

"Levi refused his safety harness, so there's only a small chance that the insurance company will pay up. I've lodged the claim anyway. Maybe you could – well, pray about it?"

"I'll certainly do that." Emma knew that *Gott* always worked in mysterious ways, his wonders to perform. Emma wasn't quite sure what that last part meant as it ran through her head – it was part of a Scripture, she was sure of that.

"I don't know why he refused his harness." Mr. Weeks scratched his head.

"He was a very stubborn man and very sure of himself. He'd organized a lot of barn-raisings and did a lot of work at a great height; I guess he thought that he didn't need one." Emma placed the sugar cookies and a pot of tea down on the table. She glanced at Mr. Weeks' worried face. "Surely you don't hold yourself accountable?"

"In a way, I do."

"Nee, please don't. It was his decision, and he wouldn't want you to feel that way."

Mr. Weeks' eyes misted over. Emma hoped he wouldn't cry. She wasn't used to seeing men cry, and she wouldn't know what to do. "*Gott* wanted him home. It was his time to go."

Mr. Weeks nodded.

"He's in a much better place now. I know that in my heart."

"Thank you, Mrs. Kurtzler. You're very kind." Mr. Weeks took a sip of the hot tea then picked up a sugar cookie. "Will you be staying on here – on the farm?"

Why was everyone so interested in whether she was staying on the farm? Was the whole town trying to make her sell? That's certainly what it felt like. "The farm is leased, so it's enough for me to live on. I've no reason to sell." Especially if the insurance money comes through, she thought.

"I see. So you lease the whole farm? To a wheat farmer?"

"We..." She caught herself. "I mean, I lease out all the land except the *haus,* the barn and a little plot where I grow vegetables. Henry Pluver uses it. He's an Amish man who leases a few parcels of land around the area. He's got his own farm too, but I've heard that it isn't very big."

Mr. Weeks scratched his chin. "He's Amish, you say?"

"Yes, he is."

"Pluver is an unusual name."

"I guess it is. Come to think of it, his is the only Pluver family in the community. I'm not sure of their history."

Mr. Weeks looked thoughtful as he nibbled on the sugar cookie. "Are you friendly with the Pluver family?"

"No, not especially." Emma thought about the Pluvers – the sour-faced Mrs. Pluver, the creepy son, Bob, and Mr. Pluver, who was just a typical Amish farmer. "It's certainly good news about the insurance money, if it comes through."

Mr. Weeks held up his hand. "I wouldn't go spending it just yet."

Emma smiled at the thought of going on a spending spree. She was very frugal with money, as was all her *familye.* She'd been taught from a young age to make do with what she had. She could cook and sew and had need of very little. The money would just sit somewhere in case the farm needed something or the *haus* needed repair.

"Emma?" came a voice from the front door.

"Come in and join us, Wil."

Wil walked through to the kitchen. Mr. Weeks stood and nodded his head as a greeting. Wil did the same.

Emma noticed that the two men didn't shake hands. They are probably still at odds with each other over the incident at the funeral. Emma considered that Wil had been rather rude to

Mr. Weeks at the funeral when the older man had only offered her help.

As Wil sat at the table, Emma saw that his face was flushed, and she figured that he must have rushed over when he saw a strange car parked in her driveway.

There was an awkward silence and Mr. Weeks took a large gulp of tea. Wil's hostility towards Mr. Weeks was obvious, and Emma was not the only one who sensed it.

She stood. "I'll fix you some tea, Wil."

"Denke, Emma. So, Mr. Weeks, what brings you here today?"

"I'm visiting Mrs. Kurtzler, as I mentioned I would. I can assure you I have no ill intentions. Levi Kurtzler was a respected member of my team and I'm sure he would want me to see that his wife has everything she needs."

Emma let out the breath that she had been holding onto. She hoped those words would put Wil's overprotectiveness to rest.

"As I told you the other day, we look after our own. I appreciate your visit but I will see that Emma has everything she needs." Wil's tone was bordering on hostile – again.

Emma nearly dropped the teapot she had just picked up. "Wil."

Wil looked at her, stony faced.

Mr. Weeks stood abruptly. "I'll be going now then, Mrs. Kurtzler. Please, you've got my number if you need anything, and we'll discuss that other matter if anything comes of it."

"Yes, thank you. I'll see you out." Emma walked Mr. Weeks to the front door. "I'm so sorry about that," she whispered.

Mr. Weeks shook his head. "Doesn't matter. It didn't bother me." He gave her a smile and a little wink before he turned and walked to his car.

Emma marched straight back to Wil, who had a mouthful of cookie. "Wil, don't you think that was a bit rude?"

"Nee, I don't. There was only one thing he was doing here, Emma. He's attracted to you and you're a woman on your own. You have to be more careful. You can't just let people into the *haus* like that."

Emma folded her arms across her chest and looked down at him as he sat at the table eating cookies. "Well, you're in the *haus* aren't you?"

He shook his head, and his eyes turned to the ceiling. "That's different. You're like my little *schweschder.* We've been friends forever."

So that's what he thinks of me. He doesn't see me as a woman; he sees me as his little schweschder. Emma didn't know why, but she was a little disappointed to know that he thought of her in that way. Although, neither did she want the aggravation of him being attracted to her – it was far too soon for her to consider another man in her life.

Why was she so upset by his words? Maybe she was trying to make up for her loss in some way. She sat down opposite him, picked up a cookie and took a bite. They sat in silence for a moment; the only noise was that of crunching cookies.

"Before Mr. Weeks arrived, I was packing Levi's clothing into boxes."

"Do you need help?"

Emma shrugged her shoulders. She didn't know what she needed. Maybe she wanted help, and maybe she didn't. Maybe she wanted to be alone while she packed up Levi's clothes. "I'm planning to take them over to Bessy's place."

Wil took a mouthful of his tea then placed the teacup down on the table. "I'll take them to Bessy's for you."

"That would be a help. You could carry the boxes down the stairs for me too."

"Of course."

Emma was grateful for his help, but at times he was too much. Sometimes she just wanted some space. Emma's thoughts turned to Bessy. She was around the same age as Wil and she had never married either. For a moment, she wondered if they would make a match, but then Emma dismissed the idea. If they were to make a match they would've had plenty of time to get together before now. But then, who was there for Wil and who was there for Bessy? It dawned on Emma that she should be grateful that she had known real love. It was clear that many of the married people she saw about the place were not happy with their choices, and there was a handful of people in the community who remained unmarried. Levi and she had been happy and very much in love; for that, she was thankful.

A smile flickered across her face. She had found something to be grateful for, just like the bishop had said – and to think, only days ago, she'd thought she had nothing.

CHAPTER THREE

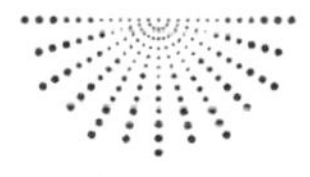

And God shall wipe away all tears from their eyes; and there shall be no more death, neither sorrow, nor crying, neither shall there be any more pain: for the former things are passed away.
Revelation 21:4

Maureen arrived at Emma's house to give her a ride to the widows' meeting. Emma saw her out the window, and hurried to her.

"You've baked?" Maureen asked as she glanced at the plate of food Emma held in her hand.

Emma climbed into the buggy. "*Jah,* I thought I'd bring something with me."

"Well, put it in the back with my lot."

She stretched her arm to put the plate on the back seat next to two larger plates.

"I've baked a couple of things too," Maureen said.

Emma looked across at Maureen and noticed that she looked a little weary. "Are you okay, Maureen?"

"Jah, I'm all right. Just a little tired. I started work early this morning."

Maureen worked at a restaurant, cleaning of a morning and sometimes of an evening. "Not working tonight then, I guess?"

"Nee. Three days a week I work in the evenings, and six days a week in the mornings. It's odd hours, but that makes the pay better."

Maureen was in her late thirties, which was quite a bit older than Emma. She was very confident and sure of herself, except when she spoke of her late husband. It was clear to Emma that Maureen missed her husband dreadfully.

Ten minutes later, they arrived at Ettie and Elsa-May's *haus.* It was a tiny little place and it glowed like a beacon, surrounded as it was by large, dark trees.

"Looks like Silvie's here already," Maureen said as she tipped her head toward the other buggy in the drive. "You go on ahead with the food – I'll just tie up the horse."

Emma struggled with the three plates, but somehow managed to knock on the door.

"Come in, dear. Nice to have you here," Ettie said, letting Emma in.

Elsa-May came up behind Ettie and greeted Emma.

"We brought some cookies and things," Emma said, handing Ettie one of the plates.

"Ahh, denke. We won't say no to food," Elsa-May laughed,

taking the other two plates from her and heading to the kitchen.

Emma hung around the doorway until Maureen came and ushered her into the living room where Silvie sat. There was no couch, which might have been more comfortable – just hard wooden chairs.

The two older widows came into the living room; Elsa-May had knitting in her hands and Ettie had needlework. Elsa-May held up the knitting, which was a soft yellow color. "I'm to be a *grossmammi* again." She offered the information to Emma. It was clear that the other ladies already knew.

"That's so exciting. How many *grosskinner* do you have?"

"I've six others, and this will make seven."

Although Emma smiled, she tried hard not to think of the fact that she had no *kinner* to remind her of Levi, and she would never have any *grosskinner* either.

Ettie leaned slightly forward. "Does that upset you, Emma?"

"Nee, I'm happy for Elsa-May."

The ladies all looked at her – they could see straight into her heart.

Maureen explained. "The group is here so we can tell each other our inner thoughts and feelings. What you tell us will not leave this room."

Emma looked at each lady in turn. They had their eyes fixed upon her. She could see they were all filled with love, united by the bonds of loss. "All right then. If I'm totally honest – I'm upset that I don't have *kinner.* I thought that I might be having a *boppli* and I just found out that I'm not." Tears ran down Emma's cheeks. She could feel her face contort into something ugly, but she didn't care. She cried harder.

Silvie was the closest to Emma, and she put her arms around her. "Let it all out. It's fine to cry."

The other ladies murmured their agreements with Silvie's advice. Emma put her arms around Silvie's graceful, slender neck and cried some more.

Ettie placed her embroidery on the floor and disappeared, returning with a handkerchief.

"Denke," Emma managed to say. After a while, Emma stopped crying and blew her nose. "I'm so sorry." She looked at their concerned faces. "I feel so foolish."

"Nee, don't. We've all been through it. You might find you cry at odd times because you're so used to holding it all in and putting on a brave front," Silvie said.

"Jah, when you feel like crying, it's best to let it out," Maureen added.

"I'll have to get used to hearing that people are having *bopplis,* I suppose, and seeing couples happy. I just don't know why *Gott* had to take Levi now. Couldn't I have had a few more years with him and at least a *boppli* – or maybe two?" Emma asked.

"Who knows the mind of *Gott?"* Elsa-May said.

Ettie added, "No one does. We just have to trust Him; we're not called to understand Him."

"Anything else on your mind, Emma?" Maureen asked.

Emma managed a smile. "Nee, nothing else." She wanted someone else to say something. She felt as if she'd dominated the group with her problems for long enough.

"I longed for a *boppli* as well, Emma. I know how you feel," Maureen said.

Emma acknowledged Maureen's admission and smiled. It

was at least *gut* to know that someone knew the pain that she was going through. "Tell me, does it get easier?"

Maureen smiled, revealing the slight gap between her two front teeth. "Oh, *jah.* It does. I find I have to keep myself busy, though. Busy with lots of things, and working helps as well."

"I find it best not to think about him at all. I got rid of everything he owned, and I put him out of my mind. Every time I think about him I still want to cry," Silvie said, tears in her eyes.

A silence fell over the group. Elsa-May clapped her hands. "Let's eat." She rose to her feet and they all followed her to the kitchen. It appeared that Emma and Maureen were not the only ones who'd brought food. There were chocolate cookies, sugar cookies, cheesecake, chocolate fudge bars, roasted almonds and dried figs.

Ettie asked, "Everyone having meadow tea?"

Everyone said 'yes' to meadow tea with the supper. Emma followed the others' lead and sat at the table in the kitchen. Even though the chairs in the kitchen were wooden as well, they were far more comfortable than the chairs in the living room.

Emma looked around at the ladies and said, "I want to thank everyone for sharing their feelings. It makes me feel so much better. Now I don't feel so alone."

The elderly Ettie put a hand over hers briefly. "That's why we meet."

Emma picked up a chocolate chip cookie and took a bite. Silvie sat opposite Emma. She was quite young to be widowed, and Emma wondered if she had ever considered getting married again. Surely *Gott* would have someone else for her, seeing as she was such a lovely girl and so pretty. Her hair was blonde, her skin creamy and her eyes the bluest of blue that Emma had ever seen. Maureen was also attractive – a little older than Silvie, but still a very handsome woman, and she was wise and intelligent. *Surely Gott could find menner for these women,* she thought. Maybe they are like me and don't want another man.

"Emma, anytime you're feeling sad you can always come visit me. I don't live that far from you," Silvie said.

"Denke, I'll remember that."

Emma knew that Maureen and Silvie had jobs. Maybe that's what she needed. If she had something to do, perhaps it would take her mind off things.

~

THE NEXT DAY, Emma forced herself out of bed and, once she'd fed the animals, threw herself into gardening. Keeping busy was her new way of coping with life without Levi.

"There you are."

Emma looked up when she heard Wil's familiar voice. "Hello. I'm gardening."

"I can see that."

Emma stood up from her crouched position. "I'm all right, Wil. You don't have to visit me every day."

"I'm just making sure you're okay – not being hassled by vultures or anyone else."

"Nee, no one's been around."

"Gut. Well, if you have everything under control, I'll be on my way."

Emma didn't want to rely on Wil. She had to be self-sufficient if she was going to get through these next few months – everyone told her it was going to be tough. *"Denke,* Wil, for everything you've done."

Wil turned to leave. As he walked away he put a hand in the air and gave a wave.

She was comforted by the knowledge that Wil was on the farm next door. If she ever did need anything, he was only a few minutes' walk away.

Emma crouched down again with her garden fork in hand. "Where do all these weeds come from?" she asked herself out loud.

A few moments later, Emma heard a car in the driveway. She stood up and walked around to the front of the house. Rarely did she have a visit from anyone in a car. The vehicle was large and black, and she couldn't see inside as the windows were dark. The driver's-side door opened slowly, and Emma suffered pangs of anxiety when she saw 'The Vulture' emerge from the car.

Emma didn't wish to have to contend with this man again, this man who wouldn't take 'no' for an answer. She glanced up the road hoping that Wil was still around, but she could see no sign of him.

CHAPTER FOUR

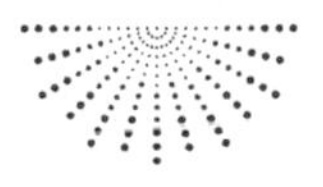

Truly my soul waiteth upon God:
from him cometh my salvation.
He only is my rock and my salvation;
he is my defence; I shall not be greatly moved.
Psalm 62:1

"Mrs. Kurtzler, I hope you don't mind me visiting you."

Emma took a step back toward her *haus.* "I most certainly do. You've been told already that I am not selling. Please leave my property."

He took a step closer to her. "It's a big place for you to manage just by yourself."

Emma folded her arms and held her head up high. "Well, it's

none of your concern. Anyway, I lease it out, so it's all under control."

The Vulture was not going to give up easily. He moved clear of his car and walked toward her. "Mrs. Kurtzler, if you invest the money that I pay you for the farm, I'm sure it will make you a far greater profit than a lease would." He moved another step closer, which left only four feet between them. "What we need to do is sit down and go through the figures."

Emma considered him condescending. He spoke as if she wouldn't know how to manage money just because she was a woman. "Mr... Whatever your name is, it's not all about money. I'm trying very hard to be polite to you, but I don't know how much longer I can do so. Please leave my property now, or I shall call someone and have you removed." Emma lifted up her chin some more and tried to look confident, while secretly wishing she had a telephone installed in the barn like a lot of other Amish folk did. She couldn't call someone even if she wanted to, but The Vulture didn't know that.

"An attractive woman like you shouldn't be out here by herself – you never know what might happen."

A ripple of fear ran down Emma's spine – she was alone, and if this man got nasty she had no defenses. Out of the corner of her eye she spied the gardening fork. If he got violent, she would be forced to use it to defend herself. "Leave my property now."

"I'm just trying to be helpful. What I'm offering you is a good deal."

"Please go." Maybe she was too polite; she tried again, a little louder. "Just get in your car and go." She glared into his eyes.

He turned and walked back to his car slowly. Once he'd

opened its door, he said, "My office is above the post office if you change your mind."

Emma stared him down as he got in his car and drove away. She threw her head back, let out a groan and then went inside, careful to lock the door after herself. Sitting at the kitchen table, she tried to calm herself down. A cup of tea is what I need, Emma thought. Once she had relaxed a little, she put the kettle on the stove. *Should I tell Wil that The Vulture came to the haus? Nee, he's already concerned enough; I don't want him coming over twice a day to watch me. Once is plenty.*

In the back of Emma's mind, she wondered why Wil was so fast to get to her place when he saw Mr. Weeks' car, but he'd done nothing to rescue her when The Vulture appeared. Surely The Vulture's car would have passed Wil on his way home.

While she drank the hot chamomile tea, she decided to go into town and get some needlework. That would give her something with which to occupy herself. She also considered getting some sort of a weapon, something a little better than a gardening fork. Was The Vulture threatening her, talking about her being all alone, or just trying to scare her? She wasn't sure. Maybe she would look around the barn and see what she could use to defend herself.

Emma hitched the buggy for her trip into town and then had a look around the barn for a weapon of self-defense. The best she could find were a pitchfork and a spade. She put them both in the back of the buggy just in case she had any trouble on the journey to town and back.

The wool and craft shop was more crowded than Emma had ever seen it. It was as if everyone had decided to go there that day. She spotted her friend Maureen at the back of the shop. "Maureen."

"Hello, Emma. I was going to visit you later today."

"Please still come. I'd love it if you did." Seeing Maureen's smiling face always made Emma happy.

"I'll come see you in a couple of hours, if you'll be home by then."

"I'll be home. I just came here to get something to sew." Emma held a couple of things that she had chosen in the air. "Trying to keep busy and all."

Maureen smiled, revealing the familiar gap in her front teeth as she did so.

Before long, a queue formed in the shop as people waited to pay for their goods. Maureen was first in the queue; she paid for her things and left. Emma was five back from the register. The next person to be served was taking a long time, and Emma wondered whether the sales assistant was having a gossip session instead of serving the woman.

Emma impatiently shifted her weight from one foot to another, and then glanced out the window. Across the road, she saw Wil, but who was the man he was talking to? She looked a little harder and saw that the man Wil was speaking to was The Vulture.

"Next," the sales assistant shouted.

Emma looked around, but she was still three from being served. She turned again to study the two men. They were speaking to each other in a civil manner, as though they were friends. Emma frowned. *That can't be right – why would Wil be talking to that horrid man? They certainly look to be friendly, but Wil was so rude to him at the funeral. Why is he being nice to him now?*

"Next."

Emma looked up to see the bored sales assistant waiting for her to bring her items to the counter.

Once she paid for the goods and was ready to leave the shop, Emma looked out the window again, but the two men had gone. She stepped out of the store and looked both ways up the street, but there was still no sign of either man. Confused and upset at what she'd seen, she hurried back to her buggy. She passed the post office and remembered the terrible man saying his office was located above it. She stopped and stepped through the doorway that led to the upstairs offices. Ah, there it was: 'McAllister Realtor.' I just don't like the way the man conducts business by harassing people. She stepped back out onto the pavement.

What she needed was something to make herself feel better, and she knew just the thing. Nearly every time Emma came to town, she stopped at the specialty chocolate shop. The hand-made chocolate tasted so much better than regular store-bought candy. Emma had once tried to make her own at home, but nothing compared to the chocolate from the little store that she had found in town. She felt that she deserved a little indulgence every now and again.

After she paid for her favorite soft-centers, she decided to buy a cake for Maureen's visit. The next store she came to was a café with a bakery attached, and she wondered if she might buy a few cookies as well. Before Emma got to the front door, she happened to glance through one of the two full-length windows. It was through one of those windows that Emma saw an odd sight: Wil and The Vulture were sitting together having lunch, and they were laughing as though they were old friends.

Nee, surely not – that can't be The Vulture I see with Wil. Emma looked harder, and her first sighting was confirmed; indeed, it was the horrid little man himself. Emma continued walking past the café window, hoping that neither man would see her.

Emma strode on, quite forgetting the idea of cakes or cookies. She climbed into the buggy and drove her horse toward home.

Usually, the clip-clop of the horse's hooves soothed whatever disagreeable mood she might be in, but today her nerves were shattered beyond repair. She couldn't shake the sight of the two men talking amicably. What on earth would they have to laugh and chat about? A few days earlier, Emma had concerns of Wil's rudeness to the man, and now they appeared to be the best of friends. It didn't make sense. Emma forced the two men out of her mind and concentrated on Maureen's visit.

After Emma put the buggy away and tended to the horse, she walked out of the barn to see a gray buggy heading towards the house. She recognized it as belonging to Henry Pluver.

Emma met the buggy and noticed that Bob, Henry Pluver's adult son, was also there. Emma always felt uneasy around Bob, and Levi had told her never to let him around the *haus* if she was there by herself. Bob never talked to anyone and that unnerved many people.

"I'm sorry to hear what happened to your husband," Henry said.

"Denke."

He would only be there to discuss the lease; Emma knew that for sure and for certain. She and Levi weren't close with the Pluvers even though they were in the same community. They might not have spoken at all if it weren't for the lease.

"My lawyer said that the lease is fine and can carry on as is." Well, what her lawyer had actually said was that as long as Mr. Pluver was happy to carry on as usual the lease would suffice, but since the lease was in Levi's name as well as her own, it did give Pluver an 'out' if he wanted one.

He avoided eye contact with her as much as possible when he said, "That's why I'm here. I can't carry on with the leasing of your property."

Another blow, Emma thought. It had never occurred to her that Pluver would want to stop leasing her land. That was how he derived his income, after all. What would she do now? With no money coming in, she would surely be forced to sell the farm unless she could find someone else to lease it quickly.

"Why is that? You've been leasing the land for years."

"The business is going in another direction. Anyway, I will pay you until the end of the month and that's all."

Emma felt the weight of the generations of Levi's ancestors who'd worked the farm fall heavily on her shoulders. "What prompted your decision?"

"The business is going in a different direction," he said again.

That told Emma absolutely nothing. "Is there a chance you'll change your mind?"

Bob stood beside his father, never looking at her or speaking to her once. Mr. Pluver said, "Nee, everything's set in place. I'm sorry to do it at a time like this."

Emma nodded, and Henry and Bob wasted no time in getting into their buggy and driving away.

What would she do now? She didn't even have Levi to talk things over with. She was on her own and about to lose her husband's legacy. She wondered what else could go wrong. Emma walked back to the buggy, took out the pitchfork and the spade, and placed them in the utility room of her kitchen. She was not going to be without some self-defense in her *haus* tonight. She might even keep one of the objects under her bed. Bob Pluver sent shivers up and down her spine, and so did McAllister, The Vulture.

~

HALF AN HOUR LATER, Emma was pleased to see Maureen's happy face at her door.

"So, how are you handling everything? It can't be easy with Levi gone."

Emma inhaled deeply. "I'm glad I went to Elsa-May and Ettie's place. I think I've found new friends in them, and Silvie, of course."

Maureen remained silent and sipped her tea. "John, my *bruder,* can come help if you need anything done around the place."

"Denke, Maureen, but Wil's only next door. He comes over nearly every day to make sure everything's okay."

Maureen raised her eyebrows. "Does he?"

"Stop it, Maureen. Don't say it like there's something going on."

Maureen pursed her lips and leaned toward Emma. "I've always thought that he had feelings for you. I wouldn't be surprised if he's never married because he's in love with you."

"What? Don't be ridiculous. He's always been Levi's best

friend and nothing more." The situation with The Vulture and Wil kept playing on Emma's mind. "Oh, I've had a dreadful day."

"Why, what's happened?"

Emma swallowed hard and braced herself to speak. "Did you see a small, balding *Englisch* man at the funeral?"

Maureen put her elbow onto the table and cradled her full face in the palm of her hand. "There were a few *Englischers.* Do you mean the one that John and I nearly ran over in the buggy?"

Emma recalled the scene of The Vulture nearly being trampled by a horse as he backed away from Wil. "Oh, was that your buggy?"

"Jah, we saw he'd grabbed onto Wil's horse. Who is he?"

Emma pushed her lips out. It was hard for her to talk about the farm. "He wants me to sell the farm to him."

"Nee. And he asked you at the funeral?"

Emma nodded.

Maureen's green eyes flashed. "You wouldn't sell, would you?"

"Nee. I mean, I had no reason to sell until today. Henry Pluver just came and told me he wouldn't be leasing the farm any longer. Anyway, that's not all I was going to tell you."

"What else?"

"At the funeral, Wil scolded the man and told him to leave me alone, but today when we were at the craft store I saw them across the road. They were speaking to each other, looking very friendly."

Maureen frowned and pouted her lips out in an exaggerated manner.

Emma continued, "Then later, I saw them together in a

coffee shop, having lunch. What do you think of that? They were speaking as if they were great friends."

Maureen placed her teacup back on the table and then nibbled on a cookie. "It's quite clear actually. It would appear that the two of them are in cahoots."

"Ca-what?"

"You know, in it together. Either they are trying to buy your property together or the short man has paid Wil to encourage you to sell – like a spotter's fee or something. There could be a number of scenarios."

"Nee, Wil would never do anything like that."

Maureen completely ignored Emma's comment. "Or maybe Wil wants to purchase the land and he's instructed the short man to act as his agent so you won't know it's really Wil buying it."

Emma considered what Maureen had said. "Nee, I can't see that any of those things are possible. Wil wouldn't deceive me. What reason would he have for doing that?"

"Think about it, Emma. You've a large piece of prime farmland and it joins on to Wil's property. They'd both be worth a heck of a lot more together than they would as two single farms."

Emma looked at Maureen's beady eyes. "Would they?"

Maureen nodded enthusiastically. "It's too much of a coincidence that Pluver has pulled the plug on the lease now, too. Someone's trying to force you off your land."

A chill ran down Emma's spine. She would definitely take the pitchfork up to her bedroom with her tonight. Emma recalled how Wil was always looking for opportunities to make money, but would he really try to use her to make his fortune – the widow of his best friend? She hoped it was not true.

"You were in the same friendship group as Wil and Levi growing up, weren't you?" Emma had not grown up in the area – she had met Levi at her cousin's wedding and stayed on to marry him, leaving her family and friends a hundred miles away. Although Emma had not grown up in their community, Maureen had.

"*Jah,* I was."

"Wil was trustworthy then, wasn't he?"

"*Jah,* I thought he was trustworthy, but people can change. There's something funny going on with your farm, I just know it. If something smells like a snake, it usually is a snake."

Emma nodded as she wondered what snakes smelled like.

"Oh, golly. I promised John and his *fraa* that I'd visit them for dinner. Anyway, you should tell the group about this next time we meet. They're very good at figuring things out."

"Really? I might do that. *Denke* for visiting me, Maureen." Emma rose to her feet to walk Maureen out to her buggy. "You brightened up my day."

"Come and visit me. And watch out who you trust, it sounds like someone really wants your farm."

"I will. I will on both counts – I will visit you, and I will watch who I trust."

Emma closed her front door and bolted it. She never bothered much with locks – even when she went to the stores or the gatherings she rarely locked her doors – but today she didn't feel safe. Could she trust Wil? Yesterday she would have trusted him with her life, but today she was not so certain. Her once-perfect world seemed to be growing less-so every minute. Since Levi had died, things seemed to get worse every single day.

She wouldn't cook dinner tonight; she was not the slightest bit hungry. Emma pulled out the embroidery and chocolate she'd bought earlier and sat on the couch. Although she wasn't hungry, the chocolate should sooth the sore throat she felt coming on. Emma got a sore throat every time the seasons changed. Chocolate was the only answer, and she had a lot to get through. She pulled a rug over her knees to make herself cozy.

I'll make a start on this sampler to keep myself busy. I wonder if I should ask Wil why he was talking to that man. Nee, I'll just wait and see if he says anything to me. At least she knew she wouldn't have to wait long – Wil would visit again tomorrow, just as he did every day.

Emma popped her feet up on the coffee table, smoothed out the fluffy blanket, and placed a soft-center strawberry chocolate into her mouth. As the chocolate melted away on her tongue, she concentrated hard on the embroidery so she wouldn't have to think about Wil and what possible reason he could have for speaking to The Vulture.

~

AT THE NEXT WIDOWS' meeting on the Wednesday night, Maureen encouraged Emma to tell the ladies what had gone on with Wil, The Vulture, and Pluver.

After Emma had explained the whole thing, with a little emphasis on certain points from Maureen, Emma asked the group, "So what do you all think of that?"

As usual, Elsa-May was the first to speak. "Something stinks. Someone's out to diddle you, girl."

"You think so? But even if they did buy the land, I would make sure that I got a fair price. How would they diddle me?" Emma asked.

"Well, dear, perhaps they think that you don't want to sell, so they have to find devious means to get what they want. They may not diddle you financially, but they may diddle you to encourage you to sell when you don't want to." Ettie was soft-spoken, and Emma had to make a special effort to hear what she said.

The other ladies made murmurs of agreement.

"What should I do? I kind of don't feel safe with The Vulture coming to the *haus* and all, and now I'm worried about Wil." Emma chewed on the end of her fingernail.

"More tea?" Ettie picked up the fine china teapot.

Emma nodded and held the teacup toward Ettie, hoping Ettie wouldn't spill the boiling tea on her with her shaky hands. "*Denke,* Ettie."

While Ettie filled everyone's nearly empty cups, Silvie said to the group, "What should we do about it? How will we get to the bottom of things?"

Elsa-May's eyes narrowed. "You, Silvie, will go and pay The Vulture a visit and pretend that you want to buy land in the area."

Emma turned to look at Silvie thinking she would be horrified with the idea.

Instead, Silvie nodded enthusiastically. "*Jah,* and I'll say my husband and I want to buy it, so he might believe it a bit more."

Ettie added, "Wear makeup so you'll look pretty, and be sure to make eyes at him."

Emma gasped at Ettie's words. Ettie was normally so quiet and proper.

When Ettie noticed the look on Emma's face, she said, "That means to flirt with him."

"I know what it means. I'm shocked that you'd encourage Silvie to flirt," Emma said.

"It'll help her get information, Emma," Elsa-May said.

Silvie held her chin up high. "I know what to do."

Emma swung around from looking open-mouthed at Ettie, to look open-mouthed at sweet, little, blonde-haired Silvie. Was she really going to go against the *Ordnung* to wear makeup – and flirt? "Should we go against the *Ordnung?"* Emma felt in her heart she would be just as guilty if she let Silvie go ahead with the plan.

Elsa-May's loud voice boomed, "Would *Gott* want you to be homeless with no place to lay your head?"

"Nee, but He does say in the Bible that vengeance is His," Emma pointed out.

"Humph." Elsa-May stuck her bottom jaw out as she said, *"Gott* gave us a brain so we could use it."

"We're using a little more than our brain here, though," Emma said. "We're using our womanly ways – would *Gott* approve of that?"

Everyone's attention was now on Emma.

"We just want to help you, Emma, that's all," Maureen told her.

"Jah. You're one of us now," Silvie said.

"Gott put you in this group with us for a reason," Elsa-May

said. "Besides, the *Ordnung* changes all the time. The bishop's allowing some people tractors now, and others can have computers for their businesses. Think of it like this: we're just ahead of our time, and *Gott* is not constrained by time; He is eternal."

Ettie chimed in, "She's right, Emma, and we're not hurting anyone; we're just trying to protect you."

The others nodded and continued looking at Emma. She could feel everyone's love and concern. Being protected was just what she needed right now – visions of her pitchfork and spade came to mind. "All right then. *Denke.* I didn't mean to sound ungrateful. I'm very thankful that you all want to help."

"Okay, we'll call it 'Operation Vulture Takedown'," Elsa-May said as she pulled out a yellow notepad and began to write.

Silvie giggled while Emma wondered what she had just agreed to.

CHAPTER FIVE

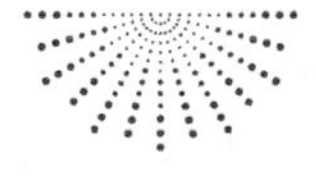

And he said unto me, My grace is sufficient for thee: for my strength is made perfect in weakness. Most gladly therefore will I rather glory in my infirmities, that the power of Christ may rest upon me.
2 Corinthians 12:9

'Operation Vulture Takedown' was to begin tomorrow, according to the plan on Elsa-May's notepad. The first step was for Silvie to visit The Vulture's office, flirt a little and see what she could find out.

Emma stepped out of Maureen's buggy and thanked her for driving her to Elsa-May and Ettie's *haus* for the widows' meeting. Emma was grateful to have some new friends who cared about what happened to her and her farmland.

She stood on her doorstep and waved goodbye to Maureen as the buggy trotted up the driveway. She was glad to be home

– while she was lonely sometimes, at least it was a place where she felt safe.

Although she was happy to be back at the farm, it was late at night and Emma hated coming home to a cold, dark *haus*. Next time she would leave a light on. She turned on the gas lantern just inside the front door followed by the main gas light in the center of the living room.

In the kitchen, she boiled some water so she could take a hot water bottle to bed with her. Maybe she would also sip some lemon tea. Emma didn't think she'd fall asleep; normally she found it hard enough, but tonight, with all the surprises at the widows' meeting, she was sure that she'd be awake for many hours yet.

Emma had passed Wil's *haus* on the way back in Maureen's buggy, and saw that it was cloaked in darkness. Never being out this late, Emma didn't know if that was unusual for him or not. Farmers usually go to bed early, but Wil was not a farmer and Emma was not really sure how he made his money. Maybe he lived on the lease money from his farm as she did.

She filled up her hot water bottle and waited for the iron kettle to boil once more for her lemon tea. Emma hugged the hot water bottle as she waited. What would Levi think of all this intrigue? He would be glad I've made some new friends, I guess.

With lemon tea in hand and hugging her hot water bottle, Emma made her way up the stairs to her bedroom. She set the tea on her nightstand, placed the hot water bottle in the bed and went back downstairs to fetch her weapons. She remembered she had a hammer in the utility room – that would save her carrying the big pitchfork upstairs. Emma found the hammer, carried it back to her room and placed it under her bed. She sent up a quick prayer to *Gott* asking Him to protect her through the night.

Emma was conscious of the space on the other side of her bed – that which had once been filled now lay empty. She still kept to her half of the bed even though she could have slept in the middle. Somehow it felt right to stay sleeping on the same side. While she sat drinking the tea, she moved the hot water bottle a little further under the blankets.

How did Maureen and Silvie cope, living alone? They still lived in the houses they'd lived in with their husbands and they seemed to manage all right. Maureen had her *bruder* to help her with things, but Emma was not sure who helped Silvie.

~

THAT NIGHT, Emma had a troubled sleep. Every time she nodded off, she woke after only a few minutes. She'd tossed and turned due to the bad dream that The Vulture was chasing her away from her *haus* and she couldn't find her hammer. Emma woke with her heart racing and her body covered in sweat.

She sat up in bed and noticed the teacup on the floor, realizing that she'd left half a cup of tea in it from the night before which was now spilled all over the floor. She must have knocked it over in her sleep. Emma slumped back under the covers. Somehow she felt safer in the daylight, and she managed to drag herself out of bed.

Elsa-May's plan was that they would all meet at her *haus* again at three o'clock. Hopefully by then Silvie would have gleaned some information from Mr. McAllister, The Vulture.

As Emma made herself breakfast, she looked down at the floorboards. They needed cleaning, as did the rest of the *haus.* It had been sorely neglected since Levi had gone. She decided that she would spend the first part of the day cleaning the *haus,* starting with the kitchen.

On hearing a buggy approach, Emma dried her hands and went to the front door. It was Wil, which surprised her – he usually walked to visit since he lived so close.

"Hello, Wil."

"I'm just on my way into town. Do you need anything?"

"Nee." Emma had to stop herself from saying that she had been there yesterday. *"Nee, denke.* I'm stocked up with all I'll need for a while."

Wil got out of his buggy and walked toward her. "Well, why don't you come somewhere with me?"

Emma looked up at the handsome Wil. If she were ready for another man, she would have been delighted to be asked to go somewhere with him. But as it was, the timing was totally off. "Why?"

"It's not *gut* for you to stay in the *haus* by yourself all the time."

"I visited yesterday; I had dinner last night at Elsa-May and Ettie's. I have been out."

Wil laughed. "You had dinner with Elsa-May and Ettie?"

"What's so funny?"

"Nothing at all. They are a funny pair and make me laugh, that's all. I'm not being disrespectful."

Emma knew what he meant. They were a couple of funny old dears.

He touched her shoulder lightly. "Come on Emma – come

on a picnic with me."

Emma hoped that Wil was not starting to like her as more than a friend. It was far too soon for her to entertain thoughts of another *mann*. Surely he can't be interested in me; nee, surely not, but he has been over here an awful lot. Maybe it's just because he was such a *gut* friend of Levi's he thinks he has to keep an eye on me, Emma thought. "I can't, I've got to..."

"Got to what?" Wil smiled widely and laid his hands casually on his hips.

"Clean the *haus*. It's in a dreadful state."

"A day will make no difference at all. Do it tomorrow. Let's go on a picnic."

Emma shook her head. "It wouldn't look right if someone saw us out together. I mean, if someone saw me enjoying myself." *Whoops, I've just admitted that I would enjoy myself with him. I hope he didn't notice what I said.*

"Just because Levi died doesn't mean you have to lock yourself up forever. Levi wouldn't have wanted that. He would want you to be happy. How about a compromise?"

Emma raised her eyebrows. She was beginning to like the sound of leaving the cleaning until the next day, but she had to be at Elsa-May's at three o'clock; after all, that's what the plan was, and she was not about to go against the plan.

"How about we go somewhere we won't be seen? That way we won't be gossiped about," Wil said, in a half mocking tone.

Emma was wavering; maybe she would enjoy a picnic. "I'd have to be back well before three."

"We can do that easily."

Emma thought of the floorboards. They didn't look that

poorly – maybe another day wouldn't matter. "Don't you have to go into town, Wil?"

"I can do that later, or do it tomorrow. You stay right here and I'll pick you up in ten minutes. I'll go home and pack us a hamper."

"Okay, I'll bring some cheesecake."

Ten minutes would be enough time for Emma to sweep the floor and stave off her guilt for not giving it and the rest of the *haus* a thorough cleaning.

Emma wondered whether she was doing the right thing. Maybe she should've put the picnic off until tomorrow, and that way she would have had more information about the whole Vulture situation. Now, she'd have to hold her tongue about seeing Wil speaking to McAllister.

Half an hour later, they sat on a grassy hill overlooking a meadow. Emma considered that if she had been there with Levi it would have been very romantic. She had met Wil briefly before she had met Levi and they had gotten on very well together, but then Levi burst onto the scene and swept her off her feet. The bishop's wife, Mary, had once told her in confidence that Emma was the only girl that Wil had ever been interested in, but by then she was betrothed to Levi, and happily so.

"So what is it that you do for a living anyway, Wil? I've never really known."

Wil took a mouthful of cider and as he placed the glass back on the blanket, he said, "Quite a few things. It's too hard to explain."

"Because I'm a woman?"

Wil smiled and looked at Emma. "Nee, I didn't mean that."

Emma loved the way that Wil smiled, but she had to fight her attraction to him. It was far too soon to let herself think loving thoughts toward him. "I don't see why it would be hard to explain what you do." Normally Emma wouldn't push a point so far, but she had to find out what was going on. Why was he trying to hide what he did for his money?

"I lease the farm to Henry Pluver, as you know, and apart from that I have a few investments. Nothing to speak of, really. Then I have the inventions I work on."

Emma didn't know what more she could ask without him getting suspicious.

After talking and eating a lot of food, Emma was no closer to finding out why Wil had been speaking with Mr. McAllister. Maybe she should just ask him straight out. Is he behind all this fuss of someone trying to force me off my land? Anyway, what was the purpose of this picnic? Maybe he's keen on me. That must be the answer. If what the bishop's wife said was true, maybe with Levi gone he wants to court me. But surely he would wait a respectable amount of time and not rush things, she thought.

"We'd better get you home." Wil stood up and held out his hand. Emma looked at his powerful outstretched arm. Of course she wanted to be held in those strong arms of his. Was it loneliness that led her to want to be held in a *mann's* arms once more, to feel them around her waist? She had always felt safe when Levi put his arms around her. Maybe she just longed for that feeling of safety once more.

She put her hand in his, and he helped her to her feet. She stumbled a little as the leg she had been sitting on had gone to sleep. He reached an arm behind her back and caught her. She could have easily pulled away, but instead she looked up into his deep brown eyes and saw his gaze slowly move to her mouth before he pulled himself away.

"I'm sorry, Emma. I... Are you all right?"

"My leg's gone to sleep."

"Sit for a while with your leg outstretched while I pack the buggy." He helped her sit back down on the blanket.

Emma sat looking out over the fields. She was upset with herself that she was not the one to pull away first. What would Levi have thought of her? He had only just gone and she was already craving another man's touch.

Even though she was mad with herself, she couldn't stop wondering what would have happened if she pressed her body into him and touched her lips to his. She remembered that Levi once joked that Wil never married because he was in love with her. Surely he was just teasing, but that, coupled with what the bishop's *fraa* had told her years ago, gave Emma something to think about.

Maybe he'd had a little crush on her a long time ago, but even if Wil was in love with her, he was not the kind of man to move in so quickly after his best friend's departure. That led her to another thought – if he had her best interests at heart, surely he wouldn't be deceiving her regarding her property. For all the time she had spent with Wil today, she was none the wiser of his motives regarding his possible interest in her or his talking to McAllister.

Once Wil had finished packing the buggy, he returned to crouch beside her. "Better now?"

Emma moved her leg. "*Jah,* better."

"Well, bring the blanket and let's go."

Ah, Emma thought, he's not going to risk giving me his hand. He does not want to be close to me again. Emma bundled up the blanket and placed it in the back of Wil's buggy. All the way back to her place, she contemplated asking him about The Vulture, but thought she was best to discuss it with the widows' society before she did or said anything.

As they drew closer to Emma's home, she saw three buggies pulling away from her drive. Emma was immediately worried, but tried not to act like it in front of Wil. "Looks like I've had visitors."

There was one buggy in her driveway when she pulled up. As soon as Emma saw the distinctive brown and white markings of the bishop's horse, she knew she could relax. The bishop's wife, Mary, was standing on her porch.

Wil stopped the buggy and Emma walked toward Mary. "Mary, it's nice of you to visit."

"I was just going. A few of the ladies have given your *haus* a *gut* cleaning and we've got a week's worth of food for you." She took Emma's hand. "You won't have to do anything for a whole week." She pulled Emma forward and gave her a kiss that she always gave people, calling it a 'holy kiss.'

Emma turned to look at Wil, who was still in his buggy. "You knew about this?"

"Of course. I was instructed to get you away from here for a few hours."

She turned back to Mary. *"Denke* so much, and thank the other ladies. This is just *wunderbaar."*

"I'll be on my way, then." Mary bustled over to her buggy.

"I'll go too, Emma." Wil tipped his hat and drove back up the driveway.

Emma felt a little foolish for thinking that Wil liked her, and that was the reason he had invited her on a picnic. Wil was simply getting her out of the *haus* so the ladies could surprise her. What a fool she would have been if she had leaned into his hard body, thinking that he was keen on her. She would have to be more careful in the future. Missing Levi's strong arms around her had left her vulnerable to another man's touch. She wouldn't let that happen again.

Emma pushed her front door open, realizing she must have left the door unlocked. She couldn't do that again, not with The Vulture hanging around, but was certainly nice to come home to a clean *haus.* Emma put her hand to her mouth and giggled as she wondered if any of the ladies had seen the hammer under her bed.

Emma looked around at her spotless home, thankful that she had run the broom over the floor before she left, otherwise what would the women have thought of her housekeeping skills?

CHAPTER SIX

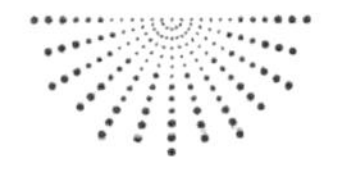

While the earth remaineth, seedtime and harvest,
and cold and heat, and summer and winter,
and day and night shall not cease.
Genesis 8:22

On the dot of three, Emma pulled up to Elsa-May and Ettie's *haus* as arranged. Maureen was already there, and they all had to wait fifteen minutes for Silvie to arrive.

"Sorry I'm late," Silvie said.

"Come in." Elsa-May pulled on Silvie's arm and hurried her to the chairs where the other ladies waited eagerly.

Silvie looked very pretty with the subtle makeup. Her face didn't look painted; her skin looked smooth, her lips very glossy and a little darker than normal. Her normally pale lashes were dark and very long, which accentuated her beautiful, clear blue eyes.

"Well, I asked Mr. McAllister if he had a farm for sale. He showed me brochures of farm land and I said that I wanted land close – in a ten minute radius – by buggy."

"Go on," Ettie said as she sat on the edge of the old timber chair.

"He said he could have a very large piece of land coming up, but he already had a buyer for it."

Ettie gasped and covered her mouth. "Emma, he already has a buyer for your land."

"It could be Wil," Maureen said.

Emma lowered her head and rested it in her hands.

Elsa-May lifted up her hands to quiet everybody. "We can't be sure, though. This is all hearsay."

Ettie nodded. "Quite right. What else, Silvie?"

"He stepped out of the office to take a phone call in private. So I dashed to the front of his desk and looked in his top drawer and found this." Silvie opened her palm to reveal a key. On the key was a tag, which said, 'Spare Office Key.'

Elsa-May clapped her hands. "Well done, Silvie, well done."

Emma stared at the key in disbelief. "What can we do with that?"

Elsa-May pointed at her. "You, Emma, will go there tonight – no, not tonight. Friday night. You will go into his office and look through his files, his messages – anything you can find until you know what's going on."

Maureen interrupted. "Tomorrow night is Friday night."

"So it is. Well, you must go tomorrow night." Elsa-May was insistent.

Emma clutched at her throat. "Isn't that against the law? I don't want to go to jail."

Ettie leaned forward. "It's breaking and entering. No, wait – it may not be breaking if you have a key. But if you have stolen the key, I'd say it's still breaking, and it's most certainly entering."

Emma jumped to her feet. "This is absurd – I can't do it. I can't!"

"Jah, you can. I'll come with you," Maureen said. "There's something going on, Emma, and you have to find out what it is. Don't you want to know if you can trust Wil or not?"

Emma thought back to the romantic picnic she had just had with Wil. What if she had kissed him or something awful, only to find out he was not to be trusted? *"Jah,* but *Gott* reveals all things in time."

"How much time do you have, though, Emma? With Pluver not renewing his lease? Maybe this is an answer to prayer – *Gott* gave you a brain to use and two feet. He didn't say that He'll work everything out and for us to sit on our bottom, did He?" Elsa-May said in her usual booming voice.

Emma considered how hard Levi's *familye* had worked on the farm for the past few hundred years. Now what was to become of it if she sat on her hands and did nothing? She didn't want to be the one to lose Levi's farm to strangers or land developers. Emma exhaled a large breath. "Okay, I'll do it." She nibbled on a fingernail, hoping that she wouldn't regret the decision she had just made.

Ettie said nothing, but all eyes were on her as she feebly walked across the room to a cupboard. She slowly opened the cupboard door and pulled out a plastic bag, tipping the contents on the floor. Out fell three pairs of thin rubber gloves, a flashlight, three black ski masks and a pocketknife. Crouching over the contents, Ettie looked up at Maureen and Emma. "You both going?" They each nodded and Ettie passed the equipment to them.

They only had a day to organize the break-in. Maureen met Emma at her farm the next morning to go over the finer details.

"How should we get there? We can't really clip-clop down the street with all the buggy lights flashing in the dark and then park outside his office. If anything should happen, people would surely remember a buggy parked outside," Emma said.

"Quite right. We'll leave from my *haus* by taxi, have the taxi take us to the other end of town, and then walk the rest of the way.

Emma nodded. It seemed a reasonable plan.

When the time came for Emma to go to Maureen's place in order to get a taxi into town, she just wanted the whole thing over with. She'd spent all night tossing and turning in nervous anxiety. Would she really find something in The Vulture's office that would make sense of it all? Was Wil her friend or her foe? Why did Mr. Pluver suddenly pull out of the lease after years farming the land? Had Pluver pulled out, or tried to pull out, of Wil's lease as well? Emma made a mental note to find that out. Was it all a coincidence or was there some larger conspiracy happening, and if there was, would they find out from snooping in The Vulture's office?

As planned, they had the taxi drop them at the top of town. They walked down the street dressed in their black coats, black stockings and black boots. Thankfully, it was cold so they didn't draw too much attention from having their coats wrapped around themselves. Instead of their white prayer *kapps,* they had their black over-bonnets on.

"Don't look so worried," Maureen whispered. "You need to look as if you don't have a care in the world and you're just taking a stroll in the cool night air."

Emma nodded and forced a carefree expression on her face.

"That's better. Now stay like that until we get there – just a couple of blocks to go."

The streets weren't crowded. A few restaurants were open and a handful of people wandered to and fro. No one paid them much attention. As they got to the block where the office was located, Maureen looked around. The entrance to the upstairs offices was set into the building, and they came to a locked door that protected the stairwell.

Maureen looked down at the key. "Oh no, we don't have a key for this door. Silvie said it was the key to the office, not the key to the downstairs door."

"We should try it anyway, Maureen." Maureen was about to put the key in the lock when Emma spoke again. "Wait. We must put the gloves on and wipe the key, too." Emma drew two sets of gloves out from inside the front of her dress. When they had both pulled them on, Maureen inserted the key in the lock and turned it.

To their amazement, it unlocked the door. "Well, I hope it works on the one upstairs as well," Maureen said.

Emma gave Maureen a little shove. "Quick, let's just get in before someone sees us."

They both slipped through the door and were faced with a well-lit staircase.

"Silvie said it was just one flight up." Maureen made her way up the stairs and Emma followed close behind, grateful that she had Maureen to lead the way. When they reached the top of the stairs, they saw three office doors. The closest one to them belonged to an accountant, the second was a financial advisor and the one farthest away had 'McAllister' written on it.

"Come on," Maureen whispered over her shoulder.

"I'm right behind you."

Maureen put the key in the lock, and the slight pressure on the door pushed it wide open. She swung around to Emma. "It was unlocked."

"He must have forgotten to lock it," Emma whispered back.

When they were both inside the office, Maureen closed the door behind them and turned on the flashlight.

"Careful to keep it away from the window. Keep it down low." Emma knew nothing of breaking into a place, but it made sense to keep the light away from the window. They didn't need any witnesses.

Maureen gave the flashlight a couple of sharp hits. "We should've put some new batteries in this thing."

"Here, give it to me." Emma wanted to read the papers that were sprawled across his desk. She picked up the first stack of papers stapled together and Maureen peered over her shoulder. She read names on the paper out loud and then said, "I don't know these people, do you?"

"Nee."

Emma leaned over the desk and searched the papers some more. The name Levi Kurtzler caught her eye. She snatched up the paper. "Look, Maureen, Levi's name."

Maureen leaned closer. "Looks like a contract for the sale of your land, but was the land in your name as well as Levi's?"

"Jah, Levi had the land put into my name as well, as soon as we married."

Maureen took the flashlight from her and had a closer look. "Weird. Anything else?"

"Here, shine the light on this one," Emma instructed.

Maureen shone the light on the papers and they both looked at each other as soon as they saw the names: Emma and Levi Kurtzler. "It looks like it's a contract for the sale of my land." Emma looked into Maureen's face. "I never ordered a contract."

"Take it with you, and let's keep looking."

It was hard for Emma to look since there was only one flashlight and Maureen was holding it. Emma moved closer to the window, hoping to read under the dim light filtering in from a street lamp. As she made her way behind the desk toward the window, she caught her foot on something and tripped over, letting out a squeal on her way down.

"Hush, Emma." Maureen turned the flashlight toward Emma's face, and it was then that the light lit up something large on the floor next to her.

Emma gasped, jumped to her feet and ran to stand behind Maureen, who trembled as she held the flashlight with both hands. "I think it's a person."

"Is it? Is it a person?" Emma asked.

Maureen took a step closer and touched the lump on the floor with her foot. There was no reaction. She reached out, moving the flashlight closer to the figure. The light shone on a face. Maureen gasped. *"Jah,* it's a person, but I think they're dead."

CHAPTER SEVEN

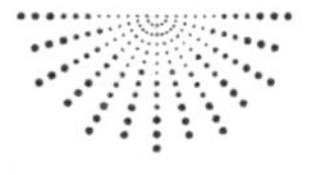

And now abideth faith, hope, charity, these three;
but the greatest of these is charity.
1 Corinthians 13:13

"Quick, Maureen, we have to check to see if he's still alive."

Maureen was speechless and stood as still as a statue.

Emma snatched the flashlight from Maureen's hands and shone the light on the face of the body once more, only to see that it was Henry Pluver. Through her plastic gloves, she could tell that his neck had no pulse. She checked his wrist as well, although she imagined that the neck would be the better source of information. "He's dead, for sure. And it's Henry Pluver."

Maureen gasped. "What will we do?"

"Get out of here, of course. Then we'll call the police."

Emma pushed the contract for her property down the front of her dress, grabbed Maureen's arm and hurried her outside the building. "Now remember Maureen, we have to walk up the street as if we're having a nice stroll and nothing more."

Maureen's eyes were wide, like saucers.

"Well, maybe just pull your bonnet down." Emma adjusted Maureen's bonnet so it hid the majority of her face.

They got in a taxi and went straight to Elsa-May's *haus.*

"We should call the cops and let them know," was Elsa-May's first response when she heard the news.

"Shall I go and call them from the public phone down on the corner?" Emma offered.

Elsa-May shook her head. "*Nee,* I'll call them from my cell phone."

"Your what?" Emma nearly choked. The Amish were not to have technology such as phones. Some had phones in their barns, and some had a telephone in a shanty outside their *haus,* but no one had a cell phone, at least no one that she knew of – until now.

"Cell phone. I just use it for emergencies such as these."

Did she just say emergencies 'such as these'? How many dead bodies has she had to call the police about? Emma realized her mouth was open very wide as she looked at the elderly lady in disbelief. "How do you even know how to use a cell phone?"

Elsa-May tipped her head slightly to the side. "Easy; it came with instructions."

"Elsa-May, we're not supposed to have the outside world coming into the home," Emma said, referencing the unwritten rules of the *Ordnung.*

"I'll use it outside then."

Emma was too flustered to argue. "Well, what will you say to them?"

"I'll say there's a body in an office in town." Elsa-May pressed a button on her cell.

Ettie spoke up. "Why don't we just wait until they discover it in the morning? Emma can call there just after nine. By then the place will be swarming with cops and she can gather information. Maybe get friendly with one of the cops."

Elsa-May was silent for a time. "You know, Ettie, I think you've just had your first good idea."

Emma looked at Ettie; she wasn't sure if what Elsa-May said to her *schweschder* was a compliment, but by the look on Ettie's face she had certainly taken it as one.

"Wait, I have to go back there?" Emma thought the idea a bad one.

"Of course you do. A man's been killed just after telling you he can't lease your land anymore and you find a contract for the sale of your farm. You have to go back there." Elsa-May switched off her cell phone and placed it back in the sideboard drawer. "What was he doing in The Vulture's office? You need to find all these things out."

Ettie touched Emma lightly on her arm. "*Jah,* dear. You have to go back there and get all the information you can."

"What will I say that I'm doing there?" Emma swallowed hard.

Maureen spoke up, "You could say that you're there to speak to Mr. McAllister about your farm. Say that you're thinking of selling and you want to talk it over with him."

"I'm a little scared. What if someone saw us there?" Emma asked.

Ettie shook her head. "*Nee,* don't worry about it. No one would have seen you. Besides, you didn't kill him, did you?"

Emma shook her head.

Elsa-May said, "See, nothing to worry about. Anyway, all Amish look the same to the *Englischers.* If someone saw a couple of Amish ladies, just don't say it was you. They can't prove anything. Ettie, hitch the buggy and take these two girls home – they look like they need a *gut* night's sleep."

"*Jah,* Elsa-May."

Emma was concerned by the late hour. "*Nee,* we'll get a taxi."

"*Nee,* it's no problem. I'll be two minutes." Ettie left the three women in the *haus* and went to the barn.

"I should help her," Maureen said as she walked out the front door.

"Elsa-May, sometimes I feel that you've been involved in this sort of thing before, with the flashlight, the rubber gloves and all."

"Let's just say we look after our own." She gave Emma a wink. "We'll get to the bottom of this mess, don't you worry."

Emma studied the capable old lady. Somehow she believed her words, but Emma was worried about exactly what they would uncover. She hoped that Wil had nothing to do with whatever was going on.

CHAPTER EIGHT

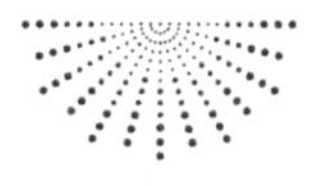

And the peace of God,
which passeth all understanding,
shall keep your hearts and minds
through Christ Jesus.
Philippians 4:7

It was just as Ettie had said it would be. The place was crawling with police when Emma arrived there at nine the next morning. She walked up the stairs and found that The Vulture's office had police tape across the door. People in white coats were brushing things; Emma assumed they were looking for prints.

"Can I help you with something?"

Emma turned to see a solidly-built man. His appearance was such that Emma immediately recognized him to be a policeman or perhaps some sort of detective since he was wearing plain clothing. "I'm looking for Mr. McAllister."

"He's not here."

"What's happened in there?" Emma pointed toward the office. As she did so, she noticed a girl in the corridor crying.

"The forensics team is combing the office."

Emma gasped in a suitable manner. "Forensics? Did someone die?"

The detective studied Emma carefully. "I'm afraid so. I stationed someone on the door downstairs – how did you get up here?"

"I didn't see anyone down there. I just walked up. So, Mr. McAllister died?"

"No, it wasn't McAllister. It was someone else, but we can't release the name until we inform the family." The detective pulled a small notepad and pen from his pocket. "And what's your name?"

"My name is Emma Kurtzler." Emma lowered her voice. "Is that girl all right?"

"She's Mr. McAllister's secretary. She's the one who called us. We've got a policewoman on the way to interview – uh, to look after her."

Emma couldn't take her eyes off the young girl, whom she guessed to be in her early twenties at the very most.

"Simpson, can you take Liza Weeks downstairs?"

A uniformed police officer stepped out of the office and guided the girl down the stairs.

The detective turned his attention back to Emma. "And what business do you have here?"

"Mr. McAllister has asked me a couple of times if I want to sell my property. I've just come here to talk about it."

"Was he expecting you?"

"No, he wasn't. I just thought I'd stop by. He gave me his card, see?" Emma pulled out The Vulture's business card and tried to think quickly. How could she possibly get some information out of the detective? "How did the man die? I assume it was a man?"

"Yes, it was. We think it was foul play, but it's too early to tell."

"You mean like murder?"

The detective nodded and turned his attention back to his small notepad. "And where can you be reached? Do you have a phone number?"

"I don't have a phone at all."

"What's your address?"

After she rattled off her address, she asked the detective, "Do you know where Mr. McAllister is?"

"No, I don't. I will need to ask you some questions later." He looked her in the eyes and leaned forward. "Don't leave town."

"Me?" Emma's hand flew to her throat. "Why would you need to ask me questions?"

"I can tell you that the man who was killed was an Amish man. You turn up here today first thing, and you're Amish – maybe there's a connection." The detective rubbed his chin.

"He was an Amish man?" Emma tried to act distressed. "That's awful."

"Yes, any murder is awful."

Emma nibbled on a fingernail as she always did when she

was nervous. "I might know him, then, if he's from around here."

"I suspected you might."

Emma took two steps back. "Well, I'll leave you to it."

The detective looked at his notepad and repeated her address.

"That's correct," she said before she turned and walked away. When she got out onto the sidewalk, she tried to steady her thumping heart. That had not gone very well. She was sure she was a suspect now, from turning up like that first thing. Ettie would be upset to find out that her first good idea had not been a good idea at all.

Emma went straight home without speaking to any of the widows. They hadn't exactly given her the best guidance, since she was now most likely the main suspect. As soon as Emma put her foot on her porch, she noticed that Wil was walking down the road directly to her *haus.* She waited for him.

"Hello, Wil."

"Hi, Emma. You're out and about early this morning, aren't you?"

"I've just been into town, to McAllister's office, but I didn't see him because the police were there."

Wil stopped still. "What for?"

"It seems that someone was murdered in his office."

Wil scratched his chin. "Who was it?"

"They wouldn't tell me the name, but they did say it was an Amish man."

"Really? I wonder who it could have been. Murdered, did you say?"

"Jah, they think it's murder, but the detective I was talking to said it was too early to know for sure. Let's sit in the kitchen."

Once they were both seated at the kitchen table, Wil spoke again. "What did McAllister say about it?"

"Like I said, I didn't see him. I don't know if the police even know where he is. The detective is coming here later to ask me some questions."

Wil reached out and grabbed Emma's hand. "You? Why's he coming to ask you questions?"

Emma was a little shocked at his touch but left her hand where it was. "The man who was murdered was Amish and I went there this morning so they think that there's a connection."

He let go of her hand and threw back his head. "Nonsense, there's hundreds of Amish in town every day."

"I suppose they have to follow every lead." Emma nibbled on her fingernail.

"That's nonsense." Wil shook his head. "Why did you go to see McAllister anyway? Have you changed your mind about selling?"

"Nee, not really. I just wanted more information from him. Maybe find out how much it's worth." *He does seem concerned about me selling,* Emma thought.

"I'll stay with you until the detective comes."

Emma shook her head. "That's not necessary, Wil."

"Jah, I think it is necessary. You're a woman alone, Emma, and I'll not have you bullied." Wil was insistent.

"He's a policeman. I don't think that he'd bully me."

"You can't be too careful with these things. You need

someone to protect you now that ..." Wil looked away from Emma's face.

"It's all right, you can say it. Now that Levi's gone."

Wil looked into her face once more. "He would've wanted me to look after you."

"Denke, Wil."

Two hours later, a police car pulled up. Emma hoped that no one in the community would see the police car in front of her *haus,* otherwise she would have to answer too many questions.

The detective got out of the car and looked up at Emma and Wil, who were standing outside the front door. Emma noticed that there was a uniformed policeman in the driver's seat who stayed in the car.

"Hello, Mrs. Kurtzler." The detective looked up at Wil. "You Mr. Kurtzler?"

"No, I'm not. Mr. Kurtzler is deceased."

The detective stood in front of Wil, and Emma noticed they were exactly the same height.

"Oh, I see. Then who would you be?" the detective asked in an unpleasant, blunt tone.

"William Jacobson. I'm Mrs. Kurtzler's neighbor and good friend."

Emma sensed tension between the two men. "Come inside, Mr. – oh, I don't think I got your name this morning."

"It's Detective Crowley."

Once they were inside Emma showed him to the kitchen table so they could sit. "Would you like a cup of tea or a cup of coffee, perhaps?"

"No." He looked at Wil. "Would you excuse us? I'd like to ask Mrs. Kurtzler some questions in private."

Wil pulled out a chair and sat at the table opposite the detective. "No, if you don't mind, I'll stay."

The detective clasped his hands on the table. "It would be better if you didn't."

Wil leaned slightly toward the detective. "It might be better if Mrs. Kurtzler got a lawyer – then you wouldn't get your answers straight away. If I stay, however, I'm sure Mrs. Kurtzler would agree to answer your questions right now." The two men continued to glare at each other.

The detective was the first to look away. "You can stay then, as long as you keep silent."

The detective took a small notepad and pen out of his pocket. He noisily clicked the end of his pen and turned to look at Emma, who was rattling around making tea. "I said no tea for me, Mrs. Kurtzler."

"I'm just getting some for myself and Wil. I can still answer your questions while I'm making it."

The detective sat with his back very straight and said, "The man who was murdered was Henry Pluver."

"No, not Henry," boomed Wil.

The detective looked directly at Wil. "You know him?"

"Yes, of course I do. I just saw him the other day. He leases my farm right next door, and he leases Mrs. Kurtzler's farm too."

"He does?" The detective turned to Mrs. Kurtzler.

Emma nodded. "That's right. Oh, I need to sit. It's so unexpected." Emma abandoned the idea of making tea and tried to look suitably shocked and shaken.

Wil scratched his head. "I don't think we've ever had a murder within the community."

"Did Henry know Mr. McAllister?" Emma hoped it was a good time for her to start asking questions. Maybe it was a good idea to have Wil there after all.

"We'll know more of that soon. How long have you been widowed, Mrs. Kurtzler?"

"Just weeks," Wil answered on her behalf.

"I'm sorry to hear that." The detective's response showed no hint of sincerity.

Emma looked into her lap and nodded slightly.

The detective scratched something in his notepad while he asked, "And how long has Mr. Pluver been leasing your farms?"

"A good five years, I'd say." Emma got in quickly so Wil wouldn't answer all the questions. The detective had come to speak to her after all, and Emma didn't want to annoy him further. She hoped that the policeman wouldn't ask whether Pluver was happy to continue leasing. Thankfully, he didn't. It would only look bad for her if he found out that Pluver didn't want to lease her land any longer. Maybe that would seem like a motive for doing away with him.

"Tell me, Detective Crowley, have you located Mr. McAllister yet?" Emma wondered if she should tell him that she was there and she was the one to discover Pluver's body, but that would also implicate Maureen and she was sure that Maureen would want to keep silent on the matter. Besides, it looked as though she was enough of a suspect already. It wouldn't look good that she had been untruthful from the start.

"Yes, we have. He arrived late to the office today. He couldn't believe what had happened. He said there was a key missing, a key from his drawer."

"Is he a suspect?" Wil asked.

"At this stage, Mr. Jacobson, everyone is a suspect."

"Surely Emma isn't a suspect?" Wil asked.

Emma swallowed hard, but quickly hid her guilty expression as the detective swung around to face her. "Where were you last night between six and ten o'clock?"

"She was with me," Wil answered as quick as a flash.

Emma felt her heart pump wildly, yet she had to maintain a cool exterior.

"Is that correct, Mrs. Kurtzler?"

Emma nodded and forced a smile. She wished Wil hadn't said that; Emma was dragging too many people into this mess with her. First Maureen and now Wil. That reminded her, she had to get to Maureen fast to tell her - well, to tell all the widows - about the detective and the fact that she was most likely a suspect.

"Is that a 'yes,' Mrs. Kurtzler?" he asked again, apparently waiting for a verbal response rather than a half-hearted nod.

"Yes." Emma hated to lie, but she had done no wrong, and for the purposes of the investigation she was innocent. Surely a small fib wouldn't affect the detective's work - she wasn't guilty, after all. If the detective knew she and Maureen had found the body, it wouldn't help him in his investigation one little bit since they didn't know who'd killed Pluver.

As the detective left, Wil and Emma stood on Emma's front porch and watched the police car speed up her driveway back to the main road.

Wil slapped his hands against his thighs. "Looks like we've got another funeral to go to."

Emma nodded and thought about Pluver's widow. She was a very disagreeable woman, and Emma was sure she'd never seen her smile – not once. Now she would have absolutely no reason to smile with her husband gone. "Wil, why did you say that you were with me?"

"I knew it wouldn't look *gut* to say you were alone here in the *haus."*

"Why? I'm not guilty of anything." In the back of Emma's mind, she wondered if perhaps Wil was giving himself an alibi by saying he was with her. *Nee, that's ridiculous – I'm getting too carried away,* she thought.

"Of course you're not, so what harm would it do for me to say that you were with me?"

Emma nodded. "I suppose so. *Denke." Once again, he's come to my rescue.*

"Are you okay, Emma?"

Emma realized that she'd been staring off into the distance. She laughed a little. *"Jah,* I'm okay. Lost in my own little world."

Wil put a warm, comforting hand on her shoulder. "Do you want me to stay a while?"

Emma knew she was in dangerous territory as his touch sent tingles throughout her body. *"Nee,* I think I might go and visit one of the girls."

He then put his other hand on her shoulder and faced her directly. "I can drive you there. You look like you're a bit weary."

She had to get away from him fast. She stepped back from his hands. *"Nee,* I'll go alone."

"You stay here; I'll hitch the buggy for you."

"Denke, Wil." Emma smiled as she watched Wil walk toward the barn. He was fine to look at; he was tall with wide shoulders and strong arms. She wondered whether the detective thought

it odd that they were together so late at night, as Wil had fibbed. Being an *Englischer,* he probably thought nothing of it.

Her attention was taken again with Wil's strong frame. *It's a wonder he's never married,* she thought once more. Having Wil do something simple as hitch her buggy felt good. It was nice to have a man around.

Emma hoped that she wasn't doing the wrong thing in going straight to Maureen's *haus* to fill her in on what had just happened with the detective. Surely the policeman wouldn't follow her or anything like that. She would likely notice someone following her, anyway, because cars went much faster than the buggies. There she was, being too suspicious again. First she'd thought that Wil was using her as an alibi, and now she thought herself so interesting to the detective that he would have her followed. Maybe, with all that was going on, she was losing her mind.

She pulled up in the buggy outside Maureen's *haus* and ran to the front door. As she put her hand up to knock, Maureen opened the door.

"What happened? You look terrible," Maureen said.

CHAPTER NINE

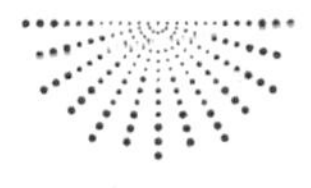

And we know that all things work together for good to them that love God, to them who are the called according to his purpose.
Romans 8:28

Maureen ushered Emma inside her *haus* and they both fell into the soft couch in the middle of Maureen's living room.

"Oh, Maureen, it was terrible. I went there this morning to McAllister's office, and there was a detective there, and he started asking me questions."

Maureen interrupted, "You didn't tell him anything, did you?"

"Nee, hush and just listen. He said the man who was killed was Amish, and since I'm Amish and I was the first person to

show up there, there must be a connection. Then he came to my *haus* and asked me a lot of questions."

"Okay, slow down. Breathe. Now, what did he ask you?"

Emma battled hard to remember what the detective had asked her. Her head was all muddled. "Well, Wil was there too, and the detective asked me how long ago my husband died and how I knew Pluver – that's really all I can think of."

Maureen patted Emma's leg. "See? Nothing to worry about."

"Oh, he did ask me where I was last night."

Maureen's eyebrows flew up and nearly met her hairline. "He did?"

"*Jah*, but Wil said that he was with me."

Maureen's eyebrows lowered into a frown. "Why would he do that?"

"I've been thinking about that. I think it's because he knew I'm alone every night and he wanted to give me an alibi."

Maureen nodded and looked thoughtful. "Maybe."

"Oh, it was awful. My heart was beating so fast the whole time he was there."

"Did Wil say anything else?"

"*Nee*, not really. He doesn't suspect a thing. He did ask me what I was doing at McAllister's office this morning, and I just said that I wanted to know more – things like what my farm would be worth. He seemed to believe that."

"That's good."

"Maureen, who do you think killed Pluver? Do you think they might try and kill me?"

"I don't know. We have to find out who killed him and why. You should go and talk to The Vulture and find out if he knew Pluver at all."

Emma made a face. "What makes you think that he'd tell me?"

Maureen shook her head a little. "I don't know, but at this stage that's all we've got. Unless ..."

"Unless what?"

"Unless you go and visit Mrs. Pluver."

Emma squealed. "Me? I don't even like the woman." Emma bit her lip. That had come out before she could think. She never liked to speak ill of people. "I shouldn't have said that, but she always looks so disagreeable. I've never even seen her smile – she scares me a little."

Maureen gave a little sound from the back of her throat. "You don't have to be polite around me. I agree with you; she never looks happy."

Emma put her hand on Maureen's arm. "Why don't you come with me?"

Maureen covered her face with her hands.

"Oh, come on. Please, Maureen?"

Maureen chuckled. "All right then."

Emma pushed her head into the high back of the couch. "So, what kind of things can we find out from her? See if she knows The Vulture, I guess. That would be the first thing. We'd have to wait a few days, wouldn't we? Should we wait until after the funeral to visit her?"

"Most likely that would be best, but *nee*, we should go soon. We'll go first thing tomorrow, and maybe take Mrs. Pluver some fresh baked bread and some beef casserole."

"Good idea," Emma said.

"You bake the bread, and I'll make the casserole. I've got some nice beef already. Now, let's pick up Silvie and we'll go to

Ettie and Elsa-May's *haus* so we can tell everyone what's going on."

~

AFTER VISITING with all the widows, Emma arrived home as the sun was going down. None of the ladies in the widows' group had any better idea than the plan she and Maureen had come up with – to go and visit Mrs. Pluver. Emma would bake the fresh bread in the morning. Tonight she was too tired to do anything.

~

SOMEHOW EMMA MANAGED to get a little sleep and she had no bad dreams. She woke early, and as she waited for the bread to bake, she heard someone at her door.

"Hello?"

She knew that the deep voice belonged to Wil. Emma flung the door open. "Come in, Wil."

"Mmm, I smelled the bread and came for breakfast."

Emma laughed. "Well, it'll be ready soon. I've baked a few loaves; I'm taking some over to Mrs. Pluver's *haus* later today. I'm going there with Maureen."

"That's nice of you."

"Sit down and I'll make a pot of tea." When Wil was comfortably seated at the table, Emma asked him, "Tell me, Wil, how long was your lease to Pluver?"

"No idea. I'd have to look it up. It's a five by five lease, I know that much. We're into the second lot of five years, but I've no idea how far along it is." He leaned back in the chair. "Why do you ask?"

"Pluver told me the day before he died that he wanted out of the lease."

"Did you agree?"

"Apparently I had no choice. With Levi gone, that left Pluver with a loophole to get out of the contract." Emma shrugged her shoulders.

"I wonder what he was doing in McAllister's office," Wil said.

Emma remained silent, hoping to find out more about McAllister from Wil. When Wil offered no further information, Emma said, "Did Pluver ever tell you that he didn't want to farm your land anymore?"

"*Nee,* but he was still on the lease; I'm pretty certain it goes for quite a while. He made no mention of wanting to end the lease. I would've let him out of it if he didn't want to farm the land any longer – he was the one who wanted the papers drawn up rather than a handshake agreement so that he could be secure in his farming."

"I guess that's understandable." Emma could be silent no longer about seeing Wil with The Vulture. "Wil, I have to tell you that I saw you with The Vulture the other day."

Wil looked confused. "Really, where?"

"I saw the two of you talking and then I saw you having lunch together. You looked pretty cozy."

"I didn't see you anywhere," he replied. "Anyway, I asked him to keep away from you. Then I thought I'd make friends with him in an effort to have him keep his distance." Wil looked at her. "You do believe me, don't you? What other business would

I have with the man? He did agree to stay away from you – we even shook hands on it."

Emma pursed her lips. "Did he say anything to you?"

"About what?"

"Well, what did you talk about?" Emma asked.

"He wants to buy up a lot of land. He even asked me if I wanted to sell."

Emma poured the hot water over the tea leaves in the pot. "Is he buying it for himself or is he acting as an agent for someone?"

"I'm not sure. The way he spoke, I would think that he was buying the land for himself; I couldn't say for sure, but he is a realtor." Wil fixed his gaze intently on her. "Emma, you don't think I'm deceiving you in any way, do you?"

Emma placed the teacups on the table. "So many things have happened in such a short space of time. I guess I don't know whether I'm coming or going sometimes. I just want to feel safe again." She slumped into one of her kitchen chairs.

Wil moved to sit beside her and reached out his hand. Emma knew it was a friendly gesture, not a romantic one, so she placed her hand in his. "I'll always be here to look after you, Emma."

That's exactly what Levi used to say to me, but he isn't here now. Levi had left her alone – whether he'd wanted to or not, he'd left her alone.

Wil suddenly looked up. "Smells like the bread's ready."

"Oh, goodness me." Emma jumped up. "Just as well you said something or it might have burned."

Emma wrapped her hands in dishtowels and pulled the loaves of bread out of the oven.

Wil sniffed the air. "Mmm, they smell great, don't they?"

"They smell delicious. I'll cut you some pieces."

"I'll do it." Wil rose to his feet, took the large bread knife out of the drawer and sliced up the loaf.

As they sat and ate warm bread and butter together, Emma found it comforting to have a man in her kitchen, sitting and speaking with her.

The sound of Maureen's buggy pulling up out the front disturbed the two of them.

Wil jumped up and looked out the window. "It's Maureen. I'll be on my way, then. *Denke* for the fresh bread."

She followed Wil to the front door and said goodbye before calling out to Maureen. "Won't be a moment!"

Minutes later, Emma hurried to Maureen's buggy with the fresh baked bread under her arm.

"You two looked very cozy when you were saying goodbye. Come to think of it, he was over at your place quite early."

Emma laughed. "Stop it. He smelled the bread and came over to have a few slices. That's all. He's a friend and nothing more."

"All right. You don't need to convince me so thoroughly. Now, let's go over our plan with Mrs. Pluver."

"I do feel a bit awful going to see her since I don't really like her. I do feel sorry for her, of course – who wouldn't? It's just that under normal circumstances I wouldn't visit so soon after her husband's death."

"Relax, Emma. You think too much. We've got to do this; there's no other way around it. We've got to find some things out."

As they drove down the Pluvers' driveway, a police car was

driving the other way. Emma saw Detective Crowley in the passenger's seat. The police car stopped, and the detective got out and flagged the buggy down.

"Stop, Maureen. It's the detective."

Maureen pulled the horse up quickly and Emma got out to greet Crowley.

"Ah, Mrs. Kurtzler, we meet again – that's an odd coincidence."

"Yes, I was just heading to give my condolences to Mrs. Pluver. That's what we Amish do." Emma hoped she hadn't sounded too cheeky.

"Carry on, then." The detective got back in the police car, and continued back down the driveway toward the road.

"He's intimidating. I don't like the way he looked at you," Maureen said.

"Jah, I know. He seems to be suspicious of me for some reason. I wish I hadn't gone there that morning – to The Vulture's office."

"It'll all work out in the end, I'm sure," Maureen said.

Mrs. Pluver stood at her front door and waited for them to get out of the buggy.

Maureen was the first to speak to Mrs. Pluver as they walked toward her. "We're so sorry to hear the news, Ethel."

Emma nodded in agreement and said, "We've brought you some food."

"Denke, come in." Ethel Pluver stepped aside to let them enter the *haus.*

Ethel made them tea and they sat down together.

"Was that a detective that we passed?" Maureen asked.

"Jah. You may as well know that they think that Henry was murdered."

Maureen and Emma kept silent.

"I suppose you've heard the talk already?" Ethel asked.

Both women nodded, and Emma said, "I'm afraid I found out fairly early on. I went to McAllister's office early that morning to talk to him. The police were there."

"I see." Ethel dropped her gaze away from the ladies.

"Did your husband tell you that he didn't want to lease my farm anymore?"

Ethel turned to Emma. *"Nee,* he didn't tell me anything about his dealings. When did he tell you that?"

"It was about a week ago."

Ethel Pluver looked into her tea and then set the teacup back on the table. "He was acting quite strangely, but I thought nothing of it."

Maureen cleared her throat. "Do you know Mr. McAllister?"

"Nee, I don't know him at all."

Maureen and Emma exchanged looks without Ethel Pluver seeing them. They knew they had asked enough questions. They stayed a little longer talking with her and made sure she had all that she needed. Just before they left, the bishop and his wife arrived to visit.

On the way back to Emma's home, Maureen said, "So what do you make of it all?"

"She said that Henry was acting funny – 'strange' is the word she used, I think. I wonder what that was about?"

"Mrs. Pluver doesn't know McAllister, but obviously Henry Pluver knew him, or why would he be at his office?"

CHAPTER TEN

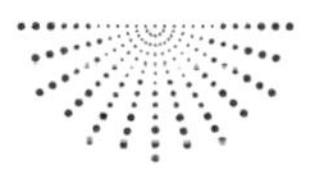

Ask, and it shall be given you; seek,
and ye shall find;knock,
and it shall be opened unto you:
Matthew 7:7

Maureen came to get Emma to take her to Mr. Pluver's funeral. They were silent for a while as they traveled in the buggy before Maureen said, "I heard whispers that Mrs. Pluver was being unfaithful."

Emma laughed. She thought that Maureen was telling her a joke. When Maureen didn't join in with her laughter, Emma turned to see a serious look on her face. "You can't be serious."

"Well, I'm just saying what I heard."

"Unfaithful with whom? The Vulture?"

"I don't know, Emma, but you should keep an open mind

about things. Where there's smoke, there's fire. Have you ever heard of that saying?"

"Jah, but Mrs. Pluver? Grouchy old Mrs. Pluver? She hardly seems the type of woman to be unfaithful. I mean, what sort of man would be interested in a cranky old lady like her?" Emma asked.

"Don't know. A cranky old man perhaps?"

Maureen and Emma giggled. Before too long, they had reached the cemetery. Maureen pulled on Emma's arm. "Look, that's The Vulture isn't it? Over there."

Emma looked to where Maureen pointed. It was indeed Mr. McAllister, and he was standing next to Bob, Mr. Pluver's son.

The widows knew they had to keep their eyes open for any strange sights at the funeral. There was one such thing that Emma noticed: the pretty young secretary from McAllister's office was there, crying. Both times Emma had seen this girl she'd been in tears. "Look up there, Maureen. That's a most odd sight."

"Jah, it is a most odd sight indeed, and I don't think it's gone unnoticed by Ethel Pluver."

Emma studied Ethel for a few moments and noticed her glancing more than once at the *Englisch* girl standing a short distance from the grave.

~

IT WAS LATER that day that the detective came to Emma's door.

"Can I come in?"

"Certainly." Emma stepped aside for the detective to enter. "Come through to the kitchen. How can I help you, detective?"

"We have a witness who saw an Amish woman near McAllister's office at seven p.m. That's the estimated time of death."

"I see. And how can I help you with that? There's a lot of Amish women around town. Do you suspect me? Is that why you're telling me this?" Emma was sure that she and Maureen had been at McAllister's office around eight or nine.

"Mrs. Kurtzler, is there anything that you wish to tell me? If you cooperate, things will go better for you."

Emma gasped and looked at the detective in horror. "I didn't do anything, Detective Crowley, and I would never kill anyone." Emma frowned at the nerve of the man accusing her of something so horrendous.

"You were annoyed that Mr. Pluver no longer wanted to lease your land."

Emma wondered how he knew that. She didn't remember telling him anything of the sort. "It's true, he didn't want to lease the land anymore, but I wouldn't have killed the man because of it. I can't even kill a fly on a hot summer's day. Do you have any suspects – besides me, I mean?"

"I know that he was killed around seven and there was an Amish woman seen there at around that time. McAllister said there was a key missing from his office."

"What did Mr. Pluver have to do with Mr. McAllister?" Emma asked.

A wry smile crossed the detective's face. "Not Mr. McAllister. It seems that McAllister's secretary and Mr. Pluver were quite friendly, if you know what I mean."

Emma's mouth fell open. *Pluver and the pretty young girl she'd seen that morning at McAllister's office? Surely not!* "That's very hard to believe." Emma wondered which story was more likely

– cranky old Mrs. Pluver having an affair with The Vulture or Henry having an affair with the young secretary. Neither story seemed plausible.

"Mrs. Kurtzler, I have to ask you this straight out – were you also having an affair with Henry Pluver?"

Emma sprang to her feet. "Detective Crowley, that is the most horrible thing that I've ever heard in my life. I most certainly was not! Please leave immediately." Emma could feel her whole body shake as she walked to open the door. The detective had to be grasping at straws – there was absolutely no basis for him to have asked her such a dreadful thing.

"I'm sorry. I didn't mean to upset you – I'm just trying to piece things together."

Emma said nothing, but held her chin up high while she showed him out the door.

When he stepped down from the porch, he turned around and said, "I might need to ask you some more questions at another time."

Emma couldn't bring herself to speak. After shutting the door, she immediately went to the window to watch him drive away. Once she was certain that he had gone, she bolted the lock on the door then walked out to her garden. She always felt peaceful in her private garden. A few minutes later, she heard Wil's voice at the front door.

"Emma!"

"I'm 'round the back, Wil."

"I saw that detective drive away." As Wil walked closer, his expression changed and he hurried toward her. "What's the matter, Emma?" He put his arm around her shoulder.

"Oh, Wil, it was horrible. That horrible detective." Emma buried her face into Wil's hard shoulder as she sobbed.

Wil lifted her away slightly and asked, "What happened?"

Emma did her best to stop her sobs and took a couple of deep breaths. "He asked me if I was having an affair with Henry Pluver."

"That's ludicrous. I don't want you talking to that detective again unless I'm here." Wil pulled her toward him and placed his muscled arms around her.

Emma let out all her bottled up emotions and sobbed some more. She was sure she was crying against him for three whole minutes before she stopped. When her sobs turned into sniffles, Wil offered her his large, white handkerchief.

She managed to smile a little. *"Denke."* She wiped her face and noticed that she had made his shirt wet. "Look what I've done to your shirt."

Wil looked down at himself. "That's the least of our worries."

"I suppose so." Emma's voice croaked. "Wil, can you take me to Elsa-May and Ettie's *haus?"*

Wil looked down at her and frowned. "Really? Why would you want to go there?"

"I just want to speak to them, and I'm sure they can bring me home later." Emma knew that she was in no state to drive a buggy.

"Of course I'll take you there."

CHAPTER ELEVEN

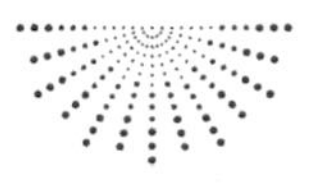

The name of the LORD is a strong tower:
the righteous runneth into it, and is safe.
Proverbs 18:10

As soon as Emma arrived at Elsa-May's and informed her of the latest news, Elsa-May gathered Maureen and Silvie for an emergency meeting. When they arrived, Emma explained to the widows what she'd learned – all of them except for Ettie, who was in town on an information-gathering expedition.

Emma finished by saying, "So, I can't work out which of the stories is true, if any of them are true at all."

Elsa-May bustled over to a drawer in her sideboard and took out a notepad. "Let's see what we know so far. Pluver is dead; he may or may not have been having an affair with McAllister's secretary. Mrs. Pluver may or may not have been having an affair with McAllister."

Silvie laughed then swallowed her laughter as Elsa-May glared at her.

Maureen spoke up. "So what would the motive be to kill Pluver?"

Elsa-May looked at her pad as she wrote. "Well, Emma's just told us that the detective has a witness placing an Amish woman around the scene of the crime at approximately six, or was it seven?"

"Just around the building; I don't know if she was seen entering or leaving or anything like that," Emma added.

"Nevertheless, we're just going on the information we have at hand. If Pluver was having an affair and Mrs. Pluver found out, she would be none too happy about it."

"That's right," Silvie agreed. "We all know that mostly people are killed over money or love."

Emma noticed that the ladies all nodded. That was something she'd never given much thought to – the main reasons for murder.

Elsa-May continued, "Now, if Mrs. Pluver was having an affair with The Vulture and Mr. Pluver found out, he would be none too happy."

"But …" Silvie held up her hand. "What does it have to do with Pluver telling Emma he can't lease her land anymore? And what about Bob, Pluver's son? Maybe he did it so he could inherit his father's business. From what I hear, they don't get along at all."

Bob Pluver had always made Emma feel uneasy. Maybe he was capable of killing someone, even his own father. He always seemed to be skulking around and he never looked anyone directly in the eyes. In her mind, that had always been a sign that someone couldn't be trusted.

Elsa-May said, "But why was Pluver killed in McAllister's office?"

Silvie pushed out her lips. "That has to be the key to the whole thing. The reason that Pluver was in the office."

"Maybe that was his meeting place with the secretary," Maureen said.

"It's unlikely that McAllister would kill someone in his own office. He would surely come under suspicion," Emma said.

There was silence for a while until Maureen said, "What about Wil?"

Emma turned to look at Maureen. "What about him?"

"Why was he speaking to The Vulture that time, acting all friendly and having lunch with him?"

Emma felt all eyes on her. "He said he was trying to get The Vulture to be nice to me. What? Do you think Wil might have killed Pluver?" Emma suddenly realized that Wil would also be disadvantaged by Pluver's death, unless Bob was prepared to take over all his father's leases. She hadn't even stopped to give a thought to the fact that Pluver leased Wil's land as well. Surely that meant that Wil was not a suspect.

Maureen grabbed Emma's arm. "Emma, do you still have that contract of sale that you took from Pluver's office?"

"*Jah,* I do, but I haven't even thought to look at it with everything that's gone on."

"Let's all go to your *haus* now and take a look at that contract."

Everyone squeezed into Maureen's buggy. Once they

arrived at Emma's house, Emma took the contract from her kitchen drawer. Her eyes scanned the page until she saw the name of the potential buyer – Henry Pluver. She threw the contract onto the table. "It's Henry. He's the one who wanted to buy my land."

"So Henry does know McAllister?" Elsa-May said.

Maureen said, "Seems like Pluver was trying to buy some cheap land."

"He probably thought that he would get it cheap because of what happened with Levi," Silvie added.

"We're no closer to finding out who killed Pluver, though," Emma said.

"I'd reckon it was Mrs. Pluver," Maureen said.

"I heard Bob never got on with his father, and someone told me that last week they had a terrible row," Silvie said.

Emma turned to Silvie. "What about?"

"I don't know," Silvie replied. "I couldn't find that out."

"Maybe Bob found out that his father was having an affair and he threatened to expose him?" Maureen said.

"Who did it, Bob or the mother?" Elsa-May said, focused on her yellow pad as if that would provide the answer.

The widows all heard a buggy pull up. Elsa-May leaned back in her chair so she could see who it was. "That's Ettie. By the way she's running in the door, I'd say she's found something out."

Emma jumped up, but Ettie burst through the door before Emma could reach her.

Ettie was breathless and had to sit a while before she could speak. "I have a friend who works in the travel agency, and guess what I found out?"

"What, Ettie? What?" her *schweschder* urged her.

Ettie held up her hand. "Hang on ... Too puffed to speak." A few seconds later, she continued, "Two plane tickets, one for Henry Pluver and one for Liza Weeks." When the ladies were silent, Ettie said, "She's the secretary of McAllister."

Elsa-May scratched on her note pad and said, "So Henry had plans of running away. To give his boy security, he was trying to buy your land, Emma. It joins onto the Pluvers' land at the back."

"So if I sold, that would make him feel that he had provided for his boy at least? I wonder why he wouldn't approach me himself – why go through The Vulture?" Emma asked.

Maureen said, "He didn't want his wife to know what he was doing."

"Well, she would've found out," Silvie said.

"But not until he was well gone," Maureen replied.

Elsa-May placed the yellow pad down on the table in front of the couch and looked up at Emma. "I think we should call your detective and tell him what we know."

Emma put her hand to her chest as she recalled the detective's attitude. "He's not my detective."

"You know what I mean. I'll call him – what's his name?"

Elsa-May produced her cell phone and stood up. "Don't worry, I'll call from outside."

Emma opened her mouth to say something to Elsa-May of the dangers of bringing the outside world into the *haus,* but then she stopped herself. After all, Elsa-May did say she was going to call from outside the *haus.* She made an excuse for everything she did; there was hardly any point in protesting. "His name is Detective Crowley."

"Ah, Detective Crowley. I've met him before."

Emma followed Elsa-May outside to listen to her call. It was clear that Elsa-May already had his number in her phone as she only pressed one button before she got his voice mail. Elsa-May left a message saying to come to Emma's place as soon as possible.

"Well, what happens now?" Emma said.

Elsa-May stated in a firm tone, "We wait."

Two cups of tea and three plates of cookies later, Detective Crowley knocked on Emma's door. The ladies told Crowley everything they knew, leaving out the part about Emma and Maureen being the ones to find Pluver's body in the first place.

"Looks like I'll be asking Mrs. Pluver some questions. Once again, thank you Elsa-May, and you too, Ettie." He looked at Emma, and said, "Mrs. Kurtzler, I'm sorry that I got the wrong end of the stick with you."

Emma nodded and gave the detective a forced smile, although she didn't take kindly to the man. He had as good as accused her of wrongdoing, but an apology was an apology and she had to accept it.

Detective Crowley turned to Elsa-May. "What have you got going here? A secret widows' society?"

Elsa-May remained straight-faced. "We just might have."

The ladies left soon after the detective. Emma hoped the detective would get to the bottom of things and she could feel safe once more.

Nothing seemed the same. How would she cope with no income and without Pluver's lease money? Hopefully the insurance money would come through from Levi's work, but she couldn't rely on that; Mr. Weeks had said that it was a long shot.

It was then that it occurred to Emma that Mr. Weeks had the same last name as McAllister's secretary. She was sure of it. She hitched the buggy and went to Elsa-May's *haus* as fast as she could.

She scrambled to the front door, and Elsa-May answered it with Ettie close behind her. "Elsa-May. What was the name of McAllister's secretary again?"

"Come in, Emma." Elsa-May scrambled through her notes. "Liza Weeks."

"Levi's boss' name is Devin Weeks; I wonder if they're related?"

"There's one way to find out." Ettie walked over to the same cabinet where she stored the rubber gloves and pulled out the cell phone.

Emma opened her mouth in shock. Again, Emma knew it was no use saying anything – besides, maybe the *Ordnung* would change in a few years.

"How will that tell us anything?" Emma asked.

"Emma, all young people have Facebook. We simply find her Facebook account and scan through her photos to see if we can find one of ... What was his name? Dustin?"

"Nee, Devin. Devin Weeks."

Ettie turned on the phone and tapped some things. "There are a few named Liza Weeks here; which one is she?"

Emma looked at photos of three people with the same name before pointing to one. "That's her."

"Hopefully she's lax on her privacy settings," Ettie mumbled, more to herself than anyone else. "Bingo. Devin Weeks – it's her father all right, and he's got himself a Facebook account as well."

"Well thought-of, Emma," Elsa-May said.

Ettie said what they were all thinking. "Maybe Mr. Weeks found out that his daughter was going to run away with Pluver, so he killed him."

Elsa-May tapped her fingers on her chin. "Hmm, now we have another suspect."

"This is too much; I think I need to go home," Emma said.

"I'll tell the detective to meet us all here tomorrow at twelve," said Elsa-May.

"Okay." Emma agreed just to get out of the place. It was all so baffling. So many people could have killed Pluver: his son, his wife, the father of his lover – maybe even his lover herself, if they'd had an argument.

CHAPTER TWELVE

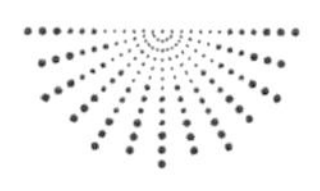

Yea, though I walk through the valley of the shadow of death, I will fear no evil: for thou art with me;
thy rod and thy staff they comfort me.
Psalm 23:4

As Emma drove her buggy past Wil's place, she saw him waving her down from the front of his house. She pulled up in front of him.

"Emma, where have you been? I've hardly seen anything of you."

"I've been spending a lot of time with Maureen and Silvie." Emma was sure that sounded more believable than spending time with the two elderly widows.

"Have dinner with me tonight?"

"I'm too tired to go anywhere. I just want an early night. I'm sorry, Wil, some other time?"

"I've already cooked chicken and vegetables. Besides, it will save you having to cook, and you can leave straight after you eat to get an early night. I'll even walk you home."

Emma knew she didn't have anything ready for dinner, but she had all that food there that the bishop's *fraa* had left her; all she had to do was heat it up. "*Denke* that would be *gut*." She decided to accept his invitation so she wouldn't have to heat up food or clean the dishes afterwards.

"Come over whenever you're ready."

Emma noticed some wood he was working with. "What have you got there?"

"I'm working on an invention. It's a new plough."

"I'll see you soon, then." Emma smiled and moved her horse on toward home. Wil was always working on some new gadget or other. She knew better than to ask too many questions; he got rather enthused when he had a project, and she wanted to get home before dark rather than listen to a long tale about the new plough.

After dinner that night, they sat on Wil's porch.

"What's the matter with you lately? You seem so worried. Is everything all right?" Wil asked her.

"Levi's just died – I'm allowed to grieve, aren't I?" Emma fiddled with the strings of her prayer *kapp*.

Wil pushed his fingers through his dark hair. "I'm sorry, of course, you're allowed to. I just meant that you seem to be worried about something else. Am I right?"

"I'm a bit worried about the farm. I'll have to find someone else to lease it, I suppose."

"Well, you'll find someone. There's a handful of men I can think of who'd most likely lease it from you. The Amish are always looking for farmland, you know that."

Emma nodded.

"Anything else?"

Emma looked up across the darkness of the fields in front of her. "I'm worried about who murdered Henry Pluver."

"Emma, you can't spend the rest of your days worrying about things."

Emma looked into Wil's eyes. He never seemed bothered by much at all. If he had any advice for her, she would like to hear it. "How can I spend the rest of my days, Wil?"

"Spend them with me, as my *fraa.*"

Emma laughed a little and put her fingertips to her mouth to stifle her giggles.

"I'm serious, Emma. I want to look after you and protect you from harm."

Emma didn't know if he loved her or just wanted to look after her. She wouldn't marry again unless it was for love. *"Denke* for your offer, Wil."

What followed between the two of them was an awkward silence. Emma considered it best to go home. Wil walked her the five minutes to her house.

As Emma lay in bed that night, she considered Wil's offer. What was to become of her, all alone? Sure, Maureen and Silvie were young and alone, but were they happy? What better man would there be for her in the whole community than Wil? Maybe she should seriously consider his offer, even if he were not in love with her. She could see herself falling for him, but did he feel the same? If he were in love with her, surely he would have said as much.

Emma closed her eyes. She felt she'd been on a very fast horse for a very long time, and she wanted to get off and just have a quiet, normal life without worrying about who had killed Pluver and why.

When Emma woke up the next morning, she decided to pay Mr. Weeks a visit at his work before she met with the widows at Elsa-May and Ettie's place.

She knew that he worked out of a van at one of his construction sites. The van had been converted into a high-tech office.

She had the taxi drive her straight to the site, which was deserted except for Mr. Weeks' car parked near his office. She walked up to the van and knocked on the door.

Mr. Weeks pushed the door open. "Mrs. Kurtzler, come inside."

"Hello, Mr. Weeks. I hope you don't mind me calling in on you unexpectedly."

Mr. Weeks shuffled the papers that were on his desk into a drawer. "Not at all. What can I do for you? Have you come to find out about the insurance claim?"

"Well, not really. I came to find out about your daughter."

Mr. Weeks sat down in his chair. He motioned for Emma to sit in the other chair. "What about my daughter?"

"Is Liza Weeks your daughter?"

"Yes, she is."

"Did you know about the rumors regarding Liza and Mr. Pluver?"

"Come for a walk with me, Mrs. Kurtzler." At her question,

Mr. Weeks' face had contorted into someone whom she didn't recognize. She was scared to go for a walk with him, but she needed some more information.

Mr. Weeks pointed to the door, and Emma turned and stepped through with Mr. Weeks close behind her.

"Your husband was a valued employee."

"Yes, he was a hard worker."

Mr. Weeks pointed to the building that was not yet complete. "This is not the building your husband fell from."

Emma nodded as she looked up at the unfinished building. She hadn't wanted to know any details.

"Let me show you the view as we talk." Emma followed Mr. Weeks into an elevator at the side of the building.

"I'm a little afraid of heights." She looked at the small elevator. "And closed-in spaces."

"It's a lovely view from the top. I'd like to show it to you. It's quite safe; the other side has a viewing platform where we take potential buyers."

Emma hesitated at the door.

Mr. Weeks added, "It's passed all safety regulations."

Emma stepped into the elevator. *Maybe there were private papers that he didn't want me to see in his office, and he might feel better walking and talking at the same time,* she thought.

As they rode in the elevator, Mr. Weeks said, "I know that my daughter was set to run away with that old man."

"You knew?" The elevator stopped and Mr. Weeks held the door for Emma to step through.

Once she was out of the elevator, she turned and waited for Mr. Weeks to answer.

He nodded. "I wouldn't let that happen. I knew she was slipping away at night to see someone. I had her followed, and she was going to your property, to the barn at the end of your farm."

Emma recalled the rarely used barn at the end of her property as well as one close to her home.

"That's why I thought it was your husband she was going to run away with – because it was your farm she was meeting the man on. I didn't know that Pluver had a lease on your property. I found out soon after."

A chill ran down Emma's spine. "No, Levi would never do anything like that, never."

"I found that out too late, Mrs. Kurtzler. I'm very, very sorry. I didn't mean it to happen like this."

Was he saying what she thought he was saying? If he thought Levi was having an affair with his daughter, then maybe he killed Levi and maybe he also killed Henry Pluver. Emma didn't know what to do. She asked meekly, "What are you sorry for?"

"I didn't mean to kill him."

Emma's hand instinctively flew to her heart. "You killed Levi?"

Mr. Weeks' face was grim as he slowly said, "I had to kill him. I had to protect my daughter. When I visited you at the farm, I knew it wasn't your husband I was after. I lodged that insurance claim for you."

Emma covered her mouth; she felt as though she would be sick. It was much worse that Levi was killed at the hands of a madman rather than in an accident. Emma knew she'd made a big mistake by going to see him alone, but she wouldn't let this man do the same thing to her as he'd done to Levi and to

Pluver. She looked out of the corner of her eye for an escape route. "You killed Pluver, as well?"

"I had to stop him ruining my daughter's life." Mr. Weeks took a step toward Emma, and she stayed very still. "You don't have children, do you Emma?"

Emma shook her head.

"When you have children you'll do anything to protect them. Anything."

Emma glanced behind her and saw that there was a sheer drop, five floors down. "Well, your secret's safe with me, Mr. Weeks. I won't tell anyone."

Mr. Weeks laughed. "I'm afraid I can't trust you with the information I've just given you." He walked toward her.

Emma pleaded, "No, don't kill me. They'll know that you did it."

"No, they won't." Mr. Weeks laughed again, and his eyes flashed with the black evil of the devil himself. "You were so distraught over your husband's death that you killed yourself."

Emma closed her eyes so she wouldn't have to look at him. "No one will ever believe that."

"They will if that's how I say that it happened." Mr. Weeks was three paces from her and he closed the gap between them quickly. His face turned white and his hands shook as he stretched them out towards her.

There was nowhere for her to go and nothing she could use to defend herself. Emma sank to the floor and closed her eyes. She prayed – she didn't want to die, not here, not like this.

CHAPTER THIRTEEN

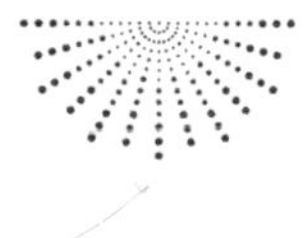

But without faith it is impossible to please him: for he that cometh to God must believe that he is,
and that he is a rewarder of them that diligently seek him.
Hebrews 11:6

"FREEZE! Weeks, put your arms in the air," a voice boomed through a microphone.

Emma opened one eye and saw that Mr. Weeks had his hands up. She closed her eyes and continued to pray.

The voice boomed again. "Step away from the lady. Make one false move and we'll shoot."

Mr. Weeks took a step away from her. Sirens of police cars sounded; there would have been at least two, maybe three.

"It's all over, Weeks," the voice boomed once more.

Emma opened one eye just slightly to see Mr. Weeks lowering his arms and taking a step toward her.

"Keep your arms up or we'll shoot."

Weeks raised his arms.

Emma glanced over the side of the building to see two uniformed policemen getting into the elevator. Mr. Weeks remained silent with his arms straight above his head.

Emma must have blacked out for a moment, because when she next opened her eyes she saw Mr. Weeks being handcuffed by two police officers.

Another officer ran toward her. "Are you hurt, miss?"

Emma shook her head.

"Stay still," the officer ordered. "We've got an ambulance coming."

Emma watched Mr. Weeks being led into the elevator.

She closed her eyes and thanked *Gott* that He listened to her prayers. "I'm fine. I don't need an ambulance. I'm fine." Emma went to stand up, but her legs were like jelly. "Maybe I'll stay here for a few moments."

"I'll stay with you," the officer said.

Emma sat on the floor, and all she could think of was Wil. She was certain that she wouldn't feel safe until Levi's strong arms were around her, but they never would be again.

Detective Crowley appeared out of the elevator. He walked over to Emma while shaking his head at her. "What did you think you were doing? You nearly got yourself killed."

She was still slumped on the ground. "I didn't know he was a murderer – I was just going to ask him a few questions." Emma heard her voice and it didn't sound like her own; it was much more high-pitched than normal.

"Well, you're very lucky. When you didn't turn up at Elsa-

May's place, she thought you might have done something silly. Ettie and Elsa-May figured out what happened. They went to find you when you didn't show. They then called me and told me what their suspicions were."

"I'm so pleased they did."

"They do have their ways about them. Let's get you out of here. Are you okay to move?"

"I'm okay." Emma got to her feet and then rode down in the elevator with Detective Crowley. She had nearly gotten killed – murdered. Nothing seemed real to her anymore.

The paramedics arrived on the scene quickly afterward. She was given the all-clear from the medical staff, but was told to rest. Crowley had a policewoman take Emma home.

~

WHEN EMMA OPENED her front door, she was never more pleased to be there.

She sat on her couch, wrapped herself in a blanket and waited for Wil. She knew it wouldn't take him long to get there to find out why a police car had just been there.

"Emma!" Wil burst through the door without knocking.

"Come in."

Wil sat next to her and asked all the questions that Emma knew that he would. She answered them all, leaving out the part about nearly being murdered. He didn't need to worry about her anymore than he already did.

"Emma, you can never do anything silly like that again." He moved closer and put his arm around her. "You should never have gone there." He pulled her toward himself, and she rested her head on his shoulder. "Do you want me to get you anything? Some tea or some soup?"

"*Nee,* I couldn't have one thing." Emma sighed. "But perhaps you could drive me to Elsa-May and Ettie's *haus* tomorrow."

"Of course."

~

IT WAS eleven in the morning when Emma arrived at Elsa-May and Ettie's place; Ettie phoned Silvie and Maureen, and it didn't take them long to show up.

The group was finally assembled, and each woman hugged Emma tightly and made a fuss over her. They had all heard what had happened from the detective.

Ettie made Emma a strong cup of tea with three heaped teaspoons of sugar, saying she needed the sugar to help her get over the shock. Elsa-May insisted that she stay wrapped in the warmth of a blanket. Emma tried to explain that she was fine and not in shock; after all, it had happened a whole day ago.

Emma was glad to be alive and finally safe. She didn't even mind sitting on the hard wooden chairs in Elsa-May and Ettie's living room.

"So, Mr. Weeks killed Mr. Pluver because his daughter was going to run away with him? He originally thought that his daughter was having an affair with Levi and killed him too?" Silvie asked.

Emma was too shaken to speak. Maybe she *was* still in a little bit of shock.

Elsa-May spoke instead. "That's right. And I guess Pluver wanted to buy the land so he could give it to his boy, Bob – maybe to appease his guilt from leaving, who knows."

Emma's thoughts turned to Wil – she hadn't given him all the information. She had told him that Mr. Weeks had killed Levi, but she hadn't told him that she was nearly murdered as well. How could she have ever thought that Wil could have anything to do with deceiving her over her land? She smiled a little as she remembered his proposal.

Yes, it was most likely too soon after Levi's departure and tongues would wag, but Emma decided she could overlook that, just as she had overlooked Elsa-May and Ettie's cell phone. The first time she'd married for love. Would the second time be for companionship, and just to feel safe?

Maureen interrupted her thoughts, "Does Wil know about all this?"

"Some. I told him the main parts."

"Ettie called Wil and he's coming to take you home," Maureen said.

Emma frowned. "Wil's only just brought me here."

Maureen smiled widely. "He answered his phone in the barn when Ettie called him. He said he'd just arrived home."

"Why is everyone fussing? I'm fine, and I've only just gotten here. Anyway, surely someone else could have taken me home." She looked at the widows in turn, and each one smiled at her. "You're all up to something," Emma said.

"*Nee* we aren't," Elsa-May insisted.

Half an hour later, Ettie said, "I hear a buggy."

Elsa-May walked over and lifted Emma to her feet.

"There's nothing wrong with me, Elsa-May. I'm just a little shaken. Well, I was shaken yesterday, but today I'm fine."

Elsa-May opened the door to Wil.

"Emma, are you all right?"

Emma could feel her cheeks flush. She wanted to run into his strong arms, but she couldn't, not with all the ladies around. All she could do was nod in answer to his question.

"Well, I'll get you home." Wil looked up at the ladies and smiled. "*Denke* for calling me. Good day, ladies."

It was clear to Emma that the ladies were stifling giggles as they said goodbye to her and Wil.

As Wil led her to the buggy, Emma said, "You must have only just arrived home before having to turn around and come get me."

Wil glanced over at her. "I'm not about to say no to anything Elsa-May asks me to do. She scares me."

Emma laughed, but had to agree. Elsa-May was a very forthright woman.

As soon as Wil's buggy was out of the sight of the house, he pulled over to the side of the road. "Emma, what did you think that you were doing? I nearly lost you." He touched her cheek softly with the back of his hand. "Ettie told me everything. She guessed that you wouldn't have told me all that happened."

Emma closed her eyes and savored his touch. "I don't know what I was doing. I didn't know that the man was a murderer."

"You're safe now, so that's all that matters. I'm going to get you home and look after you properly."

Emma giggled and looked into Wil's eyes. In her heart she still loved Levi, yet Levi was her past, and she knew at that moment that Wil was her future.

To every thing there is a season, and a time to every purpose under the heaven: A time to be born, and a time to die; a time to plant, and a time to pluck up that which is planted;

Ecclesiastes 3:1-2

HIDDEN

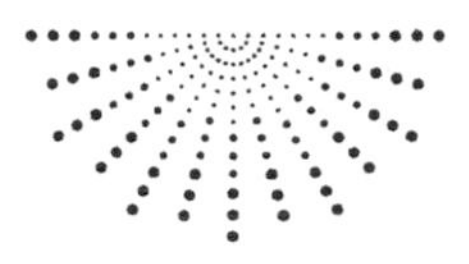

AMISH SECRET WIDOWS' SOCIETY: BOOK 2
(AMISH COZY MYSTERY)

CHAPTER ONE

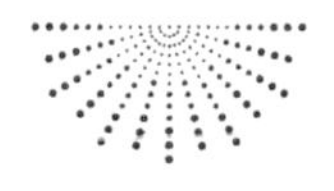

But without faith it is impossible to please him:for he that cometh to God must believe that he is, and that he is a rewarder of them that diligently seek him.

Hebrews 11:6

Emma sniffed the air; it smelled as though the chocolate chip cookies she was baking were ready. She had burned the first batch that morning by talking too much, so she hurried to save this batch. Even though a wave of heat enveloped her when she opened the oven, she still managed to listen to what Silvie had to say.

"My *mudder* sat me down when I first started being interested in boys. I could have been fifteen or sixteen. I'll never forget what she said to me." Silvie swallowed hard, and her fragile complexion turned another shade of pale. "She said that there is no such thing as 'hearts and flowers' love between a man and a woman, then I said, '*What about true love?*' And, do you know what she said?"

Emma nibbled on the end of her fingernail, hoping that this batch hadn't been in for too long as well. "What did she say?"

"She said 'love shmuv' and then said, 'humpf.' What do you think of that?"

Emma shook her head. She was pleased that she and Silvie were growing closer as friends. "Some people do find true love; I found it twice."

"*Jah,* but John and I were never in love because I never expected to find true love like you had with Levi and now you have with Wil. John might have been in love with me, in his own way. My *mudder* insisted that things would go better for me if I weren't *deerich,* foolish, about love from the start and didn't expect too much." John, Silvie's husband, had died many years before.

"I guess some people don't find that special love, but a lot of people do. My *mamm* and *daed* are still very much in love; I'm sure of that," Emma said.

"I hope I find someone to love. It must feel good. Well, I mean I did love John in the end; I grew to love him as I would love any member of my *familye.*"

"You're still young, Silvie. Why don't you ask *Gott* for a special *mann* to come into your life?" Emma studied Silvie's pretty face. She had the loveliest, pale creamy skin, which enhanced her pure blue eyes. She was truly an attractive woman.

"Do you think I should do that? It has always seemed selfish to me, to pray for something for myself instead of pray for someone else."

"I'm sure that *Gott* wants to hear about everything we care deeply about; He loves us so much."

Emma glanced at Silvie and saw a smile float across her face.

"Are you two still talking?"

The girls looked up to see Wil standing in the doorway of the kitchen. Since Wil and Emma had started courting, Wil forgot about the need to knock, and waltzed into the *haus* as he pleased.

Surely he could knock before he entered, Emma thought.

Wil took a seat at the kitchen table, reached out and took a sugar cookie. "Why did the conversation stop when I came in?"

The two girls smirked at each other.

Emma said, "We were talking about you."

Wil laughed and turned to Silvie. "Was Emma telling you how she couldn't wait to marry me?"

"Hush, Wil," Emma said quickly.

A look of delight crossed Silvie's delicate features. "Are you two getting married soon?"

"Eventually, but not right away." Emma was annoyed with Wil for saying such a thing to Silvie. Everyone they knew most likely suspected that they were courting, but it was only six months since Levi's death, which was far too soon for a wedding. It was most likely far too soon to court and Emma struggled daily with the guilt of having feelings for another *mann* so soon. Emma often wondered why she loved Wil so much when she spent half her time being annoyed with him.

Wil laughed. "You know how I like to tease. Emma, do you have a cup of tea for me, or is this a ladies only meeting?"

Without drawing a breath, he added, "Are those chocolate chip cookies I smell?"

"*Jah* and I'll get you a cup of tea as soon as I put these cookies on a cooling rack."

While Emma tended to the cookies and got the tea, Wil bit into another sugar cookie and continued to speak to Silvie. "So, how have you been?"

"I've been fine. Busy at work that's all."

"I see."

Emma placed the tea in front of Wil, a little irritated that he had interrupted her girl-talk with Silvie.

Wil looked around to talk to Emma. "Since you won't marry me straight away, I've decided to take the bishop up on his offer."

"What offer?" Emma frowned. If they had private and important decisions to make, she would rather do that in private.

"There's a young man who wants to become Amish and the bishop has asked if he can stay with me for a time. His name is Bailey Abler."

"That's odd," Emma said. "Don't they usually place people with a *familye* before they join?"

Wil shrugged his shoulders. "They normally do. He's been staying with the bishop for the past few days."

Given their conversation before Wil walked in, the girls shot each other a look of amazement. Was this new man *Gott's* answer so quickly, before Silvie had even had a chance to ask Him?

"How old is he?" Silvie asked, trying to keep the smile from her face.

"I haven't met him yet, but from what the bishop said, I'd guess him to be around thirty."

Emma put some of the warm chocolate chip cookies on a plate and placed it in the middle of the table before she sat down again. "What do you know about him?"

Wil wasted no time in taking one of the warm cookies. "Not much at all; the bishop hardly told me anything about him. He's alone in the world and used to work in the restaurant business. That's all I know."

"Well, I'm on the late shift at the bakery. I'd better get going." Silvie said.

"Late shift? I thought bakeries started around three in the mornings," Wil said before he took another bite of cookie.

"We've got a café attached now. We do light meals eight in the evenings and I stay there and clean up afterwards too."

Wil wiped some crumbs from his mouth. "I see."

"You and Emma should come in and have dinner there one time," Silvie said.

Wil smiled at Emma. "Maybe we will."

After Silvie left, Wil said, "I've invited Frank to dinner on Saturday night."

Frank was an elderly man who lived on his own in one of the Amish housing settlements. Wil was one of the many Amish people who cared about him.

"So, does that include me?" Emma asked.

"Of course it does."

Emma giggled. "So, I do the cooking?"

Wil chuckled. "*Jah*. You cook much better than I do."

Emma had guessed that he wanted her to cook. She mostly

cooked when he had guests for dinner, but he never asked her straight out, she always offered. "Who else is coming then?"

"That's all. Just you and me, and Bailey will be here by then. I thought it would be *gut* for Bailey to get to know a couple of people to ease him into the community slowly."

"Why don't we have dinner here at my place instead of yours? I know my way around this kitchen so much better."

"*Jah,* okay. I'll stop over and tell Frank that I've changed the dinner to your place. I can't do it today I've got too much to do. I'll do it tomorrow."

"I've got to go into town later. I'll stop by and tell him if you like. I also think it wouldn't hurt to have Silvie over to meet Bailey. What do you think?"

"*Jah,* that will be fine, but don't you think you should meet Bailey first before you start planning to marry him off to someone?"

"I've just got a feeling about the two of them. Besides, if he's made the decision to become Amish, he must have a *gut* heart toward *Gott.*"

"And what is your feeling about you and me?" Wil moved next to Emma and pushed his shoulder against hers.

Emma giggled. "You know how I feel about you, Wil."

"Just checking, wouldn't want you to change your mind or anything." Wil stood up. "Well, I've got work to do.

Emma admired his strong, tanned arms as he reached for more cookies. "Another invention?"

Wil smiled. "I'll see you later on." He took two cookies off the plate, gave Emma a quick kiss on the forehead and walked out the door.

Emma wondered if she would have as much time with Wil

when his *haus* guest arrived. She walked outside to bring the washing in off the line.

While she unpinned the washing, Emma's mind was drawn to the time when, as a young girl, she used to unpin the *familye* washing. She would pretend that her *bruders'* shirts were her sons' shirts. Emma had expected to marry and have many *kinner.* Emma knew that death was a part of life, and her grieving was eased by knowing where Levi was. But what of her plans of *kinner?* For so long she had dreamed of having children with Levi and now she had to switch her thinking to having children with Wil one day. Why did she struggle so much with that?

CHAPTER TWO

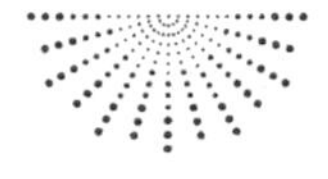

He that believeth and is baptized shall be saved;but he that believeth not shall be damned.

Mark 16:16

Emma pulled up, stopping her buggy in front of Frank's old wooden *haus*. The front garden had become a little overgrown, and Emma made up her mind then and there to get some of the ladies over to give his garden a *gut* weeding. Surely Frank wouldn't mind the company of a few ladies. Frank had lived alone since his wife, Sally, died years earlier.

As she knocked on the door, she noticed that the door could do with a repaint and remembered Wil had mentioned he would soon do some minor repairs on Frank's *haus*. She knocked again and waited a while, but still there was no answer. She figured that he could be out somewhere since many people in the community called on him. Maybe he had taken a walk. "Frank," she called out, but there was no answer.

She stepped out onto the street, and seeing no sign of him up or down the narrow road, she walked back up to the front door and turned the door handle. What if he'd had a fall?

The door was unlocked, and Emma stepped through. "Frank," she called out once more. "You home?"

Emma immediately sensed that something was wrong. A step later she saw that the floor was covered with paperwork; the stuffing was pulled out of the couches, and drawers were pulled from cabinets. Emma knew that this was more than someone being untidy; it appeared as though Frank had been robbed. She called out his name again as she raced into one of the two bedrooms.

The mattress was shredded completely as if someone had ripped it with a knife; she ran to the other bedroom to see the same thing. She heard a clanging noise behind her and turned around. As she couldn't see anything, she slowly approached the kitchen. She ignored her fast pumping heart and before she looked around the corner into the kitchen, she glanced over her shoulder for an escape route. Seeing the front door open, she took a deep breath. *One, two, three, now,* she told herself as she stuck her head into the kitchen.

Emma heaved a sigh of relief; the noise she heard was just a cat. The large, gray tabby was busy lapping something from a saucepan on the stove. Emma moved toward the cat, and it didn't acknowledge her presence. "Shoo, cat," Emma yelled. She flailed her arms to get it off the stove.

The cat remained as he was. Emma hoisted the cat into her

arms, and as she did so, she saw Frank spread out on the floor behind the kitchen table. Emma jumped and screamed, which caused the cat to yowl and jump from her arms. "Frank!"

Emma crouched over him. He was facing to the floor with one of his arms underneath him. Emma turned him over and felt for a pulse. It appeared that there was none. She guessed he had not been dead for long. Emma knew she would have to drive her buggy to the telephone shanty at the end of the road. Being in the midst of an Amish settlement Frank would not have had a phone in his home, nor would his neighbors.

After she made the phone call, Emma hung up the telephone. She looked down at her hands and could not stop them from shaking. She wanted nothing more than to tell Wil about Frank. Wil had a telephone in his barn, but was hardly ever in his barn and only used the telephone for outgoing calls. She called him anyway on the chance that he might be close to it, but as she suspected, there was no answer. She went back to Frank's *haus* to wait for the ambulance and the police, daunted that she would have to handle this all by herself.

When Emma got back to the *haus,* she peeped around the kitchen corner, a little scared to go back in. She saw that the cat was sitting on the kitchen table. She called to the cat, "Rude cat. Get off."

The cat looked at her, yowled and stayed put.

Emma tried a different approach. "Poor thing. Are you hungry?" Trying not to look at poor old Frank on the floor, Emma enticed the cat off the table with some cold meat she found in the cold box.

An ambulance and two police cars arrived within seconds of

each other. Emma took the paramedics through to the kitchen; the uniformed police officers followed closely behind.

"Are you his next of kin?" one of the officers asked as the paramedics examined Frank.

"No, I'm just a friend. I know he has two sons, but I don't know how to contact them. A friend of mine would have their phone numbers; I'm sure of it."

Emma heard the paramedics murmuring between themselves about taking the body to the hospital.

"I guess you need to take him to a funeral home?" Emma asked.

"We'll take him to the hospital first, but we have to wait for the police."

"Ah, Mrs. Kurtzler, we meet again."

Emma looked around with a fright. "Oh, Detective Crowley. I didn't think I would see you again so soon."

Crowley took out a notepad from his pocket. "Were you the one to find the body?"

Emma didn't like to hear Detective Crowley refer to Frank as *'the body.'* "Yes, I came and found Frank on the floor. He wasn't moving, and I turned him over to feel for a pulse and couldn't find one." Emma heard people coming through the front door and looked up to see three people in white suits.

"Forensics," is all Crowley said before he guided her into the living room.

Detective Crowley continued to stare at Emma, so she said, "I took the buggy up the road to find a public phone to call the police and the ambulance." Emma watched him scratch some things onto his notepad. She looked around for somewhere to sit, but the two couches were shredded.

"What brings you here, Detective? Do you come to every death in the area?"

"Death or murder?" He looked down into her eyes and then down to his notepad. "Why were you visiting him?"

"My… well, my friend and I were going to have Frank to dinner on Saturday night, but instead of having it at Wil's *haus* we were going to change it to have it at my *haus*. I was just coming here to tell Frank of the changed arrangements."

Detective Crowley scratched in his notebook. "Ah, yes, William Jacobson."

She raised her eyebrows at the detective's memory. It would have been a *gut* six months ago when they met the detective. Emma recalled that Wil and the detective did not get along well.

"Did Frank have transportation?"

"*Nee*, he walks or someone in the community drives him where he needs to go."

"So Mr. Jacobson or yourself would have picked him up to take him to your house for dinner then driven him home again?"

Emma nodded. "That's correct."

After Crowley had penned some more things in his notepad, he looked up. "Why did he need to know of the changed arrangements? Couldn't you have picked him up and driven him to your place? If he wasn't driving himself, surely there was no need for the special trip to tell him of the change of the dinner location, was there?"

Emma chewed on a fingernail as she thought through what the detective had just said. He was right; there was no need to tell Frank at all since Wil would have driven him there and back. If only Wil didn't have his head in the clouds all the time. But, then again, she was also to blame. "I see. I guess I didn't think about it too much. Anyway, he's an old man on his own; it doesn't hurt to visit him every now and again."

"Hmm."

Emma wondered what *'hmm'* meant.

"Do you, or did you – I should say, know the deceased very well?"

"*Nee,* not that well. Wil knows him well and did a lot of things for him; like repairs and anything he needed done around the *haus.* He used to take him places, but so did others in the community. We look after our own, you know."

"Hmm, I know."

Emma studied the detective's sharp, angular facial features and figured that they matched the sharpness of his tongue and his blunt personality.

The detective walked around the living room and Emma followed him. As he circled one of the couches, he said, "It looks as though someone was looking for something, wouldn't you think? Someone's done a thorough search for something."

"Can I go now, detective? I'll have Wil call one of Frank's sons, and I'm sure they'll take care of things."

As she walked toward the door, the detective said, "Mrs. Kurtzler, have you forgotten something?"

Emma spun around to face the detective. "No, I don't think I have."

Detective Crowley looked down at the cat that was purring around his legs.

"Oh dear, the cat."

"Looks like it was the old man's cat. Why don't you take it home, Mrs. Kurtzler?"

"I can't have a cat. I've got enough animals to look after." She stared at the large tabby; he had stopped purring around the detective's legs and was staring at her, as was the detective. "I've never liked cats. Besides he'll likely chase all the birds that come into my garden."

"Don't trouble yourself. I'll call animal welfare and have it put down."

"No, you can't do that." The cat looked at her as if it knew what the detective had said. Emma felt guilty and sighed. "All right. I'll take the cat." Emma crouched down. "Come on, kitty." The cat slowly walked toward her and did not object when Emma picked him up and tucked him under her arm. "Oh, he's such a heavy cat."

"Yes. It doesn't look like he's gone without too many meals."

"Well, goodbye, Detective."

"As usual, Mrs. Kurtzler, I will need to ask you some more questions; don't leave town."

Emma headed to her buggy, glad to get away from the detective. She put the cat on the seat next to her, half hoping that he would jump out and run away. She'd had dogs before, but never a cat. Despite her hopes, the gray cat curled into a ball and immediately fell asleep. He looked so peaceful and cuddly that Emma felt bad for hoping he'd run away.

When she pulled up in front of Wil's *haus,* he came out to meet her.

"Wil, it's Frank."

"What's happened, Emma? You look as white as a sheet." Wil put his hands on Emma's shoulders to steady her.

"Frank has died. The police think that he's been killed. I found him on the kitchen floor and then waited for the ambulance to come. He had no pulse."

Wil's face was blank. "Is he dead?"

"Murdered, killed, *jah,* dead." Emma collapsed into his arms.

Wil held Emma tightly for a moment, before he said, "I should have gone. I never should have sent you."

"I offered to go. There shouldn't have been any harm in going. You weren't to know." Emma gave a couple of sniffs. "That horrible detective was there too."

"Crowley?"

Emma pulled her head back from Wil's shoulder. "That's the one. He said that from the look of the place that someone was searching for something."

Wil shook his entire body. "I'm having trouble taking it all in. Come and sit inside and tell me everything from the start."

Wil led Emma into his *haus.* She sat down and told him exactly what had happened, from start to finish.

"I'll have to find the phone numbers of his sons," Wil said.

"I thought you'd have their numbers."

"I think I do. *Jah,* I'm sure that I do."

Emma's hand flew to her forehead. "Oh, I forgot I've got Frank's cat."

"*Ach, gut*; Frank loved Growler. Where is he?"

"Asleep in the buggy. He was asleep when I left the buggy anyway." Emma looked out the window at the buggy and could not see a cat walking around anywhere.

"He's not a barn cat, Emma. You'll have to keep the cat in the *haus.* His name is Growler."

Emma pulled a face. "Growler? I suppose I can keep him in the *haus* just until one of Frank's sons come and get him."

"*Jah,* I'm sure one of them would love to take him."

Emma knew nothing of Frank's two sons, except that neither of them had stayed in the community. Both boys decided on the *Englisch* lifestyle many years ago.

With Frank in his early eighties, the boys would be in their fifties, Emma guessed.

As she usually did when she got home, Emma unhitched the buggy and tended to the horse. All the while Growler stayed in the buggy until Emma picked him up and carried him into the *haus.* Once inside, Growler jumped out of her arms, walked around the living room then sprang onto the couch, curled up and went back to sleep.

"You know how to look after yourself," Emma murmured to Growler. Emma put a couple of old saucers at the back door for his food and filled up a bowl with water.

Later that night Wil went over to Emma's *haus* to check on her. "You feeling better now?"

"*Jah, denke.* Have you had dinner?" Emma knew that Wil wasn't much of a cook and did not look after himself as he should.

"Have you?" Wil asked.

"I've just finished and I was in the middle of washing the dishes. Come into the kitchen." Emma continued to wash the dishes while Wil sat at the kitchen table. "Have you called Frank's sons yet?"

"*Jah,* Clive is out of the country and Andrew is coming tomorrow."

"*Gut.* What do you know about them?" Emma asked.

"Nothing. I remember them from years ago, but only vaguely. Frank just gave me their phone numbers in case anything should happen to him."

"Was Frank expecting something to happen to him?"

"*Nee*, but he was old, that's all he meant. Even though his sons left, he still spoke to them. Well, from what he said, they hadn't visited him in five years, but he did get the occasional letter from them."

Emma nodded at what Wil said; she knew that many Amish parents had no contact with their *kinner* when they chose to leave the community, but it sounded as though it was the boys who did not keep in contact with Frank.

Wil said, "Why don't you come to Frank's *haus* tomorrow to meet Andrew?"

"I could, I guess. I'll ask if he can take Growler."

"Where is Growler?"

Emma looked around. "He was asleep on the couch last time I saw him." Emma looked by the back door to see that all the food had disappeared from the saucer. "Well, he's eaten." She pointed to the saucer. "That was full of food. I did leave the door open for a little while before, just in case he wanted to go out for a while. He might still be out there."

Wil jumped to his feet. "Emma, he might have run away."

"I have no litter tray. I had to let him out."

Wil went outside through the back door. "Here, Growler. Here kitty, kitty."

Emma followed him. "It's a little dark to see."

"Frank loved that cat," Wil said.

"Don't worry, we'll find him." Emma bit her lip and wished she'd taken better care of him.

After ten minutes of looking for him, they gave up. It was too dark to see very far.

"Hopefully, he'll be back in the morning," Emma said.

"*Jah*, I hope so. Night, Emma. Sweet dreams," Wil stepped in close to her.

"Night, Wil."

"It will be lovely when we can be together so I can cuddle you all night," Wil said as he put his arms around Emma's waist and pulled her to him.

Emma loved to feel his arms around her; she breathed in his masculine scent then giggled and pulled away. "Go on with you," she said with a laugh in her voice.

Wil walked down the road to his *haus*.

After Wil left, Emma felt a little better. It wasn't every day that she discovered a dead body and she was still a little shaken. There was also the unknown element of whether Frank died of natural causes or whether he was killed. She would hate to think that someone might have deliberately killed poor old Frank.

Emma made sure that she locked and bolted the back door and the front door after what had happened to old Frank. Emma re-boiled the kettle and made herself a chamomile tea hoping that it would help her sleep. She took the lamp up the stairs in one hand and her hot tea in the other ready for an early night. When she walked through her bedroom door, she saw Growler asleep in the middle of her bed. She hadn't even thought to look inside the *haus* for him. Emma laughed. "Make yourself comfortable, Growler."

Emma pushed Growler over to one side and thought it funny that he totally ignored her. Emma slipped under the covers, propped herself up with pillows and sipped her hot tea. She did want to share her bed once more with someone, but had hoped it would be with a *mann,* not a cat.

As she closed her eyes, Emma hoped that the widows would help her find out how Frank died.

CHAPTER THREE

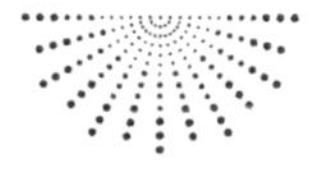

Now faith is the substance of things hoped for,
the evidence of things not seen.
Hebrews 11:1

As they walked from the buggy to Frank's *haus,* Emma noticed that one of the neighbors was peeking through their window at them. Emma knew it was Thomas Graber.

Emma whispered to Wil, "Do you see Thomas Graber staring at us through the window?"

"Wouldn't be surprised. Frank and he never saw eye to eye on anything and recently they had quite an argument over a large fence that Thomas wanted to put up. Frank said that it would block the sunlight on his vegetables."

Emma looked at the messy front garden. "It's odd that the garden in the front is neglected and he spent all his time in the vegetable garden out the back."

"He loved his vegetables."

Wil and Emma waited in the *haus* and before too long a red sports car zoomed to a halt in front of the *haus.*

Andrew looked much like Frank except a younger version. He was tall and wide just like his *daed* had been. He had a younger woman with him and Emma wondered if she was Andrew's *dochder.*

"Nice to see you again, Wil," Andrew's voice boomed. He turned to Emma. "And who do we have here? I don't remember you and I'm sure I'd remember such a pretty face."

Emma smiled and wondered if Andrew was a salesman of some kind; he certainly knew how to compliment and flatter people. "Hello, I'm Emma. We've never met; I wasn't in the community when you were."

"Did you convert?" Andrew asked.

"*Nee,* I've always been Amish, but not from around these parts." Emma smiled at the girl on Frank's arm as she spoke.

"Oh, forgive my manners. This is my girlfriend, Lacey."

Emma noticed that Lacey was quite a fancy woman. She had shiny red lips, long red nails and her dress was way above her knees. Emma glanced at Lacey's four-inch heels and wondered how anyone could possibly walk in shoes that high.

Emma nodded hello to Lacey.

"Pleased to meet you, Lacey," Wil said before he turned back to Andrew. "I would have hoped we would meet again under different circumstances. Let's talk inside the *haus.*"

Andrew stepped inside the *haus* and turned about in a circle.

"What a mess; apart from the mess, nothing has changed. Wil, how much do you think the *haus* would be worth? I'm not sure what the value would be."

"I don't know. Would you sell it or rent it?"

"I think Clive and I would want to sell. I've only spoken to him briefly; he's still overseas, but he'll back home in a week. I told him there's no need to rush home."

Emma was taken aback that the first questions Andrew had were about the value of the *haus* rather than about how his *daed* died, but then again, he could have already talked to the police.

Wil lowered his head and asked, "Do you want us to delay the funeral 'til he gets here?"

"Wil, can you handle all that stuff, the funeral? Clive and I aren't Amish anymore and most likely won't even go to the funeral. If the community is happy to look after things, that would be good."

Wil remained silent. Emma knew that Wil was struggling with judgment. Surely, they would want to be certain that Frank would be buried in the same Amish cemetery where Sally was buried, the one that they shared with the Mennonites. And why would they not attend their own *daed's* funeral?

"We'll cover the expenses, out of dad's estate. I'll have to go to the bank to see about his money. I'm guessing he had a stash of money since he sold the farm and bought this place after mom died. He would've had quite a sum left over."

"I'd say so. Well, if Clive and you don't want to be involved in the funeral, would you mind if we hold the service at my *haus*? The body is always in the *haus* for viewing and my *haus* is much bigger than this one. There'll be a fair crowd."

"Do whatever you want. Clive and I will have someone get

the house ready for sale at some stage– clean it up and that sort of thing. Did dad have anything else of value?"

Lacey took a small step forward. "Like any antiques or jewelry?"

Wil laughed. "Lacey, Amish have no need of jewelry and if something is antique, it would have been something passed down through Frank's *familye*." Wil motioned with his hand toward the furniture in the living room. "Look around and see if you think the furniture is antique."

Lacey walked around the room looking at the odd pieces of furniture scattered here and there. Lacey spun around to Andrew and said, "I don't care for any of it."

"It's not our style, Wil. I suppose it can be sold with the house. I'd dare say Clive wouldn't be interested in any of it either. It's basically junk."

Emma could not stop her eyebrows from rising. Lacey was far too interested in something that was hardly her business since she was only Andrew's girlfriend and not his *fraa*. Emma knew that Wil too would have been taken aback by Andrew and Lacey's manner. Andrew seemed to have no thought or care for his own father's funeral. "I'm looking after your *daed's* cat, Growler. Would you like him? I hear your *daed* was very fond of him."

Andrew held up a chubby hand and shook his head vehemently. "I don't want animals."

Emma looked to Lacey hoping she would say that she'd take the cat.

"I'm allergic to cat hair," Lacey said.

Of course, she would be allergic to cat hair, but not allergic to makeup, perfume, hair dye, acrylic nails and money, Emma thought before she could stop herself.

"So, Wil, anything else of value apart from this old house here?" Andrew asked.

Wil took his hat off and ran his hand through his hair, "He sold all the farm equipment at the same auction he sold the farm in. He sold the horses and the buggies. So that's it."

Andrew shook his head as if he was disappointed. Emma knew that Wil had to bite his tongue. Andrew seemed more concerned about the value of everything rather than the fact that neither he nor his *bruder* had visited their *daed* in the five years before he died.

Andrew took a handkerchief out of his pocket and mopped the sweat off his forehead. "Are you aware of any safe-deposit boxes my father had then? I'm sure he mentioned to me when I was a child that he had something special for us boys in a safe-deposit box."

Wil scratched his chin. "He told me nothing of the kind. Anyway, Andrew, Emma and I are very sorry for your loss."

Andrew nodded. "Thank you."

"I suppose the police have spoken to you about it all?" Emma asked.

"Yes, they think that he was startled by an intruder then fell and hit his head."

Emma raised her eyebrows once more. "Is that what they think?"

"Well, the place was trashed. I guess if there was anything of value here, it's well and truly gone by now," Andrew said then looked at Lacey who pouted her shiny, red lips.

"Wil, do you mind if I leave you in charge of letting a realtor through to look at the place, seeing that you live so close by and all?"

"Of course, Andrew."

"I'll have a realtor contact you in a week or two, or however long everything takes. I've never inherited anything before; I'm sure there will be probate and the property will have to be changed into our names before we sell."

Wil said, "I'm not sure how it works either; sorry I can't help you with that one."

"I'll be in touch then, thank you, Wil, Emma." Andrew and Lacey walked back to their red sports car.

~

THE NEXT NIGHT Emma met the widows at their regular gathering. They were a close-knit group that included the two elderly sisters, Elsa-May and Ettie. Elsa-May was a large-busted, solidly built lady with a big dominating personality to go with it, whereas her *schweschder* was small and fine boned and a little timid, but no less shrewd. Also at their regular meetings were Silvie and Maureen, younger widows, only a little older than Emma.

As usual at their secret meetings there was a lot of food. There were chocolate fudge bars, chocolate brownies, cheesecake and cup cakes. Emma looked forward to the regular widows' meetings that they held, but she did not like the hard wooden chairs in the living room. Ettie and Elsa-May did not have a couch or a sofa; the two old ladies did not seem to miss having a couch one little bit. Emma wondered whether they had been brought up to sit on hard chairs and that's why they thought nothing of it - they had never known anything else. Emma knew that the younger widows found it uncomfortable as much as she by the way they kept moving and shifting in their seats.

"They're not releasing the body," Elsa-May said before she bit into a chocolate chip cookie.

"Frank's body?" Emma felt silly for asking such a thing as soon as she said it; there was no other 'body' in the community of which they would be speaking.

"*Jah*. The bishop told me that he organized for the funeral director to pick up the body, but they aren't releasing it."

Emma knew that Elsa-May was very *gut* friends with the bishop and his *fraa,* and regularly went to visit them.

Ettie leaned forward. "Obviously, they suspect foul play."

"Who would kill harmless old Frank?" Silvie slid forward slightly.

"I'm sure they'll find that it's all a mistake in a couple of days," Maureen said.

Emma bit down on her lip. "The detective said that someone was looking for something."

"I hope poor old Frank didn't suffer," Ettie said. "More tea anyone?" Ettie rose to her feet and picked up the large china teapot and peered at each lady in turn.

Emma thought it amusing that Ettie referred to Frank as old; she was sure that Frank was younger than Ettie. "*Jah,* I'll have a top up, *denke,* Ettie." Emma stretched her hands as far as she could towards Ettie. She knew she risked being burned by hot tea as Ettie's shaking hands poured the tea into her cup.

"Do you remember seeing anything odd when you were at Frank's *haus,* Emma?" Elsa-May asked.

"He had some old soup or something of the kind on the stove; there were things all over the floor and the mattresses were shredded. That's all I can think of."

"Definitely sounds as though they were looking for something all right," Ettie said.

"They would've gone over the place for fingerprints already," Emma said.

"They won't find any fingerprints," Elsa-May said in a very firm voice. "The person who did this was looking for something and most likely something small since they shredded the mattresses." Elsa-May drummed her fingertips on her chin. "I wonder what old Frank could have been hiding."

"What do we know about Frank then?" Silvie said.

"He wasn't always Amish you know. He came to the community when he was in his late twenties. He married Sally soon after." Ettie gave a little giggle. "Tongues wagged when they got married so soon. Some said he only joined the community to marry Sally."

Emma dropped her gaze while she wondered if tongues would wag about her and Wil if they got married too soon. She was sure that they would.

"Sally was a little older than Frank, but he didn't seem to mind," Ettie said.

"What line of work was he in before he came to the community?" Maureen asked.

"That's a *gut* question, dear, but I don't know. If I did know, then I've forgotten." Ettie turned to her older *schweschder*. "Do you know, Elsa-May?"

"It's such a long time ago and I was busy with my *kinner* and raising a *familye* back then. I didn't really pay much notice; I never spent much time in Sally's company. We were never that close with them were we, Ettie?"

"*Nee*."

"He bought a farm and farmed the land. No one ever talked about what he did before, because his old life was buried when he got baptized," Elsa-May said with the hint of a smile on her face.

"I think the key to all this is what he did before he joined the community. We must find out what he did before," Emma said. "Can you Google him on your cell phone, Elsa-May?"

The widows' giggled at Emma.

"I know, I know. I was shocked when I first learned that Ettie and Elsa-May had a cell phone, but we need to find out who did this to Frank. What if they haven't found what they want and they kill someone else?"

"We weren't laughing at you," Elsa-May said.

"If there was any other way we could investigate, we would use it," Ettie said.

Elsa-May pulled out her cell phone from the drawer in the dresser. She pressed some buttons and waited a while. "I'm afraid it's gone dead. I haven't charged it lately. I'll go into town tomorrow and use the electricity at the library to charge it."

Ettie shook her head. "That's my fault. I'm supposed to be in charge of keeping the battery full."

"*Jah*, I distinctly remember telling you to always keep the thing charged." Elsa-May glared at Ettie.

"I will. I will. No need for anger. It goes flat over time; it's hardly my fault. Not really," Ettie said.

"I wasn't angry, Ettie. I just don't know why you can't keep the thing charged. I thought you would've learned that lesson by now. You remember that other time you didn't have it charged?"

"What time was that?" Emma knew these old ladies had done more investigating before, and investigating Henry Pluver's murder six months ago was not their first.

"Nothing, don't you worry about a thing, Emma. Ettie will have it charged tomorrow and we can all meet back here at the same time tomorrow night and find out Frank's background – that is, if there's anything about him on the internet."

"He's been Amish for so long that there may be nothing about him on the internet at all," Ettie said.

"We'll find that out then won't we, Ettie. But now, we'll have to find that out tomorrow instead of tonight because you didn't have it charged."

Ettie hung her head. "*Jah*, sorry, Elsa-May."

"Well, do it tomorrow, Ettie." Elsa-May shook her head at her *schweschder's* incompetence.

"Can we meet the day after tomorrow?" Emma knew she was brave making such a request. She did not want Elsa-May's attitude toward her *schweschder* to transfer to her. She added quickly, "I've got Wil and someone who's staying with him coming to dinner tomorrow night and Silvie will be there too."

"Do tell," Maureen said.

Emma giggled, remembering she hadn't told Maureen about Bailey. "There's a man who wants to join the Amish and the bishop asked Wil if he could stay with him for a while before he makes the decision to get baptized. He's been staying with the bishop for the last few days." Emma turned to Elsa-May. "Did you meet him at the bishop's *haus*, Elsa-May?"

Elsa-May looked away from Emma as she spoke. "*Nee*, I haven't met him yet. I know of him, that's all. He was out in the fields when I visited recently. Well, everyone all right to meet the night after next?"

Everyone agreed to meet back at Elsa-May and Ettie's *haus*.

CHAPTER FOUR

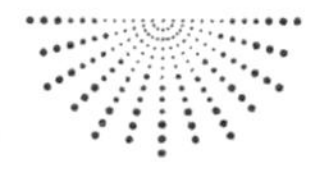

Even so faith, if it hath not works,
is dead, being alone.
James 2:17

Emma relaxed on her porch. She had just cleaned her *haus* from top to bottom and she had planted some snow peas, pumpkin and squash. She figured she deserved a little break while dinner cooked. Today, Wil was coming to dinner with the new man, Bailey. She had vegetables and chicken roasting in the oven.

She looked across her farm that was once leased by Henry Pluver and was now leased and farmed by his son, Bob. Bob kept to himself and that suited Emma just fine. He seemed to be doing a *gut* job since taking over his *daed's* leases and had even employed a couple more people to help him. Wil told her that he was going to try and get Bailey a job with Bob, or have him work for Bob without pay, just to see what it was like to work on an Amish farm and mix with the Amish folk.

Maybe with Bailey living with him, Wil wouldn't come around as much. Emma smiled at how Wil would stop by to see her at odd times; it never entered his head that some times may not be convenient. How different her late husband, Levi, was from Wil. Levi had been grounded and practical whereas Wil had his head in the clouds most of the time.

How funny it was that she could find love with two totally different *menner.* Levi was all about work; even when he was at home he found things to work on. Wil was happy to live on the income that came to him from leasing out his farm and from his investments. Wil lived life at a much slower pace than Levi had. Wil found enjoyment with his tinkering with silly inventions. Levi had always seen Wil's inventions as a waste of time and energy. Emma realized she had adopted Levi's attitude about them.

Emma looked to the trees on the horizon. She noticed how the sky just above the trees was much paler than the sky up higher. The sky high in the sky was the bluest of blue. She looked over the wheat that gently blew in the breeze. Peace filled her being as she closed her eyes and pushed all thoughts and worries out of her mind.

Silvie was the first to arrive, interrupting Emma's quiet time. After she tied up her horse, she walked toward Emma.

"Hello, Silvie. Come and sit with me for a while. Wil and Bailey haven't arrived yet and I don't have to do anything with the dinner for a few more minutes."

"I brought some apple pie and bread. I'll just take it into the kitchen."

When Silvie returned, she slumped into the porch chair beside Emma.

"You seem tired, Silvie."

"I've done a lot of work today. I worked this morning at the baker's and then I did some chores this afternoon. There's a lot to do when you live by yourself and don't have someone to help you and these odd shifts are a lot to handle. Sometimes I'm on the late shift and then the early shift. It doesn't give me much time to sleep."

"I guess I'm blessed to have Wil help me with things," Emma said.

"*Jah,* and Maureen has her *bruder,* John, do things for her."

"Silvie, if you have anything you need done, just say so. Wil would happily do anything and I'm sure John would too."

Silvie forced a laugh. "Well, it's mainly the little things. Like have someone make me a cup of tea when I'm feeling poorly. Or have someone feed the animals once in a while."

"*Gott* will have someone for you, don't be concerned, and just trust."

Silvie nodded. "I have been trusting, but I'm starting to worry that I'm getting too old to have *kinner.* What if *Gott* doesn't bring me someone until I'm too old? You know it gets harder to conceive the older you get."

Emma bit her lip and looked across her farm. "I've always wanted *kinner* too. I used to take it for granted that I would have some one day." She had pushed thoughts of *kinner* right out of her mind. Maybe she was doing the wrong thing in keeping Wil at arm's length for so long while she waited an acceptable time before marrying him, but what if in so doing she was destroying her chances of having *kinner?*

"I didn't mean to worry you, Emma."

Emma turned to look at Silvie. "You're right, Silvie. I've heard that too, about being too old to conceive. It seems that older women in the community don't have a problem conceiving if they've already had *kinner,* but first timers like we are have trouble if it's their first. Oh dear, you know what I mean, don't you?"

"*Jah,* I do. If a woman in her late thirties has already got four *kinner* she has another easily, whereas if it's her first, it's harder."

Emma nodded. "Exactly. I don't know why that is, but I've noticed that pattern of things before."

"Me too," Silvie said.

"We can't worry about those things though. If *Gott* blesses us with *kinner,* we will have them, but if not, then that's not in His plan for us. We can't worry about it."

Silvie smiled a tight-lipped smile.

Emma said, "Look at the beautiful view, the colors, the gentle swaying of the trees in the breeze. Listen to the birds."

After a moment, Silvie said, "I don't take enough time to appreciate the simple things."

"Me either, we should do more of it."

"When do you think you and Wil might marry? He'd marry you tomorrow. I'm sure of it."

Emma chewed the end of her fingernail. "It's too soon, don't you think? It's only been six months since Levi died."

"If you love him, I don't see that there's anything wrong with it," Silvie said.

"People might talk. I just want to do the right thing. I don't want people to talk about me."

"What would the right time be? What if Wil doesn't wait for you?"

Emma laughed. "I know that he'll wait for me. We are committed to each other in that way; he knows I'll marry him at some point."

After a moment's silence, Silvie asked, "Do you need any help with the dinner?"

"*Jah,* come on let's go inside." Both women stood up and went inside.

Moments later, there was a knock on the door. Emma was surprised. *Could this be Wil, knocking all of a sudden rather than barging in?*

Emma opened the door. "Wil."

"Hello, Emma. This is Bailey."

"Hello, Bailey; pleased to meet you. Please, come in. Come through to the kitchen. The meal is nearly ready."

Emma's kitchen was huge, plenty big enough for the long table that would comfortably sit twelve people, but today she had one end of it set for the four of them.

Emma watched Silvie's face as she looked at Bailey. It was obvious from the look in Silvie's eyes that she found Bailey pleasing to look at. Emma turned to study Bailey and saw that he had the same look on his face. Wil introduced the two of them.

Bailey was a very good-looking man. He was tall with a medium build, thick light brown hair that was cut in a typical *Englisch* cut with short sideburns, parted at the side with a little length on top. He appeared to have a day's growth of whiskers.

Emma could see why Silvie was so taken with him. To top everything off, he had a beautiful smile.

Everyone sat at the table and Emma placed the roasted chicken and vegetables, and the cold-cuts, in the middle of the table, so all could help themselves. There were two fresh loaves of seeded bread that Silvie had brought from the bakery where she worked.

Wil said to Bailey, "You probably already know that we each say our own silent prayer of thanks to *Gott* before we eat?"

Bailey nodded and closed his eyes.

Once everyone had finished giving thanks, they opened their eyes and began to eat.

Bailey helped himself to chicken and some roasted sweet potato.

"What made you want to join the community, Bailey?" Emma asked.

"I've been doing a lot of thinking about life and God and I could see that I was living a shallow life with no meaning. I came to realize that what's important is God's salvation."

Silvie giggled. "You'll have to learn to speak Pennsylvania Dutch."

"I can do that. I don't think that will be a problem. You could help me."

Emma secretly smiled at the way the two of them were speaking to one another. It was clear that they were attracted to each other and very much so. Emma hoped that this was the right man for Silvie.

They would certainly have beautiful *bopplis*. Bailey's hair would have surely been blonde as a child and his eyes were as blue as Silvie's.

But, they would have to wait a while if they were interested in one another. Bailey had yet to be baptized and would have to wait a time to see if he wanted to live the Amish ways.

Ideally, Bailey should not be influenced by the love of a woman. But what was ever ideal? It wasn't ideal for Levi to die and leave her childless and alone. Did anyone ever lead an ideal life or live the life that they imagined for themselves? Surely disappointment and struggle was a part of life.

Wil quickly swallowed the food in his mouth. "Bailey, it's an important commitment. If you decide to join you will have to commit before the whole church to serve *Gott* with your heart, soul, mind and body. You will be bound to that for life."

"The bishop has explained it all to me, Wil. I've already made that decision. It's just the bishop I'm waiting on. He says I have to wait a time. He didn't tell me how long I must wait before being baptized. I'd be baptized tomorrow if I could."

"*Nee,* it would be far too soon. You'd only have an idealized view of what being Amish is. You have to live it to know it." Wil put his fist to his heart.

Emma stared at Wil; she had never heard Wil speak so definitely on any matter.

"I'll have to take your word on that since I haven't lived it much so far," Bailey said.

CHAPTER FIVE

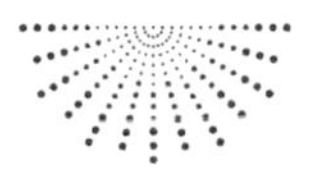

Thou shalt not make unto thee any graven image, or any likeness of any thing that is in heaven above, or that is in the earth beneath, or that is in the water under the earth.

Exodus 20:4

When their visit with Emma was over, Wil and Bailey walked home.

"Wil, what should happen if I want to take a lady on a date?"

Wil laughed. "Silvie?"

"You noticed?"

Wil nodded.

"How do I get to know her better; how do the Amish do that?"

Wil scratched his chin. "I don't know if you should be

distracted by a woman at this stage, Bailey. Did the bishop tell you that you should learn our ways first?"

"I know I shouldn't, but it's a bit hard not to be distracted by a beautiful woman. I'll keep my intentions honorable of course."

Wil slapped Bailey on the shoulder. "What we do is take them on a buggy ride or sometimes we take them out for a meal, as the *Englisch* do."

"A buggy ride sounds the thing to me, nice and romantic."

"Do you know how to drive a buggy?"

"*Jah.* The bishop showed me how to hitch a buggy and drive one. I know all the road rules too."

"*Wunderbaar.* You can take one of my buggies."

"Thank you, Wil. I'll do that. Should I stop by her place? Do you know where she lives?"

Wil hoped he was doing the right thing and would not get into trouble with the bishop. "*Jah,* it's the old red *haus* just before you turn onto the road that takes you into town. Don't get too interested in her though; you're supposed to learn our ways first." Although Wil considered he should have dissuaded Bailey, he knew what it was like to love a woman and he found it difficult to stand in love's way.

"I might see her tomorrow."

"One more thing, Bailey. The Amish, I suppose you know, are not physical before marriage."

"I know that, Wil. I'll be a gentleman."

Wil was a little concerned; he hardly knew Bailey and if anything went wrong he would hold himself responsible.

Once they arrived back at Wil's *haus,* Bailey went up to his bedroom and Wil stayed downstairs in the living room. Wil hoped that Emma would accept his proposal of marriage soon. She had said that she would marry him, but had given him no timeframe. He would wait for her because he understood that it was important for her to be ready to love him fully, but that did nothing to stop his yearnings for her.

~

SILVIE WAS SWEEPING her small patio when she heard a buggy. Her heart raced when she saw that the man driving the buggy was Bailey.

Her hands flew to straighten her apron and prayer *kapp* before she stepped down to meet him. "Bailey, this is a nice surprise."

Bailey got out of the buggy. "Hello. I hope you don't mind me stopping by to see you like this."

"Not at all."

"Would you come on a buggy ride with me sometime?"

Silvie was delighted and a little shocked. It had been years since she had been asked such a thing. She wanted to look away and laugh, but she could not keep her eyes from him. "I'd like that."

"How about now?"

"Right now?" Silvie's heart beat faster and harder. She would have preferred some time to lead up to this, but then if she had time to think she may refuse his offer.

"Why not? I'm sure your sweeping can wait. Come with me now." Bailey held out his hand.

Silvie looked at her *haus*, stifled a giggle and then said, "All right."

A huge smile spread across Bailey's face, which made him even more handsome.

Once they were both in the buggy, Bailey said, "Now, you'll have to tell me which way to go because I don't know these roads yet."

"Go left at the top of this road. I can show you around a little." Silvie took him on some quiet roads in the hope that not too many people would see them. Her late husband, John, had been gone for some time and Silvie knew that she was ready for the *mann* that *Gott* had chosen for her. Maybe it was Bailey. She looked across at him and he smiled back at her.

"Do you have *bruders* or *schweschders*, Bailey?" Silvie hoped that Bailey would be close with his *familye*.

"I know that means brothers and sisters and yes, I have two *bruders* and two *schweschders*, but I haven't spoken to them in years. What about you?"

"I have five older *bruders*, and one younger *schweschder*. I'm from Ohio originally. John, my late husband, and I moved here just after we got married. There were more job opportunities here for him." Silvie's shoulders drooped slightly as she remembered John.

Bailey took his eyes off the road and glanced over at her. "I'm sorry; no one told me that you'd lost your husband."

Silvie gave a nervous laugh. "Amish get married very young; I know that's not the same for the *Englisch*. Most of us get married before twenty years of age. It would be a little unusual for someone of my age never to have been married. Of course, there's the odd one who never marries." Silvie wanted the conversation away from herself. "Have you ever considered marriage, Bailey?"

"I'm divorced." He glanced at her just in time to see her purse her lips. "What was that look for?"

Silvie felt heat rise to her cheeks. "I didn't mean to have such a reaction. It's just that there's no divorce amongst the Amish."

"I know. The bishop told me all about things like that. The bishop said that I wouldn't have been allowed to enter an Old Order Amish community because of the divorce. He said if a couple really cannot get along, rather than divorce they live separately, but divorce is not an option. Since I was an *Englischer* when I divorced, the bishop is prepared to overlook my first marriage. He said that the past sin is washed away by baptism and repentance."

"That's right; marriage is forever. So it's important to make the right choice to start with."

"Would you ever get married again, Silvie?"

Silvie took a slow deep breath. "John died years ago and for the first few years I knew I would never marry again, but lately I've been thinking that it would be nice to have someone to look after and someone to cook for." Silvie noticed that Bailey smiled.

"That's good," he said.

"You drive the buggy very well for an *Englischer*."

"The bishop gave me a few lessons and Wil made sure I could drive before he let me loose with one of his horses." Bailey ran his eyes over the countryside. "It's so peaceful out here. Why don't we go for a walk?"

"Okay, it's a perfect day for it."

Bailey tied the horse to a fence post beside the road. "It's so quiet and peaceful out here and the air is so fresh."

Silvie glanced up into his face as they walked. She could see herself falling in love with this man, but she had to wait. She would not give her heart too quickly. She would wait until he was baptized and integrated into the community.

"Did you know old Frank, the man who died?" Bailey asked.

Silvie held her long dress up just a little so it would not trail along the long grass. "Just a little. It was horrible what happened to him, but he's gone home to be with the Lord so he'll be happy now."

Bailey stopped walking. "You know that for sure, do you?"

Silvie stopped when Bailey had. Warning bells went off in her head; it sounded like this man was having problems believing. "Of course I know that for sure. I know it in my heart."

Bailey put a finger to his chin. "What if it's all not real?"

"Bailey, if you have doubts like that, then what are you doing here?"

He looked up to the sky and turned back to look into her face. "I believe in my heart, but I have – sometimes I have a tiny doubt. That's allowable, isn't it?"

"*Nee,* I don't think so. It's a real commitment for an *Englischer* to become Amish. Being Amish is so much more than wearing these clothes, living simply and driving a buggy. We live our lives for *Gott* with all our heart, mind and soul. Where there is doubt then faith is not there. You have to believe with faith and block out any doubt." Silvie licked her lips and hoped that she was getting through to him. "It's only fear that causes the doubt."

"I'm just being honest with you, Silvie. I guess you're right. The Scripture says perfect love casts out fear. Perfect love of *Gott* causes fear to run away."

Silvie smiled at him quoting Scriptures. "That's right. Just believe, that's all we have to do. It's not hard."

"*Denke*, Silvie."

Hearing that Bailey was divorced, Silvie knew she would have to wait a while if this was the *mann Gott* had for her. She did not want to become the second woman that Bailey divorced. *Maybe Gott is testing me with this mann, testing my faith,* Silvie thought.

Bailey looked up again, to the sky. "I don't think I've ever heard so many birds chirping. And so many different birds."

Silvie closed her eyes and listened to them. "*Jah,* I didn't even hear them until you mentioned them."

Bailey pulled on her arm. "Let's sit over here and listen to them."

The two of them sat on a large boulder and closed their eyes. The sun warmed their faces and a gentle and cool breeze enveloped them as they listened to the birds make music.

As she opened her eyes, Bailey took hold of her hand. She pulled her hand away. "It's too soon, Bailey."

"What's too soon, Silvie?"

"It's too soon for anything like this. You and me."

Bailey moved closer to her. "How long will I have to wait?"

Silvie's body stiffened. "It's not about waiting."

"Then why should I wait? I know what my heart wants."

Silvie covered her mouth and giggled. "We've only just met."

Bailey gave her a smile that melted her heart. If *Gott* was testing her, he picked an excellent *mann* with whom to test her. "There's a bigger decision you have to make first and that decision should not be clouded by me."

He chuckled. "Too late for that."

Silvie put her head down and looked into her hands. "Maybe we should go back."

"Maybe we should stay here."

She looked up and stared into his eyes for some time before she could take his gaze no longer. Silvie looked straight ahead into the fields. She could see out of the corner of her eye that Bailey was still staring at her.

"You are the most beautiful woman I've ever seen, Silvie. Not only that, you're kind and sweet as well."

His words could have sounded insincere, but the way he said them made Silvie sure that he meant every one of them. Silvie rose to her feet. If she stayed sitting any longer she just might have to kiss him and she knew that would be the wrong thing to do. "We should be getting back."

"*Nee,* sit with me a little longer, please? Let's enjoy this beautiful day that *Gott* has given us."

Silvie sat down again. "Just for a little longer then."

"Have you known Wil and Emma long?"

Silvie was pleased by the change of subject. *"Jah,* I've known them since I moved here, but I was never close with them until Emma's husband died. Now that we're both widows we have something in common."

Bailey nodded. "And you didn't know Frank well?"

"*Nee,* not well at all." Silvie was sure that it was the second time that Bailey had asked her about Frank. "Why do you ask?"

"Just interested in everyone, that's all."

Silvie wanted to know why Bailey got divorced. Did his wife want the divorce or did he? She did not ask because she did not want to speak of unpleasantness. "What kind of work will you do here in the community?"

"I've always worked in restaurants. I've owned a few, but Wil has the idea that I should work on a farm to get to know other Amish men and see what the traditional Amish man does."

Silvie could not see the sense in what Wil had advised him to do. "But you're not the traditional Amish man."

"I know, but I have to do something, start somewhere. I have to prove myself; I have to prove that I'm a hard worker."

Silvie nodded. "What do your *familye* think of you living here?"

"I don't have much contact with them."

Bailey's face hardened as he spoke of his *familye.*

"That's sad," she said.

"Why didn't you move back to Ohio after your husband passed away?"

"This is my home now. I need to go forward with my life not backwards. I miss my *familye,* but I have the community here and they're like my *familye.* The community will become your new *familye* too. If you stay, you'll see what I mean."

"Of course I'll stay. I would have been baptized right away, only the bishop wouldn't let me."

Silvie looked into his eyes. She hoped that he would take hold of her hand again, but he didn't. "I suppose the bishop knows that there will be some big changes for you and you might not like them."

"*Jah,* I know. I know his reasoning."

Silvie could tell by the way he looked into her eyes that he was smitten with her. She glanced at his lips and wondered what they would feel like on hers. "We should go."

"All right, we'll go." Bailey stood up and held out his hand.

Silvie put her hand in his and rose to her feet.

"We will go back as soon as we go for another walk. It's a shame to ignore this beautiful countryside."

Given that Bailey still had hold of her hand and was walking away, Silvie had no choice but to go with him.

They walked for fifteen minutes and on their return to the buggy, Bailey stopped still. "Silvie, I need to tell you that I want to kiss you. I know I can't and I'm showing great restraint."

Silvie looked into his face. He spoke with such sincerity that she knew that he was a *gut* man and one who could be trusted. A nervous sound escaped from the back of Silvie's throat. She wanted to be held tightly in his strong arms. She forced herself to say, "We have to wait."

He drew her hand to his lips and looked into her eyes as he pressed his warm lips into the back of her hand. The touch of his lips sent tingles spiraling through her body. She giggled nervously and pulled her hand away. "We must get back."

He stood still watching her while she climbed into the buggy. "*Kumm*, Bailey."

Bailey let out a noisy sigh, untied the horse and climbed into the buggy.

All the way back to her place Silvie regretted not kissing him. *What harm could a tiny kiss do?* It had been so long since she'd been kissed. She had kept away from *menner* since John died. Bailey was the first *mann* to hold her interest.

"Well, here you are." Bailey pulled up the horse in front of Silvie's door.

"*Denke* for a nice time, Bailey."

With one strong arm, Bailey took hold of her behind her waist and pulled her quickly to him. Silvie did not resist and before she knew what was happening, his lips were softly against hers. He released her at once. "Forgive my boldness."

Silvie made an attempt at a smile and shook her head. She quickly got out of the buggy and swallowed hard. "Bye, Bailey."

He nodded his head and clicked the horse forward.

Silvie put her hand to her fast beating heart and hurried into the safety of her *haus.*

CHAPTER SIX

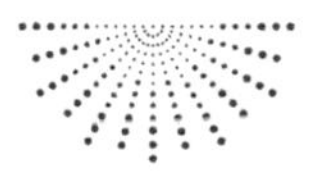

But the fruit of the Spirit is love, joy, peace,Meekness, temperance: longsuffering, gentleness, goodness, faith, against such there is no law. And they that are Christ's have crucified the flesh with the affections and lusts.
Galatians 5:22-24

As arranged, the widows met once again and this time they were to hear what Ettie had found out from the internet, about Frank.

Emma was the first to speak. "What did you find out, Ettie? Anything?"

"It's convenient that one of Frank's relatives has researched the family history. Frank's father was an art dealer back in the old country, and before Frank came to join us he worked at an auction house in Chicago as an auctioneer."

"What sort of auction house?" Emma asked.

"Seems to be an art auction house as far as I can tell. I looked them up and they don't sell anything but paintings."

"So, he followed in his father's footsteps." Maureen tried to lean back in the chair.

"It appears so," Ettie said.

"Anything else, Ettie?" Silvie asked.

"*Nee*. I've asked the people in the community who knew him best and he never spoke of his life before he joined us," Ettie said.

"Maybe someone thought that he had a valuable painting hidden or something. Maybe it was a stolen painting," Maureen said.

"Excellent point, Maureen, but I already thought of that. There are too many to track though. There are many, many missing paintings from Germany during the war and there are many stolen paintings over the years from Chicago. So even if he did have a stolen painting, we would have no way of knowing which one he had."

"It sounds all very far fetched," Silvie said. "It could have just been random thieves after money. Remember that it's often the most logical explanation that is the right one," Silvie said.

"Random thieves don't kill people though, Silvie. Thieves run if they're seen. They don't usually turn around and kill people," Elsa-May said.

"Wil's going to have Frank's body at his *haus* for the viewing and everything. Frank's sons don't want to be involved in the funeral," Emma said.

"Why don't we clean Frank's *haus* and that way we can look for clues?" Ettie said.

"Great idea, Ettie," Elsa-May said.

"The police have combed right through it; I doubt there will be any clues left," Emma said.

"*Jah*, but we have to start somewhere," Elsa-May said.

As they were getting into their buggies, Silvie shared with Emma that she went on a buggy ride with Bailey.

"Silvie, I know he's handsome, but he's not even properly one of us yet. Don't you think you should wait?" Emma asked.

"I should, I know, but it's hard."

Emma nodded and said goodbye to Silvie. On her way home, anger welled up within her. Wil had to know of it because he would have use of one of Wil's buggies. Emma stopped at Wil's on her way home.

Wil answered the knock on his door. "Emma, come in."

"I would prefer to speak out here." She spoke in a low tone so Bailey would not hear her. "I just heard from Silvie about her time with Bailey."

Wil nodded.

"Don't you think it's a bit soon for him to be taking someone for a buggy ride? What would the bishop think of that?"

Wil remained silent, so Emma continued, "Bailey's been entrusted into your care. Can't you take anything seriously, Wil?"

Wil rubbed his forehead. "I know what it's like when you love someone, Emma."

Emma scoffed. "Love? They've only just met."

"What about us?" Wil asked.

"I'm not speaking of us."

"You never want to speak of us, Emma."

"It's things like this that make me unsure about you, Wil, if I have to be truthful."

Wil raised his eyebrows and stepped closer to her. "What do you mean?"

"I need someone in my life who'll be stable and solid and not do things without thinking. You surely did not think things through if you gave Bailey a buggy to take Silvie out. What about Silvie, what if she gets hurt?"

"Sometimes people have to take a chance, Emma. That includes you. Now, if you'll excuse me. I've some things to do before I turn in for the night."

"What? Like a silly invention?" Emma bit her lip as soon as she said it. She opened her mouth to say sorry, but Wil spoke before she had a chance.

"Goodnight, Emma." Wil closed his door.

CHAPTER SEVEN

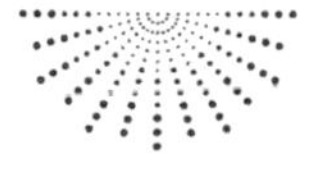

Behold the fowls of the air: for they sow not, neither do they reap, nor gather into barns; yet your heavenly Father feedeth them. Are ye not much better than they?
Which of you by taking thought can add one cubit unto his stature?
Matthew 6:26-27

Emma arrived early at Wil's home for the viewing on the day of the funeral, as did Maureen. They were fixing the food for the people who would want to return there from the cemetery for a light meal. Maureen and Emma decided on cold-cuts, coleslaw, and two hot dishes. The meal after a funeral was never a lavish affair.

The bishop and the ministers were the first to arrive. It wasn't long before there were rows of buggies outside Wil's *haus.*

"Look at everyone, Maureen. I'm glad Wil decided to have the viewing here because Frank's *haus* would have been far too small for all these people."

Maureen looked out the kitchen window. "Well, we've done all we can do in here for the time being. Let's go and greet some people."

The two ladies left the kitchen and went into the living room where everyone had gathered.

After the viewing, everyone got into their buggies to follow the funeral buggy to the cemetery.

Everyone gathered around the grave and then one of the ministers, rather than the bishop, gave a short talk on life and death, explaining that it was all a cycle, birth to death, and it was a natural thing that everyone has to go through.

Maureen and Emma were next to each other and Emma saw that Maureen's eyes misted over. Emma knew that she was thinking of her late husband. She squeezed Maureen's hand.

Emma coped with her own grief by trying not to think too much of Levi. It was hard, but she kept as busy as she could rather than face the pain of her loss. Emma could only keep reminding herself that Levi was in a better place.

After prayers were said, the coffin was lowered into the ground. Emma looked up and noticed Elsa-May and Ettie standing next to Silvie. Wil and Bailey were standing in a group with some of the men.

Emma and Maureen knew that they would have to be the first to leave so they could go back to Wil's *haus* to get the meal ready. As they both turned around, they saw that Bob Pluver had been standing directly behind them. Emma immediately got the chills. Bob Pluver was such an odd character.

"Hello, Maureen and Emma." Although he addressed Emma as well, his eyes were focused the whole time on Maureen.

"*Ach,* hello, Bob." Maureen glanced across at Emma. "Um, did you know Frank very well?"

"*Jah* I did."

Emma had to fight the smile that was trying to spread across her face. It was clear that he had a liking for Maureen because this was the most she'd ever heard Bob say unless he was talking farm business.

"Were you friends with him, Bob?" Maureen asked.

Bob nodded.

"*Gut* friends?"

"I'd say so." Bob folded his arms in front of him and leaned back.

"Did you visit him much?" Emma asked.

"I visited him every Thursday."

Emma realized that Bob must have been at Frank's *haus* on the very day that he died, but this was hardly the time or the place to ask him questions. She would have Maureen ask him questions tomorrow.

"He was a nice man," Bob said slowly.

"*Jah,* he was a nice man. I didn't know him well, but I'm sure he was a nice man," Maureen gave him a big hearty smile revealing the slight gap in between her front teeth. "If you can excuse us, Bob, we have to go and prepare the meal back at Wil's *haus.* You're very welcome to come join us, Bob."

Bob smiled at Maureen. "*Jah* I'll come, *denke.*"

As they hurried to the buggy, Emma said, "That's the most I've ever heard him say. I think he's sweet on you. He couldn't take his eyes from you and also that's the first time I've ever seen him smile. He looks a different person when he smiles."

Maureen smiled and shrugged her shoulders. "He's a sweet boy."

Emma thought she could think of a few better descriptions for him other than sweet, but she kept her opinions to herself. "He'd have to be our age, wouldn't he, Maureen?"

Emma was in her late twenties and Maureen was in her early thirties, Emma was sure of that.

As they traveled back to Wil's *haus*, Emma said, "Be careful then if you don't want an admirer, Maureen."

~

SILVIE WAS STILL at the funeral. Bailey had been on her mind every second of every day. She looked for him and saw him talking to some people. She walked over so she would be close to him, hoping that he would speak to her. As soon as Bailey saw her he excused himself from the couple he was speaking with.

"Hello, Silvie."

His smile melted her heart. "Hello. What did you think of your first Amish funeral?" Silvie asked.

"Pretty much the same as the other funerals I've been to. Not too different."

There was an awkward silence as Silvie searched for something to say.

Bailey leaned into her and spoke softly, "I enjoyed our buggy ride."

Silvie nodded and felt her cheeks heat up. She knew she was blushing and she hoped that Bailey did not notice. "Me too."

"Do you know everyone here?" Bailey asked.

Silvie looked around. "*Jah,* I think I do. Or at least I've seen all these people before. I may not be able to tell you all their names. I would've expected Frank's sons to be here and they don't appear to be."

"*Nee*. Wil told me that the sons said they wouldn't be coming to the funeral. They asked Wil to look after things."

Silvie raised her eyebrows in surprise at his sons being so disinterested in their father that they could not even go to his funeral.

Bailey spoke softly. "It seems a little odd, doesn't it? That they don't even want to go to their father's funeral, to pay their respects?"

"It is very odd. Maybe they feel awkward because they left the Amish; they might feel they have no place here."

"Maybe. Wil said they hadn't visited Frank for some years," Bailey said.

"*Jah,* that's what I heard." After a small silence, Silvie said, "I'll see you at Wil's *haus* then." Silvie turned and walked away. She could feel Bailey's eyes on her as she walked. She dared not turn around.

~

THERE WERE some hundred folk gathered at Wil's *haus.* Emma kept herself busy in the kitchen in an effort to avoid Wil. When the people had nearly all gone home, Maureen, Silvie and Emma stayed to clean afterwards.

Emma looked out the kitchen window and saw that Wil was outside saying goodbye to some people. She took her opportunity. "We've nearly finished. Do you two mind if I leave you to finish up?"

Both girls looked at her as though they wondered what she was up to. Any other time, she would've wanted to stay there to have more time with Wil. She did not want to share with them that she'd had a little tiff with him. "I've got some things I need to take care of at home," she explained.

"Of course, go," Maureen said.

Emma wrapped a portion of left over meat for Growler and slipped out the back door and hurried home.

As she opened her front door, Growler was sitting there as if he was waiting for her. "Hello, I brought you some meat."

Growler meowed and walked toward her.

"Over to your saucer, then." The cat followed Emma to the saucer at the back door. Growler appreciated the meat. Emma smiled as she watched him eat it. Even though she did not like cats, she was beginning to see why some people did. It was nice to come home and have someone waiting for her even if it was a cat who ignored her most of the time.

Emma filled up the kettle and placed it on the stove. A nice cup of hot tea was just what she needed. As she rinsed out the cup in the sink, she remembered that day at Frank's *haus* when she had found him; there had been two cups in the sink.

Why would he need two cups? He must have had a visitor there that day and it must have been someone that he knew. If someone had come to steal from him, he would not sit down and have a cup of tea with him.

Finished with his meat, Growler jumped on the chair next

to her and looked at her. "You know something don't you, Growler. What did you see that day? If only you could speak."

~

THE VERY NEXT DAY, Emma knocked on Detective Crowley's open office door.

Detective Crowley stood up behind his desk. "Mrs. Kurtzler, what brings you here this fine day?"

"Hello, Detective, it's about Frank."

He pointed to the chair opposite his desk and sat down. "Have a seat."

As soon as Emma sat down, she said, "I just thought I'd mention that there were two cups in the sink at Frank's *haus*."

"Yes, I noticed that. We had those cups tested and that's where we found the poison."

"So, he was poisoned?"

"Yes. Why are you only just telling me about the two cups now?"

Emma's heart started to race. The detective always made her feel as though she were guilty. "I only just remembered, only just this very morning."

"Have you been withholding any other information, Mrs. Kurtzler?"

Emma knew quite a bit, but thought she'd keep quiet about Bob being there the very day of the murder. She was sure that Bob was no murderer. Bob was a little odd, but not a murderer. "Frank had ongoing disagreements with his neighbor, Thomas something or other. His last name escapes me for the moment."

"Yes, Thomas Graber; he's known to the police."

Emma tilted her head slightly to the side. "He is?"

Detective Crowley nodded. "Let's just say we've had dealings with him over other matters. What else have you found out?"

Emma was surprised that the Amish *mann,* Thomas Graber, would have had previous dealings with the police. "Did you find any prints on one of the cups that didn't belong to Frank? I mean the one that the other person might have drunk from?"

Crowley shook his head, then pushed back in his chair and let out a deep breath. Did the detective think that she was wasting his time?

"Mrs. Kurtzler, what's the real reason you've come here?"

"To tell you about the two cups. You said if I think of anything to let you know."

"Mrs. Kurtzler, Emma, I have to tell you that I do not need your help to solve a crime."

Emma gasped and jumped to her feet. "I'm trying to be of help. You told me to come to you if I thought of anything and that's what I'm doing."

The detective stayed seated and interlocked his fingers in front of him. "It's funny that I come across you again, in another murder case. Would that be fate or destiny?"

"I thought I might be able to help you, that's all. Seeing that I was the one who found him and I'm looking after his cat, and all." Emma knew she was not making any sense. Why did she mention Frank's cat? "I'll be going now, then." Emma walked straight out of Detective Crowley's office without saying goodbye to him.

She was glad that she didn't mention Bob was there the day

Frank died. Bob wasn't good with words, and he would never be able to explain himself to the police.

All the way home, Emma felt sick to her stomach. *Why is that detective so mean all the time? He always finds the very thing to say that would upset me.*

The next morning, Emma stopped by at Wil's. She knew it would be awkward to see him. She was not ready to speak of their disagreement.

Emma took a deep breath when he opened the door. "Can you give me the keys to Frank's *haus*? The ladies and I want to go and give it a *gut* clean."

"*Jah,* I've got a spare key. I'll fetch it for you. Do you want to do that today?"

"Both Maureen and Silvie aren't working today, so today suits all of us."

Wil rubbed his chin. "Do you think it will be safe? They haven't found who did it, you know."

"*Jah,* it'll be safe with the five of us. Elsa-May and Ettie are going too."

Wil went around the corner into the kitchen and then came back with the key and handed it to her. "Emma, can we talk?"

"Not now, Wil."

~

THE WIDOWS MET at Frank's *haus* at noon, as they had planned. Maureen was to arrive as soon as she talked to Bob Pluver.

"What exactly are we looking for, Elsa-May?" Silvie asked.

"I don't really know. Tell me if you find anything, anything at all."

They were immediately disturbed by a knock on the door. Elsa-May opened the door to see Thomas Graber, Frank's next-door neighbor. "Hello, Thomas."

"Hello, Elsa-May. What are you ladies doing in here?" Thomas seemed jittery as he shifted his weight between his feet.

"We've come to give the place a *gut* cleaning," Emma said.

"Sad news about old Frank, wasn't it," Thomas said.

"*Jah,* that it was," Elsa-May said.

Thomas tipped his hat slightly back on his head. "Wonders me that anyone would have anything against old Frank and wish him harm."

Emma knew that the two men had many disagreements, the last one being about a fence that Thomas wanted to build between the two houses, but did that mean that Thomas would wish him harm? Surely not.

"Did you notice anything unusual in the last few days? Any strangers or visitors hanging around?" Elsa-May asked.

Thomas scratched his cheek. "Can't say so. Except the day he died, I heard some kind of ruckus. Someone was yelling I'm sure of it."

"I see, did you tell the police that?" Emma asked.

"*Jah,* there was a detective who questioned everyone in the street. I'm sure no one heard or saw anything, just me and the yelling."

"Okay, well thanks for popping by." Elsa-May tried to close the door and Thomas put his hand up against the door to hold it open. "Are you sure you ladies are supposed to be here?"

"Of course we are. Did you want to help us clean? We've got a spare scrubbing brush and soap. We could use some muscle power on the floors, especially the dried blood that's still there on the kitchen floor," Emma said.

"*Nee,* I've got to be somewhere soon." Thomas stuck his head through the door and had a good look around. "Carry on then."

When Elsa-May closed the door, Emma joined her in a fit of giggles. "What would you have done if he said he'd help with the dried blood only to find that there was none?"

"I was sure he wouldn't help," Emma said.

Elsa-May and Emma walked into the kitchen where Frank had been found. "Found anything?" Elsa-May asked Ettie and Silvie, who were on their knees.

"*Jah,* a long strand of pale hair, could be gray or could be blonde, and a flake of red."

"Did you bag it?" Elsa-May asked.

"*Jah.*" Silvie held up two plastic bags in her gloved hand.

"Wouldn't forensics have found everything?" Emma asked.

Elsa-May shook her head. "Not necessarily. Where's Maureen?"

"She's talking to Bob Pluver and then coming here, remember?" Ettie said.

"*Jah,* that's right. Now, Emma, let's think, what would the murderer do, where would he have gone?"

"Seems that he went right through the entire *haus.*"

At that moment, Maureen came through the front door. "Well, I have some news."

"We'll sit at the kitchen table," Elsa-May said.

When everyone was seated, Maureen began. "Bob said that he arrived here on the Thursday, at the time of his normal visit, and Frank seemed shaken by something. He had Bob drive him to the bank. Then Bob watched him as Frank walked to another bank. Then he had Bob drive him to a lawyer's office."

"Which lawyer?" Ettie said.

"I wrote it down, but I left it in the buggy. I think from memory it was Wagners & Sons, or something like that."

"Winters & Sons?" Silvie asked.

"*Jah,* that's the one."

Silvie sat up very straight. "I know George Winters. He comes into the bakery every single day."

"Okay, so it seems like old Frank might have taken his money out of one bank and put it in another? Then he changed his will?" Elsa-May looked at all the other widows.

"He could have taken something out of a safe-deposit box," Maureen said.

"Did you ask Bob which banks he went to?"

Maureen shook her head.

"You'll have to go back and find out which banks. Not all have safe-deposit boxes and we need to know what he did at each bank."

"Couldn't the detective find that out?" Emma asked.

"*Ach, nee,* we can't tell him that Bob was here the day he died," Maureen said.

"Maureen's right, Emma. We don't want innocent people to get blamed for things they didn't do," Elsa-May said.

Emma nodded.

"Silvie, you will have to find out from George what Frank was doing there that day, the day that he died."

"*Jah,* I'll do that today," Silvie said.

"Off you go now then," Elsa-May said.

Silvie looked down at her clothes. "I'm a mess. I'll have to go home and change first."

Elsa-May lowered her head and glared at Silvie. "Nonsense, you look fine. Go now."

"Okay," Silvie said as she headed quickly to the door.

"We'll wait for you; come straight back here," Elsa-May yelled after Silvie.

"Do we know anything of Frank's will?" Ettie asked.

"*Nee*, not that I've heard. Andrew said he was going to have Wil let a realtor come through to put a price on it, but he hasn't done that yet. Maybe that means that the *haus* is not left to Andrew? I'm not sure," Emma said.

"He only had Andrew and Clive and I'm sure he wouldn't have left something to one son and not the other," Maureen said.

"Maureen, you go back right now to Bob and find out what two banks Frank went to."

"Do I have to go back now? I don't want him to think that I like him," Maureen said.

Ettie giggled.

"That's the least of our problems, Maureen. Just go and find out those two things, hurry," Elsa-May said.

Maureen headed out the door with a most reluctant look on her face, which caused the three remaining widows to giggle.

"Poor Maureen," Emma said. "I do think that Bob is keen on her."

"He'll be pleased to answer her questions then," Elsa-May said with a grin on her face.

"Well, come on girls; this place isn't going to clean itself," Ettie said.

Half an hour later, Maureen arrived back. After she told the widows which banks Frank went to, it was clear that he hadn't gone to the banks to take something out of a safe-deposit box, as neither bank had them.

"*Gut* work, Maureen," Elsa-May said.

"*Jah,* now I have to have dinner with him next week," Maureen said.

"He's the strong silent type, Maureen. There's nothing wrong with that boy and now he's inherited his *daed's* business, he's quite a catch," Ettie said with a twinkle in her eye.

"I hear a buggy, must be Silvie back," Emma said.

A minute later, Silvie burst through the door, quite breathless. "Phew, it took me a while and two cups of coffee, but old Mr. Winters told me that Frank insisted on changing his will there and then, so his 'useless' sons would get nothing."

Elsa-May leaned forward and asked, "So who did he leave his money to?"

"Bob, Bob Pluver. And Bob's to see that Growler is looked after."

Emma covered her mouth. "Bob."

Elsa-May said, "That means that Bob is now our prime suspect. That's not *gut*. It means that we can't listen to what he told us. If he killed Frank, he could've made up the entire thing he told Maureen."

"He was right about going to the lawyer, though," Maureen said. "He didn't lie about that."

"*Jah,* That's right, Maureen." Ettie laughed. "But that was to his advantage to know where the most recent will was kept."

Maureen shook her head. "I don't believe that he did it."

"Neither do I, but he does move to front place as far as the suspects are concerned," Elsa-May said.

"Are you going to tell the detective, Elsa-May?" Maureen said.

Elsa-May narrowed her eyes. "I don't know. I think we should sit on the information for now."

The widows had been silent for a moment, before Ettie asked, "You've got the cat, haven't you, Emma?"

"I'm afraid so. He just ignores me all the time; I don't know how the old man got so attached to him. He just sleeps and eats, and he's taken over the whole *haus*."

"You must look after him well, Emma. That was Frank's wish," Silvie said.

"I will. He already has the run of the *haus*." Emma gave a little giggle; she was not brave enough to tell the widows that the cat slept on her bed. They would consider her far too soft in the head.

"Why would Frank suddenly decide to leave everything he owned to Bob on that very day? What had him so shaken?" Elsa-May drummed her fingertips onto her chin. "Ettie, go out to the buggy and get me my writing pad."

Ettie came back into the *haus* within moments with a pen and Elsa-May's writing pad.

Elsa-May began writing. "Suspects? We have the old man next door, the two sons and Bob."

"*Nee*, not Bob," Maureen said.

Elsa-May glanced up at Maureen and then set her eyes once more to her writing pad. "As I was saying, Bob, and who else would have had something to gain from the man's death?"

"When Andrew and his girlfriend were here the other day,

he mentioned something; he thought his *daed* had in a safe-deposit box somewhere," Emma said.

Elsa-May pushed out her lips. "Maybe he did have something in a safe-deposit box somewhere. Did we find a key anywhere?" The widows all shook their heads. "Perhaps the detective found a key. I'll pay him a visit and give him what we found and ask him a few questions."

Elsa-May scribbled down a few more things on to her writing pad. "Let's re-cap. Frank was upset by something –most likely to do with his sons, because he had Bob drive him to town where he went to two banks and then changed his will at the solicitor's. And that's only if Bob was telling Maureen the truth."

"He was, I'm sure of it," Maureen said.

"Did Bob come into Frank's *haus* on the Thursday, the day that Frank died?" Silvie asked.

"He said that he didn't," Maureen said. "He had to go back to work."

"So we can't say at what time Frank's home was broken into and wrecked. Frank was upset, went to banks, solicitor, back home, and that's all we know until Emma came later in the day and found him poisoned on the floor," Elsa-May said as she studied her writing pad.

"*Jah,* seems to be all we know so far," Ettie said. "His boys had to have been upset with him because he changed his will. That part is obvious."

"Would one of his sons have killed him if Frank told them what he'd done about changing the will?" Emma asked.

"*Nee,* because then he'd never be alive to change the will back," Elsa-May said. "It's pointing more and more to Bob."

"Can't we rule out the man next door? It's a bit weird to think someone could kill someone over just a fence," Silvie said.

"Ahh, but it's never just a fence. The fence could be the last straw, as the expression goes; the last straw that broke the camel's back. We can't rule anyone out."

CHAPTER EIGHT

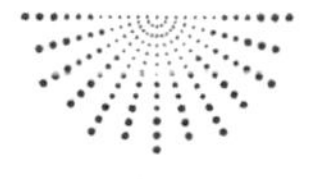

Be kindly affectioned one to another with brotherly love; in honour preferring one another;Not slothful in business; fervent in spirit; serving the Lord.

Romans 12:10-12

It was on the Saturday after the funeral that Silvie heard a knock at her door. She opened it to see her younger *schweschder,* Sabrina, with a suitcase in her hand. Silvie looked up the road to see a taxi driving away. "Sabrina, what are you doing here?"

Sabrina pushed past Silvie into the *haus*. "*Mamm* sent me."

"She did? How did you get here?"

"I came on the Greyhound." Sabrina put her bag down just inside the door and took off her coat.

Silvie took her coat from her. "I don't mean to sound rude, but why are you here?"

"*Mamm* heard that you were very friendly with an *Englischer* at a funeral."

Silvie was surprised how fast news traveled. "There is a man, but he's staying in the community because he wants to become Amish, that's all. There's nothing going on with me and him."

"Really?" Sabrina raised an eyebrow and stared at Silvie. It reminded Silvie of how her *mudder* had always stared at her when she'd done something wrong. Silvie's *mudder* was a dominating force and Silvie had escaped that domination when she married John. At that moment, Silvie realized that getting away from her *mudder* might have been a major factor in her decision to marry John.

"Why do you come to my *haus* and question me? I'm a grown woman and can do as I please," Silvie said as she hung up Sabrina's coat.

"Do what you want." Sabrina laughed. "I just had to get away for a while and this was a *gut* excuse. Besides, it'll give me a chance to meet the *menner* in the community. Is there anyone who might suit me?"

Silvie reached for Sabrina's suitcase. "I'll take this up to the spare room. Come, I'll show you where it is."

"Silvie, you didn't answer me. There are no *menner* for me in Ohio so I'm hoping there might be someone here for me. You'd like to have a *schweschder* here, wouldn't you? It must be lonely out here all by yourself."

Her *schweschder* or for that matter, any member of her *familye* staying in Lancaster County, was far less than an ideal situation for Silvie. "It's the second Sunday tomorrow so there'll be a meeting; come see for yourself."

Sabrina clapped her hands together. "Goodie. You don't mind me staying a while, do you?"

"Of course not," Silvie said as she heaved the heavy suitcase onto the bed. "I'll be pleased of the company." Silvie wondered who there might be for Sabrina. "There are a few single *menner* you might like."

"*Ach,* I can't wait for tomorrow to see for myself."

"*Mamm* sent you to spy on me?"

"She sent me to make sure that you don't make a mistake. She was worried when she heard about the *Englischer.*" Sabrina sat down heavily on the other side of the bed. "Who is he, the *Englischer*?"

"No one important. Just someone who might become Amish soon, that's all, but I'm a grown woman and can make my own choices; I wish *mamm* would realize that. Apparently, I'm not far enough away from her." Silvie wondered who it was who reported back to her *mudder*.

"Silvie, that's a terrible thing to say. *Mamm* would be so upset to hear you say a thing like that about her."

Silvie laughed. "You only just said that you needed to get away too."

"I didn't say it was because of *mamm*. I mind what I say." Sabrina pouted.

"Okay, then I'll mind what I say as well. You get settled; unpack your clothes, and then you can help me with the chores."

"Chores? I'm a guest. I don't want to do any chores; I have to do chores at home."

Silvie shook a finger at Sabrina. "If you stay here, you'll stay as *familye,* and you'll be doing chores."

Sabrina pouted once more. "If I'd known that, I would not have come."

Silvie turned and walked toward the bedroom door. "If you want to stay with me, you have to do chores. I'll give you fifteen minutes to unpack." Silvie walked out of the bedroom pleased with herself. If her *mudder* had sent Sabrina to spy on her, she had to turn things to her advantage in the best way that she could.

As Silvie finished washing the dishes, she looked out the window and remembered her prayer of just days ago. She shared with *Gott* that she didn't want to be alone. Was this *Gott's* answer, to send her Sabrina? She meant she wanted a *mann* in her life, not her spoiled *schweschder* to come and stay with her. She would have to be more specific with her prayers in the future.

CHAPTER NINE

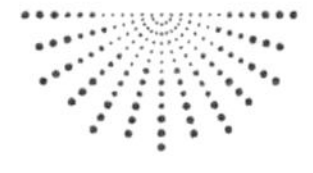

For as the body without the spirit is dead, so faith without works is dead also.
James 2:26

Emma drove herself to the Sunday meeting rather than go with Maureen or Wil. Sometimes she liked to be alone driving to the gathering and back home.

Walking toward the group, she saw Silvie and was sure that the woman next to her had to be Silvie's *schweschder.* She had the same fine features and the same delicate coloring with the blonde hair and the blue eyes.

Silvie looked up, caught her eye and walked over to her with her arm looped through her *schweschder's*. "Emma, this is Sabrina, my *schweschder*."

"Hello, Sabrina." Up close the girl was even more beautiful than Silvie.

"Nice to meet you, Emma."

Emma noticed that Sabrina was hardly paying her any attention as her eyes darted to and fro over the crowd. It was clear to Emma that Sabrina was single and looking for a husband. Most young girls of her age thought of little else. "I guess you're from Ohio too, Sabrina?"

"*Jah,* I don't know how long I'm staying yet, maybe just a week or so."

Sabrina and Silvie sat with Maureen and Emma during the service.

When the meal was being served afterward, Silvie pulled Emma aside. "*Mamm* sent her to spy on me because she heard that I was sweet on an *Englischer.*"

"Really? I guessed that she was looking for a husband."

"*Jah,* that too."

Emma laughed, and they both turned to look at Sabrina only to see her approach Wil. "*Ach,* look she's gone over to Wil. Emma, you have to stop her."

Emma scoffed. "I'm not concerned. Wil had plenty of time to find someone else besides me; he's never been interested in anyone else."

Silvie frowned. "You're very confident, Emma."

Emma was not confident at all, not after the argument they'd had. "We've talked of marriage."

"You haven't said 'yes' though, have you?"

"*Nee,* but we have an understanding. He knows it's too soon for me to say 'yes.'"

Although Emma knew that Wil loved her, Silvie's words

concerned her. "Let's go closer to hear what they are talking about," Emma said.

Wil immediately looked up as they approached. "Ahh, Silvie you have a delightful *schweschder.*"

Silvie smiled and looked at Emma.

"Emma, have you met Sabrina?"

Emma noticed that as Wil spoke he shifted his weight from one foot to the other.

"*Jah,* we met earlier." Emma looked at Sabrina and was sure that she looked disappointed that her talk with Wil had been interrupted. *Could Sabrina see Wil as a potential husband even though she was only about eighteen and he was in his thirties? Surely not.*

"Sabrina's interested in my inventions."

Emma raised her eyebrows. She didn't see how anyone could be interested in Wil's inventions. How did they come to speak of his inventions so quickly? "Is she?"

"*Jah,* I do a little fiddling with inventions myself." Sabrina was certainly more animated in her conversation when there was a man around.

"Such as?" Emma asked, wondering if Sabrina would dare to make up such a thing.

"*Mamm* has a gas powered iron and I've made it into a battery powered iron by fitting it with a battery pack that I made myself."

Emma laughed and before she could stop herself, she said, "What would be the use of that?"

Wil stared at her and Emma knew that he sensed something was not right with her. Did Wil know that she was a little jealous of this new girl?

Sabrina tilted her chin high. "Well, *mamm* liked it. She found it more convenient."

"*Jah*, I'm sure it's got many convenient uses." Emma tried to sound sincere to cover her previous cruel outburst.

Sabrina ignored Emma's words and said, "Why don't you show me some of your inventions, Wil?"

"Of course, have Silvie bring you for dinner one night this week. That'll be okay, won't it, Silvie?"

Silvie smiled. "*Jah*, we could come tomorrow night."

"Tomorrow it is then."

"Come on, Sabrina." Silvie linked her arm through Sabrina's. "I've got some people I want you to meet. Excuse us, Wil, Emma." Silvie pulled Sabrina away, leaving Wil and Emma alone.

"You'll come to dinner tomorrow too, of course?" Wil asked Emma.

"Do you want me to?" Emma asked.

"Of course, all my dinner invitations include you."

Emma folded her arms and looked into the distance. She had never experienced the emotion of jealousy, but now she knew what it was. She was annoyed at Sabrina for speaking to Wil and not just speaking, she was flirting with him. Outrageously flirting and she even invited herself to his *haus*. *The sheer nerve of the woman.* "Don't you know that Sabrina is attracted to you? She's only here from Ohio to look for a husband."

"That's a little harsh, Emma. You've only just met the girl. You were also rude to her."

Emma's mouth fell open at Wil's words. "I was not."

Wil rubbed the back of his neck. "You've never understood about my inventions have you?"

"What do you mean? I do understand about your inventions."

"When someone invents something, it's important to them. You have never shown any interest in my inventions - ever." Wil nodded his head in a definite manner as he spoke.

Emma remained silent; she was not the slightest bit interested in his senseless tinkering with useless objects, and why should she be? They were a sheer waste of *Gott's* time. Why couldn't Wil see that for himself?

Wil continued, "Think of it like your needlework. You spend hours on your needlework and show me what you've done and I show interest in your work – the fine stitches, the different colors. But, if I try and speak about my inventions or try to show you, you just don't pay any mind. You make no effort to even pretend to have a tiny piece of curiosity."

Emma looked up at Wil. He was scolding her. He had never spoken crossly like that to her before.

Wil continued, "You even told that girl that her invention was of no use. How would you feel if someone told you your needlework was of no use to anybody?"

Emma jutted out her bottom lip as she thought of Sabrina's invention. "Well, I think the battery iron was silly and I do think it's of no use. I have to be truthful." Couldn't Wil see that a battery pack on an iron was pointless when a gas-powered iron would've done the same thing? Why was he defending the girl? Was it because she was pretty and young?

"What use is your needlework? What use is it to anybody?"

Emma scoffed. "It's hardly the same thing, Wil."

"It might not be the same thing, but it's about people's feelings. Think about other people for once, Emma." Wil put his hands on his hips and his eyes flashed with disappointment.

"Are you saying that I'm selfish?" Emma asked.

Wil slowly nodded his head. "*Jah,* something like that. If you'll excuse me, I see someone I need to speak to." Wil walked away from Emma with long, fast strides.

Emma's eyes filled with tears. Never had he spoken to her like that. Wil had been her rock ever since Levi had died. Wil was her best friend and now he had said mean things to her and for no reason.

Feeling all alone in the world, Emma walked directly to her buggy, hoping that no one would see her in tears. She drove all the way home with tears brimming in her eyes. She was pleased that she had decided to drive there alone that day.

Was she selfish? Could Wil be right? No one else had ever called her selfish.

She opened her front door, lay down on the couch, closed her eyes and thought on Wil's words. He was as *gut* as saying that she was selfish for not showing interest in his silly inventions. She had an ache in her tummy. It was true she never showed any interest but he had never been angry about it before, not 'til she hadn't shown any interest in Sabrina's useless invention. Maybe Wil was sweet on Sabrina. Could it be more than a coincidence that he picked a fight with her immediately after he met the young and pretty Sabrina?

No one had ever said that needlework was a waste of time. *At least I have something to show for all my time,* Emma thought of her sewing.

Emma went into the kitchen to make herself something to

eat. Growler was finishing the last of the meat she had put out for him that morning. "Hello, Growler." As usual, Growler ignored her and kept eating. She leaned over and stroked his gray, silver fur until he purred.

She walked past Growler into the utility room and spied some chocolates and decided that she needed something to cheer herself up. Emma took the chocolates back to the couch and covered herself with a blanket.

As the chocolate melted in her mouth, she thought of more than a few times that Wil had tried to show her what he was working on. Sometimes she would laugh, or scoff and sometimes she would say she'd look later, but never did. Perhaps she should show interest in what he did with his time, but couldn't he see that his inventions were useless? Even Levi had said that they were a waste of time.

Maybe she wasn't a match with Wil in spite of what she had thought. Maybe loneliness was the only factor that had driven her to find comfort and companionship with Wil.

CHAPTER TEN

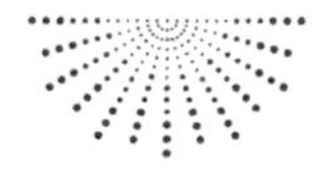

And the multitude of them that believed were of one heart and of one soul: neither said any of them that ought of the things which he possessed was his own; but they had all things common.
Acts 4:32

Typically Emma would have offered to cook when Wil had guests but considering their cross words of late, Emma thought she would leave Wil to cook on his own. She thought by doing so he would appreciate her more and not speak to her so meanly in the future.

She arrived at Wil's *haus* at 6 p.m. only to find that Silvie was already there so she assumed that Sabrina would be as well.

Silvie and Bailey were talking on the porch on two large wooden chairs. "Hello, Emma," Silvie said.

"Hello, you two. Where are Wil and Sabrina?"

"Sabrina's helping Wil in the kitchen."

The nerve of the girl; she's trying to step right into my shoes. Emma was angry with herself for not helping Wil as she usually did. Because of her pride and selfishness, she had unknowingly opened a way for Sabrina to work her way into Wil's heart.

Emma looked down at the apple pie in her hands. "I'll be back in a minute. I'll just take the apple pie into the kitchen." Was she going to be the odd one out tonight? Silvie and Bailey were attracted to each other and Wil and Sabrina had their inventions to chat about. Emma walked quickly into the kitchen. "I brought apple pie."

"*Denke,* Emma. I love your apple pie."

"I know. I made it especially for you." Emma tried to make it sound as though they were a couple in front of Sabrina. "Hello, Sabrina. *Denke* for helping Wil; I usually help him with the cooking, but I was busy with other things today."

"Hello, Emma. I couldn't see Wil do all the cooking himself. He needs a *fraa* to look after him." Sabrina shot an adoring look at Wil, which annoyed Emma greatly.

Wil and she were courting, didn't Sabrina know that; hadn't Silvie told her to keep away from him?

When Wil remained silent, Emma walked out of the kitchen and sat out on the porch with Bailey and Silvie. They stopped speaking when she approached.

"How are things doing with you, Bailey?" Emma asked.

"Fine, *denke,* Emma. I'm learning a lot and taking it all in. I'll be Amish in no time."

"That's *gut.*" Trying not to clench her mouth, Emma asked, "Silvie, how long is Sabrina staying with you?"

"I don't know. She's enjoying a little freedom away from *mamm*."

That was the answer that Emma didn't want to hear. She had no one to discipline her and she was set loose on the *menner* in the community, in particular Wil.

Wil and Sabrina came through the front door. "I'm just going to show Sabrina some of my inventions in the barn. Do you want to come with us, Emma?"

"*Jah*, I'll go and have a look." Emma considered that she was in a difficult position. While she was glad that Wil asked her, she didn't want to appear to Sabrina as though she was jealous of her. She would also have to leave Bailey and Silvie alone with each other.

While Wil showed Sabrina and Emma all the things he had invented, Sabrina made all the appropriate oohs and ahhhs while Emma found it difficult to muster the appropriate enthusiasm.

The whole night Emma felt totally out of sorts. Sabrina took over her role as hostess and Emma spent the night forcing a smile on her face.

Once everyone had gone, Emma turned to Wil. "I'd better get going too."

"*Nee*, wait, Emma. I'm sorry for what I said to you on Sunday. It was mean."

"You were right, Wil. I've been so consumed with myself and feeling sorry for what happened to me that I haven't been aware of other people's needs. Well, your needs."

Wil said, "I'll walk you home."

Although they had both apologized to one another, something had changed. Emma knew in her heart that things between them were not the same.

~

THE TENSION between Wil and Emma played on her mind so much that Emma knew she had to have a straight talk with Wil about it. The next morning, Emma stopped in at Wil's on her way to town. "Are you there, Wil?"

Wil came to the door with a coffee cup in his hands. "Emma, come in."

"How about we sit out here, in the morning sun?"

"Okay, would you like a *kaffe*?"

"*Nee*, I just had one at home. Wil, I feel things between us are different."

Wil smiled. "Are they?"

"If something's important to you, I will try and understand why it interests you."

Wil reached out and took hold of Emma's hand. "Let's not speak of it again. We said all we needed to say last night."

"Okay," Emma said.

"Let's just enjoy this beautiful sunny day before the cold weather sets in."

Emma took a deep breath and let it out slowly while she enjoyed the sunlight on her face. She was happy not to speak of things that they would disagree on.

"Have you heard the latest about Frank?" Emma tried to change the subject.

"*Nee*, what's happened?" Wil asked.

"Oh, I know nothing. I wondered if you'd heard anything. It

was a little difficult to talk last night with all the people around."

"*Nee,* I've heard of nothing. They are trying to locate Frank's will and that's all I know," Wil said.

Emma bit her lip. She had to keep quiet about the will since she wasn't supposed to know about it. "Ettie did a bit of digging about Frank's past before he came to the community. Anyway, he was an auctioneer and Ettie seems to think that he might have some paintings hidden away somewhere." Emma giggled nervously knowing that she should not have talked about things that came out of the widows' meeting.

Wil sprang to his feet. "Emma, I completely forgot about the paintings."

Emma rose to her feet. "What paintings? Wil, what do you mean?"

"It was years ago; that's why I forgot about them. One day, Frank brought some paintings to me. That was just after his *fraa,* Sally, died and before he moved into the smaller *haus.*"

"Go on."

"He asked me to look after them for him."

"Where are the paintings now?" Emma asked.

"I wrapped them in brown paper and a large blanket and put them up in the attic."

"Go and see if they're still there, but don't tell Bailey what you're doing."

"Okay, I'll be back soon. I think Bailey's out with Silvie anyway."

"*Gut*. Wait, I'll come with you."

The two of them walked quickly into Wil's *haus.* Wil had a ladder already at the back door as he'd been working on his roof. He climbed the ladder and pushed aside the board covering the entry to the attic. "Hand me that kerosene lamp, would you?"

Emma lit the lamp and handed it to him.

"*Jah,* seems they're still here," Wil called out.

"That's far enough. Both of you stay where you are."

Emma held her stomach at the sight of Bailey Abler with a gun in his hand. Wil ducked his head back into the room.

Bailey took a step closer. "Emma, stay where you are and put your hands in the air. Wil, get the paintings and come down the ladder nice and slow."

Emma obeyed him and raised her hands above her head. Once Wil got to the bottom of the ladder, he placed the paintings still wrapped in a blanket onto the floor.

"What is the meaning of this, Bailey? What are you doing pointing a gun at us?" Emma asked.

Bailey kept his eyes fixed onto Wil. "I need to ask you, Wil, what are you doing with stolen art work?"

"Stolen? Frank asked me to take care of them. Emma has just jogged my memory of them. He placed them in my care years ago and never mentioned them to me again." As Bailey slowly walked closer, Wil asked, "Whom are they stolen from? Or do you think that we stole them?"

Emma was relieved to hear the sound of a buggy stopping outside the *haus.* Emma glanced at Bailey's startled face. Surely he couldn't shoot everyone. Emma lowered her hands.

"Bailey, what are you doing?"

Emma knew that the booming voice belonged to Elsa-May. Behind Elsa-May she saw Ettie and Maureen.

Bailey addressed Elsa-May. "I just found that these two are in possession of stolen paintings."

"Nonsense." Elsa-May pushed down the gun in his hand.

Emma quickly told Elsa-May, "Wil remembered that Frank had given him the paintings to look after. How did you know to come here?"

"We were coming to visit you when we saw your buggy here at Wil's place." Elsa-May ignored Bailey and walked right past him. "Did you say paintings? Well, let's unwrap them and take a look."

Bailey put his hand agitatedly to his forehead. "Aunt Em, you can't just walk into my investigation like this."

Elsa-May swung around to Bailey. "Wil, Emma, meet my and Ettie's nephew, Bailey Rivers. He's a detective."

Emma gasped and Wil asked, "You're Elsa-May and Ettie's nephew?"

Emma was relieved that he was not a thief or a murderer.

Bailey nodded. "Well, great nephew, really."

"So you don't want to join the Amish? Your name's not Bailey Abler?" Wil asked.

"Sorry to do that to you, Wil. I'm Bailey Rivers. You've been very kind to me, showing me how everything works, the traditions and the customs."

"This is such a shock." Emma put her hands to her head.

"I think the person you should apologize to should be Silvie," Wil said with deep furrows in his brow. "Does the bishop know of this deception?"

Bailey lowered his head. "The bishop knew from the start."

Wil shook his head.

"I'm afraid I'm the one who organized things for Bailey to be here, Wil," Elsa-May said, "Now, let's have a look at these paintings."

Elsa-May and Bailey carefully unwrapped the paintings while Wil and the others looked on.

There were three small paintings. "This one looks to be a Chagall, that one is by Otto Dix and I don't know who that one was painted by, but it looks to be a 16th century painting." Elsa-May rose to her feet. "You see a lot of art went missing in World War Two from Germany."

"How do you know all these things, Elsa-May?" Emma asked.

Elsa-May flung a hand in the air. "I studied art history at the library when I was younger."

Emma's head felt as though it was spinning with all the surprises. "So Frank was murdered for these paintings? They don't look like they're worth much at all," Emma said.

"We could be looking at millions, Emma," Elsa-May said.

Emma's hand flew to her mouth. "Millions?"

"What have you found out, Aunt Em?" Bailey asked.

Emma knew she should be concentrating on the paintings, but all she could think of was how devastated Silvie would be.

"Well, you obviously knew about Frank's father's art dealings and you knew that he'd have these paintings hidden somewhere," Elsa-May said.

"Yes, I've been on the trail of the paintings for a long time. Funny that they should bring me here to the same community where you are," Bailey said.

"And the same community that Silvie's in," Emma said, hoping he would see that she was cranky with him for leading her dear friend up the garden path.

"If only you'd come a little earlier, you could have saved old Frank from being murdered," Wil said.

"Do any of you have any idea who could have done it?" Bailey asked.

"Yes, that was my question," Detective Crowley said as he walked through the door. He glanced at the three paintings on the floor. "So you've found the paintings, Rivers?"

"Yes, seems that the old man gave them to Wil to look after, and Wil's only just remembered about it."

The detective raised his eyebrows. "How convenient."

"Look here, what are you implying?" Wil said with a raised voice.

"I can vouch for Wil and Emma, Detective. They're just innocent bystanders in all this," Elsa-May said. It appeared that Elsa-May had a fair amount of influence over the detective.

Was the detective also a relative of Elsa-May and Ettie's? Emma wondered.

"Well, if neither of them did it, who killed Frank?" Crowley asked.

"I don't know, but I will have to take these paintings and have them verified. I'll call for a photographer first and have them catalogued before I move them." He looked at Detective Crowley. "I should also probably have them dusted for prints."

"Yes, if it's not too late," he said looking at Elsa-May and Wil.

"I was careful only to touch the corners of the frames," Elsa-May said.

"I only touched them years ago," Wil said.

Emma remained silent until the detective stared at her. "Oh, I haven't touched them at all."

"I'll get the fingerprint team down here." Detective Crowley walked out the door while pushing buttons on his cell phone.

"They promised me full co-operation," Bailey said nodding his head to Crowley.

"What prints would you expect since the person looking for them at Frank's *haus* didn't find them? It wouldn't have their prints on them," Elsa-May said.

"I know; it's just routine. We have to do things properly." Bailey lowered his voice, "Especially with Crowley breathing down my neck. I can't do anything unless it's completely by the book."

CHAPTER ELEVEN

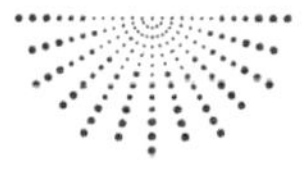

And on the seventh day God ended his work which he had made; and he rested on the seventh day from all his work which he had made. And God blessed the seventh day, and sanctified it: because that in it he had rested from all his work which God created and made.
Genesis 2:2-3

"Detective, have you found anything out?" Elsa-May asked him when the detective came back inside the *haus* after speaking on his cell.

"It so happens that we have new information from the son, Andrew. He admitted to being there that morning. Andrew had fallen on hard times and thought his father had something of great value that he might be able to sell. His father denied having anything at all and a shouting match broke out."

"Must have been these paintings that Frank was protecting," Wil said.

The detective took a step forward. "Well, no one will get them since they're stolen."

"Not so fast." Bailey held up the paintings one by one, taking a good look at each of them. "I dare say that these aren't any of the paintings I was chasing. Two of them are very similar. These could be stolen as well, though. These might very well be the real deal."

"What do you mean, the real deal?" Detective Crowley asked him.

"They might not be stolen. There is every chance." Bailey carefully looked at the back of the paintings with gloved hands. "Just as I hoped. It appears something is stuck to the back of each painting; no doubt it would be the receipts and authentication if the old man knew what he was doing. It's a hunch, but I think we will find that these aren't stolen."

"So the sons will come into an inheritance?" Maureen's eyebrows rose.

"Appears so," Bailey said.

The sound of a car screeching to a halt made everyone's heads turn toward Wil's front door. Wil went outside the *haus* to greet Andrew, Frank's son.

"Wil, I've just been to the bank and all the money was cleaned out of dad's account, all of it."

Wil jerked his head back. "Did they say when the money was taken out?"

"The day he died. The very day he died, all the money gone." Andrew put a hand on Wil to steady himself and looked as though he was about to collapse.

"Detective Crowley is here. Come inside." Wil helped Andrew into the *haus.*

Wil told Crowley what Andrew had just told him, while Andrew sat breathing heavily on the couch with his hand on his chest.

Detective Crowley sat opposite Andrew and scratched in his notebook. "Did anyone at the bank see if he was accompanied by anyone?"

Andrew shook his head. "They didn't say."

"Should be on their CCTV. I'll check into it."

Wil said, "Andrew, these are your *daed's* paintings. He told me if anything should happen to him to give them to you and Clive. I'm sorry, but I only just remembered them."

Andrew hurried over to the paintings and sank to his knees. "This must be what he told us about. Something of tremendous value for us boys."

Bailey stepped forward. "You can't touch them. We need to have them fingerprinted and authenticated to check that they aren't stolen first. I'll need to take them for a while."

"My *daed* was a man of *Gott.* He would never steal," Andrew said.

"I don't mean to offend you. I'm Detective Bailey Rivers."

"What's going on here? Why would you think that they were stolen?" Andrew asked. When Wil told him about Bailey being on the trail of stolen paintings, Andrew asked Bailey, "How long will you have to take them for?"

"Three days, I've got someone coming in from Chicago. Hopefully, they'll be here tomorrow so we can get this thing wrapped up. I've been chasing some stolen paintings, but I'm sure I'm on the wrong trail with these ones."

"Do what you need to do. I'm confident that they're not stolen," Andrew said.

"Andrew, what's keeping you?" Andrew's girlfriend called out to him from the doorway. "I'm coming, Lacey, and I've got some good news."

Emma noticed that Lacey had long blonde hair and today her long nails were pink, but the day Emma met her they were red. An alarm bell went off in Emma's head, the long strand of hair, the red flake, which could've been a piece of red nail polish. Emma looked up at Elsa-May and by the look on her face Emma knew that she was thinking the same thing.

While Andrew was showing the girlfriend the paintings, Elsa-May pulled the detective aside and whispered in his ear.

The detective stood behind the girl and asked, "Tell me, Lacey, were you at Frank's *haus* the day that he died?"

"No, she wasn't there. She waited in the car for me," Andrew answered for her.

"I'm asking this young lady, not you, sir." The detective looked back at Lacey. "Well, young lady?"

"No, like he said, I was in the car."

"In that case you wouldn't mind giving me a DNA sample would you?"

Lacey's face stiffened. "No, I'm not going to waste my time with such a thing." Lacey looked at Andrew. "Tell them, Andrew."

"How long will it take, detective?" Andrew adjusted his trousers. "We've got lunch reservations."

"I'll have someone here in ten minutes." The detective stepped outside and made a call on his cell phone.

"Is Lacey a suspect?" Andrew asked when the detective came back inside.

"Not especially, but everyone is giving DNA samples and we haven't got one from her yet. I could get a warrant, if need be."

Andrew slumped into the couch and wiped the sweat off his forehead. "We can wait ten minutes. You don't mind if we inconvenience you for ten more minutes do you, Wil?" Andrew asked.

"*Nee,* of course not."

"I'll make us some tea," Emma said and hurried to the kitchen with Elsa-May close behind her.

"What do you think?" Elsa-May whispered to Emma.

"She does have the long, pale hair and that red flake we found could be that nail varnish she was wearing," Emma whispered back. "She was after the thing of value that old Frank had spoken of. She could have come back after Andrew ransacked the place and tried to get it out of the old man, where the valuables were."

"*Jah,* that makes sense because he was poisoned with a lethal dose of sodium pentothal." On seeing the blank look on Emma's face, Elsa-May said, "Truth serum."

"When did you find that out?"

"Crowley told me as soon as he found out. I didn't put two and two together at the time. Now, it makes sense."

"What about all his money disappearing from the bank? Do you think Bob could've had anything to do with it?" Emma asked.

"I'd hate to think so. I don't think Bob would've done such a thing. He's always been honest in his dealings," Elsa-May said.

When they brought the tea into the living room, Andrew and the detective were speaking to each other on the couch.

"I've admitted to looking through the house, but I didn't kill him and I didn't ransack the place," Andrew said.

The detective said, "You've told the police all this in your statement, haven't you?"

Andrew nodded.

The detective continued, "Did you see Bob Pluver?"

"I was parked up the road with Lacey later that day and we saw him go past in the buggy with Bob Pluver."

"Then where did you go?" the detective asked.

"Lacey had a hair appointment…"

Lacey interrupted as she bounded to her feet. "I don't want to wait for the DNA people. I already told you that I've never been to the house."

"I could get a warrant; it'll only take me a couple of hours." The detective's tone was firm.

Lacey walked toward the door. "Come on, Andrew. Let's go."

"We should just wait and get it over with, Lacey. He said he could get a warrant and then you'll just have to go to the bother of doing it another time."

Lacey's voice rose. "I said that I don't want to stay, Andrew."

Andrew looked shocked as if he had never heard Lacey raise her voice. "Whatever's gotten into you? Just stay. It won't take long."

"We found some hair and some other material we can identify. The hair was long and blonde. Is there anything you'd like to tell me, Lacey? We can also check with the hairdresser to see if you kept that appointment."

Lacey looked at the floor. "It was an accident. I didn't mean to kill him. I just wanted him to tell me where the valuables were. I gave him truth serum, only a bit. He must've had an allergic reaction or something."

Andrew jumped to his feet. "You did what?"

Lacey burst into tears, ran to Andrew, and put her head on his shoulder. "I'm sorry. I'm sorry. I didn't give him much at all."

Andrew whispered to her. "Don't say anything until we get a lawyer."

"Where did you get the sodium pentothal from?" The detective asked.

Lacey shrugged and raised her head slightly. "I'm not saying any else."

"One more thing I should tell you, Andrew." Detective Crowley said.

"And what's that?" Andrew asked.

"The will you have in your possession has been superseded. He wrote a new will the day that he died. I'm afraid that you and your brother are no longer the benefactors."

"No. It must be a fake will. It can't be real."

"He had a lawyer witness it. I can assure you it is real," Detective Crowley said.

Lacey jumped back from Andrew. "You idiot, Andrew. Can't you do anything right?"

"Shut up, Lacey. Clive and I will contest it. Who's the benefactor?"

"Bob Pluver is the sole benefactor. I wouldn't waste your time or your money contesting anything, not after you both terrorized the old man and finally killed him."

Lacey hurried to the door. "Let's go, Andrew."

The detective stepped in front of her. "Lacey, you have to come with me."

Sirens sounded and everyone stayed still. Seconds later, two police officers ran into the house.

Emma remembered she saw the detective on his phone minutes before and realized he had called for backup.

The detective pointed to Lacey as he spoke to the officers. "You can take this one back to the station."

As the officers led Lacey away, Andrew said, "I'll follow them in my car, sweetie."

The detective sat down.

"Tea?" Elsa-May said as she held up the teapot.

The detective grunted. "I'll need something stronger than tea, but I suppose tea will do for now."

"Did I hear you right? Bob inherited everything?" Emma asked.

"It appears that Bob was preparing to have the old man move into a small *haus* that he'd built on to his own. He called it a *daadi haus*. You Amish look after your own, I'm told." He smirked at Emma.

Emma smiled back. "That's right; we do."

Wil said, "His sons hadn't visited him in years so I don't see that they would've taken him in when he got too feeble to look after himself. Bob was doing a *gut* thing."

"I knew Bob wouldn't have done anything bad," Maureen said.

Emma signaled to Bailey to meet her in the kitchen.

"Bailey, have you thought of how upset Silvie will be when she knows that this was all not real – you intending to join the community?"

"Yes, I have and it's upset me from the start. I feel such a pull toward her that I couldn't bring myself to stay away from her."

Emma was annoyed with Bailey for pursuing a relationship with Silvie in the first place when he knew that he would not be staying. "She took quite a liking to you and she has never shown interest in any other man since her husband died."

"I'll go straight to her place and tell her, as soon as I can. I'm sorry to deceive you and Wil too, but that's the nature of my business, I guess."

Emma folded her arms. "Maybe you should get into a different business then."

Bailey nodded. "Excuse me, I'll have to arrange to take the paintings away."

"Once again, Elsa-May, thank you for your assistance," Detective Crowley said, and then quickly drank the rest of his tea. "I must be going – paperwork."

"Detective, I must ask. Was the hair that we found useable for the DNA test? Did it have the root follicle attached?"

Detective Crowley grinned. "They weren't able to use it, but we don't need it now that we have a confession."

SILVIE SAT at the kitchen table and took a moment to enjoy the peace and quiet in the *haus* now that Sabrina had taken the buggy into town. A car pulling up in her driveway disturbed her peace. As she opened her front door, she saw Bailey getting out of a car.

"Bailey, why are you driving a car?"

Bailey hurried toward her. "Silvie, can we speak inside?"

"*Jah*, of course."

Bailey led her by the hand to her couch, sat her down, and said, "I've a lot of things to tell you. You just missed all the action at Wil's *haus*."

"I did? What happened?"

He filled Silvie in on what happened with the paintings, Lacey's confession and Bob inheriting Frank's estate.

Bailey reached for Silvie's hand and held it in his. "I've always been fascinated by the Amish. I'm a Christian and I have admired the faith and strength of the Amish for a long time."

"What are you trying to say? Have you changed your mind about joining us?"

"I'm afraid I've deceived you. I am a detective – undercover, and I've been on the trail of stolen paintings. My real name is Bailey Rivers."

Silvie tilted her head slightly to one side. "So you're a detective and you don't want to be Amish?" Silvie pushed her fingertips to her forehead. "I can't believe what you're saying."

Bailey nodded. "I'm interested in becoming Amish now, but at the start I admit I was deceiving everyone. Elsa-May and Ettie are my grandfather's sisters. He left the Amish when he was fourteen and had no contact with his *familye* for a good twenty years after that. It was Elsa-May who persuaded the bishop to let me in to do my job."

Silvie pulled her hand away from his. "So that's how you did a *gut* job in your lies, you knew all the right things to say from your Amish relations. You didn't need to act so keen to be Amish. I've been deceived."

"Please don't be like that Silvie. It was my job."

Silvie turned her body away from his. "You should get

another job." *I can't let him see me with tears in my eyes,* she thought.

He stood up and sat down on her other side. "Don't cry, Silvie, or you'll break my heart."

Silvie cried more at his words. "Would you ever join us?"

"I would, I think I would, only being a detective is part of who I am, a big part of who I am. I can't be Amish and a detective."

"It's just a job, Bailey. A job shouldn't define who you are," Silvie turned her face away from him once more.

"I can't explain it to you, Silvie. I'm sorry." Bailey put his hand gently on Silvie's cheek and turned her head to face him. "Silvie, what if I come back and join the Amish, for real?"

Silvie sniffed a couple of times. "You'd do that?"

Bailey stared intently into her eyes. "I'm seriously thinking on it, but I have to find the stolen paintings first. I can't let them get the better of me."

"How long will that take?"

He dropped his eyes from hers. "It's taken me nine years already."

"How close are you?"

Bailey shook his head keeping his gaze to the floor. "I headed down a wrong path thinking that Frank or his father had stolen some paintings. Now, I'll have to backtrack and pick up the trail again."

Silvie rose to her feet. "I hope you come back, but for now, it would be better if you left."

"I understand." Bailey stood up, walked toward the door and then turned around. "I'll always be thinking of you, Silvie."

"Don't say anything, Bailey. Just go." Silvie turned her back until she heard Bailey shut her front door. She turned around to check that he had gone then all strength left her legs and she sank to the floor. As tears came to her eyes, she knew that her *mudder* was right about love. It was all too *hatt,* and she was better off without it. Why hadn't she listened to her *mudder*?

CHAPTER TWELVE

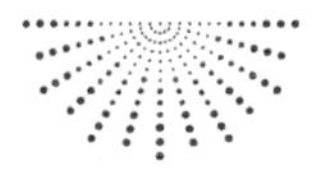

For if a man know not how to rule his own house, how shall he take care of the church of God?
1 Timothy 3:5

As the widows sat around munching cookies, Maureen said, "I knew Bob wouldn't have been involved in anything bad. Besides, he didn't even need the money that Frank left him."

"*Jah,* he seems to be doing quite well for himself," Emma said.

Silvie and Ettie giggled.

"What are you two laughing at?" Maureen asked.

"We think you're growing fond of Bob," Ettie said.

"I've found out this week that there's more to Bob than we know. Just because he's quiet and doesn't speak to anyone people think that he's simple. He's not simple; it's just that when he doesn't have anything to say, he doesn't speak."

Elsa-May said, "I know a few people who could learn from him."

The widows laughed. They all knew a few folk in the community who liked to gossip a little too much.

Maureen said, "What about you, Silvie? What about Bailey?"

Silvie shrugged her shoulders. "I haven't heard from him."

Maureen put her hand on Silvie's shoulder. "*Ach,* it's only been a week, Silvie. I'm sure you'll hear from him. I know he likes you."

Silvie clenched her jaw. "Love's too much pain. I'm better off without it."

"Nonsense," Elsa-May said in her usual booming voice. "Love is precious and if you find it, you need to treasure it. It's just like a plant; starts with the seed, you cover it with the warm earth, water it and look after it."

Emma thought on Elsa-May's words. Maybe listening to Wil prattle on about his silly inventions would be the same as watering the seed. Emma knew she showed her love by cooking the things that he liked, but maybe she could do other things like listen to him and pay attention when he spoke on things that mattered to him.

"What do you mean, Elsa-May?" Silvie said, "I'm hardly in a position to do anything. I just have to wait until he comes back to the community – if he ever comes back."

"Silvie's right, Elsa-May. She just has to wait and if he comes back, he does, and if he doesn't, then it was never meant to be and she has to forget him," Maureen said.

"Nonsense," Elsa-May said. "I think Silvie should pay the man a little visit. Remind him what he's missing."

Silvie's hand flew to her mouth. "Really? Do you really think I should visit him?"

"Why not? I would," Elsa-May said.

Silvie swung around to face Emma. "What do you think, Emma?"

Emma wished she hadn't been put on the spot. If she agreed with Elsa-May and things went wrong, Silvie might blame her. On the other hand, things could go well and Bailey might come back and join the community. "I can't say. I'm sorry, Silvie. You just have to listen to your heart. Maybe forget all those things your *mudder* told you about love; she sounds as though she was —is a very unhappy woman. I hope you don't mind me saying what I think."

"I don't at all. What do you say, Maureen?" Silvie asked.

"I think you should pray about it, then listen to *Gott's* promptings in your heart. It's your decision."

"*Nee,* I'm totally against you going out and throwing yourself at the *mann,*" Ettie said with unusual decisiveness.

Elsa-May gave a little chuckle. "Only you can decide, Silvie."

Silvie nodded. "*Denke* for all your opinions. I'll pray about it and have a think on it."

Elsa-May clapped her hands. "Okay, back to business. Lacey has been arrested for the murder of Frank."

Maureen interrupted. "What about Andrew? Was he charged with anything?"

"*Nee,* he wasn't. Bob is keeping old Frank's *haus* and he's going to rent it out."

"Maybe Sabrina might want to rent it from him." Silvie giggled.

"*Ach*, is your *schweschder* still visiting?" Maureen asked.

"*Jah*, I'm afraid so. I guess I don't mind a bit of company. She does talk about Wil a lot though." Silvie turned to Emma. "Is everything okay with you and Wil?"

Emma forced a smile. "*Jah*, everything is just perfect."

"When are you going to marry the man?" Ettie asked.

"It's not been long enough." Emma was referring to the fact that it had only been just over six months from the death of her husband, Levi.

"I'd marry him straight away. What if he starts looking around? You know what these young single girls are like," Ettie said.

All eyes were on Emma waiting for a reply. She licked her dry lips. "I just need to wait until it feels right."

"How did we get back on to love when we were speaking on the case?" Elsa-May asked.

"Sorry, Elsa-May. I think it was when Bailey's name was mentioned," Silvie responded.

Elsa-May shook her head. "The paintings were original and worth a great deal. Bob is most likely the wealthiest Amish man ever since Frank left him everything."

All eyes turned to Maureen.

"Why's everyone looking at me?" Maureen asked.

The widows giggled.

"I think I will visit Bailey," Silvie said.

"*Gut*," Elsa-May said while she reached for a chocolate fudge bar.

~

On Emma's way home, she passed Wil's *haus* and saw his lights still on. Wondering if she should speak to him, she pulled off the road and into his driveway. *Nee it's too late at night; it's not proper,* she decided. She was just about to turn her buggy around when Wil opened his front door.

"Emma?"

"*Jah,* Wil, it's me."

"It's late."

"I know, I was just returning from visiting."

Wil walked over to her buggy and stood at the door. "Emma, I was going to call and see you tomorrow. I'm sorry; I was too hard on you. I just wanted more of your attention. Maybe it's me who's the selfish one."

Emma opened the door and stepped out so she could face him. "Wil, I want to apologize to you for taking you for granted. I've been too wrapped up in myself. I've been a selfish, horrible person."

Wil smiled, pulled her toward him and held her tightly. "*Nee,* you haven't been. I've been mean because I just want to marry you and I'm impatient. It's me who needs to apologize to you. I'm sorry."

They both laughed. Emma knew she would have to take an interest in the things that mattered to Wil even if she had no interest in them herself. Wil was right; he did show an interest in her sewing and the things that she did. Why was it so hard to be interested in his hobbies? "So, you have no interest in Sabrina?"

Wil pulled back from her a little. "Sabrina? Of course not; she's a child."

"She's marrying age, Wil."

"She's a child to me. Anyway, the only woman I see is you."

She rested her head on Wil's shoulder and he held her a little more tightly.

"We should marry soon."

Emma shut her eyes tightly. "*Jah,* we should."

ACCUSED

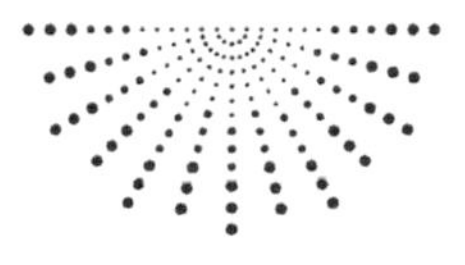

AMISH SECRET WIDOWS' SOCIETY BOOK 3

CHAPTER ONE

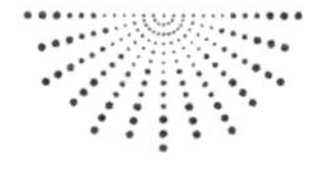

My fruit is better than gold, yea, than fine gold; and my revenue than choice silver. I lead in the way of righteousness, in the midst of the paths of judgment: That I may cause those that love me to inherit substance; and I will fill their treasures.

Proverbs 8:19-21

Feeling foolish was the last thing Amish woman, Angela Bontreger, expected when she arrived in Lancaster County. Her Aunt Elsa-May had assured her Robert would be a match. That was the sole reason she agreed to correspond with the man. Now, after at least forty letters and many months had passed, she was in his living room while he sat glaring at her as though she'd escaped from some far-away insane asylum.

"How is it that you know nothing of me?" Angela pulled a

bundle of letters, tied with a purple ribbon, from her drawstring bag. "You've written me all these." Somewhere in Angela's embarrassed fog, she hoped seeing the letters might bring something to his mind.

He glanced at the letters in Angela's outstretched hand and gave a dismissive wave. "I know nothing of them." His dark brown eyes looked directly into hers. "Is it possible that you have the wrong person?" His voice hinted at desperation—desperation to get her out of his house.

Angela shook her head and placed the letters in her lap. "I just can't understand it." She drew one of the letters from the pile and pointed to the name and address on the back of it. "That's your name and this is your address. I've been writing to you at this address for months."

Robert bounded to his feet and ran his long fingers through his thick, dark hair. "Give me a look at one of those letters." He examined the letter she passed him for a moment and then shook his head. "That has to be the only explanation."

"What?" Angela asked, "What has to be the only explanation?"

Robert either didn't hear her or chose to ignore her. He strode purposely toward his front door and yelled, "Jacob, come here."

"I'm busy, *Onkel* Robert. Can I talk to you later?"

Angela hurried to the door and stood behind Robert. She stood on her tiptoes to look over his shoulder at Jacob, who was in the field closest to the *haus.* Angela had heard of Jacob, the nephew that Robert had taken in and cared for as his own. Robert always mentioned in his letters how much he liked Jacob.

"Now," Robert repeated, firmly, pressing his hands into his hips.

Jacob lifted up the long rein attached to the horse. "I'm busy with the horses."

It appeared to Angela, from all the straps attached to the horse, that Jacob was breaking the horse into harness.

"I said now, Jacob." Robert moved out of the doorway and onto the porch.

Angela stayed a little behind Robert and watched Jacob unstrap the horse and then walk toward his uncle shuffling his feet.

"Jacob, this is Miss Bontreger."

"Hello, Miss Bontreger." Jacob smiled when he looked at Angela.

"Hello, Jacob." Angela noticed that when Jacob's eyes moved back to Robert, the smile left his face altogether.

"Do you know anything about letters? Have you been writing letters to Miss Bontreger, pretending to be me?"

Angela's mouth fell open.

So that's what happened.

She was glad she did not gasp audibly; she felt foolish enough just being there.

Jacob glanced over his *onkel's* shoulder toward Angela then looked to the ground. "Well, I thought it would make you happy if you had a *fraa*. Maybe then you won't be angry all the time."

Angela moved to stand next to Robert and out of the corner of her eye she saw that Robert was red in the face with anger.

In a controlled tone, Robert said, "I'm only angry because you do things such as these. If you didn't continue to do these things then I would have no cause for unhappiness or anger. Go to your room."

Jacob dragged his feet past Robert and Angela.

"Wait a moment," Robert said.

Jacob stopped still and looked up at his *onkel* with large, sad eyes.

"Don't you think you have someone else you should apologize to?" Robert asked.

Jacob looked up at Angela. "Sorry, Miss Bontreger."

Angela did the best she could to force a smile. She couldn't help but feel sorry for Jacob, being reprimanded in front of a visitor. "Apology accepted, Jacob."

Jacob walked into the house.

Robert turned to Angela, red-faced. "No words, I simply have no words." He put a hand to his forehead. "No words except to say that I'm very sorry. I hope you can forgive my rudeness earlier. I had no idea who you were and we're not used to having visitors."

"That's quite all right. My visit must've come as a shock."

"Jacob and I keep to ourselves most of the time." Robert ran his eyes up and down Angela. "Come back inside and I'll fix some tea and cookies."

Angela put her hand to her heart. "I feel terrible for intruding on you like this. I feel silly, so silly."

Robert put his hand up. "Not another word. It's me who's in the wrong – completely. Please, come back inside."

Fifteen minutes later, they were in the kitchen drinking hot tea. Angela was trying to keep the conversation light and off the embarassing reason she was there.

It was Robert who raised the subject again when he asked, "How many letters did he send you?"

"Quite a few and over some months. He even sent me money to travel here to meet him, I mean you did – *ach,* it's a bit confusing. I'll give you the money back, of course."

Robert shook his head. "So that's where his money went. Nonsense, you'll not give anything back. I feel deeply troubled with the disruption that Jacob and I have caused you."

Angela forced another smile even though she felt sick to the stomach. "No harm done."

Robert disappeared into the kitchen then came back with a tray of cookies.

Angela brought the teacup to her lips, saddened that the letters weren't from Robert. He was exactly the kind of *mann* she would have liked. He was tall, strong and responsible. *Robert must be a caring mann to have looked after Jacob all this time. Elsa-May was right about him. I wonder what he thinks of me? Seems he's not looking for a fraa at all,* Angela thought.

Robert put both hands over his face and rubbed his forehead. "I don't know what I'm going to do with that boy."

"His heart was in the right place. He was trying to make you happy."

"I wouldn't have dared to do a thing like that when I was a *youngin.* I would've got such a hiding I wouldn't have been able to sit for a week."

Angela knew she was partly responsible. She should have realized that it was a child writing to her, but the writing style was so mature. "Are you going to punish him?"

"I'll stop him looking after the horses for a week. He likes to train the horses. We've got a new one out there at the moment. The gray one he was working with."

"Did you teach him to break horses in?"

"I showed him the basic things, but he has a knack of knowing how to handle the horses and they respond well to him."

"*Jah,* keeping him away from the horses will upset him and make him think twice about doing such a thing again." Angela was glad that the boy escaped a whipping. She would feel horrid if such a thing happened on her account.

CHAPTER TWO

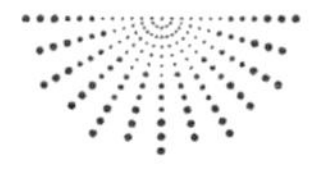

Fear thou not; for I am with thee: be not dismayed; for I am thy God: I will strengthen thee; yea, I will help thee; yea, I will uphold thee with the right hand of my righteousness.
Isaiah 41:10

The Day Before

It was a most beautiful day in Lancaster County. The sun was high in the sky and a gentle breeze kissed Emma's face. As her buggy clip-clopped forward, Emma became transfixed by the shadows made on the road as the sunlight filtered through the trees. She was glad the cold weather was over; spring was well and truly here.

Emma knew as soon as she arrived at Elsa-May and Ettie's *haus* that Ettie was in a particularly disagreeable mood. The elderly sisters had lived together for years from the time shortly after both their husbands died.

A smile widened Emma's lips as she thought of the pair. Elsa-May was the elder and usually the more outspoken of the two. Ettie mostly agreed with everything that Elsa-May said. From their appearance, no one would guess that the two sisters were related. Elsa-May was a large, robust woman whereas Ettie was small and thin. Emma guessed them to be in their late seventies or early eighties – she never asked and they never told.

When Emma tied up her horse and entered the sisters' house, she noticed that there was barely a smile on Ettie's face. Emma was at the house for the widows' meeting. The group of five widows met regularly and enjoyed a time where they were free to speak whatever was on their minds. Cake and sweets of all kinds were a vital ingredient at the meetings.

The sisters' house always had a pleasing aroma of freshly baked cake. As soon as Emma sat down with the ladies, she noticed Ettie wasn't her usual self. "What's the matter, Ettie? You don't look very happy,"

"Listen to what Elsa-May has to say and see what you think of it," Ettie said.

Elsa-May adjusted her prayer *kapp,* looking pleased with herself. "I've been writing to a niece of mine, Angela Bontreger; she's twenty eight and has never married. I told her about Robert Geiger. I simply encouraged her to write to him." Elsa-May then reached forward and plucked a chocolate brownie off the plate on the table.

Ettie narrowed her eyes at her *schweschder.* "You could've told me that before today, Elsa-May. Do you think that's a *gut* idea, to have Angela throw herself at him? Just because two people are Amish and aren't married doesn't mean they are going to get along with one another."

"Where does your niece live, Elsa-May?" Silvie asked as she pushed a few blonde strands of hair back from her pretty face tucking them under her prayer *kapp.*

"She lives in Bloomfield."

"Is she your niece too, Ettie?" Maureen asked since Elsa-May and Ettie were sisters. Maureen had always been a close friend to Emma and it was she who invited Emma to join the widows' group shortly after Emma's husband died.

Ettie shook her head and kept looking down at her needlework. "*Nee,* she's Elsa-May's late husband's niece, his *schweschder's dochder.*"

"How long has she been writing to him, Elsa-May?" Silvie asked as she blinked her attractive, blue eyes. Just like Maureen, Silvie had been widowed for quite some time. Both Maureen and Silvie were in their early thirties, slightly older than Emma.

Elsa-May chuckled. "She's been writing to him for around five months and he's invited her to visit. She's very excited. She arrives tomorrow."

Ettie pressed her lips tightly together and shook her head.

"What's the matter now, Ettie?" Elsa-May asked.

Ettie lowered her needlework and looked at Elsa-May. "No *gut* will come of it."

Elsa-May snorted. "Come of what?"

"Meddling. Nothing *gut* ever comes of meddling."

"Nonsense. We meddle all the time." Elsa-May laughed. "That's what we do."

The two sisters often ended up annoyed with each other; it

was mostly Ettie who backed down before things became too heated.

Emma spoke up to try and soothe things between the two *schweschders.* "What harm can it do, Ettie? If they meet and don't get along, then that's one man who she can cross off her list. Who knows? They might get along just fine and get married."

Emma's words weren't of much use as Ettie still wore a stony expression and her lips were so tightly pressed together that they formed a thin line.

It seemed as though Elsa-May could not keep the smile from her face despite Ettie's disapproval. "You'll all get to meet my niece of course. She's a lovely girl."

Silvie brought her teacup to her lips and before she took a sip, she asked, "Why has she never married?"

"She's quite shy, which doesn't help matters. Her *mudder* told me she was in love with a boy and was holding out for him for the longest time, but he married someone else."

"That's sad," Maureen said.

"There might not be too many *menner* in Bloomfield," Silvie said.

"If *Gott* wants her to be married, He'll put someone in her path," Ettie said. "It's not for us to do His work."

"You'd do something to help yourself though, wouldn't you, Ettie? So just keep out of things that don't concern you." Elsa-May folded her arms across her chest.

Emma was shocked by Elsa-May's words and glanced at the other widows' faces to see that they were also startled by her words.

Ettie shot her head up and dropped her needlework into her lap. The tension between the sisters hung heavily in the room.

Emma quickly spoke again to avoid any further unpleasantness. "Maybe that's what *Gott* has done now, Ettie. He's put it in Elsa-May's head to encourage Angela to write to Robert. Angela didn't have to write to him. No one forced her to do it. Now, Robert's invited Angela to meet him."

"It's still okay for Angela to stay with you, isn't it, Emma?" Elsa-May asked.

"*Jah,* I'll be pleased with the company. I get lonely in the big old *haus* with just me and Growler." Growler was Emma's cat that she had reluctantly taken in when his previous owner was murdered just months ago.

Emma turned to see Ettie staring at her open-mouthed. "What is it, Ettie?"

"You knew about all this?" Ettie asked.

"Yesterday Elsa-May asked if Angela could stay for a time. I said she could stay as long as she wanted."

Elsa-May quickly added, "She can't stay here, can she? Our *haus* is barely big enough for the both of us at times."

Maureen cleared her throat in a nervous manner. "Speaking of *haus* guests, do you still have your *schweschder* staying with you, Silvie?"

"*Jah,* she's still there. I suppose it's nice to have a little company, but I'd most likely prefer to borrow Growler as a *haus* guest." Silvie gave a little laugh. "Sabrina's like a bee in a bottle; she always wants to go places and do things. I let her take the buggy by herself. She's out most days. I have no idea where she goes; I'm just glad for the peace. I know she's scouting around looking for a husband; that's for sure and for certain. Before she goes home, she's making sure that she's met all the boys in the community."

The widows laughed.

"Have you heard from that nephew of mine, Silvie?" Elsa-May asked.

"*Jah,* Bailey writes me twice a week. Still hasn't said anything about visiting me or joining the Amish. Does he still write to you two?" Silvie asked of Elsa-May and Ettie.

"We get the occasional letter. He speaks fondly of you, Silvie," Elsa-May said.

Silvie's cheeks turned a shade of pink and she looked down into the chocolate cake in her lap.

"You can't push him, you know," Ettie said.

"I know, Ettie. It was he who suggested that he might join us in the future. I would never push him into something. It would never work that way. He has to want to join us." Silvie swallowed hard. "He has asked me to visit him."

"You should go," Elsa-May said.

Silvie met Elsa-May and Ettie's *Englischer* nephew, Bailey Rivers, months ago when he was working on a case in Lancaster County. Bailey Rivers is an undercover detective and at the time Bailey and Silvie met, Bailey was working undercover and staying within the community under the pretense of wishing to join the community.

Bailey assured Silvie that his deception was necessary for his job. Silvie suggested that he change his job. Bailey had hinted that he might become Amish when he finished the case that he was working on. The only catch was that the investigation had already taken him many years and there was no telling how much longer it would take.

"Are you unsure of leaving Sabrina alone in the *haus* when

you visit him?" Emma asked. Sabrina was Silvie's *schweschder* who had been visiting her on an extended stay.

"*Jah,* partly that and partly that I haven't traveled much outside the community." Silvie gave a little laugh. "I'm a little nervous traveling alone, finding my way and that kind of thing."

"Do you want me to go with you?" Maureen asked.

"*Denke,* Maureen, but if I go I should probably go alone. I might take you up on it. I'll have a think about it."

"The offer's there if you want it. Just give me some notice so I can arrange time off from work." Maureen offered a wide smile.

CHAPTER THREE

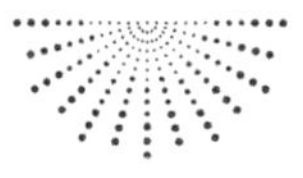

Through faith we understand that the worlds were framed by the word of God, so that things which are seen were not made of things which do appear.
Hebrews 11:3

Emma had prepared one of her upstairs bedrooms for Angela's stay. She had freshly washed the sheets, washed the floor, dusted the furniture and opened the window to air the room out. It had been a long time since Emma had visitors.

"Emma."

Emma heard Wil calling her name from the bottom of the stairs.

"Hello, Wil. I'm expecting Angela here shortly. I'm just upstairs fixing her room. I'll be down there in one minute."

Emma hurried down the stairs, anxious to see Wil. Even though they saw each other every day, her heart still skipped a beat whenever she saw him.

"It'll do you *gut* to have someone staying with you. I'll make myself scarce. I've just brought that broken kitchen chair back to you."

"*Denke,* Wil. It looks as *gut* as new."

"It is. I've put new rods in the sides. It's stronger than when it was new. Do you want it back in the kitchen?" Before Emma could open her mouth, Wil was walking into the kitchen carrying the chair.

"*Jah,* in the kitchen." Emma placed her hands on her hips as she watched Wil's strong body walk away from her. She knew things hadn't been easy for Wil. He wanted to marry her way before now, but Emma was worried that an acceptable time hadn't yet passed after Levi had died, to marry. She was thankful that Wil had been patient.

"I'll go before Angela comes, so you two can get to know each other by yourselves without me around."

"*Nee,* you don't have to do that. Stay and have the midday meal with us."

"I've got errands to run this afternoon and I'd best start them now." Wil walked toward Emma and gave her a quick kiss on the forehead before he strode out the door.

Emma stood on the porch and watched Wil's buggy drive up the road. Just as his buggy was a speck in the distance, a taxi appeared beside it traveling toward Emma's *haus. I wonder if this is Angela,* Emma thought. The taxi continued right to her front door. Emma stepped down from the porch to meet Angela.

Angela opened the taxi door. She had a dark green dress in a full style, which was more gathered than most of the Amish women wore in Lancaster County. Emma noticed that the prayer *kapp* was a little smaller and made of sheer material. The white apron she wore was the same as the aprons that Emma was used to. Angela was a tall girl with dark hair and dark eyes. She was not unattractive.

Emma reached out her hands. "Angela?"

"*Jah,* and you're Emma?"

The two ladies gave each other a small kiss on the side of the cheek. The taxi driver dropped a bag at Angela's feet. "Would you like me to take it inside for you?" he asked Angela.

"*Nee.* I can do it, *denke.*"

"Here let me take it." Emma picked up the bag and Angela followed her into the *haus* as the taxi drove away.

"I've got you in one of the upstairs bedrooms. Follow me," Emma said.

As Angela followed her up the stairs, she said, "I can't thank you enough for this, Emma."

Emma glanced back at her. "It'll be *gut* to have some company." Emma passed her own room and saw that Growler was asleep in the middle of the bed. She stopped in the doorway and nodded in his direction. "That's my cat, Growler. He'll most likely ignore you. He ignores me most of the time unless I'm late with his dinner."

"By the look of him I would say that you're never late with his dinner. He must be the largest cat I've ever seen. My cats are nowhere near that size."

Emma continued to the next doorway. "This is your room." She placed the suitcase on the bed. "You can unpack now if you like and come down when you're finished. The midday meal is nearly ready."

"*Ach,* it's a lovely room." Angela walked to the window. "Such a pretty view from here."

Emma looked out the window. "I know. I should appreciate it more, but there always seems so much to do and so little time."

"I'll help you while I'm here. You just tell me what you'd like me to do," Angela said.

Emma smiled. "There's not much to do today. Are you hungry?"

"A little hungry."

"Leave the unpacking then, and we'll have the meal now."

They made their way downstairs. Emma had already prepared most of the meal ahead of time and only had to heat a couple of things on the stove. "Cup of hot tea?" Emma asked.

"*Jah*. Let me get it," Angela said.

Emma showed Angela around the kitchen, so she knew where everything was kept. Moments later, they sat at the kitchen table sipping hot tea.

"Elsa-May tells me that you're to meet Robert Geiger soon."

Angela made a face. "I'm a little nervous. He's arranged for me to meet him tomorrow. He's even sent me money to get a taxi from here."

"I could've driven you."

Angela gave a high-pitched giggle. "It'd make me more nervous if someone else was there. What if we didn't like each other at all? Then things would be really awkward."

"I suppose so. Has he told you all about himself?" Emma asked.

"He told me he's got his *bruder's* son, Jacob, living with him. He said that he's a very smart boy."

"I've heard Jacob can be a little bit of a handful."

"What do you mean, Emma?"

"*Ach,* nothing to worry about, I'm sure. You heard of how Jacob's parents died?"

"In a buggy accident, wasn't it?" Angela asked.

Emma nodded. "Unfortunate circumstances. Jacob's *daed* was Robert's *bruder.* I'd say Robert hasn't married up until now because he's been too involved with looking after Jacob."

"*Jah,* that's what his letters as *gut* as said. It must be awful for Jacob. He's blessed his uncle took him in. From his letters I can tell that Robert adores him."

"You're going to visit Robert tomorrow then?"

"*Jah,* I've got his address. Elsa-May said it's not too far from here."

"Not far at all," Emma said.

Angela leaned forward. "Is there anything you can tell me about Robert?"

Emma thought for a while. "*Nee,* I don't know him well enough."

Angela took a deep breath. "That's all right. I guess I'll just have to see for myself."

Emma could imagine how nervous Angela would be after months of writing to a man and now finally about to meet him.

CHAPTER FOUR

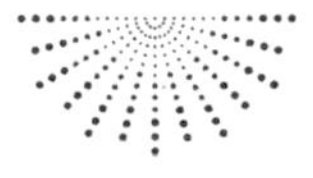

Because strait is the gate, and narrow is the way, which leadeth unto life, and few there be that find it.
Matthew 7:14

Angela sat with Robert and tried to get over the shock of Jacob being the one to write the letters. Despite the shock, she did feel a little more comfortable than when she had first arrived.

"It was my *Ant* Elsa-May who suggested I write you." Angela felt the need to explain that to him, since he hadn't had the benefit of reading any of her letters.

Robert smiled. "I recall she did try to tell me of someone who might suit me, on more than one occasion. I did try to tell her about the boy and how it complicates things for me."

Angela did not quite know why he thought he could not be

married because of Jacob. Jacob had said himself that he wanted Robert to have a *fraa*.

"I heard you took Jacob in when his *mudder* and *vadder* were killed in a buggy accident."

Robert stared straight ahead and took a mouthful of tea. "Jacob's *daed* was my *bruder*, Ross. What you might not have heard was that my *bruder* had been charged with murder and was out on bail when he and Jacob's *mudder* were killed in the accident."

"*Nee*, I didn't know about that."

"I've been trying to clear Ross' name for the sake of the boy. That's what Ross would've wanted."

"Does Jacob know that his *vadder* was accused of such a thing?"

Robert shook his head. "If he's heard things here and there, he hasn't mentioned anything to me."

"How far have you gotten trying to clear his name?" Angela asked.

"Not very far. I've got small pieces of information and that's all."

"Elsa-May's had some success with things like this in the past. Have you considered getting her help with it?"

Robert tipped his head back and laughed. "Dear old Elsa-May being of help in a matter like this?"

"It might seem unlikely, but it's true. Elsa-May and her *schweschder*, Ettie, have had success; they even know detectives. In fact, one of their nephews is a detective."

Robert drummed his fingers on the long, wooden kitchen table. "Really?"

Angela nodded enthusiastically.

"Your coming here might be an answer to prayer, Miss Bontreger."

Angela's heart beat faster when he looked at her. He was a handsome man and even more so when he smiled. She had been waiting on a time like this, a time where *Gott's* favor would shine upon her.

Robert was silent as he slowly raised the hot tea to his lips. He took a mouthful, placed the cup carefully onto the table and looked once more into Angela's eyes. "Write a *gut* letter, did I?"

Angela smiled. "I'm here, aren't I?"

Angela and Robert laughed, which eased any leftover tension between them.

"I'm staying at Emma Kurtzler's *haus*, and Elsa-May and Ettie are coming for dinner tonight. Why don't you tell me everything you know and I'll pass it on to Elsa-May and see what she makes of it?"

Robert ran his fingers over his chin. "Wouldn't hurt, I guess. I kept in contact with the police for a time, but I think they came to see me as a pest at some point. They'll hardly speak to me now when I go in there. They certainly don't listen to anything I have to say. I've given them new information, but I think they don't want to put any effort into the case. They appear to be happy to leave things as they are. Every time I've been to there to talk to one of the police, I've overhead at least one of them grumbling about paperwork. I came to realize that all they want to do is drink coffee and eat donuts."

Angela smiled at his comment. "They're not all like that."

Robert rubbed his right eyebrow and then looked back at Angela. "Why don't I take you back to Emma's *haus* and I'll tell you everything on the way?"

"Jah, denke."

Robert leaned his body back slightly. "Forgive me. I've put you in an awkward position. You came here expecting something quite different and now I'm saddling you with all my burdens."

Angela instinctively put her hand on his arm. "*Nee,* not at all. I'm happy to be of help."

Robert sat up straight, put his fingers lightly on her hand and stared into her eyes. Angela pulled her hand away and looked down. She wanted to keep her hand there, but she did not want him to think that she was anxiously looking for a husband. The last thing she wanted was to appear to Robert as though she were desperate.

"I'm sorry, Angela. I'm not used to a woman's soft hands against my skin."

Angela smiled and kept her gaze away from him. "Robert, you must stop apologizing to me; it's not necessary." Angela could scarcely breathe as she felt his gaze upon her. She stood up. "Should we go now?"

"Visit me tomorrow? I mean, to tell me what Elsa-May makes of the whole thing?"

"*Jah,* I will."

Before Angela could say more, Robert called out to Jacob who was still in his bedroom. "I'm going out now, Jacob. You can come out of your room. I'll be back later. I'll tell you of your punishment when I return." He turned to Angela. "Let's go." He walked out the door toward the barn with Angela hurrying behind him.

Angela leaned against the barn door and watched Robert as he hitched a buggy to one of his horses. She scrutinized his strong arms lift the buggy and strap the leather onto the horse. He spoke to the horse in a low, soothing voice as he worked. Angela liked people who were kind to animals.

Elsa-May was right; this could be the mann for me, she thought. *We both felt something as we sat in the kitchen just now; I'm sure he felt it too. His touch sent tingles right through me; surely that means something.*

During the ride home, Robert told Angela everything he knew about his *bruder's* case wherein he was falsely accused of murder. Angela wrote everything down so she wouldn't forget anything.

CHAPTER FIVE

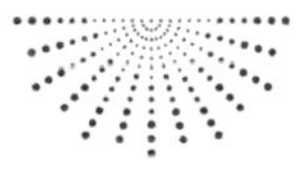

A hot-tempered man stirs up strife, but he who is slow to anger quiets contention.

Proverbs 15:18

That evening, not only did Elsa-May and Ettie come to Emma's *haus* for dinner, Silvie and Maureen came as well.

Angela was well aware of her *Ant* Elsa-May's crime solving abilities and she guessed that these widows helped her.

As the ladies were all helping to prepare the meal, Elsa-May pulled Angela aside for a quiet word. "How did you like Robert?"

"*Ach,* it was terrible. It wasn't he who wrote the letters; it was Jacob."

"His nephew, little Jacob?"

"Yeah, he's most likely eleven or twelve. He admitted to it and he said he wanted his *onkel* to be happy. I still find it hard to believe that I was fooled by a child of his age. It's obvious that he is a very smart boy."

Elsa-May chuckled. "Bless his little soul."

"I was extremely embarrassed. I felt such a fool going there to meet someone I thought I might marry and he knew nothing of me, nothing at all."

Elsa-May waved her hand dismissively. "Apart from all that, what did you think of Robert?"

Angela giggled a little. "He was lovely. Just the sort of *mann* I'd like. You were right about that, *Ant*."

Elsa-May leaned toward her and spoke quietly. "Don't give up; *Gott* works in mysterious ways."

"Did you know about his *bruder*, Jacob's *daed*?" Angela asked.

"*Ach, jah.* A terrible business, on bail for murder and then killed before he could clear his name. Both Ross and his *fraa*, Linda, died in that buggy accident."

"So, you believe he was innocent?" Angela's eyes grew wide.

Elsa-May filled her cheeks with air. "I don't know any details. I've always assumed he was innocent. No Amish *mann* would ever have done what he was accused of."

"Robert wants to clear his *bruder's* name for Jacob's sake. He thinks that's why Jacob has been unruly. Although, he's not sure whether Jacob knows or not, but he must have heard some kind of gossip. Anyway, I said I'd get your help."

Elsa-May nodded slowly. "*Jah*, I'll help. We'll all help. Did he tell you anything?"

"He told me everything he knows and I even wrote it down."

Elsa-May patted her on the arm. "Tell the ladies over

dinner."

Angela drew her chin backwards. "*Ant,* that's not very nice dinner conversation for the ladies."

Elsa-May held Angela's arm firmly. "Believe me, they'll appreciate the conversation more than talking about the last quilt they sewed or the batch of strawberry preserves they've just bottled."

Once the dinner table was set, they all sat down to eat.

Elsa-May began, "Now ladies, you all know Robert Geiger and how his *bruder,* Ross Geiger, was accused of murder before he died in the buggy accident?"

The ladies nodded.

"We are going to try and clear his name," Elsa-May said.

"What if he's guilty?" Ettie said.

Elsa-May glared at her *schweschder.* "Then things remain the same, but if he's innocent, we will be able to clear his name for his son's sake." She looked at all the widows. "All in?"

"*Jah,*" the widows chimed.

"Tell us what you know, Angela." Elsa-May said.

"This is what Robert told me. Two years ago a man was found dead, tied to a wooden cross. He was found by a couple of children on their way to *skul.* A witness came forward and said that she saw Ross hitting the man on the head with a rock and she saw him tie him to the cross. It was the woman's testimony that had him arrested, even though Ross' *fraa* said that he had been home all evening. The police believed that it was an Amish person because of the religious implications of the murder, with the cross and all."

"Who was the man who was killed?" Maureen asked.

Angela shrugged her shoulders. "I don't know. Robert says

that no one knows."

"How did Ross get bail if he was charged with murder?" Emma asked.

Ettie said, "From what I remember of the case, they did not think he was a flight risk since he had no passport and did not know anyone outside of the community."

"Is that all you know, Angela?" Elsa-May asked.

"*Jah,* that's all I know. I'm seeing Robert again tomorrow. Is there anything I should ask him?"

The widows looked at each other.

"*Nee,* that's all we need for now until we think of some questions," Elsa-May said.

Ettie said, "Elsa-May, you'll have to go and ask Crowley some questions."

"Indeed." Elsa-May nodded. Detective Crowley had been a source of information to them in the past and was always more than willing to help. Although, not everyone liked Detective Crowley even if he was helpful.

"Better you than me." When everyone looked at her, Emma said. "He always makes me feel guilty and uncomfortable."

Ettie pointed a long, bony finger at Emma. "He always helps us."

Emma nodded and put her head down and wished that she hadn't spoken at all. She knew Ettie was right.

Silvie said, "What's the plan, Elsa-May?"

Elsa-May placed her knife and fork down and swallowed her mouthful of chicken. "Let's see now. I'll visit Crowley to find out what he can tell me about the case. That's really all we can do until we have more information. I'll go first thing in the morning."

Angela turned to Emma. "I hope you didn't mind having this conversation over dinner, Emma."

"*Nee,* not at all. Everyone here has had a little experience in these matters. We're all happy to help in whatever way we can."

"You came here to see Robert?" Silvie asked.

Angela's face flushed scarlet. "I suppose it doesn't matter if everyone at this table knows. Elsa-May had me write to Robert, but it appears my first letter was intercepted by his nephew, Jacob." Angela put her fingertips to her forehead and continued, "Jacob wrote back to me and he's been writing to me ever since, pretending to be his *onkel.* Both Robert and I only just found out today."

Maureen giggled. "*Ach,* that little - naughty boy."

Silvie asked, "So what's the plan, Elsa-May, where do we start?

"Ettie, you go visiting people and see what you can find out. People like to talk to you."

"Okay," Ettie said. "I'll start visiting tomorrow and ask a lot of questions."

"Emma, you go and visit Crowley," Elsa-May said.

"Me? Why do I have to visit Crowley? Didn't you say you were going to do it, Elsa-May? You're the one he respects. I told you he makes me feel uncomfortable and guilty all the time."

"Just do it, Emma. The rest of us will spread out, visit people and ask questions without appearing obvious. Everyone in the community should recall the incident. We have to find out who the witness was and who the dead man was."

"You're going back to Robert's place tomorrow aren't you, Angela?"

"*Jah,* I am. In the afternoon," Angela said.

"Ask questions about the witness and the dead man. Find out if Robert knows anything about them and find out what other little things he might have forgotten to mention."

Angela nodded. "I will."

"Now, if we're all done with that business, we've got dessert," Emma said.

Angela looked up to see Emma and Maureen carrying desserts to the table. There was a tall chocolate cake with pink and white marshmallows on top, chocolate fudge, ice-cream and round chocolate balls covered with coconut.

"Someone likes chocolate," Angela said with a laugh.

"Chocolate is a weakness of mine," Emma said as she sat down.

Maureen took a large knife and cut the tall chocolate cake into slices. "I hope no one here is watching what they eat."

"Not anymore," Ettie said.

After a large meal and an even larger dessert, the widows went home.

"I'll dry the dishes, Emma. That way we can talk," Angela said.

"*Denke*. How are you liking Lancaster County so far?"

"Everyone seems really friendly. I like the countryside; it's quite similar to back home."

"I heard you tell Elsa-May that you like Robert," Emma said.

"*Jah*. I don't know what he thinks of me. A strange lady showing up at his *haus* expecting that he should know of me. It was the most embarrassing moment of my life."

"He's a *gut* man, from what I know of him. He would have felt bad when he found out what Jacob had done."

Angela looked thoughtful. "He did."

"Seems to me as though Robert is always sad or distracted by something. Now I know more of what happened to his *bruder,* it all makes sense. Mind you I didn't know the Geigers that well."

"I appreciate you letting me stay here, Emma."

"You're doing me a favor. I like having company. I told Elsa-May you are welcome to stay as long as you want." Emma took the opportunity to try and find out more about the cases Elsa-May had worked on in the past. Emma was involved in the Pluver case and the more recent murder of old Frank, but she knew that Elsa-May and Ettie had worked on many more cases with Detective Crowley. "You're aware then of Elsa-May working on similar cases to try and solve them, and such?"

"*Jah,* someone was murdered once, down my way, and Elsa-May helped with that," Angela said.

A smile spread across Emma's face. "I see. I knew she'd done these things before."

"Don't tell her I told you; she's very secretive about these things. I don't want her to be cross with me."

"I won't tell," Emma said.

"My *daed* used to say that Elsa-May's every bit as smart as a *mann.*"

Emma raised her eyebrows and bit her tongue to avoid making a comment, although she couldn't help but say, "I guess your *daed* would see that as a compliment."

"Very much so." Angela laughed. "I guess he thinks that *menner* have to be smarter."

Emma vigorously scrubbed a saucepan. "Women are just as smart, I'm sure."

"Elsa-May said you might be married soon?"

"*Jah,* to Wil Jacobson. He lives next door. You met him yesterday, didn't you?"

"*Nee,* I didn't meet anyone," Angela said.

"That's right; he left just before you arrived."

"That's right, I do remember passing a buggy that looked as though it was coming from your place. Is he nice?"

"He is. I'm blessed to have had two *gut menner* in my life. Why have you never married before now, Angela?"

"Where I come from isn't like here. There's not many *menner* to choose from and they get snapped up pretty quickly. I'm quieter than the other girls so it made things that much harder for me. The other girls can talk to the boys easily. I never had any *bruders,* so I'm not used to boys. There was one boy I liked once." Angela rubbed her neck. "I was too nervous to speak to the boys especially the ones I liked. Anyway, before too long, they were all married."

"That's the disadvantage of a small community, I suppose."

"My *Ant* Elsa-May's been telling me about Robert for a long time. I finally gave in and wrote to him and well… you know the rest."

Emma put the last saucepan in the cupboard and wiped down her long, wooden table in the kitchen. "All done; just a quick sweep with the broom and we can sit down."

"Let me do it, Emma." Angela rushed for the broom.

"*Denke,* I'll make us some hot tea." Emma put the kettle on the stove and got the tea ready. "Don't fuss too much with the floor, Angela. I'll wash it tomorrow."

Once the tea was poured, Emma carried the tea, chocolate cookies and her favorite chocolate soft centers out to the living room.

"This is a nice big room, Emma," Angela said as she sat on the couch.

"*Jah,* it's just as we wanted. Levi, my late husband built the *haus* for us." Emma passed Angela the tea.

"Will you live in Wil's *haus* when you get married?"

Emma sat down opposite Angela and put the pink flowered teacup to her lips and took a sip. The teacups had been a gift from Levi on the announcement of their marriage. They were far more fancy than the china she had been used to, which was plain white with maybe a small pattern. As she placed the cup down onto the saucer, she said, "We haven't even decided that." Emma looked around the room. "This *haus* reminds me of Levi. I wouldn't want someone else to live in it, neither would I feel comfortable living in it with Wil, especially when he has his own *haus* on the next door farm."

Emma watched Angela bite into a chocolate cookie.

"You know, now I say that out aloud I realize that's what's stopping Wil and I moving forward. I just can't see where we could live," Emma said.

"That makes sense."

"Does it? Sometimes it seems as nothing makes sense to me. Nothing has fallen into place. Nowhere feels right for us to live."

"Perhaps you're thinking ahead too much? I know it would be hard to leave this place, but it is after all just a *haus,*" Angela said.

Nee, it's not just a haus, Emma thought. Emma drew comfort from living in the *haus* that Levi had built for them. It was as if part of him was still there. Angela's words seemed harsh. Emma studied Angela as she sat in front of her, nibbling on the cookie.

She hadn't meant any offence; Angela couldn't know the feelings that she had for the *haus* or the comfort it filled her with.

Angela looked up and caught her eye. "I didn't mean to upset you, Emma."

"I'm not upset. I'm realizing just how attached I am to this *haus*."

Angela nodded sympathetically and passed her up the plate of cookies. Emma took a cookie and held it in her hand. What was the answer? Where would she and Wil live after they married?

Angela broke through Emma's pondering when she said, "Robert asked me to go back there tomorrow."

Emma was pleased that they had arranged to meet again. "I'll drive you there."

"*Denke,* would afternoon suit you? He's hoping I'll have some word from Elsa-May helping to clear his *bruder's* name. I'm hoping we might have some information by afternoon."

Emma raised her eyebrows. "That seems a little hopeful since he's gone two years with no information."

Angela gasped and covered her mouth. "I hope I didn't give him false hope when I told him of Elsa-May's abilities."

"We'll all do the best that we can. Besides, it'll give you reason to keep speaking to him." Emma giggled.

"*Jah,* I know it will."

"I saw when he brought you here this afternoon that he had the look in his eye that a *mann* has when he likes what he sees."

Angela's face brightened. "You think so?"

Emma smiled at the look of delight on Angela's face. "I do."

Angela breathed in and let her breath out slowly. "I'll sleep well tonight."

CHAPTER SIX

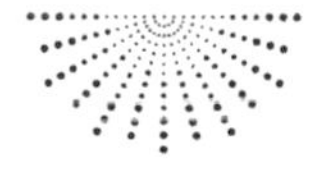

But without faith it is impossible to please him: for he that cometh to God must believe that he is, and that he is a rewarder of them that diligently seek him.
Hebrews 11:6

Emma was woken by a shaft of light entering her bedroom from where her two curtains met in the middle. She had forgotten to close the gap the night before. She always woke at the slightest light.

Most nights before she went to bed, she would adjust her curtains so they would blanket the morning light. Too late – she was already wide-awake.

As she stretched her hands over her head, she recalled that today she had been designated by Elsa-May to visit her very least favorite detective.

She had to go that morning because she had told Angela she would drive her to Robert's *haus* in the afternoon. Emma got out of bed and hurried to get her chores done so she could make an early start, figuring that Crowley would get into his office at around nine.

~

THE MORNING HOURS passed quickly for Emma and now she stood outside Detective Crowley's office, knocking tentatively on his door.

"Come in," Crowley said.

She stepped through the doorway and he rose to his feet when he saw her. "Mrs. Jacobson?"

"*Nee*, it's Mrs. Kurtzler."

"Yes, of course, I was getting confused with Wil Jacobson. So you haven't married Mr. Jacobson yet?"

Did the detective know that she was conflicted over the prospect of marrying Wil so soon after Levi died? Could he possibly be that good of a detective?

"Detective, with all due respect, I did not come here to discuss my marital status." Emma silently reprimanded herself; she knew that was a silly thing to say if she was to keep him on side. But he seemed to have a way of getting under her skin. Why would he call her Mrs. Jacobson? He knew her name very well and Emma knew for sure and for certain that he had an excellent memory.

A smile softened the detective's sharp features. "Have a seat." He motioned to the chair in front of his desk.

They sat at the same time.

"What brings you here then, if it's not to discuss your marital status?"

Keep calm, he's trying to bait you again, Emma cautioned herself. "Elsa-May sent me." Emma knew that the detective respected Elsa-May, so she congratulated herself on thinking to use her name.

The detective leaned forward. "I'm listening."

"Do you remember a case some years ago involving an Amish man called Ross Geiger?"

"I do. Strange case that one. The body was tied to a cross."

"That's the one," Emma said pleased that he remembered it.

"What of it?"

"Elsa-May sent me to ask you who the witness was and who the dead man was."

The detective rubbed his left ear. "I recall the accused man died in a buggy accident shortly after he was granted bail."

"Yes, he and his wife, before he could clear his name. Before proper investigations could take place."

The detective bit on the end of a pencil. "So, that's what this is about? Elsa-May is looking to clear his name?"

Emma nodded. "Were you working on the case?"

"No, but I knew about it. It should all be on the computer." The detective turned his attention to the computer on his desk. He pressed a button and tilted the screen to face him. After a few moments and a few clicks, the detective asked, "How long ago? What was the accused's name again?"

"Roughly two years ago and his name was Ross Geiger."

"Got it. Here we go. The dead man was never identified, but we do have his DNA records, dental records, body measurements and fingerprints. He did not fit the description of any missing person at the time or since." The detective looked at Emma. "The dead man had no criminal history because his fingerprints weren't in our database."

Emma nodded. "Does it give a description of him?"

The detective turned back to the computer screen. "Five foot ten inches, light brown hair, brown eyes and no identifying marks or scars. He was wearing dark blue jeans, brown leather boots and a blue shirt with a collar."

"What does it say about the witness?" Emma asked.

"Mrs. Kurtzler, you know I can't give you sensitive information like that. But, if you should happen to overhear me talking to myself as I'm looking at the computer, then I wouldn't be breaking any rules." The detective looked again, at the computer screen. "The witness was, or I should say is, Juliana Redcliffe." The detective was quiet for a moment as he read the information. "She said she couldn't sleep that night and went for a walk down by the river. She heard a noise and looked through the undergrowth to see Ross Geiger hit the man in the head with a large stone several times then he tied him to a wooden cross."

"Does that sound odd to you, Detective? That someone would go for a walk alone in the woods if they can't sleep? Do people do that? Especially a woman alone at night?" Emma asked.

"Sounds odd, but how is someone to say that she didn't go for a walk?" The detective kept his eyes fixed on the screen. "It happened two miles away from Ross Geiger's house and five hundred meters from the witness' house."

"And where's that?"

The detective lowered his head and looked up at Emma, and said, "What?"

"The witness' house."

The detective leaned back in his chair. "This is a murder. Only a trained professional should stick their nose in."

Emma stared back at the detective and held his gaze for some time.

"All right, I'll speak to her today. If she still lives there," the detective said.

Emma wriggled in the chair. "Could you possibly do it this morning?"

The detective cocked his head to the side and frowned. "It's an old case. What's the rush?"

"Well, you see. We really want to clear Ross Geiger's name for his son. He's becoming a handful to look after and Ross's *bruder* is taking care of him and Angela, who's staying at my place, was writing letters to..."

"Spare me the finer details, I'm sure they're very interesting – to someone." He looked back at the computer. "Yes, we have Robert Geiger's details here, on file. It would appear he's been to see us several times." The detective stood up. "I'll talk to the witness and then come to see you. Do you still live at the same place?"

"*Jah*, still the same *haus*."

As Emma was walking out of his office, the detective called after her, "Mrs. Kurtzler."

She turned to face him. "Please, call me Emma."

The detective smiled. "Do you still have that fat cat?"

Emma smiled at the thought of Growler. "Yes, I've still got Growler. He's part of the *familye* now."

A look of amusement crossed the detective's hard face. It was the detective who suggested that Emma take Growler to live with her after his owner had been murdered. At the time, Emma hardly had a choice, it was take Growler or the detective was going to have him put to sleep.

Or was he?

That's what the detective said that he would do at the time. She remembered distinctly that the detective said that he'd call animal welfare and have the cat put to sleep if she didn't take him.

Had he been bluffing?

He seemed interested in Growler's welfare. Emma shook her head. She'd never know what went on in the detective's head.

CHAPTER SEVEN

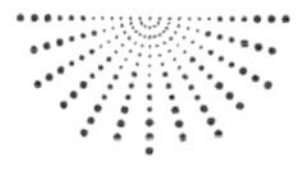

Let us come before his presence with thanksgiving, and make a joyful noise unto him with psalms.
Psalms 95:2

Emma drove her buggy home, pleased with the fact that Crowley was going to question the witness. It was still early in the day and Emma knew that Angela would not expect her back for some time, so Emma pulled up her buggy outside Wil's front door.

Wil came out to meet her. "Emma, I was just about to put some *kaffe* on."

"Lovely, I'll have one, *denke*."

"You sit here and I'll put the hot water on to boil."

Emma sat on the white porch chair and looked out across Wil's farm. What a coincidence it was that they both owned farms adjacent to one another. He'd been a *gut* friend to her late husband and she knew without a doubt that Levi would wholeheartedly approve of the two of them getting married.

Wil fell into the seat next to her. "What's on your mind, Emma? I can tell something is."

Emma smiled. Wil could read her like a book. "You still want to get married next wedding season, don't you?"

"Or as soon as the bishop can marry us and as soon as you are willing."

"It occurred to me that I've been hesitating because of my *haus.* Because it was the house Levi built for us to live in." Emma studied Wil's face and noticed that he did not look happy. "Wil, don't be like that. I need to speak to you about these things. I want to be able to tell you all things that trouble me."

"*Jah,* Emma, we need to discuss these things. I know that. I didn't realize how you felt about the *haus.*"

"I don't know what to do about the *haus*. I mean, where do you see us living?" Emma nibbled on the end of her fingernail. She had nearly beaten the habit, but every now and again she realized she was chewing her nails.

Wil turned his body toward her a little more. "I always thought that we'd live here in my *haus*. It's plenty big enough and I'll change it to whatever suits you. I can make the kitchen bigger and better. Did you have other ideas?"

Emma shook her head slowly. "*Nee,* I guess it's either my *haus* or your *haus*."

"I wouldn't feel right living in another *mann's* house even though Levi was like my own *bruder*." Wil picked up Emma's hand. "Emma, if it means that much to you I'll be happy living anywhere as long as I'm with you. It doesn't matter."

"*Denke,* Wil. We don't have to decide now, do we?"

"*Nee,* don't upset yourself. We've got time to decide, a few months anyway."

Emma smiled and was pleased that she could bring up the subject of the *haus* even though she knew it would remind Wil that she was once married to another *mann.*

She left Wil sitting on his porch and drove her buggy the short distance to her *haus.* Emma knew she should be sewing for her wedding and planning things as she had with her first wedding. With her first wedding, she took pleasure in every stitch she sewed in her special linen dress.

Now her second wedding was approaching, she knew that the marriage was the important part and not just the wedding day. Besides, she could get all the sewing and organizing done in a very short space of time; she'd only need weeks before the wedding.

Angela was sweeping the porch when Emma pulled the buggy up. "*Denke,* Angela. You're my guest you don't have to do anything."

"Idle hands and minds are the devil's playground, my *mudder* always said." Angela smiled as she leaned on the broom. "I prefer to stay busy."

"I'll fix the horse up and then I'll come inside and tell you what I found out from Detective Crowley."

Since it was nearing the middle of the day, they sat out on the porch to eat the midday meal. They ate chicken and coleslaw while Emma told Angela all the information that the detective gave her.

"*Denke* for all you've done, Emma."

"I always get nervous speaking to the detective. He did tell me all he could which surprised me. He said he's coming straight here once he talks to the witness. I hope she still lives around these parts."

"*Jah,* I hope so too."

"I suppose you could take the buggy rather than have me drive you to Robert's *haus*. I didn't think of that earlier. I don't have to go anywhere else today, so you're welcome to use it." Emma said.

"*Denke,* Emma that's kind of you."

They both looked up the road when they heard the car coming toward them. It was a police car and Detective Crowley was being driven by a uniformed police officer.

"I don't know why he never drives himself," Emma whispered to Angela. "He always has someone drive him in a police car."

"Doesn't that defeat the purpose of wearing plain clothes?" Angela said.

Both girls giggled, but quickly regained their composure when the detective leaped out of the car and headed toward them.

"Good afternoon, ladies."

Both ladies rose to their feet and Emma said, "Afternoon, Detective. This is Angela Bontreger."

The detective nodded his head to Angela.

"Angela was the one who told me of the... the whole thing that I spoke to you about this morning. Come inside."

Once the three of them were seated around the table the detective said, "It's highly unusual to discuss these things with civilians. I'm only doing it because Elsa-May sent you, Emma. Elsa-May's helped me in the past."

"I appreciate that. What did you find out? Does the witness still live at the same place?" Emma asked.

The two girls leaned slightly forward to hear what the detective had to say.

"Yes she's living at the same place. What's more, she's sticking to her story. She went for a walk that night and saw the Amish man hit the deceased in the head several times with a rock. Then she watched from a distance as he tied him to a wooden cross."

Emma glanced at Angela and noticed she had turned pale. She patted Angela on the arm. At least Emma had heard these kinds of things before, but Angela was new to them.

"Detective, if it was dark how could she see or properly identify the person who did it?" Angela asked.

"She picked him out of a lineup. She is still sure that Ross Geiger is the man she saw commit the crime."

"Is there any new information at all?" Emma asked.

The detective shook his head. "What I can do is run the DNA again and see if any new matches are available; a lot can change in two or more years."

"In what way?" Angela asked.

"More and more DNA samples are being done and recorded on the FBI database. There's a chance we may find a match. With no more evidence and the witness sticking to her story, that's the only avenue we can go down at this stage."

Emma rubbed her chin. "Does the witness have any link to the man who was murdered, or any link at all to Ross?"

"She says no, but I'll see what I can find out." The detective looked at his watch. "I'd better get going."

"Thank you, Detective. I appreciate you following up on the matter," Emma said.

The detective smiled and said goodbye to the two ladies before he got back in the police car.

"Doesn't seem like we've got much to go on," Emma said.

"Seems odd that the witness was able to say without a doubt that Ross was the man she saw," Angela said.

Emma caught herself before she put fingers to her mouth. "*Jah,* and that was enough to have him arrested. And how would she be able to know for sure in the dark? Elsa-May and Ettie will be here soon. They might have uncovered something from all the people they've spoken with this morning."

Angela smiled and nodded. "I'm having an exciting change here in Lancaster County. At home, I'd be doing the same old thing that I do day after day. Is it always like this?"

Emma giggled. "It never was like this until I became friends with the other widows. Something exciting is always happening now. Maureen was a *gut* friend of mine and when Levi died, she brought me into her little group of widows with Silvie and the others."

~

AN HOUR LATER, Elsa-May and Ettie arrived at Emma's *haus.* Elsa-May nearly ran into Emma's *haus,* leaving Ettie to tie up the horse.

Elsa-May threw herself down on Emma's couch. "Well, we've found something out. We spoke to Bob Pluver's *mudder*;

she knew Ross and Linda Geiger quite well it seems. Before they died, she was visiting them and they told her that the woman who told the police that Ross was guilty was living with the man who died.

"How did they know?" Emma asked.

"Rumors and talk, the man had been living with the woman for weeks. That's what's rumored anyway," Elsa-May said.

"How can that be? The police don't even know that. Wouldn't that have come up in their investigations?" Emma asked.

Ettie came through the door at that moment. "Did Elsa-May tell you that the witness knew the man who was killed?"

Emma turned to Ettie. "*Jah,* she did. Wouldn't that information alone be enough to clear Ross's name?"

"It should be, if it's true. Let's see what else we can piece together. You got any of those chocolate chip cookies, Emma?" Elsa-May asked.

"*Jah,* I've always got chocolate chip cookies." Emma went to the kitchen to get the cookies and called out from the kitchen, "I'll brew some tea. Don't talk about anything important 'til I come back."

Ettie came into the kitchen to help Emma. They fixed a large tray with tea, cookies and cakes to take into the living room.

As Emma set the tray down on a small table in the living room, she said, "*Ach,* have you two had lunch yet? I could fix you something."

"*Nee,* this will be fine for us," Ettie said.

Elsa-May said, "*Jah,* I was getting a little weak. This will pick me up."

Elsa-May was a larger lady, but Emma wasn't too worried about them going without food because she knew that everywhere they had visited that morning would've offered them food. Amish folk never like to see anyone go hungry and there's always plenty of food, if not on the stove then in the cold box.

"Wait a minute, the police don't know the identity of the man who was murdered. Did you speak to someone who knew who he was?" Emma asked.

"It seems as though he was, according to Mrs. Pluver, living with the woman who gave testimony against Ross Geiger for the murder, but no one seems to know his name or anything about him at all."

"What does this all mean in plain English?" Angela asked.

"It means, what I said before," Elsa-May's tone was slightly annoyed with Angela not being able to keep up with the information. "The man who was murdered was living with the witness and she said that she saw Ross kill the man and spoke nothing to the police of knowing the man personally."

Ettie said, "Seems pretty sketchy to me."

"I have to go and tell Robert what I've found out this afternoon," Angela said.

Elsa-May put her hand up. "*Nee*, tell him nothing. Not 'til we've figured it out. We don't want him to jump to conclusions and get in the way of things."

"What am I to say to him then?" Angela said with her fingers to her mouth.

"Tell him that we haven't been able to find anything out yet, then smile your prettiest smile," Ettie said, which caused Angela to giggle.

"I'll hitch the buggy for you now, Angela. That way you can

have more time with him before it gets dark." Emma headed to the barn to hitch the buggy then led the horse to the front of the *haus.*

Angela climbed in the buggy. "*Denke,* Emma. Are you sure you don't need the buggy for the rest of the day?"

"*Nee,* you go on and enjoy yourself. Do you remember which way to go?"

"*Jah,*" Angela said.

The three widows watched Angela drive the buggy down the dirt packed driveway.

CHAPTER EIGHT

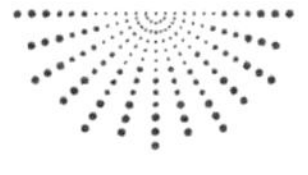

I have come as a light into the world, that whoever believes in Me should not abide in darkness.
John 12:46

As Angela approached Robert's house, her heart pounded. She hoped that he had the same attraction for her that she felt for him. She stopped her horse just past the *haus* in front of the barn.

"You looking for *Onkel* Robert?"

Angela looked to the direction of the voice and saw Jacob in a nearby field. "*Jah*. Hello, Jacob."

"He said to tell you he'd be back soon. He wasn't sure what time you'd be coming and he had to go into town for some supplies."

When Angela got down from the buggy, Jacob said, "I'll fix your horse."

"*Denke,* Jacob."

Angela watched Jacob as he unhitched the horse, rubbed him down and set him into the paddock adjacent to the barn. "That's very kind of you."

"There's fresh water in there for him. I just filled the trough. I can make you tea if you'd like some?"

Angela nodded. "That'll be lovely. I wouldn't mind a cup of hot tea."

"Follow me." They walked into the house and through to the kitchen.

"Do you want me to help you?" Angela asked.

"*Nee,* I make tea for *Onkel* all the time. Sit down here." Jacob pulled out a chair from the kitchen table.

As Angela sat, she wondered what she should say to Jacob. She was nearly going to ask him how long he'd lived with his *onkel,* but considered that might bring back memories of his parents' accident. "So, you like *skul?*"

"*Jah,* I like it *gut* enough."

"What do you think you'd like to do when you grow up?"

Jacob poured the hot water into two cups. "I'd like to be a pilot like my *daed.*"

"What? You mean, fly planes and such?"

"*Jah,* someone said that's what my real *daed* did."

"Your real *daed?*" Angela put her head to the side. "Wasn't Ross Geiger your real *daed?*"

Jacob shook his head. "I was adopted."

Angela was a little shocked, but tried not to show it. "You

were? I didn't know. Do many people know that you were adopted?"

He set a cup of tea in front of Angela. "Just my *onkel* I guess, maybe the bishop, I s'pose. And my real *daed's schweschder,* my *ant*. She's an *Englischer* too."

"To be a pilot means your real, I mean, your biological *daed* was an *Englisher*?" Angela hoped that she wasn't crossing the line talking to Jacob about his birth parents without Robert there. It seemed that Jacob was quite open with the information about his adoption.

"*Jah,* and I'm going to leave the community as soon as I'm old enough and I'm going to get my pilot's license and *Onkel* Robert won't be able to stop me."

"Do you know much about your *daed,* the pilot?"

"His *schweschder* told me that he died, some time ago."

"I'm so sorry to hear that."

Jacob produced a plate of cookies out of the cupboard and placed them on the table. "*Onkel* says that death and life are just a cycle and we shouldn't be sad about something that *Gott* has set into place."

"What about your biological *mamm*?"

"I don't know about her; my *ant* wouldn't tell me about her. She said that the least said, soonest mended." Jacob sat next to her. "I'm sorry that I wrote to you pretending to be *Onkel* Robert."

"I accepted your apology yesterday, Jacob. Don't concern yourself. All is forgiven from my part."

"I know it was wrong and I felt bad about doing it. I just wanted *Onkel* to be happy." Jacob smiled at Angela. "I think you'd make him a fine *fraa*."

Angela smiled back at Jacob. "*Denke*."

They both lifted their heads to the sound of hoof beats.

"Sounds like it might be your *onkel* home," Angela said.

Jacob ran to the front door and Angela stood behind him.

"I'll fix the horse, *Onkel*." Jacob ran to take the reins from Robert.

Robert walked past Jacob and playfully messed his hair with his large hand. "*Denke,* Jacob." Robert looked up at Angela, who was standing just inside the front door. "I'm sorry I wasn't here when you arrived. We didn't arrange a firm time so I took the opportunity to go and buy something nice for us to eat." He looked over at Jacob. "He's been taking care of you by the looks?" Robert asked.

"*Jah,* he looked after the horse, then he fixed me a cup of tea."

"Come along. A cup of tea sounds *gut*." Robert led the way back into the kitchen and made himself a cup of tea. "He's a *gut* boy most of the time." Robert placed a package on the table then sat down. "I bought some cupcakes for us."

"*Ach,* I love cupcakes."

"Who doesn't love cupcakes? I know Jacob does. We have them on special occasions." Robert looked out the kitchen window. "He's still fooling around with the horses."

"He must be a *gut* help to you."

Robert took the lid off the package of cupcakes. "*Jah,* he is. He loves the horses. I didn't punish him. I gave him a stern talking to and he saw the error of his ways. As you said, his heart was in the right place."

"I'm glad. He seems a kind and caring boy." Angela's eyes ran over the rainbow array of cupcakes. She chose a cup cake with pink icing, topped with a dark pink flower topped with small silver balls.

"I'll have a chocolate cup cake."

"Jacob's been telling me his plans of becoming a pilot."

"*Jah,* I've heard those plans too. I used to have fancy plans when I was his age, before I knew better."

"Robert, I didn't know that Jacob was adopted."

Robert put his head to the side. "He told you?"

Angela nodded. "Not that's it's any of my business, but from what he's said, his biological *daed* died and now both his adoptive parents have died. Must be hard on him."

Robert nodded. "He doesn't have things so bad. He's got me and he's got a home here."

Of course, he'd have to think of the positive side of things, Angela thought. "He talks of his biological *daed's schweschder*. Does she live close by?"

Robert lowered his head and was silent for a moment. "I don't allow her around him."

Angela remained silent, waiting for him to continue.

"It disturbs me to speak of her or even think of Jacob's *daed's schweschder,* Juliana Redcliffe. She was the one who was the witness against Ross. It seems as though because Ross told her to stay away from Jacob that she was out to get him in whatever way she could."

"Juliana Redcliffe was the one who said she saw Ross hit the man on the head, Jacob's *ant?*"

Robert nodded.

"How do you know this?" Angela asked.

"Ross told me about her. It was common knowledge at the

time; everyone knew. Made it all up, of course. Seems she wanted to get back at Ross for some reason."

"Why?"

"She wanted to visit Jacob, and Ross wouldn't have it. Ross wanted Jacob to be brought up Amish and not have the influence of the outside world. That woman would've brought the outside world into his life. She already filled his head with pilot nonsense."

"He spoke to me of her, so he must have met her at some point," Angela said.

"*Jah,* he did meet her. She went against my *bruder's* wishes and spoke to him several times when he walked home from *skul.* It went on for a while before someone told Ross that they saw an *Englisch* woman speaking to Jacob. Ross knew who it would be straight away."

Angela broke off a piece of cupcake and popped it in her mouth.

"That woman filled Jacob's head with nonsense of his *daed* being a pilot."

"Was he a pilot?" Angela asked.

"I'm not sure what he was. Ross would've known. All I knew is that Ross' *fraa,* Linda, met Jacob's biological *mudder* somewhere. She wasn't interested in bringing up the child. She wanted to adopt him out and that's all I know of his birth parents. That's all I was told."

"Do you have any idea of the name of the man who died? Any idea at all?"

Robert shook his head from side to side and looked across at her. "What have you heard?"

"I've heard that the man was Juliana Redcliffe's boyfriend or live-in lover or such. I guess that could be just a rumor and no one seems to know his name." Angela knew she wasn't supposed to tell Robert anything until the widows found out more, but now that he knew a lot more than he'd been admitting to, she considered that it no longer mattered.

"*Jah,* I heard the same," Robert said.

"Robert, this gives Juliana a motive. A motive to have your *bruder* blamed for something. It's a vital piece of information."

Robert rubbed his forehead hard.

"Do you think that she deliberately blamed Ross?" Angela asked.

"I'm sure of it. I didn't want to tell you about it before. I wanted to see what you'd find out, or rather what Elsa-May might find out, without any influence from me."

Angela blew out a deep breath. "I understand that, but the police don't know that Juliana, the witness against Ross, was Jacob's biological *ant* or that she knew the murdered man. Don't you think that you should tell them, and also tell them that she was trying to talk to Jacob and Ross told her to stay away? The detective said to Emma that there was nothing linking the witness to Ross. Ross must have never told the police."

Robert rubbed his ear. "Ross would've been confident that the truth would come out eventually."

"*Nee,* that doesn't seem right. It would've got Ross off straight away, I'm sure of it. It's a major fact and I don't know why you haven't made a point of telling the police. There must be more to it."

"Every time I'd find out a piece of information I'd go in and tell the police. I kept going in there to tell them different things

I found out, but they got irritable with me and didn't want to know. I don't know what more I can do. I even wrote them a letter explaining everything to them."

Angela knew it couldn't have been easy for Robert to speak of such delicate things to someone he'd only just met. Maybe she should talk of something else, but she could not get the whole murder incident off her mind. "Tell me if I am missing something. No one knows the identity of the murdered *mann*? The witness who named Ross as the murderer was Jacob's biological *ant*?"

"That's what I'm sure of."

Angela wound the string of her prayer *kapp* around her finger. "Have you thought that the dead man might be Jacob's biological father?"

Robert's face remained expressionless and he slowly said, "I have considered it, but it would be too terrible a thing."

Angela said, "The police said that they have a DNA sample, so all they would need is a swab from Jacob to see if they are a match. That way you'd know for certain."

Robert shook his head. "He already knows both his *daeds* died so how would that help him?"

"It's a piece in the puzzle to find who the real killer was, so your *bruder's* name will clear."

Robert cleared his throat. "Either way, it's upsetting for him."

"You're right. It's upsetting either way. You have to decide what's more important to you and what's more important to Jacob. Surely it's *gut* to know the truth on a matter."

"It's a bad situation. It seems as whatever way I turn or

whatever I tell the police, no *gut* will come of anything." Robert's eyes went glassy as if he was close to tears.

Angela put her hand comfortingly on his shoulder.

"It's been nice talking to you. I've had this burden on my own for so long that it's a relief to speak about it with someone. *Denke* for taking such an interest in us," Robert said.

CHAPTER NINE

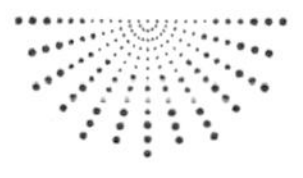

But as many as received Him, to them He gave the right to become children of God,
to those who believe in His name
John 1:12

When Angela pulled the buggy up outside Emma's *haus,* Emma came out to meet her.

"I'll tend to the horse," Emma said.

Angela got out of the buggy. "I've got a lot to tell you."

"Follow me and and tell me." Emma led the horse forward a couple of steps.

"The witness, Juliana Redcliffe, was Jacob's biological *ant,* and Robert's also heard the rumor that the dead man was living with Juliana."

Emma stopped still and looked at her, while the horse

rubbed his nose on her. "Angela that's a huge piece of information. That would've set Ross free if that connection between the two of them was known."

"Robert said that Ross told him that the birth *mudder* did not want to have anything to do with the child and they had no more contact with her. Juliana was visiting the boy and telling him about his real *daed* on the way home from *skul* and when Ross found out, he told her to stay away. I got to wondering whether the dead man might be Jacob's birth father."

"I never even considered that. *Gut* work finding all that out. We should go visit Elsa-May tomorrow and tell her everything. Had Robert known all this for a while?"

"*Jah,* he did, but he kept it from me. He said he wanted to see what Elsa-May would uncover."

"Be *gut* if he could've told you everything from the start. Would've saved a lot of time," Emma said.

"Don't you think it would've been hard for him to tell a total stranger everything? It was awkward at first when I tried to explain who I was and he knew nothing about the letters." Angela giggled. "He must have thought I was quite mad until he figured out that Jacob wrote the letters."

"I guess so. He seems to like you."

"You think he does?"

"I'm sure he does. He'd be doing well to have a fine woman like you as his *fraa*. He would well know it too." She patted the horse on his neck and then continued to unhitch the buggy.

~

THE NEXT MORNING AFTER BREAKFAST, Emma said to Angela, "I'll quickly go to Wil's *haus* and see if he's going out. If he is, I want him to deliver a message."

"Okay."

Emma wrapped her black shawl around her shoulders and walked the five minutes to Wil's *haus.*

Wil stuck his head around the barn door when he saw Emma approach the *haus,* and walked toward her. "Emma, I didn't expect to see you this morning."

"Hello, Wil. I've just come by to see if you're going anywhere today."

"I was thinking of going to the hardware store."

"If you do, can you tell Elsa-May that we all need to see her and we'll all be coming to her house this afternoon?"

"Sure."

"So, you will be going."

He smiled. "I will now."

"Denke. Please make certain to say, 'we'll all need to be there.' She'll know what you mean."

He narrowed his eyes. "Is this something I should be concerned with?"

"Nee."

"Okay then. I'll be leaving soon."

"Denke, Wil. Wait, it would be easier if I wrote a note."

"I'll get pen and paper. Don't worry I won't read it."

Angela giggled as she followed him into the house. When he handed her the paper, she sat down on the couch and leaned the paper against the coffee table in front of her.

Elsa-May, can you organize for the widows to all meet this after-

noon? I have news of the witness's identity and we have a theory on who the dead man might be.

Robert seems to think that it just might be Jacob's biological father; although he has no idea of the man's name. According to Angela, Robert knows that the witness is Jacob's biological ant. She even told Jacob that she's his real daed's schweschder. *The police don't even know the connection.*

Emma thought for a moment as her pen poised over the page.

She knew she had to make things clearer. In her mind, she heard Elsa-May ask, *Did she think that she saw Jacob's daed kill him or did she make the whole thing up, or did she see someone else kill him?*

Then Emma wrote more.

Maybe she wasn't at the scene of the crime at all and didn't see anyone. She could have just made the whole thing up. Robert told Angela that the schweschder *was talking to Jacob for a time every afternoon as he walked home from* skul. *Ross found out and warned her to stay away. He didn't want anyone from the outside world talking to his boy.*

Emma glanced up at Wil.

"That sure is a long note. More like a short story."

Emma giggled. "I'm nearly finished." Then she wrote, something she knew they should do, but wasn't too keen about.

Maybe have Crowley come to the meeting as well. He'll need to know what we've found out.

Emma looked up once more. "Done!"

"Everything all right, Emma?"

Emma walked toward Wil. "*Jah,* everything's fine."

"You know, you can tell me things. If there's any kind of trouble, I'd like to know about it."

Emma shook her head. "I know you would and if there was any trouble, or if I was in any kind of strife, you'd be the first to know."

Wil smiled revealing his straight white teeth. "You had breakfast yet?"

"*Jah,* I have. I'd better get back to Angela. I told her I'd only be a little while."

"I never see much of you when you have visitors." Wil walked toward her and put his strong arm around her back.

Emma giggled. "I hardly ever have visitors."

"*Kumm,* I'll walk you back home." They held hands until they got out of the barn and then Emma broke her hand gently from his grip. She did not feel it proper to have too much physical contact until they were married; even though she craved his touch, she knew that she would have to wait.

They took the usual short cut through the fields.

"I've been giving some thought to where we should live." Wil looked down at his feet as he walked.

"*Jah*? What have you thought about?"

"We could build a *haus* between the two properties. Half on your side and half on my side. Come here." He took hold of Emma's hand and they walked up a little rise. "Right here. What about that?"

Emma looked around about her. The land was slightly higher than the surrounding land and there were *gut* views of both properties. "It seems like a nice place for a *haus*."

"We could have the porch right here." Wil raised his arm

across in front of him. "We could sit here of a morning drinking *kaffe* and look at all this."

Emma looked over to see the soft yellow wheat blowing in the wind. Clumps of dark green trees in the distance framed the wheat fields. "It's certainly a pretty sight, but is it practical, Wil? We'd have to build another barn, as well as a chicken coup and a ..."

Wil laughed. "Listen to you. If I can build you a *haus,* I can certainly build a barn, a chicken coup and whatever else we need. I'll rent my *haus* out and you can do what you like with your *haus*. Leave it vacant, let friends stay, whatever you wish."

Emma turned her eyes back to the swaying fronds of wheat and tried to imagine what it would be like to sip *kaffe* there in the mornings in their own new *haus*. "*Ach,* Wil. I'd love it. I'd love it."

"*Gut,* I'll get working on the plans right away. After I come back from my journey this morning."

Emma smiled and tried to still her mind as it tried to wander back to the time when Levi was drawing up plans for their *haus. Levi's in the past,* she reminded herself as she consciously blocked out the memories. She knew she had to enjoy the present moments with Wil and not have memories of the past ruin what happiness she could have right now.

Wil put his arm around her waist. "We'll be happy here, Emma."

She pressed into his arms and tipped her head up to look into his kind eyes. "I know, I just know we will."

They held each other tightly for a moment before Emma pulled away. "Angela will be wondering what's taking me so long."

As they continued on their way, Wil said, "You never told me whether Angela and Robert liked each other."

Emma laughed. "That's quite a story. It seems that Jacob was writing the letters to Angela."

"Little Jacob?"

"*Jah,* he was writing to her pretending to be Robert."

Wil shook his head. "That's an embarrassment for both Angela and Robert."

"I suppose so, but it seems they like each other now they've met. Angela went back to visit him yesterday. Things look *gut* for the two of them."

"Must be difficult for Robert to look after the boy by himself. He seems to be spirited from what I've heard. I know it can't be easy for the boy losing both his parents in that accident."

Once they had arrived at Emma's *haus,* Emma said, "You coming in for a *kaffe,* Wil?"

Wil looked up. "*Nee,* I've got things to do."

Emma looked into his eyes and smiled. "I'll see you soon then."

Wil kissed Emma lightly on her forehead then turned back toward his *haus.*

CHAPTER TEN

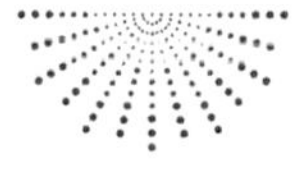

But thou, when thou prayest, enter into thy closet, and when thou hast shut thy door, pray to thy Father which is in secret; and thy Father which seeth in secret shall reward thee openly.
Matthew 6:6

That afternoon, the widows all gathered at Elsa-May and Ettie's *haus.* Angela told the ladies all they found out before Detective Crowley arrived.

"Thank you for coming, Detective," Elsa-May said.

"It sounded important." The detective sat on a creaky, wooden chair opposite the widows. "What can I do for you ladies?" Detective Crowley looked straight at Emma and gave her a glowing smile. Emma looked away because he had a way of making her feel uneasy, as if she had committed some type of crime.

Elsa-May told Crowley all about the suspected identity of the dead man and the identity of the witness.

"When it was mentioned to have Jacob do a DNA test, Robert wasn't agreeable," Emma said.

The detective was silent for a while. "The boy would've been through enough. I can understand Robert not wanting to put the boy through any more dramas." The detective scratched his chin and after a moment said, "What we can do is match the boy's birth certificate records to find his biological father's name. Once we have his name, we'll try and find his dental records and match them up to the records from the dead man's autopsy."

"*Jah,* brilliant idea," Elsa-May said.

Detective Crowley smiled at Elsa-May, "I'll get straight on to that today."

Silvie said, "If it is proven that the witness did have some kind of relationship to the dead man then would that be enough to clear Ross's name? Especially since the woman was keeping information from the police?"

"Possibly; it's not up to me. It seems there's much more to this whole case than what it first appeared. Why don't we meet back here the same time tomorrow?" Crowley said. "That should give me enough time to find Jacob's birth father's name."

~

THE NEXT DAY, Angela and the other ladies kept the appointment with Detective Crowley at Elsa-May and Ettie's *haus.*

"I found the name of Jacob's biological father from his birth certificate. His name is Wesley Conrad and he's still alive and well, living in California. We contacted him this morning. He claims he ceased all contact with his sister some years ago, and last he heard of her she was living in England. What's more, her description does not fit the description of the witness."

Crowley produced a notebook from his pocket and read his notes. "Wesley Conrad is not a pilot and he works for civil service. He has no wish for any contact with the boy that he gave up for adoption. He said that he barely knew the mother of the baby. He continued to say that he suggested to the mother that she abort the baby and she refused. She eventually agreed to adopt. Wesley heard that after she gave the baby up, she tried to get him back."

"Who is the mother; did you find that out detective?" Emma asked.

"Ah, that's the bit I was saving 'til last. The mother's name is Juliana Redcliffe."

The widows gasped.

"That's right. Jacob's birth mother, the woman who is named on his birth certificate, is the woman who has claimed to witness Ross killing the man."

Angela asked, "Why would she tell Jacob that she was his *ant*, when she's really his *mudder*?"

"Most likely she didn't want the boy to get confused by having two mothers, who knows," the detective said.

Ettie said, "If the witness is the mother, why would she wish harm on Ross?"

Angela said, "Robert said that Ross warned her to keep away from Jacob. He would've known who she was."

Elsa-May said, "Have you talked to Juliana again now that you've got the new information, Detective?"

"Not yet. I'm going to see her tomorrow in the afternoon. Just wanted to check with you ladies first, to see if you've found out anything else." Detective Crowley leaned forward, stretched out his hand and took a square of chocolate fudge. "Mmm, this is very nice."

Maureen said, "Emma made those."

Emma glared at Maureen wishing she had not said that. The detective smiled at Emma and Emma managed to force a smile back at him.

"As I was saying, I'll go and see the woman and see what she says about the whole thing." The detective continued to bite into the slice.

Ettie said, "Why didn't all this information come out before? Why wasn't more investigation done into it?"

The detective swallowed his mouthful. "With no known identity of the deceased and with the arrested man dead, the case came to a stand still. We still don't know the murdered man's identity."

"Convenient wasn't it? The investigation ceased because Ross died; might not one suppose that Ross was killed to prevent further investigations?" Elsa-May said.

Ettie pushed a bony finger into the air. "Yes, the real killer might have killed Ross off to cover his tracks."

"Or hers," Silvie said.

The detective licked chocolate from his lips. "I've already thought of that. I checked into the buggy accident that killed Mr. and Mrs. Geiger and there were no suspicious circumstances. None whatsoever."

"Can you double check, detective?" Elsa-May asked.

"No point. I checked it all again this morning. It was a drunk driver who was already known to the police. He was badly injured and was charged with manslaughter. There's no connection to him whatsoever." The detective brushed some crumbs from around his lips and stood up. "I'll check back in with you ladies after I speak to Juliana Redcliffe tomorrow."

Ettie pushed her lips tightly together. Emma knew that Ettie was not convinced that there was no connection, particularly when no one knew the connection of the witness and the dead man until very recently.

When the detective left Ettie said to Silvie, "Onto a happier subject. Elsa-May and I have a surprise for you, Silvie."

"For me?" Silvie smiled brightly. "What is it?"

"Bailey is coming to stay nearby for two days next week. He called us today to let us know. Since you have no phone he would've arrived before a letter reached you. It was a good thing that I called him, and this time he actually answered which is rare."

Silvie clasped her hands together. "He is? He's coming?"

"*Jah,* and I'd say he's only coming to see you. He said to be sure and tell you. He only has two days here."

"Who's Bailey?" Angela asked.

"Bailey is Ettie and Elsa-May's nephew; he's a detective," Emma said.

"*Ach, jah,* I've heard about him from Elsa-May," Angela said.

"He's not a relative of yours too, Angela?" Maureen asked.

"*Nee,* I'm related to Elsa-May's late husband."

Emma continued to explain who Bailey was. "Bailey stayed with Wil months ago when he was working undercover. He was pretending he wanted to become Amish and he fell in love with Silvie."

"That's romantic," Angela said.

"Well, it wasn't too romantic when I found out that he wasn't who he said he was," Silvie said. "I know it was his job and everything, but it was still deceiving people."

Emma said, "He was sorry about it. He didn't intend to hurt anyone. Now, he might even come and join the community."

"Really?" Elsa-May and Ettie chimed together.

"He said that again, just recently?" Elsa-May asked.

Silvie frowned at Emma. "Emma. That was something private I told you."

Emma's hand flew to her mouth. "I'm sorry, Silvie. I forgot. I was just excited about it."

Silvie looked at both Ettie and Elsa-May. "I didn't want to tell anyone his thoughts unless they didn't happen."

"That would be *wunderbaar* if he joined the community," Ettie said. "It would be a real answer to prayer."

"We'll have to wait and see. No *gut* getting excited about something that might not ever happen," Elsa-May said.

Ettie pouted. "But it might happen, Elsa-May. Why can't you ever let me be happy about anything?"

The other ladies looked at each other and smiled; they were used to Elsa-May and Ettie getting under each other's skin.

"You can be happy about whatever you want, Ettie. I'm just saying that he might not join us. Why get excited about something that might never happen? It doesn't make sense. He only said that he might, and he only told Silvie in private. He likely doesn't want anyone to know his private thoughts, only Silvie."

Ettie lowered her head. "I won't say anything to anyone, Silvie."

Emma said, "*Nee,* we'll all keep quiet about it. Sorry for mentioning it, Silvie; I was just happy for you."

"No harm done," Silvie said.

Elsa-May turned her attention to Angela. "Angela, I made a phone call to Robert just before everyone arrived just now, to see how he was. He has a telephone in his barn. He wanted to know if he could call on you tomorrow morning at Emma's *haus.*"

Angela gasped and drew both hands to her mouth. "What did you say?"

"I said *jah,* of course. I told him to do it."

Maureen said, "Angela, you seem to like Robert quite a bit."

"I do like him, but he just probably wants to know what I've found out so far."

"*Nee,* he asked me questions. He wants to see you, plain and simple," Elsa-May said.

Angela's face glowed just as Silvie's glowed.

"I'm feeling all left out now," Maureen said. "Everyone's got *someone* but me." She looked at Elsa-May and Ettie. "Do you have *gut* news for me? Did you just happen to call someone for me?"

Everyone laughed except Elsa-May, who looked quite serious. "Ettie and I don't have anyone," she said.

"You two don't want anyone, do you?" Emma asked.

Ettie chuckled, "I'm too old now. I might have been interested years ago."

"I'm too old and set in my ways now," Elsa-May said.

Silvie asked, "What happened with Bob Pluver, Maureen?"

Emma shivered at Bob Pluver's name. She found him an odd character.

"I went to dinner with him a few months ago." Maureen's mouth turned down at the sides. "He hardly said a word."

"He never says much, Maureen. You never know what's going on in his head. That's what unnerves me about the man." Emma bit her lip. She often spoke without thinking and this was one of those times. "I'm sorry; I didn't mean to be unkind."

"It's hard to get to know someone if they don't speak," Maureen said.

"Do you like him?" Ettie asked Maureen.

Maureen gave a little shrug of her shoulders. "I think I do, a little."

"He might need a little encouragement. I heard his *daed* was hard on him and used to beat him. *Spare the rod and spoil the child* was his saying. I heard he didn't spare the rod at all. That has to have affected him and made him unsure of himself," Elsa-May said.

"I need a *mann* who'll look after me. I don't want to be a *mudder* to a *mann*," Maureen said.

"I agree with you," Emma said.

"He might have potential in the future," Maureen said.

"If he changes?" Emma asked.

"*Jah*," Maureen agreed.

Silvie put her arm around Maureen's shoulder. "You never know who *Gott's* got for you."

"His ways are not our ways," Ettie said with a smile.

Maureen smiled and nodded.

~

Robert said he'd be there at 10 a.m. the very next day. Angela had been ready and waiting since 9 a.m. She was excited to spend time with Robert. Jacob would be in *skul* so they would have no distractions. Angela wondered where they would go.

"Excited I see?" Emma said.

"Jah. It's been a while since I've had the interest of a man. My heart keeps beating fast." Angela put her hand lightly over her heart.

"I suppose you don't know where he's taking you?"

"Elsa-May didn't say. Maybe he's taking me back to his *haus* to talk some more."

"I'm glad you've come to stay with me. It's been nice having someone else around. Someone else in the *haus* besides Growler."

"I've never lived alone, always with *mamm* and *daed*. I've got three cats at home. I've an old white fluffy one, a ginger tabby kitten and a black cat. The white one is the only one allowed in the *haus*. The other two are happy to prowl around and catch mice."

"I never liked cats until I got Growler. He's not friendly, but he's *gut* company for me."

Angela laughed. "Cats can be moody sometimes."

Emma nodded. *"Ach,* sounds like that might be Robert."

Angela dashed to the window. *"Jah,* it is." Angela smoothed down the apron that covered most of her dress and touched her prayer *kapp* to be sure it sat properly on her head. "See you later today, Emma."

"Goodbye." Emma stayed inside the *haus* and watched them drive away. The look on Robert's face as Angela walked toward the buggy confirmed Emma's suspicions that Robert liked Angela very much.

Emma hurried to Elsa-May house. Early that same morning Wil had delivered a message that Emma was to go to there as soon as Angela left. Emma knew that meant that an urgent widows' meeting had been called.

CHAPTER ELEVEN

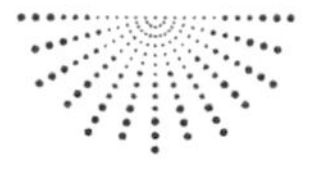

And whatever things you ask in prayer,
believing, you will receive
Matthew 21:22

As soon as they were clear of Emma's *haus,* Angela glanced at Robert's face and he caught her eye and smiled.

"I read all your letters last night," Robert said.

Angela's face lighted up. "You did? I didn't realize that Jacob kept them all."

"He did, and he presented them to me last night."

Angela lowered her head and looked at the floor of the buggy. "*Ach,* now I'm embarrassed."

"No need to be embarrassed, you wrote from your heart

with honesty. That's commendable. I know you so well now. It's *wunderbaar* what you can learn from letters."

Angela put her fingertips to her eyes. "I wish you hadn't read them."

"They were addressed to me and they were my letters." He turned to her and said softly, "I'm glad I read them. I know you much better now."

"Not fair. You know me better now than I know you. You should write me forty letters to catch up."

Robert chuckled. "While you're here, I would like to get to know you better and have you get to know me."

Angela swallowed hard which turned into almost a gulp; she hoped he hadn't heard it over the clip clop of the horse's hooves. "I'd like that."

He looked over at her and smiled. The warmth of his face sent pulses through her body like she'd never known before.

"Jacob must have written to you in a mature manner for you to think a grown man penned the letters."

"I can show you my letters. I've got them at Emma's place. He wrote well. I had no idea, no idea at all. He spoke of mature things. Jacob has a *gut* insight on life. He must care for you deeply to be hunting for a *fraa* for you."

"Angela, I'm glad that he wrote to you and had you come to visit. I know what he did was wrong, but I would never have written back to someone. If I got that first letter from you I most likely would have written back telling you that I was too busy to write or some such thing. It worked out well that Jacob replied to you."

Angela remained silent because she did not know how to respond to his candid admission of interest in her. Should she appear keen? She had already shown how keen she was to get married by writing to a *mann* whom she did not know. If she said that she was interested in him too, that might appear as if she were desperate to marry a *mann* – any *mann.*

Robert took his eyes off the road and glanced at Angela again. "Forgive me, I always say what's on my mind. I think that's always the best way. You are a lovely woman."

A giggle escaped Angela's lips, which released the tension she felt just seconds before.

"Any *mann* would be pleased to have you as his *fraa.*"

Angela searched her mind for a reply. Any reply would be better than remaining silent yet, she was not accustomed to speaking to *menner,* especially not ones as handsome as Robert.

"In your letters you mentioned that you were looking to marry," Robert said.

Angela nodded knowing that she could admit to wanting marriage as all the girls in the community wanted a happy *familye.* "I am. I'm looking for a *gut mann* to marry and raise a *familye* with. What about you?" Angela silently reprimanded herself for her blunt question. She might have been better off to remain silent after all.

"I'd like nothing more to have a *fraa* and *kinner,* but I need to get Jacob settled first. I've taken on Jacob as my responsibility. I'd like to clear his *daed's* name and then I would feel free to live my life and find a *fraa.*"

"I understand. Jacob's very blessed to have someone who cares for him so deeply." They sat next to each other in silence as the buggy clip clopped through the winding, narrow roads. Angela was at peace in Robert's company. There was something about being with Robert that made her feel safe. As well as his obvious physical strength, she sensed that he also had an inner strength.

"I'm taking you to my favorite place," Robert said.

"Where's that?"

Robert laughed. "There's an old stone bridge not far up here. I used to play underneath the bridge when I was a child. I would fish from the top of it as well. I haven't been there in a long time."

"I'd love to see it."

Robert pulled the buggy off the road and tied the horse in the shade. "It's just down here."

Robert held Angela's hand and helped her through the undergrowth. They walked a little further until the bridge came into view.

"Is that it, Robert? It's beautiful."

"That's it all right." As soon as they were on the bridge, Robert said, "It's called a kissing bridge." He glanced at Angela. "Don't look worried. That's what they're called, but I didn't know that until recently."

"Why's it called a kissing bridge?"

Robert looked over the edge of the bridge. "They're romantic places to go, I'd guess."

Angela looked at the reflective surface of the water as it rippled its way underneath the bridge. The birds chirping and the rustle of the wind in the treetops made a perfect melody for their special time alone.

It's a perfect place for a first kiss, Angela thought. *I wonder if that's why he brought me here.* She looked up at Robert. He took his eyes off the horizon and looked deeply into her eyes. He moved his body so it was directly in front of hers. He caressed her cheek with his fingertips. Her body shuddered at his touch, however she did not move away.

"Your skin is so smooth." Robert's words were whispered.

She smiled at his compliment, but words escaped her. All she could think on was what his mouth would feel like against hers. Angela had never desired to be kissed by a man until that very moment.

As if he sensed her longing, his gaze fell to her mouth. He lowered his head until his lips lingered over hers. Was he asking for her permission to touch her lips? She arched her back and moved her lips just a fraction until their lips met.

All feeling left Angela's body and her head swam. She was not aware blackness had engulfed her until she woke with her body on the hard ground and her head cradled in Robert's manly arms. She made to move.

"*Nee,* stay still. You've fainted; it must be the heat."

Angela obeyed his command, closed her eyes and enjoyed being close to him, inhaling his manly aroma.

Angela was aware that it was a hot day, but was that why she fainted? Surely it was the closeness of Robert's hard, body and his soft lips against hers that caused her to loose consciousness. "I'm alright."

He lifted her head up a little.

"I don't know what happened," Angela said.

"Have you been unwell?"

"*Nee,* I'm always in *gut* health."

"It's a hot day. Stay here. I've got some water in the buggy." Robert helped position Angela's back against the side of the bridge.

While Robert fetched the water, Angela recalled that she had not drank any water the entire day, when normally she drank quite a few glasses by this time of the day. Angela admired how caring and attentive Robert was. She touched her lips softly with her fingertips as she remembered their kiss.

"Here you go." He poured the water from a large container into a metal cup.

She slowly drank two cups of water. "I remembered that I hadn't drank any water at all today."

Robert sat down next to her. "I said that it was a kissing bridge, not a fainting bridge."

Angela smiled. "Did I dream that we kissed?"

Robert whispered. "That was real."

His whispers sent tingles soaring down her back. They sat and talked for a time and they didn't even notice that dark rain clouds had gathered overhead. Raindrops began to spatter down upon them in large droplets. They both looked upwards at the gray sky.

"We're going to get caught in the rain," Robert said.

"Moments ago it was bright sunshine."

They looked at each other and laughed.

Never had Angela dreamed it would be possible to have such a time with a man. She knew now what she had missed out on. Being quiet and shy had done her no favors in the past. But if she hadn't kept away from *menner* she might be married to someone else by now and she would never have gotten to meet Robert.

"Are you all right to stand?" Robert asked.

"I'm sure I am."

Robert put his arm around her waist and lifted her to her feet. "Let's go."

Once they were both inside the buggy the rain began to pour down in shafts.

"I made a picnic for us. I imagined we would sit in the sun on a grassy bank overlooking my bridge. How would you feel about eating here in the buggy?"

"*Jah,* let's have the picnic right here in the buggy."

Robert reached over to the backseat and unwrapped a package of ham and relish buns. "The weather's not usually like this here. It usually stays as it starts out in the morning. We don't normally get sudden downfalls of rain like this."

"I love the rain, especially at night. I love to hear it beating against the window pain and pouring down the pipes at the side of the *haus,*" Angela said.

CHAPTER TWELVE

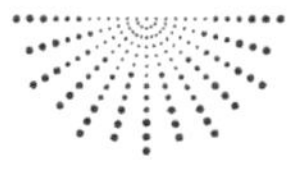

Surely goodness and mercy shall follow me all the days of my life: and I will dwell in the house of the Lord for ever.
Psalms 23:6

While Angela was with Robert, Emma was at the emergency widows' meeting that had been called. Detective Crowley was to meet them again that afternoon.

"I heard that Juliana took a different man home with her nearly every weekend. The particular weekend when that man was murdered, she had left the bar with the same man for the third Saturday in a row. It was a Saturday, wasn't it, that the murder took place?" The widows all nodded so Ettie continued, "Why would she go for a walk on her own because she couldn't sleep? What's more, she was seen leaving with the man by more than one staff member of the bar."

"Why hasn't this come out before? Why don't the police know about it?" Silvie asked.

"She told the police that she was alone, but she wasn't. The police wouldn't have known to ask the bar staff because they wouldn't have known she was there in the first place," Ettie said.

"You think that the man murdered was the same man taken home by Juliana that night?" Emma asked.

Ettie nodded. "He fits the description and no one knew him; he wasn't from around here, from what the bar staff told me."

Silvie said, "How do they remember something from so long ago?"

Ettie said, "Marg, one of the staff, was concerned when she heard of the murder. She even asked Juliana about it. Marg asked Juliana if she'd seen the man alive after that time. Juliana told her that the man she'd taken home couldn't have been the same man who was murdered because he was at her house when she'd gone for that walk. The walk where she said she saw Ross hit that man over the head."

Ettie took a deep breath and continued. "Marg asked Juliana why the man wasn't around any longer and Juliana said she'd sent him on his way because he'd gotten violent with her. She even showed Marg bruises on her arm, two days after the murder."

"Did Marg ever think to go to the police? Or were the police aware that Juliana had someone staying at her *haus* the night of the murder?"

"The detective didn't mention a thing about it." Ettie turned to Elsa-May. "Did he mention anything to you?"

"*Nee* he didn't. I've spoken to him twice about that murder and he never once mentioned that she had some strange man at her house that night," Elsa-May said. "Silvie, why don't you knock on Juliana's door and pretend you're from the college doing a paper on witnesses and ask her if she wouldn't mind answering some questions?"

Silvie's face went pale. "Why me? I can't do things like that. I wouldn't know what to ask. I can't fool someone like that. She'd never believe me. Amish don't go to college, so how do I explain that?"

"*Jah* she will believe you, I'll write the questions for you and you'll have to get yourself some clothes that will pass as *Englisch*. All you say when she answers the door is, *Good morning. Are you Juliana Redcliffe? I'm Silvie Brown and I'm doing a paper on the effect that witnessing a crime has on people. Do you mind if I ask you some questions?* She'll either say *no* and slam the door on you or invite you in. If she invites you in, you'll produce my list of questions and write down her answers. It's simple, Silvie," Elsa-May said.

Silvie nodded, "*Jah,* I suppose I can do that, but I'm a little frightened. What if she killed that man and blamed it on Ross? That means I'll be alone with a murderer."

Elsa-May tapped her chin. "I'll have Maureen go with you."

Maureen made a sour face. "All right, I'll go with you, Silvie. As long as you do all the talking; you're better at that kind of thing than me."

"You need to do that today. There's no time to waste. You have to speak to Juliana and make sure you don't bump into

Crowley; he wouldn't be too happy to see you anywhere near Juliana," Elsa-May said.

~

An hour later, Silvie and Maureen, both wearing *Englisch* clothes, pulled up in a taxi up the road from Juliana's house.

When the taxi drove away, Silvie said, "I hope she's home. Remember, I'll do all the talking and you help me take notes on what she says."

Half an hour before, when they were at Silvie's *haus* dressing in *Englisch* clothes, it occurred to Silvie and Maureen to go against Elsa-May's advice. They hoped they would not get into terrible trouble with her. They decided rather than say that they were doing a paper on witnessing crime they would say that they were doing a survey for the Department of Health on violence against women. Maybe that would have her open up about the man who was violent with her.

They had the taxi drop them a little up the road so it would appear as though they were doing a door-to-door survey.

They knocked on Juliana's door, hoping that she would be home.

Seconds later a woman who answered Juliana's description answered the door.

Maureen spoke first. "Hello, we're doing a survey."

"We're from the health department," Silvie added.

The woman looked from one to the other. "What's it about?"

"It's about violence against women. We're trying to find how wide spread it actually is and we're going door to door in the whole neighborhood," Silvie said, hoping that *Gott* would forgive her for telling a fib if it was to help someone.

"Do you have five minutes to answer some quick questions?" Maureen asked.

Juliana looked at her watch. "As long as it will only be five minutes."

"That's all it will take," Maureen said.

"Come in then." Juliana stepped back so both women could enter the *haus.* "This way." She took them through to a small room with two small couches. "Have a seat."

Once they were seated, Silvie shuffled some papers in readiness to make it look as though she was reading questions out.

"I forgot to ask for your ID," Juliana said.

"We don't have any yet," Maureen said.

"There was a mix-up with the new model of ID and they'll be ready tomorrow. We can call back and show you tomorrow if you wish," Silvie said.

Juliana shook her head, "Don't worry about it. Will this survey help other women?"

"That's the purpose of it," Silvie said. Without written questions from Elsa-May and with no time to write any of her own, Silvie had to pull some quick questions from her head. "Have you ever been the victim of abuse?"

"Yes, I have. I've been physically abused many times in my life."

Maureen leaned forward. "Have you? That's awful." After an intense stare from Silvie, Maureen straightened up.

"Thank you and yes, it was awful. First my step-father beat me on more than one occasion and I had two boyfriends who used to hit me when they got angry."

Juliana cast her tear filled eyes downward and Silvie looked at Maureen. Had they bitten off more than they could chew?

"When was the last time you experienced abuse? Could you tell us about it? If you feel you can talk about it," Maureen said.

Juliana sniffed and looked at the two ladies in front of her. "It was a while ago now. I made sure that he could never hurt anyone again."

"That's good and how did you see to that?" Silvie asked.

Juliana shook her head. "I don't want to speak about it. In fact, I'd prefer not to talk at all. It's too upsetting for me to speak about." Juliana looked at Silvie and then looked at Maureen. "I appreciate what you ladies are doing. There's too much violence towards women. I hope you can make a change, but I can't help you." Juliana rose to her feet. "I'll show you out."

Maureen stayed seated. "Before we leave can you tell me just how does one go about making sure that a man will never hit a woman again?"

Juliana shrugged her shoulders. "How should I know?"

Maureen locked eyes with Juliana. "You just said that you made sure that the last man who hurt you would never hurt anyone again."

"I've had enough questions for today. I'm done." Juliana stared at Maureen until she stood up.

"Okay, thank you," Maureen said.

Maureen and Silvie left Juliana's house and hurried to the main road. Maureen reached into the pocket of her long black *Englisch* looking skirt and took out Elsa-May's borrowed, and secret, cell phone to call a taxi.

Once the call was made, Silvie asked, "What do you think of all that?"

Maureen placed the cell phone carefully back in her pocket. "Did you hear what she said? She said she made sure the last man who hurt her would never hurt anyone again. Do you think she was referring to the man who was murdered two years ago?"

"Could have been."

~

THAT AFTERNOON the five widows waited for the detective at Elsa-May and Ettie's *haus*. He had phoned ahead and told them that he had a significant development in the case of Ross Geiger.

"What news do you have for us, Detective?" Elsa-May asked once the detective sat on one of their hard, wooden chairs.

"Juliana Redcliffe admitted to killing the man and said that it was self-defense. She claimed that she witnessed Ross kill the man because she wanted him in jail so she could get her child back. She said that it was after she killed the man and was back in her house that she got the idea to make it look as though Ross had done it. She'd seen some sticks at the scene of the crime so she took some twine back to the body, made a cross and tied him to it. She figured it would be believable that an Amish man did it if there was a religious element there somewhere."

"But the dead man was found about 500 meters away from her house. How could she get him that far away?" Emma asked.

"He chased her out there. She claims he knocked her to the ground after chasing her from the house. She saw a rock and when he turned his head that's when she hit him. The first knock stunned him and he fell to the ground and she beat him with the rock a couple more times to make sure he would not get back up."

Emma winced as she imagined the scene.

"She kept the dead man's wallet, so now we know who he was and can try and contact his relatives." The detective yawned. "Excuse me."

"How did you get her to confess it all, after all this time?" Ettie asked.

"She thought we knew already. She said something about other people being there that morning to question her – two ladies." The detective looked at each lady in turn. He did not question any of them about the matter and neither did they comment.

"Will she go to jail?" Emma asked.

"Seems it was self defense so things would've gone better for her if she had admitted to it immediately. Now she's perverted the course of justice by her false accusation. The courts don't take things like that lightly."

"Do you think the buggy crash that killed Ross and Linda was purely an accident?" Ettie asked the detective.

"As I mentioned before, we found nothing suspicious to do with the buggy accident. It seemed to be just that – an accident," Detective Crowley said.

"I've got a *haus* guest so I better get going now. Thank you for helping us again, Detective." Emma said goodbye to everyone and hurried to her buggy. She was glad that Robert's *bruder,* Ross, would finally have his name cleared. Emma could hardly wait to go home and tell Angela the news.

Once Emma arrived back home, Angela was in her room

and did not come out the whole night. It was the very next morning that Emma told Angela what the detective found out about Juliana and the murder.

"What should I do, Emma? Will I visit Robert, or should I wait for him to come here? What if he doesn't come here?" Angela asked over breakfast the next morning.

"Give it 'til after the midday meal and if he hasn't come here by then, take my buggy and go and visit him."

"*Denke,* Emma." Angela took a deep breath. "I hope the detective or someone lets him know what's going on."

"*Jah,* they would've told him. The detective knows how important it is for Robert to clear his *bruder's* name. That's what spurred this whole investigation. He has Robert's address and everything," Emma said.

CHAPTER THIRTEEN

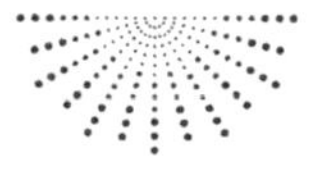

Let the word of Christ dwell in you richly in all wisdom; teaching and admonishing one another in psalms and hymns and spiritual songs, singing with grace in your hearts to the Lord.
Colossians 3:16

Bailey had already delivered the bad news to Silvie through Elsa-May and Ettie. He could not stay two days at the nearby B&B as he had hoped, but he would drive to see her. They only could have a few small hours together before he would have to leave.

Silvie waited by the window for him. He told her that his car was dark gray in color and she fixed her eyes on the road looking for his car. A dark gray car turned off the road and into her driveway. She opened the door and waited for him in the doorway. Her heart pounded in her chest as she watched him walk toward her.

He walked quickly and reached out and held her tightly in his arms. "Oh, Silvie, I've missed you so much. So much."

"Me too." Silvie managed to say. He was holding her so tight she could barely speak. Silvie pulled him inside and shut the door.

"I need to say all that's on my mind. I've been giving things a lot of thought. In particular you and me, and joining the community," Bailey said.

Silvie raised her perfectly shaped eyebrows.

"I do want to come and join the community if the bishop will allow me. I'm hoping Wil will have me back to stay at his *haus.* He's easy to get on with and I'd feel awkward with a *familye* I didn't know. I might be ready in a year. How does that sound to you?"

"I would like it very much, but the bishop would tell you that you must join the community because that's what *Gott* has put on your heart to do, not because of us."

Bailey nodded. "I know he would say that, but without you I wouldn't be drawn here. Now that I've met you, I want to be with you forever."

Silvie was pleased by his words, but disappointed she would have to wait for him. "Why must you wait a whole year?"

"My job."

"Your job is still so important to you?"

"I feel a certain obligation toward the people who are depending on me. I'm so close to finding the stolen paintings I've been chasing."

Silvie raised her eyebrows again as she remembered him

saying that he had been chasing those stolen paintings for a number of years.

"Will you wait for me, Silvie? I want to marry you, when I learn all the Amish ways and get baptized."

Silvie knew that she should have said *no* for two reasons. The first reason was that he was putting his job before *Gott* and herself, the second reason was that he should want to join the Amish whether she was there or not. Her head was conflicted with rights and wrongs, but her heart knew what it wanted. She heard herself say, "*Jah,* I'll wait for you, Bailey." The way she felt about him she had absolutely no choice.

"Thank you, Silvie. Thank you." Bailey took hold of her wrist and pulled her to himself. As he held her tightly again, he said, "You are more beautiful than I remember."

Their time together passed far too quickly for Silvie's liking. She watched with tears in her eyes as Bailey drove away from her. All she had been left with was promises, but could she trust and believe them?

"So, that's Bailey."

Silvie swung around to see her *schweschder,* Sabrina, walk out of the downstairs bedroom. "Sabrina, I didn't know that you were home."

"That sounded all very lovely dovey." Sabrina folded her arms as she walked towards Silvie.

Sabrina reminded Silvie of her *mudder*. That was exactly how her *mudder* would speak to her since she disapproved of everything Silvie did. "I love him, that's why," Silvie said, annoyed that Sabrina had overheard their private conversation.

"What would *mamm* think of you being in love with an *Englischer*? We're not supposed to be entangled with the world."

"Sabrina, you were obviously listening in on us so you would have heard him say that he's thinking of joining us."

Sabrina flung her arm in the air. "*Jah,* thinking not doing. There's a big difference. You even said yourself that his job was too important to him. Just because a handsome *Englischer* shows you a small bit of attention you go weak at the knees and put him before *Gott* and the community. You sounded all wimpy and childish when you were speaking to him. It made me sick to my stomach."

Silvie tipped her chin high. "I'm old enough to do what I wish and make my own decisions. I'm older than you, a lot older than you. Besides, you shouldn't have been listening to us."

Sabrina shook her head. "Older in years, but not in the head, it seems."

"You're staying here as my guest. I've a *gut* idea to pack you back off to *mamm* and *dat,*" Silvie frowned and mirrored Sabrina by also crossing her arms firmly in front of her chest.

A look of horror crossed Sabrina's face. "You wouldn't do that, would you? I'm only trying to protect you from getting hurt by an *Englischer.*"

"While you're under my roof, you will show me respect."

Sabrina pouted and stared at her *schweschder.* "All right, I won't say anymore about him."

"Are you sure? Not one word?" Silvie asked.

"I stayed away from Wil, didn't I, even though I had so much in common with him? I can keep to my word."

"I suppose that's true enough. You can stay then, but no telling *mamm* or anyone of any of my private information."

"All right, I won't. Can I stay?"

Silvie nodded and Sabrina turned around and hurried back into her room.

Silvie sank into the couch hoping she finally had Sabrina under control. Otherwise she surely would send her packing.

~

ANGELA DID NOT HAVE to wait long for Robert to come to Emma's *haus.* The detective had visited him and told him all that had happened. Robert was shocked to find out that the woman who had spoken against his *bruder,* Ross, was Jacob's biological *mudder* and even more shocked that she admitted to killing the man and tying him to a cross so it would be more believable to blame an Amish man.

Emma left Robert and Angela alone when she sensed the moment was right. "Excuse me, but I've something to do in the barn."

Robert stood. "Would you like some help, Emma?"

"Nee. It's something only I can do. It'll take me some time." She walked away quickly leaving them in the kitchen together.

Angela held her breath, thankful that Emma left them alone.

"Angela, I have to come right out and say this."

"What is it?"

"Would you stay here and not go home? I don't think we should rush things, but I'm feeling like we could be a good match. I think Elsa-May was right."

A grin broke out on her face. "I could stay for a little longer."

"I've never had these feelings for anyone before."

"Me either," Angela confessed.

He held out his hand and she placed her hand in his. "Let's

get out of here for a while. I'll bring you back later. We can talk better about our plans somewhere else."

"I'd like that."

They told Emma they were going to be gone for a few hours and just as they drove away from Emma's *haus*, they saw Will, walking.

"You there, Emma?" Wil called out from Emma's front door.

Emma came out of the barn where she'd been tidying up. She was a little surprised that he didn't walk into the house without knocking like he often did. "I'm here. Let's go inside."

"Robert and Angela just passed me in the buggy."

"*Jah*, they're getting along fine. Come into the kitchen while I bake cookies."

"Mmm, fresh cookies, warm cookies." Wil followed Emma to the kitchen and sat down. "I've been thinking about our *haus*."

"Our new one that you're doing the plans for?"

"Well, I don't know if that's the best way to go about things. With Bob leasing both of our farms, it's difficult to find the perfect spot for the *haus* that won't interfere with the land."

"Okay, so what have you been thinking?" Emma got the ingredients out for the cookies.

"I've got a couple of ideas. We could buy a place somewhere else, not too far from here, or we could buy land somewhere and build."

Emma opened the oven and realized she'd left it on since she made bread that morning. "I'll leave it up to you."

"What's the matter?"

"I left the oven on." She pointed to the bread that she'd sliced earlier.

Wil leaped to his feet. "I'll start looking straight away." He leaned forward and gave Emma a quick kiss on the cheek then grabbed a slice of bread before he rushed out the door.

Emma giggled at how silly he was. He reminded her of a lively child who flitted from one project to another. She knew that when they were finally living together as *mann* and *fraa* that her life would never be dull or boring.

CHAPTER FOURTEEN

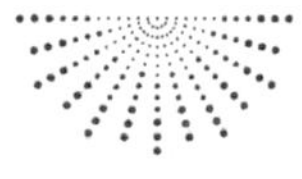

The blessing of him that was ready to perish came upon me: and I caused the widow's heart to sing for joy.

Job 29:13

A week later, the five widows were gathered again at Elsa-May and Ettie's *haus* for one of their regular widows' meetings.

"Awful that Robert wanted to clear Jacob's *daed's* name and then it turns out that Jacob's biological *mudder* was the one who did the murder," Silvie said.

"*Nee,* it was self defense that's a very different thing to murder," Maureen said.

"*Jah,* that's true," Silvie said.

"Angela tells me that Robert was very happy with the outcome and he sent his thanks to all of us," Emma said. "He's also pleased how it ended up with Angela coming to visit him. He's not too angry with Jacob anymore."

"I told them both they would suit each other well before they met," Elsa-May said. "I think they'll get married."

"I think they will too," Emma said. "Robert as *gut* as said so to Angela. They're courting now. I don't think she'd mind me telling you that."

"Is she staying with you for a while longer, Emma?" Maureen asked.

"*Jah,* she's staying on with me. She can't very well go back to Bloomfield now that she's in love with Robert."

"And I've got my *schweschder,* Sabrina, still living with me. I hope she finds a *mann* soon or goes back home," Silvie said. "I'm glad that she turned her attentions away from your Wil, Emma."

"Is she giving you trouble?" Ettie asked Silvie.

Silvie gave an embarrassed laugh. "*Nee,* it's just that I'd grown used to my own company."

Emma knew what Silvie meant. She knew that she could live by herself if she absolutely had to, but was glad that she didn't have to.

With Wil as her husband, she would be able to create a proper *familye.* If *Gott* willed it there still would be plenty of time for her to have many *kinner.* She was glad Wil had waited for her until enough time had passed to marry another man.

Emma was confident no one would whisper or point fingers at Wil and her for marrying in a few months time. By then, it would be well over a year since Levi went to be with the Lord. "If Wil and I marry soon, will I still be welcome at these meetings?"

"*Jah,* of course," Elsa-May said.

"You were once widowed so that's enough to qualify," Ettie said with a grin.

Emma smiled; she was happy that *Gott* had blessed her with *gut* friends and a *wunderbaar mann* with whom she would spend many fun-filled days. She would wait until Angela moved out and then she could concentrate on getting ready to marry Wil, at last.

Even so faith, if it hath not works,
is dead, being alone.
James 2:17

AMISH REGRETS

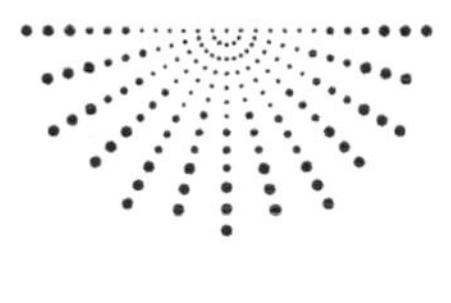

AMISH SECRET WIDOWS' SOCIETY BOOK 4

CHAPTER ONE

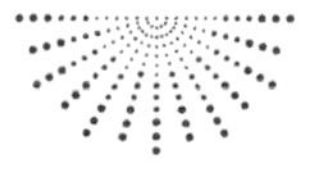

Ask, and it shall be given you; seek, and ye shall find;knock, and it shall be opened unto you:
For every one that asketh receiveth; and he that seeketh findeth; and to him that knocketh it shall be opened.
Matthew 7:7-8

"It's your turn next," Silvie whispered to Emma once the bishop pronounced their friends, Angela and Robert, *mann* and *fraa*.

"*Jah,* it's not far away now." Emma smiled and looked lovingly over at her husband-to-be, Wil. They'd finally set a date just two months away and now with Angela out of her *haus,* Emma could concentrate on her own wedding day.

"Where's Sabrina? I thought she'd be here," Emma said.

"She hasn't shown up to anything of late. I've a *gut* mind to send her packing back to Ohio. Now that she's not under *mamm* and *dat's* eyes, she thinks she can do anything she likes. She hasn't even been to the last few Sunday meetings. I wouldn't be surprised if the bishop stopped by to have a talk with her."

"What's she doing then? I thought she was looking for a husband, so wouldn't she attend everything she could, especially a wedding? Look at all the single *menner* here."

Silvie looked around. "*Jah*, that's true. I wonder what she's been up to. I'm going to have to take more notice of her comings and goings."

"Maybe we should spy on her, follow her." Emma giggled, then leaned close to Silvie and whispered, "From what you said of your *mudder* she'll blame you if Sabrina gets into any trouble. She is your younger *schweschder* after all."

What Emma said about Sabrina getting into trouble preyed on Silvie's mind and was the reason she left the wedding celebrations early. Why hadn't she thought of it herself? It was clear, now that Emma had pointed it out to her that Sabrina was up to something. But what? Sabrina freely admitted to being in Lancaster County solely to look for a husband, so why wasn't she at Angela's wedding – a perfect place to find such a *mann*?

Silvie had been so caught up in her own long wait for Bailey, the *mann* she loved, to become Amish that she had completely ignored her duty as big *schweschder*. Whatever would her *mudder* think of her?

While her horse clip-clopped home in the dark with the

mandatory lights of the buggy flashing, Silvie recalled that Sabrina had been out and about nearly every day of the past week.

Silvie had been so pleased to have some time to herself that she never thought to ask Sabrina where she went. The truth was that she hadn't cared where she was.

That was before she considered that she might be doing things she shouldn't be doing.

As Silvie drew closer to home, she was surer than ever that her *schweschder,* Sabrina, was secretly dating an *Englischer.* Nothing else fit. That had to be it.

Anger rose within Silvie as she recalled that just recently Sabrina told her she was disappointed in her for being in love with Bailey because he was an *Englischer.*

Calm down. There could be a logical explanation. Maybe she's sick and that's why she didn't go to the wedding. Silvie's body trembled in anger. *Well, she had better be sick,* Silvie told herself.

Once Silvie had the horse rubbed down and safely in his stable, she headed into the *haus* to see what she could find out about what was going on with Sabrina.

Silvie had given Sabrina the downstairs bedroom, which had its own outdoor access. Silvie realized it had been a mistake to give her a room from which she could come and go as she pleased. Silvie would have no idea what time she was coming home or whether she was sneaking out after she'd come home.

Silvie lit one of the gas lanterns, opened Sabrina's bedroom door and peeped in. There was no sign of her. Sabrina would have known that Silvie would have been home very late that night. Maybe Sabrina thought she could slip home unnoticed at a late hour. She had a good look around Sabrina's room. Nothing seemed out of place.

Silvie felt sick to her stomach and decided to help herself to a small glass of the fortified wine, which she only kept for medicinal purposes. She walked into the utility room, stretched onto her tiptoes and reached to the back of the highest shelf. Once she poured some of the dark fluid into a small glass she sank into the couch and put the glass to her lips.

Her body flooded with warmth after one sip. *Oh Gott, what am I to do?* She asked in desperation. She knew that *Gott* was the only answer. He could help her with her problems with Sabrina. The more she thought about it, the more she realized there was a problem, as things with Sabrina just didn't add up. She was angry with herself for not realizing before now and angry with herself that it needed Emma to point it out to her.

There was nothing she could do, but wait until Sabrina came home and then she would confront her with her suspicions.

Silvie was drifting off to sleep on the lounge, then jolted awake when her head tipped down suddenly. She looked up at the china clock on the sideboard. It was ten past twelve. The clock reminded her of John, her late husband. She thought of him less and less as the years passed. It wasn't a bad marriage and Silvie had grown to love John over the years. She did miss being married and having a man to care for. She hoped that Bailey would fill that gap in her life before too long.

The low hum of a car's engine outside her front door snapped Silvie out of her daydreams. She flung the door open to see Sabrina racing towards her. She collapsed in Silvie's arms and the taxi sped back up the driveway.

"What's the matter with you, Sabrina?"

Sabrina pushed Silvie inside, shut the door behind them and then sank to the floor. "He's dead; he's dead."

CHAPTER TWO

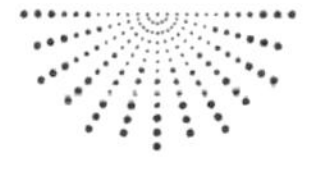

And rend your heart, and not your garments, and turn unto the Lord your God: for he is gracious and merciful, slow to anger, and of great kindness, and repenteth him of the evil.
Joel 2:13

Silvie sank to the floor beside her *schweschder.* "Who, Sabrina? Who's dead?"

"Carmello. Carmello's dead."

Silvie searched her memory banks for someone named Carmello and came up with a blank. She was sure that she'd never heard of anyone who went by that name. Her next question was one that she wasn't sure she wanted to know the answer to. "Who's Carmello?"

Sabrina looked up at her through tear-filled, blue eyes. "My boyfriend. He's my boyfriend; his name's Carmello." Sabrina sobbed uncontrollably as she sprawled herself out on the floor.

Silvie's heart began to pound fast. Carmello was no Amish name; that was for sure and for certain. Sabrina's boyfriend was an *Englischer;* her suspicions were correct. What would their *mudder* think when she got to hear about it? There was only one thing to do and that was to try and conceal everything from their *mudder* for as long as they possibly could. But, did Sabrina say this 'Carmello' man was dead?

"You mean, dead dead. Not alive?" Silvie asked.

Sabrina lifted her head, looked at her and then her mouth downturned and she sobbed louder.

"I'm sorry, Sabrina. Try and stand. Come over to the couch." Silvie lifted Sabrina to the couch and handed her a handkerchief to wipe her tear-drenched face. After a time, Sabrina's sobs lessened enough so that she was able to speak.

"I found him dead," Sabrina managed to say.

"Don't try to talk for a while. I'll get you a glass of water." Silvie hurried to the kitchen and came back to hand Sabrina the water.

Sabrina held the glass in both hands and wobbled it to her lips with shaky hands. She managed to drink a little.

"That's *gut*. Now tell me about it when you're ready." Silvie patted her on her shoulder.

Sabrina looked into Silvie's eyes. "*Ach*, it was terrible, just terrible." She placed the glass on the table and covered her face with both hands. "Carmello and I arranged to meet and when he wasn't at our usual place, I went to his office and found him dead. He was just lying there."

"Did you call the police?"

Sabrina looked down into her hands. "I heard someone coming, so I hid in the adjoining office until they left; then I slipped out."

"How did he die?"

"I don't know I didn't wait to find out."

"Who was it who came when you were hiding?"

"His wife."

"What?" Silvie felt her stomach lurch. Things were much, much worse than she ever could have imagined in a trillion years. "Did you say wife? So, Carmello was married?"

"He was separated. He was trying to get a divorce, but she didn't want a divorce unless he gave her everything. He finally agreed to give her what she wanted and she was to sign papers tonight."

Silvie wanted to ask what she was doing involved with an *Englischer* and a married one at that, but what was done was done. Silvie knew Sabrina would be in no state of mind to listen to any straight talking common sense right now. She would have to wait for a time when Sabrina would be more receptive; nevertheless, Silvie wanted to shake Sabrina for being so stupid.

"I'll make you a cup of tea." Silvie wrapped the crocheted throw that she kept near the couch over Sabrina's shoulders. "Keep that around you. You've had a nasty shock; I've heard it does you *gut* to keep warm."

Sabrina's sobs lessened to snivels and sniffs. Silvie rushed to make the tea, glad she had taken a little of the medicinal wine before Sabrina arrived home. She put two spoons of sugar in Sabrina's tea and hurried back to the living room with it, hoping Sabrina would soon be able to tell her the whole story from the beginning. "Here, drink this; it'll make you feel better."

"*Denke.*" Sabrina took a sip of tea then set the cup down on the saucer.

"Do you feel up to telling me how all this happened?"

Sabrina nodded and lifted her eyes to the ceiling. "I met Carmello when I was in a coffee shop in town. We just got to talking. Things went from there."

"Things, what things exactly?"

"Do I have to spell everything out for you? You're over thirty. You should know a bit about life. You know what I mean. We were having a relationship."

Sabrina's words were snapped and angry, but Silvie knew that she was scared and trying to keep up a front. Silvie reminded herself that it was no time for a lecture and knew she had to show kindness and empathy. After all, who was she to judge? She knew how hard it was when she fell in love with Bailey, even though he was no Amish *mann.*

"Did his wife call the ambulance and the police?"

"I left when the wife left."

"How did you know he was dead? Sometimes people can look dead, but they can be unconscious."

"His eyes were open and just staring," Sabrina said before she jumped up and ran outside.

Silvie heard the noises of Sabrina throwing up, so she went into the kitchen and wet a cloth. Silvie sat on the front doorstep and waited until Sabrina finished.

Sabrina sat on the ground after she had finished.

"Here." Silvie handed Sabrina the damp cloth then helped her back into the *haus.* "Feel a bit better?"

"I don't know how I feel. I'm just numb. I checked to see

whether he was really dead, and he was. He wasn't breathing and I felt for his heart and it wasn't beating."

Silvie knew it was important to ask Sabrina as many questions as she could right away, even though Sabrina might not want to answer any. "Come back inside. It's getting a little cold."

Once they were both back on the couch. Silvie said, "You probably don't feel like answering any questions, but it's important you tell me all you can remember."

"We were to meet at the little place where we always met. When he was half an hour late, I knew there was something wrong. He's never late. I went to where he worked, figuring he might still be busy. I could see from the road outside that his office light was still on. I went up there. Everything was unlocked. I opened his door and peeked into his office and he was right there on the floor, dead. Right in front of the door."

Sabrina dabbed the damp cloth all over her face. "I thought at first that he was playing a joke on me. He always does silly things like that. I told him to get up and that he wasn't fooling me. I scolded him for leaving me waiting. When he didn't answer me or didn't laugh, I feared the worst and reached down and touched him."

After a long pause, Silvie asked, "Then what?"

"I heard someone calling his name. I hid in the other office and closed the door. I didn't hear her scream or anything. She stayed there for a few minutes then left."

"Did you scream when you saw him?"

"*Nee* because I thought he was joking, playing a prank. When I realized he wasn't, I just froze. I hid when I heard someone coming because I didn't want anyone to know about me. We were keeping things a secret until his divorce then we were going to be together. Carmello didn't want anyone to know about me yet."

"If you were hiding in the other office, how did you know that it was his wife who came into his office?"

"I looked out the window after she left and I saw her cross the street. It was her."

"Where had you seen her before?"

"The first time I saw her was at the coffee shop that I mentioned. It was before I met him; in fact, the first time I laid eyes on him. I could tell they were having an argument and trying to keep their voices down. I got up to leave and she got up to leave at the same time and then she bumped into me and called me a 'stupid religious freak' and stormed out. She caused me to overbalance and I knocked into the table where he was still sitting. Carmello apologized for what she had said and that's how we got to talking. That's how we met."

"How long's it been going on?"

"I met him just days after I arrived here. I think it was the first time you let me take the buggy by myself."

"You should tell the police that you found him," Silvie said, hoping that Sabrina would not throw up again.

"I can't do that. I hid. What would I say to them?"

"I'll leave it up to you, but I really think you should tell them everything you know."

"I'll look like I'm guilty because I hid when the wife came."

"Guilty of what? Are you worried about having an affair with a married man, or having people think that you killed him?"

"You think he was killed?" Sabrina asked.

"We don't know. You probably should have stayed and been

the one to call the police, then you would've found everything out."

Sabrina said, "He was perfectly healthy. He looked after himself. I'll call the police if you think I should."

"I think it'd be a *gut* idea. I'll walk up the road to the phone with you." Silvie had no phone of her own. Driving to a friend's *haus* or using a public phone was the only option and considering the late hour, the best option was the public phone up the road.

"Can it wait 'til morning?" Sabrina asked.

"*Nee*, and rather than call them, I think what we should do is drive to the police station and then you can tell them everything you know."

Sabrina nodded. "I suppose nothing worse can happen than has already happened."

After Silvie and Sabrina arrived at the police station, two policemen sat with Sabrina as they prepared to listen to what she had to say.

"Would you like a lawyer?" one of the policemen asked.

Silvie's eyes opened widely. "She hasn't done anything. Why would she need one?"

"We're counting Mr. Liante's death as suspicious. It could well have been murder. We won't know for sure for a few more hours."

Sabrina told them everything she knew, about how she found Carmello and hid when Mrs. Liante arrived, and then looked out the window to see her leave. Silvie sat with Sabrina while the police asked questions.

The sisters looked at each other often as Sabrina gave her

answers. Some tiring hours later, Sabrina and Silvie were in the buggy driving back home.

"It's strange that they knew nothing of the wife coming to see him. Are you sure it was she who you saw?"

Sabrina nodded.

Silvie continued, "I overheard one of them say they had just gone around to the Liantes' house to tell Mrs. Liante and she was very distressed."

Sabrina shrugged. "I know. I heard them say that too. She's acting like she didn't know that he was already dead."

"That doesn't add up. If she'd been in his office when he was lying there on the floor, she would've already known that he was dead. They said that the janitor found him. That means that after she saw him, she didn't phone the paramedics or the police."

"Am I having a bad dream? This all doesn't seem real," Sabrina covered her face with her hands.

"I know; if it is, I'm having the same bad dream as you." Silvie considered her bad dream was that she'd get the blame from her parents about what Sabrina had been up to. They would blame her for not keeping a closer eye on her and they would blame her double when they found out about Bailey, her *Englischer* man whom she was in love with. They would claim that she'd set a bad example for Sabrina.

Silvie wondered whether that were true. Had she set a bad example for her *schweschder* by falling in love with an *Englischer*? Even though she was a grown woman, her parents still treated her as a child. "I'm sorry, Sabrina, if my entertaining the idea of Bailey joining the community had anything to do with you seeing Carmello."

"*Nee,* Silvie, it had nothing to do with it. Why would you think that? It was nothing that I planned. I never would have thought I'd fall in love with someone like Carmello. The heart wants what the heart wants."

Silvie frowned. "Where did you hear that from?"

"Carmello used to say it all the time. Do you think that they will tell Carmello's wife about me?"

Silvie made a face. "I hope not. They were separated, weren't they?" Silvie considered that it might make things slightly better if the two were officially separated before Sabrina began her relationship with the man.

"*Jah.* He told me that they were separated, but they still lived in the same *haus* until he got the documents signed. I think in the end he agreed to what she wanted so he could get divorced without waiting any longer."

"Maybe she was entitled to everything. Do you know how these things work?" Silvie asked.

Sabrina shook her head. "I know nothing of these things. All I know is that Carmello would not have lied to me. He was the nicest man who has ever walked this earth."

"What did he say about your faith? He obviously knew you were Amish by your clothing."

"He asked a lot of questions if that's what you mean."

"Did he speak of marriage with you?" Silvie asked.

"*Nee,* but he was in love with me. We would've got married; I'm certain of it. I just know it and that's why we didn't have to speak about it."

Under the circumstances, Silvie considered that it was no use telling Sabrina anything contrary to what she currently believed. What *gut* would it do to talk sense into her when the man in question was dead?

Sabrina broke down as they drew closer to home. "It's all my fault. *Gott* is punishing me because I sinned. Now Carmello is dead and it's all my fault."

"Don't be upset. *Gott* doesn't punish people like that. He gave everyone the will to choose their own path. He would've waited for you to turn back to Him. He's a patient *Gott*; he wouldn't kill someone to pay for someone else's sin. It's not your fault at all." When that did nothing to stop her tears, Silvie added, "You'll feel better when you've had some sleep."

Silvie was looking forward to some sleep as well. She was so tired she could hardly keep her eyes open and she knew that there were only a few hours before daybreak. "Sabrina, I have to go to work at eleven in the morning. Do you want me to take the day off to stay with you?"

"*Nee,* I'll be all right. You go. I'll be better tomorrow. You're right; I probably just need a *gut* sleep."

When her head hit the pillow less than half an hour later, Silvie was filled with worry. What was she going to do with Sabrina? Sabrina should go to the bishop and confess her sin, but Sabrina was old enough to make that decision on her own.

Maybe the bishop might have her confess to the whole congregation and tell them what she had done. Silvie's cheeks flushed as she considered the embarrassment and humiliation Sabrina would feel if that were the case. News travels quickly amongst the Amish and her *mudder* and *vadder* would surely get to learn of it if the whole congregation heard her confession. Silvie told *Gott* all her worries and handed them all over to Him, so she could have at least a little sleep.

CHAPTER THREE

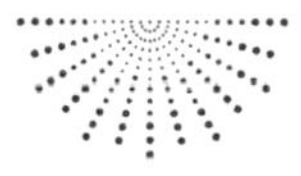

Let the righteous smite me; it shall be a kindness: and let him reprove me; it shall be an excellent oil, which shall not break my head: for yet my prayer also shall be in their calamities.
Psalm 141:5

Silvie peeked into Sabrina's room before she left for work the next morning. A china cup on Sabrina's nightstand told Silvie that Sabrina had woken and fixed herself some tea. If only she didn't need the money her job at the bakery gave her, then she would've been able to stay home and be there when Sabrina woke up. But she did need the money and things had been much harder on Silvie now she had to keep Sabrina, as well as herself.

Sabrina would not have realized the financial burden that she had put on Silvie. Sabrina had never worked a day in her life and being the youngest, she had never had to do as many chores as the older ones had. Silvie wondered whether it was her easy lifestyle and lack of responsibility, which caused Sabrina to make bad choices. Maybe she should have Sabrina pay room and board to force her to take a job and give her a sense of responsibility.

When Silvie arrived to start work at the bakery/café, the whole place was abuzz with the talk of the local 'murder.' Silvie naturally kept quiet about what she knew and the fact that her *schweschder* had been the one to find the body.

Throughout the day, Silvie kept her ears open. The rumors were that Carmello had been poisoned and his wife was distraught.

She also heard talk that Carmello Liante was a ladies' man, a charmer; some went so far as to call him a 'womanizer.' It was suggested that Carmello always had a mistress on the side and the loving wife, Stephanie Liante, had no idea.

Silvie decided it best to keep that information from Sabrina, at least for the moment. There was no point in upsetting her further, especially as it might have been nothing more than idle gossip.

Silvie learned that Carmello co-owned an accountancy firm with a business partner, Neville Banks.

After her work day, Silvie arrived home in the afternoon. She hoped that Sabrina might be busying herself with gardening or housework, but instead Sabrina was nowhere to be seen.

Silvie peeked in Sabrina's bedroom to see that she was still in bed, fast asleep.

Resentment rose in Silvie. She'd had hardly any sleep and

had to force herself out of bed to go to work so she could make ends meet. Sabrina was still asleep and had done nothing to help with the running of the household. Not only had she done nothing to help, she had added an extra burden onto Silvie with the worry of the murder and the worry of Sabrina's indiscretion.

Silvie glanced at the clock; it was nearly time to prepare dinner and with Sabrina still asleep she would have to do that chore by herself. Silvie picked up her Bible and sat in the couch. "What lesson are you trying to teach me *Gott?*" she asked aloud. She knew in her heart before she asked that He was trying to show her how to have more compassion and be less judgmental.

Her Bible opened automatically to Matthew chapter seven. She read the first few verses.

Judge not, that ye be not judged. For with what judgment ye judge, ye shall be judged: and with what measure ye mete, it shall be measured to you again.

And why beholdest thou the mote that is in thy brother's eye, but considerest not the beam that is in thine own eye?

She smiled and knew that she could not judge her *schweschder* for what she had done. Anyone could fall into temptation if they were not mindful.

As it was nearing dinnertime, Silvie forced herself into the kitchen, pulled some vegetables out of the container in the icebox and began to cut them into pieces. A loud knock on the door made her jump a little with fright.

She opened the door and in front of her stood a small, dark haired woman. Her hair was swept up on her head and she wore a cream jacket and skirt, and high heels.

"Hello. Can I help you?" Silvie asked.

"My name is Stephanie Liante; I'm Carmello's wife," is all that the woman said as she looked Silvie up and down.

Silvie's jaw dropped open and she was lost for words. The rumors said that this woman knew nothing of Carmello's indiscretions, so what was she doing standing there? Silvie realized that the woman might have thought she was the one having the affair with Carmello. Sabrina and Silvie looked very much alike except that Silvie was older. Should she say that she wasn't Sabrina?

Silvie licked her lips. "I was sorry to hear about your husband."

Mrs. Liante scoffed. "I don't think much of your religion if you think you can whore around town with other peoples' husbands."

"You're looking for me."

Silvie nearly jumped with fright when she heard Sabrina's voice coming from behind her. Silvie stepped to one side, blocking Sabrina from the woman. "I'm sorry about your husband, but I don't know what we can do for you," Silvie said, not wanting the two women to come face to face.

"I just wanted to look at the woman who thought she could get away with having an affair with my husband. The police told me that she was the one who found him. How do I know that she wasn't the last person to see him alive?"

"Are you saying I killed him?" Sabrina asked, trying to talk to the woman from behind Silvie.

"When did you last see him? Alive I mean?" Silvie asked Mrs. Liante.

"Not that it's any of your business, but I saw him at home

before he left for work in the morning after we made passionate love."

"That's not true," Sabrina spat out her words with the viciousness of a wild cat.

Silvie turned her head slightly to speak to Sabrina. "Hush." She turned back to Mrs. Liante. "You didn't see him later in the day?"

"No, I did not. It's none of your business anyway."

Sabrina successfully pushed Silvie out of the way and was now facing the furious woman. "You weren't sleeping with him. He told me you were separated. Anyway, what makes you so angry with me?"

"How dare you. We were not separated; we were happy. I was happy until I found out about you, just today. The police told me all about you. They said you were having an affair with him and you were the one who found him dead. You probably killed him, you little strumpet."

It was when Silvie tried to pull Sabrina back into the house she realized she still had the vegetable-chopping knife in one hand. While holding the knife in one hand and struggling with Sabrina in the other, Silvie said, "I'm sorry, but I'm going to have to ask you to leave."

"Are you threatening me with that knife?" Mrs. Liante asked.

Silvie glanced at the knife, which was now in the air and immediately lowered her hand. "No, I was just chopping vegetables."

The woman backed away.

"How did you get our address? The police wouldn't have given it to you," Silvie said.

"I've got resources, don't you worry about that. I'll see you both get what's coming to you. You religious freaks." The woman turned and took two steps toward her car then turned around. "No, I take that back, you are whores and tarts. I'll have you run out of town." The woman stomped back to her car, slammed the door and drove away.

Silvie pulled Sabrina back inside and closed the door with a heavy heart. What Sabrina had done was a sad reflection on all the Amish.

"What a horrible woman," Sabrina said.

After she locked the door, Silvie said, "Sabrina, her husband has just died and she's also just found out that he was having an affair with you. How do you think that she'd feel?"

Sabrina shrugged her shoulders. "They were separated."

"Whether they were, or they weren't, the woman has lost a husband."

Sabrina frowned. "So you're on her side? I've lost the man I loved; why aren't you on my side?"

"I don't have a side. There are no sides. Nothing is ever black or white. Just try and see someone else's side for once."

"So you are on her side? I think I might go back to *mamm* and *dat*; at least they like me." Sabrina burst into tears and ran into her room; slamming the door behind her.

Silvie returned to the kitchen to finish cutting the last of the vegetables. There was no use speaking to someone who was hysterical. Two minutes later there was another knock on the door. This time, Silvie was careful to put the knife down before she answered the door.

"Stay in your bedroom, Sabrina. I'll handle it." Silvie was sure it was Carmello's wife back again.

Silvie opened the door to see the two police they had spoken to in the early hours of the morning. "Oh, come in."

"Sorry to disturb you. We've got some questions for Sabrina."

"Certainly, come in."

She knocked on Sabrina's bedroom door. "It's the police."

Silvie showed the police to the living room and Sabrina joined them moments later.

"You said in your statement that you saw Mrs. Liante come to Mr. Liante's office?"

"That's correct. I've already told you everything I know. I saw him dead; I hid in the next office because I wasn't supposed to be there. I only hid because I heard someone walking in the hallway and then they called out his name. I heard someone come in the room and leave almost right away. I heard the downstairs door shut and I looked out the window and saw Mrs. Liante cross the road. No one else was around; it had to be she who was in the office."

The two policemen looked at each other.

"Why do you look at each other like that?" Silvie asked.

"Mrs. Liante claims that she was at home at the time. Her housekeeper testifies that she was there with her, all day."

"She's fibbing of course," Sabrina said. "She was just here threatening to run us out of town."

The older of the two policeman said, "Do you want to file a complaint against her?"

"Yes," Sabrina said.

"No," Silvie shouted over the top of her *schweschder.* She glared at Sabrina, as she continued, "No, we do not want to file a complaint. The woman was just upset."

"Very well. If you change your mind let us know." The policemen stood up.

Silvie and Sabrina followed suite.

"Did you find the cause of death yet?" Silvie asked.

"It looks like he was poisoned."

Sabrina doubled over and held her stomach. Silvie sat her back down on the couch and walked the policemen to the door. "What type of poison was it?"

"We're not certain yet; we have to wait for the lab reports. It could be something else, but the initial examination suggested poison. That's all I know at this stage."

Silvie lowered her voice so Sabrina would not overhear. "So do you think that it was murder? Or could he have somehow accidently taken the poison?"

"Murder," one of the policemen said, while the other nodded in agreement.

"You came here just to find out if Sabrina had made a mistake about seeing Mrs. Liante there?"

"That's correct. Seems one of them must be giving us false information. Mrs. Liante has an alibi and your sister has none. Maybe she should re-think her statement."

"Is Sabrina a suspect?" Silvie asked.

The policeman who had done most of the talking said, "Not at the moment, unless we find evidence to suggest otherwise."

"Is Detective Crowley handling this case?"

"Yes, he is. He's in charge of the investigation."

"All right. Thank you." As Silvie shut the door, she was thankful that Crowley was in charge of the investigation. Detective Crowley had helped her and her group of widow friends in the past.

CHAPTER FOUR

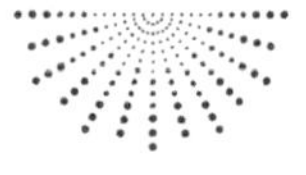

Put on therefore, as the elect of God, holy and beloved,bowels of mercies, kindness, humbleness of mind, meekness, longsuffering;
Colossians 3:12

The next night was the night of the widows' meeting. The five widows regularly met at the elderly *schweschders,* Elsa-May and Ettie's, *haus* for friendship and to discuss whatever was on their minds. Silvie brought Sabrina because Sabrina did not want to be left alone.

Emma was the first to speak to Sabrina. "I'm sorry to hear what happened, Sabrina."

"*Denke,* Emma." Sabrina shot a quizzical look to Silvie.

"All the ladies here know about what happened. We don't have any secrets and we can all help you," Silvie said.

"What way can they help me?" Sabrina asked.

Elsa-May leaned forward. "This thing's not over yet, not by a long shot. You saw Mrs. Liante cross the street after she saw her husband dead in his office. She had no reaction, neither did she call the police. She denies to the police she was ever there and had her housekeeper say that she was at home. Something stinks."

"I suppose it does," Sabrina said. "But there's nothing much I can do."

"There are things that we can do though," Ettie said as she waved one of her long bony fingers in the air.

Maureen leaned her ample body towards Sabrina, "Don't you worry about a thing; we'll find out who killed him."

"He'll still be dead though, so what's the point?" Sabrina wriggled in her chair. "How do you people sit in these chairs? Don't you have anything more comfortable?" Sabrina looked at Elsa-May and Ettie. "Why don't you have a couch like everyone else does?"

Silvie lowered her head in embarrassment at her *schweschder's* constant ungratefulness and complaining.

"What's wrong with the chairs?" Elsa-May asked.

Silvie was embarrassed at Sabrina's words. The elderly sisters had no couch, just several wooden chairs. No one had ever said anything to them about the discomfort, up until now.

Sabrina scrunched up her face. "They're hard and they're worse than what we have to sit on at the gatherings."

Silvie shot her head up. "Be quiet about the chairs. Everyone is trying to help you."

Sabrina lifted her chin to the ceiling. "I'm not in any trouble."

"*Jah*, but you might be if they start thinking you had anything to do with his murder," Emma said. "You wouldn't be the first innocent person to end up in jail."

"I'm not going to jail." Sabrina looked at Silvie. "I wish you hadn't made me come here."

"You said that you didn't want to be left alone," Silvie said.

"I didn't know it was going to be like this. You said you sat around and talked and ate cakes and things." Sabrina swiveled her head around. "Where are the cakes?"

Silvie looked at the other widows and said, "I'm sorry."

"This is not something to be taken lightly, Sabrina. A man's been murdered and they are looking for someone to pin it on. I mean they'll be looking for the person who did it." Elsa-May's voice boomed so loud that Sabrina cringed. Elsa-May continued, "Sabrina, you must tell us everything you know and don't leave anything out."

Sabrina straightened her back. "What kind of things?"

"Start with telling us if you know of anyone, anyone at all who would wish Carmello harm," Elsa-May said.

"His wife for one. He wanted a divorce and she didn't give him one until he agreed that she could have everything. She was about to sign the papers that day. I'm not sure if she did or not."

Elsa-May pushed her finger into her round cheek. "Seems silly for her to kill him if she was going to get everything anyway. Anyone else?"

"He often fought with Neville, his business partner."

"What about?" Ettie asked.

"Just business things, I'd guess. Then he had a secretary that he had to fire. She was lazy and never did anything she was told and turned up late to work and left early. When he fired her she put in a claim of sexual harassment, but then she dropped it a few weeks later."

"What was her name?" Elsa-May asked.

"I can't remember. Maybe I never heard it; I couldn't really say. Do you think that's important?"

Elsa-May ignored her question. "Have you met any of these people?"

"*Nee*, I've just seen them. I haven't actually met them. Except, Silvie and I met the wife yesterday. She came to the door and was really mean."

"What did she say?" Emma asked.

"She called us both horrible names and said she'd have us run out of town," Silvie said.

"No wonder Carmello wanted a divorce from her," Sabrina said.

"People can say awful things when they're upset," Maureen said. "She would've had a nasty shock over the whole thing."

Elsa-May read back her notes that she'd scribbled on her yellow writing pad. "Suspects so far are the wife, the secretary, or I should say the ex-secretary, and the business partner, Neville."

"That's the only people I know about," Sabrina said.

"Ettie, you do what you do best, which is scout around and talk to people. Find out what you can about Carmello. Emma, you go and speak to Crowley and see what he knows so far..."

"Me? Why do I always have to speak to Crowley? He'll ask me why I'm not married to Wil yet. Do you know that last time he called me Mrs. Jacobson, when he knows very well my last name is Kurtzler. He takes delight in making me uneasy."

"Nonsense, Emma. You were the one to speak with him most of the time on the last case and he told you everything he knew."

"*Jah,* Emma. Just put your personal feelings to one side," Ettie said.

"What do you mean last case? Are you all like detectives or something?" Sabrina asked as she looked around at each of the widows.

"*Nee,* we just help people where we can, that's all," Maureen said with a wide smile revealing the slight gap between her two front teeth.

Emma blew out a deep breath. "Okay, I'll go and talk to him first thing in the morning."

"*Gut,*" Elsa-May said then turned to Maureen, "Maureen, you try and find out what you can about the housekeeper."

"How will I do that? I don't know where they live or what the housekeeper's name is or anything," Maureen said.

"Emma will find all those sorts of things from Crowley, and then you can take things from there," Elsa-May said.

"What do you want me to do?" Silvie asked.

"You just look after Sabrina." Sabrina smiled and her face lighted up until Elsa-May added, "Keep her out of any more trouble because she obviously does not have one ounce of common sense."

Sabrina's smile vanished, replaced with an angry glower, directed at the elderly Elsa-May. Elsa-May glared right back at her until Sabrina looked away.

"You were after some cake, weren't you, Sabrina?" Ettie said as she rose to her feet.

The smile quickly returned to Sabrina's face. "*Jah,* Silvie said that there would be cake."

"Coming right up," Ettie said.

CHAPTER FIVE

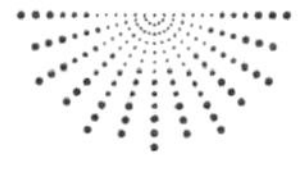

Finally, brethren, whatsoever things are true, whatsoever things are honest, whatsoever things are just, whatsoever things are pure, whatsoever things are lovely, whatsoever things are of good report; if there be any virtue, and if there be any praise, think on these things.
Philippians 4:8

The next morning, Emma reluctantly knocked on Detective Crowley's office door. She knew how uncomfortable he would make her feel, but the widows needed his help and he had always come through for them.

"Come in." His deep voice rang in Emma's ears as she stepped through his doorway.

Detective Crowley stood up from behind his desk. "Ah, Mrs. Kurtzler. Elsa-May told me you'd be coming this morning."

"Call me Emma."

He waved his hand in the direction of one of the two chairs in front of his desk. "Have a seat."

Emma sat down and licked her lips as nerves had made her mouth dry.

Thankfully the detective spoke first on the subject she'd come about. "You're interested to know about Carmello Liante?"

"Yes I am. Sabrina, Silvie's sister, found him dead before the janitor found him, but she was scared and hid when she heard someone coming."

"I know, I've read her statement. Says she heard Mrs. Liante come into the office, look at her dead husband on the floor then leave."

"That's right." Emma crossed her legs in an effort to feel more comfortable, but she nearly tipped herself off balance on the chair. She uncrossed her legs and hoped Crowley hadn't noticed her awkwardness.

His raised eyebrow and downturned mouth told Emma that he had noticed.

Then the detective lowered his eyebrow and his face returned to its usual deadpan state. "Did it occur to you that this might be a crime of passion and Sabrina might be guilty and trying to implicate Mrs. Liante?"

Emma sat tall; she was highly offended by his suggestion. "No, it didn't occur to me because I know that is not true. Amish aren't capable of violence. It's against everything we stand for."

Detective Crowley picked up a pencil and tapped it a couple of times on his desk. "Isn't having relations with a married man also against what the Amish believe in?"

He's trying to rattle you again, Emma. Think your answer through before you speak. Emma knew what he said was true and she did not like having to defend Sabrina's actions. "All people sin, Detective, even the Amish, because we are still people. To answer your question, I do not believe that Sabrina is capable of murder. She was in love with the man and she had no reason to kill him."

He pushed out his lips. "He might have told her that he didn't want to see her anymore."

Emma narrowed her eyes. "But he didn't."

"You can't know that with absolute certainty."

"I know it in my heart." Emma pounded her fist against her heart so hard that she involuntarily coughed.

"I agree." The detective leaned back in his chair.

"You do?"

"Yes. I don't think she did it at all." He swiveled slightly in his chair and then stopped.

"Why did you say those things, Detective?"

The detective gave one of his seldom seen smiles. "To see how strongly you agreed with me."

Emma tilted her head at the riddles the detective was speaking in. *Why can't he just speak straightly?* Emma thought. "You were testing me?" she asked.

The detective leaned back in his chair once more, but he remained silent. Emma wished that Elsa-May had come instead of her. She knew that the detective would cause her to feel foolish.

Emma forged ahead with the reason she was there. "Now that we have all that out of the way, what can you tell me about the case?"

"Seems that Carmello was quite the ladies' man."

Emma was disappointed to hear that and hoped it wasn't true. Sabrina would be sad to know that she hadn't been the only woman in his life. "Is it true that his wife was just about to sign some sort of contract, like divorce papers or some kind of property settlement papers?"

"We found no personal papers whatsoever in his office. I personally questioned Mrs. Liante and she told me that she had a happy marriage and was unaware of any indiscretions. When she learned of your friend, Sabrina's, relationship with her husband she was visibly shaken. She either had no idea her husband was having an affair, or she's a mighty good actress. She denies any talk of separation or divorce."

Emma knew that the woman was not being truthful, but that did not mean that she was guilty of murder. "Did she know of anyone who wished her husband harm?"

"She said that she couldn't think of a single enemy her husband might have had."

"Was he poisoned?"

"He'd ingested a lethal dose of Aconitine."

"What is Aconitine?"

"It's derived from a highly toxic plant, the monkshood plant, also know as Wolfs bane. It's nature's poison. A person can be poisoned just from picking the leaves without wearing gloves. It's lethal."

Emma chewed on a fingernail at the thought of the painful death Carmello might have had. Poison would not be the nicest way to die. "Could it have been an accident?"

"Not in that dose."

"Suicide?"

"There was no note, and no poison near him. Suicide isn't plausible."

"Elsa-May also wanted me to ask you about Mrs. Liante's address and the name of the housekeeper."

Detective Crowley shook his head.

"Elsa-May said if you don't want to give it that's okay, there are plenty of other ways she can find out."

The detective continued to shake his head as he wrote the information on a slip of paper and handed it to Emma.

Emma smiled. "Thank you, Detective Crowley."

The detective leaned forward and spoke in a low tone. "You didn't get that information from me." He gave Emma a wink.

CHAPTER SIX

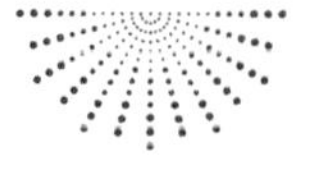

What doth it profit, my brethren, though a man say he hath faith, and have not works? can faith save him? If a brother or sister be naked, and destitute of daily food, and one of you say unto them, Depart in peace, be ye warmed and filled; notwithstanding ye give them not those things which are needful to the body; what doth it profit? Even so faith, if it hath not works, is dead, being alone.

James 2: 14-17

At the widows' meeting the next night, Detective Crowley told all the widows how Carmello Liante had died.

Elsa-May smiled. "Ah, yes, Aconitine. It's a slow and painful death resulting in paralysis just before death. It's actually a pretty plant with blue-violet flowers, but extremely poisonous. It's native to northern Europe."

"How would anyone get it around these parts?" Silvie asked.

Elsa-May tapped on her chin with her fingertips. "That's the origin of the plant; it's grown all over the place now. The roots and leaves can be dried just like any other herb."

"Interesting," Ettie said in a bored tone which sounded deliberate.

Elsa-May continued, "It is said that's how the Roman Emperor Claudius died, from the same poison. It was rumored that his wife poisoned him. Funny that Liante was Italian too and his wife is a suspect."

"Claudius who?" Silvie asked.

"Never mind, you wouldn't know him," Elsa-May said. "I'm not about to try and explain the whole of the Ancient Roman Civilization to people who probably don't even know where Italy is."

Ettie groaned. "Don't be boastful of all your library reading, Elsa-May. *Dat* always told you not to be prideful. He thought that might happen when you spent so much time reading."

Elsa-May glared at Ettie. "I was married at the time with two *kinner. Dat* had nothing to do with it and Liam was happy for me to go."

"Hmmph." Ettie shrugged. "Liam would have let you fly to the moon if you asked him."

"You spent a lot of time in the library all those years ago?" Silvie asked.

Elsa-May smiled. "I did and I'm not prideful about it. I craved learning about all kinds of things and still do."

"That's all very interesting I'm sure, but you ladies can discuss those things when I'm not here. Let's get back to the point, shall we? I found out that Mr. Liante was worth around four million dollars, possibly more," Detective Crowley said.

The widows gasped.

Silvie turned to Sabrina. "Did you know of this?"

"*Nee,* what does it matter how much he had?" Sabrina said.

The detective's eyes fixed firmly onto Sabrina as he asked, "Did you know that you, Sabrina, have been left one quarter of everything?"

"Really? Well, that's one thing he didn't tell me. Who was left the rest?"

"Sabrina!" Silvie said shocked at her *schweschders's* rudeness.

Ettie interrupted before the detective could answer Sabrina's question, "Sabrina won't have to go to the reading of the will and be in the same room as Mrs. Liante, will she?"

"No. I was getting to that. Mrs. Liante is in the hospital. It seems that there was an attempt on her life this afternoon. Someone broke into her home with a knife. The housekeeper disturbed the intruder and he fled."

The widows murmured their shock.

"That's awful," Ettie said.

"Is she hurt badly?" Silvie asked.

"She has small cuts, and she's suffering from severe shock. She's under sedation now. I've got a guard stationed on her door just in case the attacker thinks he'll be able to get to her in there. I've another piece of news. Mr. Liante's business partner has disappeared."

"You're full of surprises tonight, Detective," Elsa-May said. "Is there anything else we need to know?"

The detective shook his head. "I wouldn't mind a chocolate

slice or a cookie." The detective looked around the room. "Are you ladies on diets? There's usually food galore here."

Ettie rose to her feet. "I'll get it. We've started talking first before we eat. We seem to get more done that way. Your usual black tea, Detective?"

"Yes, please."

"What will you do with all that money, Sabrina?" Maureen asked.

"I'll stay here in Lancaster County and buy a *haus*. I'll give some to Silvie and some to *mamm* and *dat*."

Silvie said, "You don't need to give any to me, Sabrina, but it's a kindly thought."

"I want to give you some money, so you don't have to work so hard."

"I don't work that hard and I enjoy the bakery," Silvie said, pleased that her *schweschder* had a generous heart.

"Okay, I'll keep it all then," Sabrina said without the hint of a smile. "When do I get the money, Detective? I've never been left any money before."

"You'd have to wait a time until probate goes through. Could be weeks or months. There's no telling how long it will be."

"How much did Mrs. Liante get?" Sabrina asked.

"The remainder of his estate was divided amongst Miss Scotsdale, Miss Tobrill and Mrs. Liante. I should let you know that Mr. Liante's lawyer suggested that Mrs. Liante could contest the will and she'd likely have a good case."

"Who are those other two women?" Sabrina asked.

"As far as I've been able to ascertain, one was a girlfriend of some time ago, before you came along, that was Miss Tobrill. Miss Scotsdale was his former secretary."

"What does it mean to contest the will, Detective?" Silvie asked.

"She could take the matter to court and claim that the will was unfair to her since she was the lawful wife. The courts might decide that it's only she who is entitled to his entire estate. If she does take it to court, it's hard to say which way it will go."

Sabrina bounded to her feet and walked outside. Maureen stood up to follow, but Silvie said, "Leave her, Maureen. She needs to be by herself for a while."

Maureen sat down. "It must be an awful shock to her."

"She brought it all on herself thinking she could get away with such a terrible thing as having an affair with a married man." The widows remained silent and Silvie reprimanded herself for her judgmental attitude, knowing that it wasn't her place to judge anyone.

Ettie came out of the kitchen with a tray of goodies. "There you are Detective, Emma's chocolate fudge, chocolate chip cookies and a chocolate cake that I baked today."

"And my poor old sugar cookies," Maureen said.

"Everything can't be chocolate," Emma said.

The detective took a chocolate slice and said, "You ladies sure know how to cook."

"Silvie, are you sure Sabrina's alright? Should someone go and check on her?" Emma asked.

"*Nee,* the fresh night air will do her some *gut* and she'll come back in when she's ready," Silvie said.

"Who are the suspects, Detective?" Elsa-May asked.

"I think we can safely rule Mrs. Liante out. She would not have known that she wasn't left all of the money, so she would've had no motive. Now it would appear that she's in danger too. Perhaps we need to be looking for someone who had a grudge against both of them."

"Who does that leave?" Elsa-May asked with pen and paper in hand.

"The business partner has to be the main suspect now that he's disappeared."

"Detective, what do you know about these other women? Could one of them be a jilted lover out for revenge?"

"That's the next possibility. There's also the possibility that Mr. Liante told Miss Tobrill or Miss Scotsdale of their inheritance and they wanted to speed things along or have him die before he changed his will again."

Ettie shook her head. "Terrible, terrible mess."

"It's unusual for an Amish woman to get involved with a man like that, isn't it?" The detective looked at Silvie. "I mean, I know it is, but what prompted her to do such a thing?"

"She would say love," Silvie said.

The detective scoffed. "Seems Mr. Liante had plenty of that to go around."

"Do you think that Mrs. Liante knew of these other women?" Maureen asked.

Detective Crowley thought for a moment before he said, "Going on my talks with her, it seemed she was totally unaware, although she did comment that her husband worked hard and was away a lot. Generally that would be cause for suspicion or at least put some doubt in a woman's mind, but not Mrs. Liante."

Sabrina walked back in and sat down on the hard, wooden

chair. "Detective, do you think I'll get any money at all if Mrs. Liante contests?"

The widows raised their eyebrows at her comment. It hardly seemed the main concern since the man was dead, no one knew who murdered him and she'd been caught out in sin.

"It's hard to say. It's unlikely that she won't contest the will. It depends what the courts decide. They'll take into account that he was of sane mind when he wrote the will and that was his choice. You'll just have to wait and see what happens."

Silvie leaned toward her *schweschder.* "That's hardly the most important issue here, Sabrina."

Sabrina looked at Silvie and remained silent.

After he ate two more chocolate fudge squares and drank half his tea, the Detective got to his feet. "I'm off to talk to Mrs. Liante at the hospital. I'll see if she's able to speak yet, see what else I can find out. I was going to wait 'til tomorrow, but I'll see if she's up to talking tonight." The detective chuckled. "That'll be one less thing I have to do tomorrow."

As soon as he left, Elsa-May said, "Mrs. Liante was my main suspect. What do you know about the business partner, Sabrina?"

"Let me think." Sabrina pressed a finger into her cheek. "I never met him. He was *gut* at business and I know that Carmello was happy with him most of the time, apart from some arguments."

"What is his name?" Ettie asked.

"Neville Banks."

"Was he aware that Carmello was having relationships with women outside his marriage?" Elsa-May asked Sabrina.

"As far as I knew he wasn't. I thought it was only me and he told me that he was separated and living in a different room in the *haus*," Sabrina said. "I had no reason to disbelieve him especially when I saw with my own eyes how they interacted with one another. The first day I met him was after they had a big argument in a coffee shop. She knocked me over when she stormed out, and he apologized to me."

"Ahh, that's an important thing to tell the detective since she claims that they were happily married. Just a moment." Elsa-May drew her cell phone out of the top drawer of the dresser in the living room.

Sabrina gasped. "You have a cell, Elsa-May?"

"Only for emergencies." Elsa-May looked at Emma. "I know, I know, I'll use it outside." Elsa-May stepped through the front door.

"No one can judge me for what I've done if Elsa-May has a cell phone. We're not supposed to have things like that," Sabrina said.

"What you've done is much worse," Silvie snapped before she could stop herself.

"No one's judging you. It's *Gott* who judges," Maureen said.

Sabrina looked down at the floor.

"He's going to talk to Mrs. Liante in the hospital tonight. Tomorrow afternoon he'll make a surprise visit to Mrs. Liante's *haus*, question the housekeeper and have her show him through the *haus*."

"Won't he need a warrant?" Emma asked.

"*Nee*, only if the housekeeper objects, but why would she if there's nothing to hide?" Elsa-May sat back down. "We should meet back here same time tomorrow, directly after dinner."

"Why doesn't everyone come to my *haus* for dinner?" Emma asked.

Everyone agreed, but then Elsa-May said, "*Nee,* I told Crowley to come back here same time tomorrow night. Some other time, Emma?"

Emma nodded.

Ettie said to Elsa-May, "Why don't we summarize all that we've learned?"

Elsa-May looked down at her list. "Carmello was poisoned; his business partner, Neville Banks, is missing. Someone tried to kill Mrs. Liante at her home with a knife and now she's in the hospital. Carmello left money to his wife and money to three other women and it's quite likely that Mrs. Liante doesn't know of it yet and is expecting to inherit everything. Have I left anything out?"

Ettie looked at all the widows. "*Nee,* I think that's it."

"Well, we'll meet here with Crowley tomorrow and see what else he's found out. Now, we'll have to find out things as well, or Crowley will stop being so free with giving us information. Silvie, you see if you can find out which lawyer is handling the will. It could be your lawyer friend, the one who comes to the bakery all the time."

Silvie said, "George Winters? I'll see what I can do."

Emma leaned over to Maureen and said quietly, "I've got the house address of the Mrs. Liante and the housekeeper's name. Crowley gave it to me."

"*Denke,*" Maureen said.

Elsa-May overheard what Emma said. "*Jah,* Maureen. You see what you can find out."

Maureen nodded. "I'll snoop around the house, talk to the

housekeeper and see what I can find out. She'll most likely talk to me rather than the police. I'll pretend I'm there about a job."

CHAPTER SEVEN

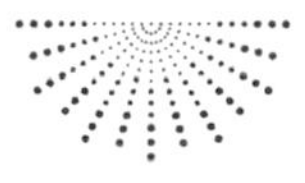

Therefore as by the offence of one judgment came upon all men to condemnation; even so by the righteousness of one the free gift came upon all men unto justification of life.
Romans 5:18

An hour later, Silvie was glad to be home.

As Silvie and Sabrina walked through the front door, Sabrina said, "I suppose you think that I should confess to the bishop what I've done."

Silvie sank into the couch. "I'm tired, Sabrina, I don't want an argument."

Sabrina sat next to her. "I just asked a simple question."

"I know, but your tone is argumentative and I can't deal with it tonight. It's too late and I've got to get up at five tomorrow morning and go to work." Silvie glanced at her china clock. "That's just five hours I'll have of sleep if I'm blessed to have that much."

"I don't want to go and see the bishop."

Silvie winced at Sabrina's high-pitched tone and covered her ears. She'd had enough of her *schweschder,* enough of her problems and enough of her constant whining. She wondered if Carmello had ever seen this side of her. "It's up to you, but I'm certain that he'll be knocking on our door soon to ask why you haven't been to the gatherings. It'll either be him or one of the ministers. They might even write a letter to your bishop in Ohio."

Sabrina sighed. "I'll think about going to see him then."

Silvie still did not understand how her *schweschder* could do what she had done. Things were worse if Carmello had been lying to her about being separated from his wife.

"If you want to stay in the community, you'll need to speak to the bishop. You may be shunned for a time," Silvie said.

"Shunned, *ach nee.*"

"*Jah,* shunned. Maybe you'll have to confess what you've done at the gathering. You'll have to stand and ask forgiveness. Maybe you'll be shunned and then have to ask forgiveness before you come back."

Sabrina was quiet then tilted her head upwards as she said, "I won't be shunned because I haven't been baptized yet."

Silvie tilted her head to the side. "I thought you had been baptized."

Sabrina shook her head.

"Have you thought about your prospects of attracting a *mann* after all this has happened? It won't help you find a *mann* once they hear of this. Your name will be associated with what you've done." Silvie knew her words were harsh; she didn't want to hurt Sabrina, she just wanted her to come to terms with the reality of what she'd done.

Sabrina stood up. "I was in love with Carmello. Don't you understand that? I'll never be able to love another man. So what does it matter?" Tears poured down Sabrina's face as she ran to her room sobbing uncontrollably.

Silvie sat by herself. She was giving her opinion and it was true, Sabrina would find it difficult to find a husband now with the scandal in her past. She was trying to prepare her for what was to come. Silvie knew that there was no use speaking to Sabrina when she was tired and crying. She would speak to her tomorrow, but tonight Silvie needed to get as much sleep as she could before her 5 a.m. start.

Silvie took off her prayer *kapp* and took the pins out of her hair. Her long, dark blonde hair fell down her back. She climbed the stairs to her bedroom hoping that the next few weeks would not be too horrible for Sabrina. At least Sabrina wasn't a suspect in Carmello's murder; that was one thing that they could be thankful for.

Moments later Silvie heard a voice in the darkness. "Are you asleep, Silvie?"

"*Nee,* not yet. Come in."

Sabrina pushed Silvie's door open. "I will go to the bishop. I'll give myself a day or two to think about what I'll say. I'll take whatever punishment I have to take. I don't want to leave the community. I thought about it and I don't want to be an *Englischer*. I want to remain here in Lancaster County with you."

While propping herself up with pillows, Silvie said, "That's *gut,* Sabrina. I'm glad you've made that choice." Silvie would prefer Sabrina to go back home, but she was her *schweschder,* she had to look after her and if she wanted to stay, Silvie would have to do what she could to make her stay a happy one.

Sabrina sat on the edge of Silvie's bed. "I'll get a job because I don't know if I'll get any of Carmello's money or not. I'll get a job to help out with money and I'll do more chores around the *haus.*"

Silvie smiled; her *schweschder* was finally taking responsibility for her life. "I'm happy about that."

"Do you think I should go to Carmello's funeral?"

Silvie shook her head violently at the thought of Sabrina showing up at Carmello's funeral. "*Nee,* I'd stay away if I were you."

"*Jah,* I think it'd be best for me to stay away, but it's hard. I loved him so much; I feel as though I should be the person arranging the funeral. I feel as though I was his wife."

"That's the way things work, Sabrina. Officially you weren't his wife and now you have to guard your reputation from any more talk or any more trouble. It won't do anyone any good for you to go to the funeral. It'll create a scene or a lot of chatter at the very least."

Sabrina lowered her head. "Do you think that I'll ever get over Carmello's death?"

"After some time, *jah.*"

"It must have been hard for you when John died."

Silvie had never shared with Sabrina the fact that she had not been in love with John when she married, and neither was she about to share it with her at this point in time. "It was very hard, but I adjusted. In life you have to learn to adapt to change, the *gut* and the bad. Life is constantly changing and most of it is out of our control."

"*Denke* for helping me through this, Silvie." Sabrina leaned over and hugged her *schweschder.* Once she straightened up she asked, "Can you come to the bishop with me?"

"*Nee,* I can't. It's best you go alone. That kind of thing has to be done by yourself."

"Please come with me, Silvie? I can't do that on my own. I really want you to come with me."

"*Nee*. I'll drive with you and wait outside, but I can't come in with you."

Sabrina bounded to her feet. "What do I ever ask you to do? I ask you one little thing and you say 'no.' I will never ask you anything ever again." Sabrina stomped out of the room and shut Silvie's door firmly on her way out.

Silvie sighed and sank back into her pillow. For a moment she thought that Sabrina had changed, but she was being nice so she would accompany her to the bishop. Silvie closed her eyes and hoped that sleep wouldn't be far away.

CHAPTER EIGHT

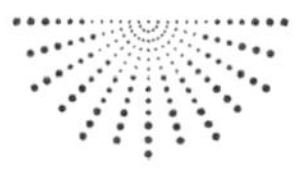

When I was a child, I spake as a child, I understood as a child, I thought as a child: but when I became a man, I put away childish things.
For now we see through a glass, darkly; but then face to face: now I know in part; but then shall I know even as also I am known.
And now abideth faith, hope, charity, these three; but the greatest of these is charity.
1 Corinthians 13:11-13

At the bakery the next day, Silvie waited for Mr. Winters of Winters & Sons lawyers to come in for coffee. He came in every day for at least one coffee, and today Silvie would question him about the Liantes and hoped that he knew them. Maybe he was their lawyer. It was after the lunch hour rush that Mr. Winters came into the bakery. Thankfully, he was alone, so Silvie seized the opportunity of her fifteen-minute break to have a chat with him.

"Sit with me, Silvie."

He always asked Silvie to sit and talk with him, and this time she was in a position where she was able.

Silvie pulled out the chair on the other side of the small round table. "I can today; I've just begun my break."

"Mr. Winters, have you heard of the death of Mr. Liante? He owned an accountancy firm just up the road here."

Mr. Winters finished the mouthful of the salad roll he had just bitten off. "Heard of him? I'm going to tell you something that's normally highly confidential, but under the circumstances, you need to know. Carmello Liante came to me last week wanting a will drawn up fast. He was a new client. He came to me because his lawyer was too slow and he wanted a new will drawn up quickly."

Silvie couldn't help the gasp that escaped from her lips.

"That's right. He told me that a couple of months ago, he had another will drawn up and he said it had taken his lawyer three weeks to prepare it. I told him if it was simple, then I could do it for him in a matter of hours."

"What reason are you telling me this? What circumstances do you mean and did you end up doing the new will?" Silvie wondered whether Crowley knew about this recent will or had he only been in contact with the lawyer who had the will from months ago?

"Yes, I drew the will up as Carmello Liante requested. It wasn't a complicated one. There was only one beneficiary."

"Are you sure it was the same Mr. Liante who was just murdered who came to see you?" As soon as she asked the question Silvie realized how silly it was. How many Carmello Liantes could there be in the world?

He looked at Silvie from under silver, bushy brows. "Silvie, I deal in facts; of course I'm sure."

"Do the police know that? Detective Crowley spoke of a will, but said nothing of it being drawn up the day before." Silvie scratched her neck. "You haven't told me yet why you're telling me all this."

"You can't sit with me and not eat anything," Mr. Winters said.

"I've got Teresa bringing me a cheese and lettuce roll."

Mr. Winters nodded. "That's good. You have to keep up with feeding yourself; there's nothing of you."

Silvie smiled at his concern. "We were speaking of the will."

"Ah, the will. The will was drawn up, but never signed."

Silvie tilted her head to one side and opened her mouth to speak, but stopped when her co-worker Teresa placed her food in front of her. "Thank you, Teresa."

"Don't hurry from your break, Silvie. We're not that busy," Teresa said.

"Thanks, Teresa." Silvie glanced around the tables in the bakery. Teresa was right; they weren't that busy. "So, you say that the will was never signed?"

"I saw him the day he died and he told me who the beneficiary was to be. He couldn't wait while I drew it up and fiddled around with the form on my computer. He said he had a busy day and asked me if I could stay late and meet him after five so he could sign it. I waited for him, but he never showed. I figured he forgot the appointment. I left a note for my secretary to phone him the next day to re-schedule."

"Can you tell me who the beneficiary was?"

"Ahh, that's what I was getting to. The reason I'm telling you all this is that your sister was the sole beneficiary."

Silvie's hand flew to her open mouth as it fell open in disbelief.

Mr. Winters continued, "I was shocked that he was leaving his estate to a woman who wasn't his wife. Someone I haven't even heard about." He leaned in close to her. "I usually hear of everything in this town. He explained the situation and said he was in love with, Sibyl, was it?"

"Sabrina," Silvie corrected him.

"Anyway, as I said, we had a chat and he told me she was Amish and I saw that she had the same last name as the one on your badge." He pointed to Silvie's name badge.

Silvie looked down at her badge and her fingers were drawn to touch it. Since John died Silvie sometimes went by her maiden name of Tildy. "So he did love her."

"I'd say most definitely."

"He told Sabrina that he wanted to leave his wife and she wouldn't give him a divorce until he agreed to give her everything. He wouldn't have had anything to leave Sabrina would he, if he got divorced?"

"He was a wealthy man and had millions in non-marital assets. His wife would only have been entitled to what is termed 'marital assets.' Marital assets are those which are attained by either party during the term of the marriage. It was the marital assets that they were at loggerheads over. I'm a personal friend of the lawyer who was handling his divorce, so I did hear snippets. Mind you, I don't know the finer details of the divorce proceedings or the property settlement."

The more Silvie listened, the more it seemed that Carmello might have been genuinely in love with Sabrina. "He did tell Sabrina that he and his wife were separated but still living in the same house. Do you know anything about that?" Silvie took a bite of her roll.

Mr. Winters leaned back and dabbed at the corners of his mouth with a white napkin. "If one party doesn't consent to the divorce, the only way to get a divorce in this state is to be separated for two years and then the divorce goes through without a hitch. There are little things she could try and do to stop it, but usually when two years has passed, it's just some more paperwork and then a divorce is granted."

"But they were living in the same house," Silvie said.

"It doesn't matter; they can still be legally separated under the same roof as long as they are not living together as man and wife." Mr. Winters took a mouthful of coffee. "They don't have relations; they don't go to family occasions together; they live totally separate lives."

"So how long had they been separated like that for; do you know?"

"From what I surmised, the two years was growing close and that's what prompted him to have the new will drawn up."

"Thank you, Mr. Winters, I can't tell you how much help you've been."

"Anytime, Silvie, anything you need, just ask."

Silvie felt bad for being tempted to judge her *schweschder* as foolish. It was clear now that the man was in love with her if he was leaving every single dime he had to her. Maybe their love was true.

She knew from her own experience that it was easy to fall in love with someone, even an *Englischer.* Maybe Carmello had been a womanizer in the past, but everyone can change and he might have done just that, when he met Sabrina.

Mr. Winters leaned over closer to Silvie. "I don't have time to tell you here because you'll have to get back to work, but there's something else you should know if you're interested in Carmello Liante."

"Yes of course I'm interested. I'd like to know anything that you know about him."

Mr. Winters neatly arranged his knife and fork on the empty plate. "What time do you finish today?"

"I should be off at around four today unless Bill wants me to stay later."

"I'll expect you just after four. Tell Bill that you've got an appointment with me." Mr. Winters gave Silvie a wink.

Silvie smiled and nodded. "Will do."

Silvie could hardly wait to hear what Mr. Winters had to say about Carmello. She was hoping it was something that would help them find out who had killed him.

When four o'clock came around, she was pleased that she was free to go and did not have to stay longer. She hurried down the road to Mr. Winters's office. She'd been in his office building many times delivering lunches and coffees.

"Come in, Silvie." Mr. Winters was just outside his office speaking to the front desk receptionist when Silvie pushed open the heavy glass door. "This way."

His office was at the end of the corridor. The suite of offices was housed in an old building. Some of the rough red bricks were left exposed and made a startling contrast with the modern glass and stainless steel of the interior of the office partitions.

"Take a seat." Mr. Winters had the largest office, being one of two partners in the firm. Apart from his large desk at one end of the room there was a group of black tub chairs in a circular arrangement. It was these chairs that they sat in as they spoke.

"You had something to tell me? Oh, I nearly forgot; I bought you a slice of cherry pie." Silvie leaned down in her bag and handed Mr. Winters the white package.

"My favorite, thank you, Silvie." Mr. Winters took the pie and placed it in his small fridge at the far side of the room. "For later." He laughed and sat back down in front of Silvie. "What I want to tell you is something that I heard from another lawyer. We lawyers talk about our clients, even though we aren't supposed to."

"What was it?" Silvie leaned forward.

"The lawyer was approached by a previous client of Mr. Liante. The client was unhappy with him and wanted to know his rights and whether or not he could sue Mr. Liante for anything."

"What did he do?"

"The client went to him with a commercial real estate opportunity and had Liante crunch the numbers – that means work out whether it was a good deal or not."

"Yes, I know. Go on."

"Liante told his client that the numbers didn't work and he couldn't recommend the deal. Next thing, his client found out that the property went under contract quite quickly. Months later the client did some checking into the company that bought the property and – can you guess the rest?"

"Liante was the owner of the company?"

"Yes, the director. The client thought that this was a breech of ethics and approached the lawyer to see if he could be sued."

"Could he have been sued?" Silvie asked.

"At best he could have been reported to the Accountancy Board. Usually accountants and professionals have their own set of criteria they are ethically bound by. He most likely breached their ethics, but legally there was no use going ahead with anything. Liante could have said that he'd already been considering the property; it was also bought in a company name and not in his own name which distances him further from any liability."

"So the man who missed out on the deal would have been very angry?" Silvie asked.

"Very angry is an understatement from what his lawyer told me."

"Thank you, Mr. Winters; you've been very helpful."

"Anytime, Silvie. I'm here to help, and to eat cherry pie." Old Mr. Winters laughed.

CHAPTER NINE

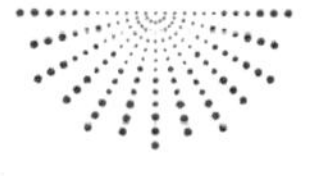

Now I beseech you, brethren, by the name of our Lord Jesus Christ, that ye all speak the same thing, and that there be no divisions among you; but that ye be perfectly joined together in the same mind and in the same judgment.
1 Corinthians 1:10

Knowing that Mrs. Liante was still in the hospital after the attempt on her life, Maureen thought it the best opportunity to go to her house and speak to the housekeeper. She went as early as she could because she knew that Detective Crowley was going to have the housekeeper show him through the house that afternoon.

Maureen took a deep breath, said a quick prayer and knocked on the Liantes' front door. She glanced down at her

Englisch clothing and smoothed down her hair, conscious of the fact that her prayer *kapp* was missing.

Seconds later the door opened a crack. "Yes?"

"Hello, I'm Mary Templeton. Would Mrs. Liante be home at the moment?"

"No, I'm afraid not." The housekeeper looked Maureen up and down. "Are you selling something?"

"No, I'm not selling anything. Mrs. Liante told me to come and see her the next time I had a day free. She said she's looking for a cook and she's interested in using my services."

"She might be back tomorrow or the day after. Does she have your phone number? I'll tell her you came by. What's your name?"

"Would she authorize you to speak to me? I know she was looking for someone rather quickly and you'd be doing her a favor. I'm not sure when I'll be free next; I'm very busy. She'll be so disappointed that she missed me."

The housekeeper opened the door a little wider and studied Maureen again, from top to toe. "Come on in then. Heavens knows that Mrs. Liante can't cook. It's about time she thought to get someone in." Maureen was led to a living room with large floor to ceiling glass windows overlooking a garden. "It'll take a weight off my shoulders. I'm no cook either."

"What a lovely home. Have Mr. and Mrs. Liante lived here long?"

The housekeeper lowered her head. "Mr. Liante died just days ago."

Maureen gasped and covered her mouth with her two hands. "How terrible. I'm so sorry I had no idea."

"It was a horrible business. Mrs. Liante was so distraught she had to be hospitalized."

"She's in the hospital?" Maureen asked.

The housekeeper nodded. "Anyway, I didn't introduce myself. I'm Maud Camry."

Maureen shook her hand. "Very pleased to meet you."

"Do you have any references that I can pass on to Mrs. Liante?"

"I don't need references. Mrs. Liante has seen my work first hand. She's been to many, many functions I've cooked at. She really just wanted to show me the kitchen."

"I can do that. I can show you the kitchen. This way." Maud walked toward the kitchen.

As Maureen followed, she noticed that the dress Maud wore was particularly well made. She knew good tailoring when she saw it since her mother was one of the better seamstresses in the community. Maureen also knew that the silk fabric would have been highly expensive. "That's a lovely dress you're wearing, Maud."

Maud stopped and turned around. "Mrs. Liante gave it to me." Maud laughed. "We're the same size and she gives me all her old clothes."

"Lucky you," Maureen said. "I'd never fit that size." Maureen patted her full hips.

"She's a size two, same as me. Some of the clothes she gives me have never been worn. It's like that with rich people. Sometimes they're far too free with their money."

"They don't even know the word *budget* do they?" Maureen laughed. "Do you live-in?"

"Yes, well nearly. I've got the garden house out behind the

main house. It's two bedrooms and it's quite roomy. It's funny that Mrs. Liante didn't mention you."

"I've met her quite a few times. She's a lovely woman."

"Lovely?" Maud laughed. "I've heard her called many things, but not many people would call her lovely."

"She seemed lovely to me."

Maud's face turned serious. "She can be lovely and she can be horrid. It depends on what mood she's in. I'm not about to cross her in any way."

"Of course you wouldn't cross her because she's your boss."

Maud smiled. "Come on. I'll show you the kitchen and then I'll give you a quick look over the rest of the house. It's quite grand."

Maureen was happy that she was getting along so well with Maud. In real life, they might have become friends. Maureen was a little saddened that she was deceiving this lady just to find out more about Mr. Liante's murder. Maureen took a deep breath and reminded herself of what she was there for and followed Maud as she took her on a tour of Mrs. Liante's home.

"Well, that's the home," Maud said.

"It's magnificent."

Maud tapped Maureen on the arm. "I've got loads of free time since Mrs. Liante's not here. Let's have a nip of sherry."

Maureen smiled. She wasn't a drinker. It wasn't forbidden in her community and many of her Amish friends drank in moderation. Maureen knew she had to keep a level head. "Yes, that would be lovely. I have a little time before I have to be somewhere."

"Excellent. We can enjoy ourselves before Mrs. Liante gets home."

Maureen followed Maud to a formal sitting room. "Sit here," Maud said while she walked to the far side of the room and pressed a button under a concave in the wall. A bar rose up out of the floor.

Maureen covered her mouth with both hands. "Well, I'll be. I've never seen anything like it."

Maud laughed. "Mrs. Liante likes her gadgets. She's got a large television screen in the bedroom that comes down from the ceiling at the press of a button."

Maureen noticed that Maud said that 'she' has the television screen in the bedroom and not 'they.' Maybe that was because Mr. Liante was no longer alive, but surely she would have said 'they've' got a television screen, if they were in the same bedroom. For being so early after Mr. Liante's death, the housekeeper hadn't made one slip with the 'they' when referring to her employers; it was always 'she.' Maureen mulled the whole thing over until she was handed a small glass of sherry in an extremely heavy and expensive looking cut glass goblet.

The housekeeper sat next to her on the blue, brocade chaise.

Maureen looked around her and then looked back at the glass. "I feel very stylish."

Maud laughed. "They do know how to live."

There it was; the housekeeper had said 'they.' Now Maureen had no reason to believe, no hope to cling to that Mr. and Mrs. Liante were separated, but living under the one roof. She had no evidence of that at all. She had hoped she could go back and tell the widows and particularly Sabrina that they had lived separately, but she could not.

"Cheers," Maud said as she lifted up her glass.

"Cheers," Maureen copied Maud as she sipped the sherry. "Very nice."

"It should be. It's the best that money can buy," Maud said.

"And they don't mind you drinking it?"

Maud laughed. "What they don't know won't hurt them. I mean what Mrs. Liante doesn't know won't hurt her."

~

SILVIE DRAGGED Sabrina along to the next widows' meeting, even though Sabrina didn't want to go because she was still cross at having to go to talk to the bishop alone. Silvie knew it would be beneficial to have Sabrina at the meeting.

"That night of the murder, how did you know that it was Mrs. Liante whom you saw? How could you see her face in the dark when she left Carmello's office? You didn't see her actually in the office, did you?" Maureen asked Sabrina.

"*Nee,* I didn't actually see her in his office. I heard someone come in and then I heard someone leave. I heard the door downstairs close and I looked out the window. Just as I looked out, I could see her face as she glanced back at the building. I remember her face and it was definitely her. There was also no one else around."

"Mrs. Liante's housekeeper, Maud, is given all Mrs. Liante's old clothing and she takes exactly the same sized clothing. She looks similar to Mrs. Liante; it would be hard to tell them apart at a distance. The only difference is that the housekeeper is older, but that would be hard to tell in the dark, wouldn't it?"

"What are you saying, Maureen? Do you think that the housekeeper killed him? Why would she?" Sabrina asked. "And she wouldn't have attacked Mrs. Liante as well, because if they're both gone she would have no job."

Maureen slumped back slightly in her chair, which caused the old wooden chair to creak. "I didn't think of that."

Ettie said, "What else did you find from going around the *haus,* Maureen?"

Maureen looked at Sabrina. "I'm sorry to say that I didn't see any evidence that they had separate bedrooms. In fact, she showed me their bedroom, the master suite, she called it, and said nothing of them leading separate lives."

Sabrina said nothing and looked sad.

"How many bedrooms do they have in the house?" Emma asked.

"Couldn't count them. Must have been around ten bedrooms. It is possible that Mr. Liante used one of the bedrooms as his own." Maureen said, looking at Sabrina. "I'm just saying that there was no evidence from what I saw. I didn't look in closets or anything."

"It's alright, Maureen. You don't have to be careful what you say. I know what I had with him. I know that it was real. Silvie's got something that she hasn't told you yet."

All eyes turned to Silvie. "I told Sabrina as soon as I got home today. Mr. Winters gave me some very useful information. It seems that Carmello had a new will drawn up, one that was never signed. Carmello was to sign it in front of Mr. Winters the afternoon that he died and Carmello never showed up."

"That's an interesting turn of events. Did he tell you what was in the new will?" Elsa-May asked.

"He was leaving everything to Sabrina. Every single thing he owned, all to Sabrina," Silvie said.

All eyes turned to Sabrina.

"See?" Sabrina said looking self-satisfied. "You all think that he was using me and I was a stupid little fool, just one of his other women, but I wasn't."

"*Nee,* we don't think that at all, Sabrina. We want to help you, dear," Ettie said.

Sabrina smiled at Ettie, which was the first time Silvie had seen a smile on her face in days.

"*Denke,* Ettie," Sabrina said.

"And then he was killed," Elsa-May said, obviously talking about the recent will, quite oblivious to the little exchange that Sabrina and Ettie had just had.

"*Jah,*" Silvie continued, "He also told me that Carmello had an extremely disgruntled client who was looking to sue him."

"Tell us more," Maureen said.

"Mr. Winters found out from another lawyer, that a client of Carmello's came to ask him whether a property was a good investment. Carmello told him it wasn't worthwhile to go ahead with and then Carmello bought it with one of his companies."

"Unprofessional, wicked and unethical," Elsa-May said. "And because he bought it in the company name, that means he was somewhat personally protected from litigation. But, technically, what he did was most likely not a crime anyway, just wicked and unprofessional."

"That makes the former client a suspect then," Maureen said.

Ettie made a noise from the back of her throat. "Now, our

suspect list: everyone named in the old will, including the wife; plus the housekeeper, and now the disgruntled client."

"That's right," Elsa-May said as she scribbled notes on her yellow pad.

"Wasn't Detective Crowley coming here tonight?" Silvie asked.

Like clockwork, Detective Crowley knocked on the door. For the next fifteen minutes, Silvie and Maureen briefed the detective about everything that they had learned.

"Maureen, I wouldn't say that was a good idea what you did. Showing up at the Liante house like that. Things like that need to be left to a trained professional."

Maureen jutted out her jaw. "I found some things out."

The detective frowned at Maureen and his cheeks went red. "You could have put yourself in danger. Please, don't do it again; leave it to us."

Maureen smiled through tight lips. Silvie knew that Maureen would do something like that again, as would they all if the need arose.

"What did you find out from Mrs. Liante, Detective?" Emma asked.

"She gets out tomorrow if the doctor gives her the all clear. She is going to increase the security on her house, by putting in an alarm system and security cameras."

"Did you go to the house?" Maureen asked.

"I stopped in on the housekeeper and asked to look around the house and she refused. She said that if I wanted to come in or look around that I'd need a warrant."

Maureen giggled. "Funny that she let me have a look around and I'm not a trained professional."

The detective grimaced at Maureen's words. "Did you find out whether Mr. and Mrs. Liante had separate bedrooms?" he asked.

Maureen did the best she could to stifle her amusement. "No, I didn't see that they did, but it was possible I suppose. There were a lot of bedrooms and I didn't look in closets or bathroom cabinets."

Silvie added, "According to the lawyer they were separated. Well, living separately, not living as man and wife."

"That's interesting," Detective Crowley said.

Silvie fiddled with the long strings of her prayer *kapp*. "Yes, and even more interesting that the two years were nearly up. Their divorce would have been a formality and it would have made it a lot harder for Mrs. Liante to formally object to it."

"It's a little odd that he changed lawyers quickly at the end like that. I'll talk to his old one again tomorrow and also Mr. Winters," Detective Crowley said.

CHAPTER TEN

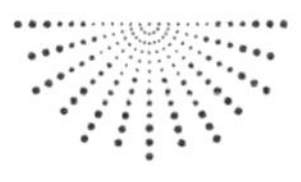

For we must all appear before the judgment seat of Christ; that every one may receive the things done in his body, according to that he hath done, whether it be good or bad.
2 Corinthians 5:10

The last thing that Sabrina ever thought she would be doing was going to the bishop's house to confess her sin. She regretted what she had done, which was to have an affair with a married man, even if he was officially separated. Sabrina would have preferred if Carmello had moved out of the house all together, but he felt he was entitled to stay because he had owned the house before he married Stephanie.

Sabrina shrugged all thoughts of Carmello off and tried to concentrate on *Gott* and the bishop. She knew she needed to get right with *Gott.* The fact that Carmello was separated and the fact that she was in love with him would make no difference to the bishop. Sabrina considered that she had no choice but to go through with the shame and the humiliation of speaking to the bishop.

If Carmello had not died, Sabrina would have most likely left the Amish to be with him. Now, Sabrina had no good reason to leave the Amish. Now that she stood in front of the bishop's front door about to knock on it, the impact of what she'd done hit her in the stomach. She pressed both hands to her tummy. *Don't be sick, don't be sick,* she told herself.

When Sabrina was with Carmello everything seemed good and right. Now that he was gone and she had to tell someone about him and their relationship, it all seemed dirty and sordid. Tears filled Sabrina's eyes as she lifted her hand and knocked on the door. No one would ever know what they had truly had.

The bishop was expecting her. "Come in, Sabrina."

Once they sat down the bishop said, "Would you feel more comfortable speaking to your own bishop back in Ohio?"

"*Nee,* I'm thinking of staying on here, with Silvie."

The bishop nodded. "What have you come to see me about?"

Sabrina liked the bishop from the time of her first gathering that she went to with Silvie. He was an elderly man, but he still had dark hair and a dark *baard.* His eyes were dark brown and filled with kindness and gentleness. Sabrina was comfortable speaking with him. While Sabrina spoke of her ordeal the bishop nodded and seemed sympathetic.

After the bishop heard the whole story, he asked, "Are you truly sorry?"

"*Jah,* I am. I'm truly sorry. I was blinded by love and *Gott* punished me by taking him away."

"I can't tell you whether what you say is right or wrong. Sometimes I don't know how the mind of our *Gott* works. Maybe He did take Carmello away from you and maybe He didn't. The important thing is that you know what you've done wrong and you confess it to Him. Shore up your weaknesses."

"I will. What punishment will I have?" Sabrina was sure that the kindly and sympathetic bishop would give her no punishment. Maybe he would say that she'd already been through enough hurt and pain.

"You will have to confess to the community what you've done."

Sabrina drew in a sharp breath. She would rather be shunned than speak about what she'd done. "I have to do that? I would be embarrassed."

"Everything that is done in secret shall be made known, the Scripture says. There is nothing secret with *Gott*."

Sabrina made a face. The bishop was speaking from Scripture, a Scripture that Sabrina had not heard of. "Do I have to do it?"

"If you want to stay in the community, you must do it. The community is all one. When one suffers we all suffer."

Sabrina nodded. "I will, then, and then I'd like to be baptized." Sabrina wondered if she should go back to Ohio to be baptized. Maybe if she went back there no one would ever find out what she'd done, but then she figured the bishop would most likely write a letter to the bishop in Ohio if she suddenly disappeared. No, she should be baptized and live life as she was supposed to live.

"This Sunday you'll stand before the gathering and speak to

the congregation," the bishop said as he scratched his dark *baard.* "Then I'll give you dates for the next instructions."

Sabrina nodded once more. Her good name would be ruined, but she would have to stop being bothered at what people thought of her and start thinking about her relationship with *Gott.* She didn't much care about being able to find a husband because Carmello was the only man she could ever see herself with. The widows didn't miss having husbands; they had good lives; she could be like one of them.

~

THE NEXT SUNDAY came all too quickly for Sabrina. She stood before the community and confessed what she had done. It wasn't so bad because she knew that soon, she would be baptized. No one could judge her.

At the end of the meeting, she said to her sister, "*Ach,* Silvie. I feel different. I feel clean."

Silvie smiled. "You're about to be born anew."

Sabrina rubbed her face. "Let's go home."

"Sabrina." The bishop approached Sabrina and took her aside to have a few words. Then she came back to Silvie.

"Can we go now?" Sabrina asked.

On the way home, Sabrina said, "I'm sorry for being so horrible. It's just that everything seems so hard for me. Everything goes your way all the time. I wish I could be more like you."

Silvie's mouth fell open. "I don't see that things go right for me any more than they do for you. It's just the way you look at things. If you look for good things then that's what you'll see; if you look for bad things then you'll only see the bad."

"I suppose so. I can't wait to get home and be by myself for a while."

~

It was around the middle of the day that Sabrina and Silvie arrived home. Sabrina had finished her bath and Silvie had tended to the horse and made the midday meal. They were just about to sit down to eat when there was a loud banging on their door.

On her way to the front door, Silvie noticed through the window that a taxi was driving away. She opened her front door to see her mother standing on the doorstep with suitcase in hand. "*Mamm*! What are you doing here?"

"What would you think I'm doing here?" She pushed her way passed Silvie and into the house.

Sabrina came out of the kitchen. "*Mamm*!"

Their mother dumped her small suitcase on the ground. "Well, I've heard what you've been up to, Sabrina, and I'm absolutely ashamed of you." Her eyes glistened as they fixed upon Sabrina. "Deeply ashamed. You've ruined our *familye's gut* name. No one in our *familye* has ever done anything like this and now we're going to be talked about because of you." She turned to Silvie. "I would've expected something like this of you." She looked back to Sabrina, "But not you, Sabrina."

"*Mamm,* I'm going to be baptized and officially join our community," Sabrina said.

Their mother collapsed into the couch. "What does that matter now? Our name is ruined. How could you?"

Silvie sat next to her mother. "*Mamm,* don't you think it's a *gut* thing that Sabrina is taking the instructions and will be baptized? She's confessed to the gathering and everything."

Their mother opened her mouth and her bottom lip quivered. "She's what? That means that everyone knows. My life will never be the same." She sobbed into her apron.

Silvie and Sabrina looked at each other, helpless to know what to do.

Silvie said, "Does it really matter what other people think?"

"Of course it matters; a *gut* name is everything. People will think that *dat* and I have been bad parents and have set a bad example. The Scripture says that a good name is more prized than great riches."

"How did you find about it so quickly?" Silvie asked.

"I heard from someone what Sabrina had done, but I didn't know she had confessed it to the congregation."

"That's *gut* though, isn't it? That's what the bishop asked her to do," Silvie said.

Through sobs she said, "Wait 'til I tell your *dat.* It would be better if she hadn't done that terrible thing to begin with, then she wouldn't have brought shame and disgrace on the *familye. Dat* and I have done all we can to bring you *kinner* up proper." Her mother cried bitterly into her apron then brought her head up again. "And then this happens."

Sabrina crouched down beside her. "Sorry, *mamm.*"

"Too late for sorries."

"How long are you staying, *mamm?*" Sabrina asked.

"I'm taking you back with me, Sabrina. We leave the day after tomorrow."

"*Nee*, I'm not going. I'm staying here with Silvie. I've got it all worked out. I'm going to get a job here and live with Silvie."

Their mother glared at Silvie. "How could you have let this happen?"

"How could I stop it? I knew nothing of it." Silvie wrung her hands.

"You should have kept a better watch on your *schweschder*. I thought I didn't have to worry about her being away from home because she was with you. Now I know that it was the worst thing ever."

"I'll go and make up the bed for you." Silvie left her *mudder* downstairs while she tended to the spare bedroom upstairs.

After a few moments, Sabrina burst into the spare bedroom. "I fixed *mamm* a cup of tea; that should keep her quiet for a while. Silvie, how did *mamm* find out so soon? I thought it would've taken at least a week for word to get to her."

"They've got a phone now, haven't they?" Silvie asked.

"Yeah, *mamm* and *dat* got a phone installed in the barn before I left."

"Someone's called them I'd say. I have no idea who. Maybe the bishop's *schweschder*. She's a bit of a gossip and a meddler." Silvie looked up from making the bed. "Don't worry about it. We'll most likely never find out who told her. At least now you can get her scolding out of the way. You'd have to face it sooner or later."

"I guess so," Sabrina said.

"You'd better go back down and speak to her or she'll think we're up here talking about her."

Sabrina giggled. "We are. Okay, I'll go down and talk to her. We don't want to upset her anymore than we have to."

"*Gut.* How long do you think she'll stay?" Silvie asked.

"I think she'll try and make me go back with her. She'll stay until she sees it's useless."

Silvie's shoulders drooped downward. "That might be a while then."

Sabrina slowly walked the stairs back down to her unhappy *mudder.*

Silvie unfolded the spare quilt that she used in the guest room, shook it out and let it fall softly over the bed. Once she was satisfied that her *mudder* would be happy with the room, she sat on the bed wishing she did not have to go downstairs. It was bad enough her *schweschder* staying with her, but it was her worst nightmare that her *mudder* had come to stay.

She had never been close with her mother as her friends were close to theirs. Silvie's mother always found things wrong with her; nothing Silvie did was ever right. In her eyes, the single thing that Silvie ever did correctly was to marry John. John had been her choice and Silvie had gone along with her mother's wishes. Silvie was happy enough to marry John; she had never found another man that she had liked more and she was getting older. She knew that the older she got, the less choice she would have, in regard to choosing a husband. Her mother urged her to accept John's offer to marry rather than be left 'on the shelf.'

A storm of angry words coming from her *mudder* and her *schweschder* forced Silvie off the bed. She took a long, slow, deep breath and then made her way downstairs.

When she reached the two of them, she saw that her *mudder*

had a bunch of Bailey's letters in her hand. Silvie froze in horror.

Sabrina looked over to Silvie. "I tried to stop her. I came down here and she was reading your letters."

Silvie put her hand to her throat and raced toward her *mudder*. "*Mamm,* those letters are mine and they're private."

Her mother leaped to her feet and put the letters behind her back. "He's an *Englischer.* You've been speaking of love to an *Englischer*. No wonder Sabrina got herself into trouble. I knew you'd be behind this somewhere. It's your fault that Sabrina got involved with that terrible man; I told *dat* that it would be all your fault."

Silvie grabbed the letters out of her *mudder's* hands.

Sabrina said, "It's nothing to do with Silvie. She didn't even know that I was seeing him. She's been nothing but *gut* to me."

"*Mudder,* you are welcome to stay the night, but tomorrow first thing, I am putting you in a taxi and you are going back home on the Greyhound bus."

Her mother gasped. "Your *mudder* is not welcome in your home? I've never heard such a thing. My bus tickets are for the day after tomorrow."

"Well, I'm sure they can be changed." Silvie left her *mudder* and *schweschder* staring at her open-mouthed as she stomped into the kitchen. Silvie had never spoken angrily to either of them.

Sabrina ran after her. "Are you alright, Silvie? I couldn't stop her reading the letters. She found them in the writing bureau while we were speaking upstairs."

"I know it's not your fault. I'm just glad she's going tomorrow," Silvie said.

"You don't mind if I stay on, do you?" Sabrina asked.

"*Nee,* not at all. You can stay." Silvie was genuine in her response to Sabrina. She would rather live alone, but if it helped Sabrina start a new life then she was more than happy to help her.

"*Denke*. What a day it's been. I get baptized and *mamm* comes here on the very same day. She must have missed her own gathering to come here," Sabrina said while Silvie served the food for the midday meal.

CHAPTER ELEVEN

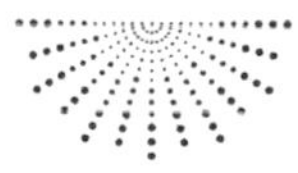

Ask, and it shall be given you; seek, and ye shall find;knock, and it shall be opened unto you:
For every one that asketh receiveth; and he that seeketh findeth; and to him that knocketh it shall be opened.
Matthew 7:7-8

Amidst her mother's protests Silvie deposited her *mudder* safely in a taxi the next morning and went to visit Emma on the way home. She hoped Emma would be home and not off on one of her visits to town. Silvie breathed a sigh of relief to see Emma out in front of her *haus* sweeping the porch.

Emma looked up and waved at Silvie. She left the broom leaning against the side of the house and went to meet her. "Hello, Silvie. It was lovely to see Sabrina baptized yesterday."

"That's not all that happened yesterday." Silvie secured her horse to the side fence rail.

"Come inside and tell me," Emma said.

Silvie followed Emma into the house.

"Now tell me what else happened. Mrs. Liante didn't come back again, did she?" Emma asked once they were both seated comfortably in the living room.

"*Nee,* it was my *mudder.* She turned up on the doorstep, didn't care that Sabrina is going to be baptized, and she chastised her for seeing a married man."

"She shouldn't have done it, but under these circumstances Sabrina must feel awful."

"That's not all. *Mamm* found and read the letters that Bailey wrote to me. She started to say horrid things to me. I'm sure she thinks what Sabrina did was my fault."

Emma shook her head. "*Nee,* she wouldn't think that."

"*Jah,* she even said so. She said that she told my *dat* that it would be all my fault somehow. Anyway, I've just come from putting her in a taxi to take her to the bus station."

Emma giggled. "That was a quick visit."

"Too long for me. Anyway, the reason I've stopped by is because I'd like you to come with me to see Detective Crowley. He said that he'd go and see the lawyer who drew up the new will, Mr. Winters, and also the other lawyer, the one who did the old will. I'm anxious to know what he's found out."

"*Jah,* I'll come with you."

Silvie knew that Emma would be reluctant to go and see Crowley as she was always saying to Elsa-May that he made her feel uneasy; she was glad when Emma agreed to go with her.

"*Gut, denke.* Ride with me and I'll bring you back home,"

Silvie said.

Silvie was grateful to have a friend like Emma. She could have asked Maureen, but Maureen was working. Emma did not have to work because she lived on the money she received from leasing out her farm to Bob Pluver.

"I'll make us a pot of tea before we go?" Emma asked.

A wave of relaxation came over Silvie. "I'd love a cup."

"Come with me to the kitchen."

While Silvie sat at Emma's long kitchen table, she wondered if she would ever plan another wedding as Emma was. "Are you excited about your wedding, Emma?"

Emma had already put the kettle on the stove and now she was fixing the tealeaves. "I think I am getting a little excited. It's a new beginning. Wil decided not to build us a *haus*. He's been looking for one that we can buy and re-build to suit us."

"It'd be nice to have a man around all the time, one you can rely on."

"It can't be easy for you and Bailey, especially since you don't know for sure whether he will join the community," Emma said.

"It is hard, but there's no one in the community for me, so it's not as if I'm passing other *menner* up while I'm waiting for him." Silvie giggled.

"I have you in my prayers."

"*Denke,* Emma. You and Wil are always in mine too."

Emma smiled. "Everything will work out for you, just you wait and see."

Silvie slouched and her shoulders drooped. "Things haven't been easy lately with Sabrina and her problems. I mean, she's not the easiest person to be around without the entire recent goings on. Then with *mamm* coming, I felt that I would explode. Have you ever felt like that?"

Emma sat down next to Silvie and placed the teacups on the table. "I didn't ask; I just gave you chamomile. It's calming on your nerves."

"*Denke*."

"To answer your question, *jah*, I've often felt like that. Sometimes when one bad thing happens it seems to lead to another then another. Sometimes there seems no end in sight." Emma took a sip of tea.

"How do you cope with problems, Emma? You always seem so serene and at peace."

Emma gave a laugh. "I think about the tide. When I'm going through tough times, I tell myself that the tide is out. But you know what? The tide always comes back in. The further out it has been, the further it has to come back in."

"Like the tide of the seashore?" Silvie asked.

"*Jah*, the tide of the seashore. Tough times never last; you just have to wait for them to stop and then the good times will come back to you."

"*Denke*, Emma. I'll look at things that way. My tide is way out at the moment; I'll hope for the change."

"Cookies?" Emma asked.

"Thought you'd never ask."

Emma brought a plate of cookies out of the icebox and placed it on the table.

Two cookies each, a cup of tea and a buggy ride into town later, they were in Detective Crowley's office.

"Morning ladies, have a seat. I guess you ladies are here for an update?" Once both ladies agreed that was why they were there, the detective continued, "I saw Mr. Winters early this morning and I saw Mr. Piper, Carmello's original lawyer, on Friday. Mr. Piper had no knowledge of a new will and had no idea why he chose a different lawyer to draw the will up and he appeared offended. Mr. Winters didn't have much information for me; he did confirm all that he had already told you, Silvie."

Both ladies looked at each other. "Are there any updates on anything?" Silvie asked.

"Mrs. Liante is out of the hospital and the funeral for her husband is on Wednesday. That's the only update I have so far. Except that the business partner turned up on Friday afternoon. He was called out of town on the very day that Carmello died. Claims that it was last minute and that he let Carmello know, mid-morning. Carmello was to pass it on to the rest of the staff that he'd be gone for a time, but he didn't have a chance, did he?"

"Why was he out of town?" Emma asked.

"Claims his father was sick in a hospital in Cleveland. We're looking into his story now."

"Sabrina said they fought quite a bit. Did you know that?" Silvie asked.

The detective scratched the side of his head with a pencil. "Yes, I heard that when I was at Elsa-May and Ettie's place. According to him, they didn't have any major fights or arguments, just very minor disagreements. He wasn't aware of the client whom Carmello essentially cheated out of that property. He knew nothing about the purchase and he was not involved in the company that purchased it."

"You don't think that he's a possible suspect in Carmello's death?" Emma asked.

"We'll have to wait until we check out his story about his father being in the hospital. I've got people looking into it. I'll know later today."

"Is there anything at all that we can do to help?" Silvie asked.

The detective leaned back in his swivel chair and crossed his arms. "You ladies are not to go around poking your noses in. I don't mind hearing what gossip you might have overheard, but I do not want you sticking your noses where they don't belong." He looked deliberately and slowly from one lady to the other. "Stick to baking cookies. I'm going to the funeral on Wednesday. That's generally a good place to get some leads and find out what's really going on."

"Mrs. Liante doesn't mind you going?" Emma asked.

"She doesn't know. I'll just show up and observe the goings on. Generally in a murder case, people like to surmise. I'll be around to hear their theories and assumptions over who murdered him. Let Elsa-May know that I'll be around to visit you ladies at her place at seven sharp, Wednesday."

"Wednesday evening? It's only Monday. Is there some little, tiny thing that we can do in the mean time? " Silvie asked.

Emma nodded in agreement and said, "We'll feel useless if we sit around and wait for Wednesday night."

The detective was silent for a while. "No, can't think of one thing that either of you ladies can do. Leave it to the professionals. If you want to try and figure things out take a look at this." The detective handed them a sheet of paper that had been lying to one side of his desk. "These are Carmello's movements on the last day of his life. There has to be a clue in there somewhere; he had to have ingested the poison that day." The detective rose to his feet. "Let me know if you find anything out."

CHAPTER TWELVE

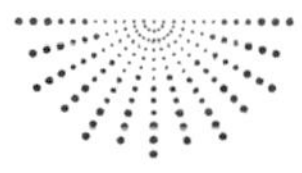

By faith Abraham, when he was called to go out into a place which he should after receive for an inheritance, obeyed; and he went out, not knowing whither he went.
Hebrews 11:8

Silvie and Emma left the detective's office and went straight to Elsa-May and Ettie's *haus* to tell them to expect the detective on Wednesday night. Wednesday night was often the night that the widows got together anyway.

"I'm stumped," Elsa-May said. "I have no idea who might have killed him. I think there might be a clue in his changing the will; that was a fairly big move. We should look at finding out who knew about the change."

Ettie moved to the edge of her chair. "Why did he change lawyers too?"

"I nearly forgot," Silvie said. "The detective gave us this." She pulled out the piece of paper and handed it to Elsa-May. "Everything he did on that last day is listed. Crowley must have got the information from Carmello's secretary or his work diary."

Elsa-May's eyes scanned the piece of paper. "He started at nine, made an appointment with Mr. Winter, then he made two other phone calls. After he went to Mr. Winters office, he came back and had back-to-back appointments until 5 p.m."

Ettie said, "Now Silvie, I think you should have Sabrina go talk to Miss Scotsdale and Miss Tobrill. See what she can find out. She would have a common bond with them since it seems they all had a close relationship with Mr. Liante."

"Do you think she should?" Silvie asked. "She's very emotional at the moment."

Elsa-May's face lit up. "You could do it then, Silvie. Pretend to be Sabrina, no one will know. Neither of these women would have met Sabrina. Besides, you're closer to Carmello's age. I heard he was in his late thirties."

Silvie lowered her head. What other things did she have to endure? Normally, she wouldn't have minded, but all this was a little too close to home.

Ettie said, "I've got a good idea, Silvie. I think you should go, posing as Sabrina."

Elsa-May's mouth dropped open. "I just said that."

Ettie frowned and stared at her. "When?"

"Just then." Elsa-May looked around at everyone. "Didn't I? Everyone heard me. What are you playing at, Ettie?"

"I wasn't listening to you. I was thinking about what I was going to say next."

Elsa-May shook her head. "See what I have to put up with? It wonders me that I'm—"

Silvie interupted, "All right, I'll do it." She agreed for two reasons. She couldn't listen to any more back and forth, and Sabrina was in no mental state to pull off something like that.

Ettie walked slowly over to the top drawer of the dresser and pulled out a piece of paper. "These are the two girls' addresses."

Silvie took the paper from Ettie; she didn't bother to ask how she got the addresses. She knew that Ettie was a whiz at finding things out. She most likely made a trip to the voter registration office and talked them into giving her the information.

"Visit one tonight and one tomorrow. That way you can spread it out a little," Elsa-May suggested.

"You can even wear your own clothing this time. Since Sabrina is Amish and if they have heard of her, it won't be odd," Ettie added, with a wide smile crinkling the lines in her cheeks even further.

"I don't have to work today, but I do have to work tomorrow afternoon. I guess Elsa-May is right. It makes sense if I go visit one of them tonight and the other in the morning," Silvie said.

"That's the way," Elsa-May said.

Silvie rose to her feet. "I'd better get Emma home and get back home myself and see what Sabrina is up to."

ON THE WAY to Emma's house, Silvie said to Emma, "You were very quiet back there."

"I was feeling a little tense for you having to go and see those two women, the two previous girlfriends of Carmello, pretending to be Sabrina."

Silvie shrugged her shoulders. "I'll try not to think about it. I'll just do it."

"What if they're angry?" Emma asked.

"They shouldn't be angry. They got money in the will so I'd think they'd be pretty happy about that. They wouldn't know that he was close to signing a new will leaving it all to Sabrina. Or, do you think that they might still be in love with Carmello and think that Sabrina came between them?"

Emma nibbled on the end of a fingernail. "I don't know, could be."

Silvie pressed her lips tightly together and drew a deep breath inwards. "I'll have to go and see, won't I?"

Once Silvie told Sabrina that she was going to speak to Miss Scotsdale and Miss Tobrill, and why, Sabrina was grateful. Miss Scotsdale's apartment was too far away to travel by buggy so Silvie would have to take a taxi. Silvie pulled the jam jar down from the very top shelf and counted out her money. Taxis were expensive and things had been a little tight with her uncertain hours at the bakery and the extra mouth to feed.

"Here you are, Silvie."

Silvie looked up to see that Sabrina had a fist full of notes in her outstretched hand.

"Where did you get that money from?"

"I saved it from raising chickens back home. Take it."

Silvie looked at the money she had counted out and it was

enough to get to where she was going in a taxi, but may not have been enough for her to get back home. She looked back at Sabrina. "Are you sure?"

"Of course I am. You're doing it for me after all."

Silvie took the money. "*Denke,* Sabrina. I didn't know that you raised chickens. You could do that here. We could build a pen out back. We've got just enough room, if we transplant the vegetables closer to the fence."

"*Jah*, I'd like that, and I'll get a job as well."

A horn blew from outside their *haus*. It was the taxi that Ettie had booked and it was right on time.

"Pray for me, Sabrina. I'm nervous."

"I will."

While the taxi drove towards Miss Scotsdale's house, Silvie played over in her mind how she thought things would happen when she got there.

She would take a deep breath, lift up her heavy hand and knock on the door of Miss Scotsdale's apartment.

"Hello?" The woman would say, as she looked Silvie up and down wondering who she was.

Silvie would respond with, "Are you Miss Scotsdale?"

"Yes."

"You don't know me, but I'm Sabrina Tildy." Silvie would burst into fake tears right on cue.

"What's the matter?" Miss Scotsdale would most likely ask.

Silvie would look at her through the tears in her eyes. "Have you heard about Carmello?"

"Yes, did you know him too?"

"I was his girlfriend." Silvie would crank her crying up a notch to gain the woman's sympathy.

"Oh dear. Don't cry, come inside."

Silvie would walk into the apartment.

"Please sit down."

Silvie would sit and then say, "I'm sorry to come here unexpectedly like this, it's just that Carmello used to speak of you and I feel like I know you."

The woman would smile, flattered that Carmello would still speak of her – think of her. "He spoke of me?"

Silvie would nod and at that point Miss Scotsdale would rise from her seat and fetch Silvie some tissues.

"Thank you," Silvie would say, and then ask, "Were you Carmello's girlfriend too? I know you worked for him."

Then Miss Scotsdale would proceed to tell her all about her relationship with Carmello and hopefully other information that Silvie could use so the widows and Detective Crowley might be able to figure out who murdered Carmello Liante.

Fifteen minutes later, Silvie stood outside Miss Scotsdale's door for real. She knocked on the door, just as she had imagined. The door opened and instead of Miss Scotsdale, a young man stood there, in front of her.

"Can I help you?" he asked, as he looked Silvie up and down just as she had imagined that Miss Scotsdale would.

"Is Miss Scotsdale home?"

"She's in New Zealand meeting Ryan's parents. They decided to get married just last week. Are you a friend of Carmen's?"

"No, I don't really know her. Ryan's her boyfriend?"

The man nodded. "Yes." He reached out his hand. "I'm Chad, Carmen's brother."

Silvie shook his hand and felt relaxed by his kind smile.

"What do you want with her? Was she thinking of running away to join the Amish at some stage?" Before Silvie could answer, he added, "She's always doing something crazy."

"I'm here to tell her some distressing news. I'm not sure if she's heard, but her old boss was murdered."

"Liante?"

Silvie nodded.

The man stepped back into the apartment. "Come in."

All of a sudden Silvie felt lightheaded. Under no other circumstances would she enter an apartment with an unknown *Englischer,* but if she didn't what chance would she have of finding out any other information?

Just as she had imagined, Silvie was asked to have a seat, but this time there were no tears in her eyes and no Miss Scotsdale.

"What is your interest in my sister and Mr. Liante?"

Silvie remembered she was still masquerading as her sister, Sabrina. "I was in a relationship with Mr. Liante before he was murdered. Do you know that he left a portion of his wealth to your sister?"

"Bad news, I'm sorry to hear it. Carmen did hear of his death. He told her that he would leave her something, but she didn't know whether to believe it or not. She certainly wasn't relying on it or anything." He leaned back in the chair and placed his right ankle across his left knee. "They had a relationship back when she was working for him. The wife found out and made him fire her. She sued him for sexual harassment out of revenge for being dumped and then he talked her into dropping the suit."

"Did you ever meet him?" Silvie asked out of interest.

"I met him briefly once. He seemed a decent sort of character, except for the fact that he was married while he was having a relationship with Carmen. It was her life; who was I to tell her what to do?"

Silvie tried to think of more questions.

"Who killed him?" he asked.

Silvie shrugged her shoulders. "They don't know yet.

"Carmen should be back in a week. Shall I have her call you?"

"Do you know of anyone who wished Carmello harm? Did your sister ever mention anything?"

Chad was silent for a while, then shook his head. "It's a wonder I haven't had a visit from the cops."

"I think you will very shortly," Silvie said. "But please, don't mention to them that I was here. They think I'm meddling and they'll get angry with me again. I'm just trying to help them, but they don't see it that way."

Silvie stood up and Chad stood up as well.

Chad said, "I won't say anything. Anyway, Carmen's the one they would want to speak with. I know nothing."

Silvie managed a smile. "You've been very helpful. Could you do one more thing for me?"

"What's that?"

"Call me a taxi?"

On the way home, Silvie thought over everything that Chad had said. He really did not give her any new information except that Carmen sued Carmello out of revenge and that Mrs. Liante had found out about their affair. Silvie closed her eyes and dozed for the rest of the drive home.

CHAPTER THIRTEEN

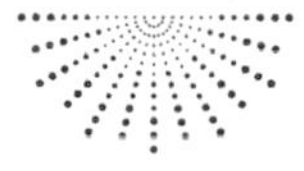

But without faith it is impossible to please him: for he that cometh to God must believe that he is,
and that he is a rewarder of them that diligently seek him.
Hebrews 11:6

Silvie had one more thing to do and that was to find out what she could from Miss Tobrill, the other ex-girlfriend of Carmello who was named in the will. Before she started work the next day, she knocked on Miss Tobrill's door. There was no answer.

Silvie used her time to go back to see Mr. Winters. As soon as she got there, the secretary showed her into his office. He seemed pleased to see her as she sat down in front of him.

"Mr. Winters, is there anyone at all who could have known about the new will?"

Mr. Winters shook his head. “Not even my secretary knew what was in it. She wouldn’t have known until after it was signed and it was ready for filing. The reason for that was that it was such a simple will with only one beneficiary. I just filled out his details on a pro-forma and printed it out ready for him to sign.”

“Couldn’t he have signed it at the same appointment then?”

“I’m a little slow with my typing. He could’ve signed it then and there, but he said he had a busy day. I said I’d stay late for him to come after work. He agreed to meet me here just after 5 p.m.”

“No one else could see it in any way, shape, or form?” Silvie asked.

“I did email it to him, as a formality.”

“Email.” Silvie thought for a while and then said aloud. “I wonder who had access to his email.”

“Maybe his secretary? No, I remember now. He had two email addresses and I sent it to his private email. Every time we have a new client we have them fill out their details on a New Client sheet. I remember that he had two emails, one marked ‘personal’ and one marked ‘work.’”

“Thank you, Mr. Winters. You’ve been a marvelous help.”

All Silvie had to do now was find out who had access to Carmello’s private email. “Oh, one more thing, Mr. Winters. Can you tell me what time exactly that you sent the email?”

“I’ll look it up right now and tell you.” Mr. Winters tilted his computer screen toward him and pressed some buttons. “It was 12:30 p.m. and I put a receipt on it which tells me what time it was opened. It was read at 12:45 p.m.”

A cold shiver ran down Silvie’s spine. What if someone else

read that email and found out that they were not in the new will? "Can you tell me what the email said?"

"I'll print it out for you."

Mr. Winters walked to the printer on the other side of the office and picked up the page as it printed out.

He handed it to Silvie and she read it out. "Attached is a copy of your Last Will and Testament. Sabrina Tildy is named as your sole beneficiary. As agreed, I will see you just after five today for signing." Silvie looked up to Mr. Winters. "Do you mind if I hang on to this?"

"By all means. I hope it helps."

Silvie folded the page in two. "I'm sure it will help."

~

ON WEDNESDAY NIGHT at the next widows' gathering, the ladies sat waiting for Detective Crowley.

Ettie and Elsa-May asked Silvie what she learned from visiting the ex-girlfriends, Miss Scotsdale and Miss Tobrill.

"Both of them weren't home when I went to see them. I talked to Carmen Scotsdale's *bruder* and he said she's getting married soon and was off meeting the future in-laws. He said that Mrs. Liante knew about his sister's relationship with her husband and she denies knowledge of any of his relationships."

"Okay, not a word to Crowley that you went to see them. We'll use that information when we need to. He won't be happy, and if you've no information to give him there's no point us saying anything to him," Elsa-May said.

Silvie agreed and at that point there was a loud knock on the door that could only be Detective Crowley.

The detective dusted off his shoes on the front doormat before he entered the house. He took a seat on a wooden chair and shared his updates on the murder. "The business partner was telling the truth, about his father at least. His father was in a hospital in Cleveland and we have Neville Banks' credit card records showing that he was on route to Cleveland at the time of Carmello's death. I really learned nothing at the funeral; there were surprisingly few people there."

"Could he have poisoned Carmello before he left?" Emma asked.

"The poison is not instantaneous; so it's possible he could have poisoned him."

"Look at this." Elsa-May handed the detective the email Mr. Winters sent Carmello, with the copy of the will attached.

While the detective read the email, Elsa-May said, "Don't you think it's possible that someone found out that they would be left out of the new will?"

"Yes, and if it was Mrs. Liante, she knew she would have a fight on her hands in court to keep the money," Ettie said.

"This is enough to allow me to get a warrant on Mrs. Liante's house."

"Wouldn't the fact that Mr. Liante has been murdered be enough to allow you to search his house?" Silvie asked.

"Normally, depends who you go to, to sign off on the warrant. Judge Bower's usually good for granting warrants, but he's away 'til next month. There's really only Judge Peters and she's a stickler for not invading privacy. This'll be enough to tip her over the edge." Crowley stared at the paper. "I will have every computer removed from the house and I'll have the computer team go right over them. If she did this, then she'd have motive."

"What about the other two women who would've been left out of the will?" Ettie asked.

"Of course, I'll get warrants for their houses as well, but it's more likely that it's Mrs. Liante. Carmello might have had a computer at his home where his personal emails went. Most people are automatically logged into their emails on their personal computers, which would make knowledge of a password unnecessary. The other two women would have only been able to access his emails by password unless he had a personal computer at their place, which is unlikely as he wasn't in a continuing relationship with either of the women." The detective looked at each of the widows. "There's a good chance that whoever opened this email is the same person who killed him."

"They would've needed access to him pretty soon after they read it too, wouldn't they? He sent the email at 12.30 p.m. How long does that poison have to take effect?" Emma asked.

"The poison in the dosage he was given takes three to four hours to take effect. We know that he had back-to-back appointments that afternoon until 5 p.m. The receptionist left at 4.30 p.m. and Carmello was alive when she left."

"Detective, how can we find out what he ate at work? Since he didn't go out, he must have had lunch in his office. Can you go to his office and find out exactly what he ate that day? Have you done that yet?" Elsa-May asked.

"Yes, we've tested everything in the office kitchen and everything in the office fridge. There's no more we can do."

"Was there any take-out ordered, or any take-out that came into the office that day?" Ettie asked.

The detective noted it in his book. "I'll check all the nearby cafes and check the logs of the reception for that day. I'll have the team go back and check for residue in all the wastebaskets in every office of the suite."

"Detective, weren't all the wastebaskets in the office checked for poison when the forensic team first came in, the day they found him?" Elsa-May asked.

The detective answered, "Only the ones in his personal office and in the kitchen."

Elsa-May raised her eyebrows and Silvie knew that Elsa-May was thinking that all wastebaskets should have been searched at the beginning of the investigation and not days later.

~

THE NEXT DAY, Detective Crowley made a surprise visit to Silvie's house. Silvie and Sabrina sat in front of him.

"We have a development in the case. There was a lunch order that came in for Carmello's business partner, Neville Banks. The secretary remembers that since Neville wasn't in, Carmello ate his lunch. He was seen in Neville's office. Traces of Aconitine were found in Neville's office. Which leads me to believe that someone was trying to kill Neville Banks. Carmello was nothing more than an innocent bystander."

"That means that Neville would be in danger." Silvie said.

"That's right, you would have no way of knowing." Detective Crowley lowered his head. "I'm afraid last night Mr. Banks had a car accident. His brake lines were cut; he plowed into a tree after he lost control of his vehicle."

Sabrina hid her face and sobbed, "Why, why?"

"We have a suspect in custody and we found Aconitine in his car. The man we have in custody is a known hit-man."

The two women looked at him blankly until he explained, "That means he is paid to kill people."

Both women gasped.

"I never knew of such a thing," Silvie said.

"I'm afraid there are people like that out there," Detective Crowley said.

"So it wasn't Mrs. Liante or any of the other women?"

Detective Crowley shook his head. "Mr. Liante was in the wrong place at the wrong time."

"Why would someone want to have Mr. Banks dead?" Silvie asked.

"Gambling. He was addicted to gambling and borrowed heavily to cover his debts. He had his house heavily mortgaged and on top of that a $300,000 personal loan, which he was months behind in. It's evident that he also borrowed money from some very dangerous people."

"I'll tell the rest of the ladies tonight what you've found out."

~

SILVIE CALLED AN EMERGENCY WIDOWS' meeting that night so she could tell everyone at the same time what she'd learned from the detective. Then they could put the matter to rest.

Before anyone said anything, Maureen began by saying, "I am positive that Mrs. Liante did it. I saw Mrs. Liante's housekeeper, Maud, driving a very expensive looking car. I checked with the motor vehicle department and it's registered in Maud's own name. Mrs. Liante is not generous with money, that's evident in her money struggles with Mr. Liante. It seems to me that Mrs. Liante paid her for her silence. Mrs. Liante probably faked that knife attack and there was no attack on her at all."

Elsa-May said, "*Jah,* Maureen. I never believed that there was any real knife attack. I think Mrs. Liante had the housekeeper cut her here and there, to make it look as though she had been attacked. Maybe she got the housekeeper to deliver a poisoned lunch to the office and that's why she's been paid off with that car. I agree with Maureen, Mrs. Liante killed her husband."

"That seems right. If someone wanted to kill her with a knife, then they'd just do it. She'd be too small from what I've been told of her to fend off a knife wielding assailant," Ettie said.

Silvie was glad that she made Sabrina stay at home because all this talk might have upset her. She held up both hands. "Stop everyone. I called this meeting because Crowley found out who killed Carmello."

A hush fell over the room.

"No one wanted to kill him at all…" Silvie said.

"That's not true, we've found plenty of people who wanted him dead," Ettie said.

Silvie shook her head. "*Nee,* just listen to me. Neville Banks was killed last night. He had his brakes in his car cut. Crowley found out that someone had been paid to kill him for unpaid gambling debts. When Neville went to visit his father unexpectedly, he had already ordered his lunch that day. Carmello ate his lunch since Neville wasn't there to eat it. They even found the same poison residue in Neville's wastebasket. He must have eaten the lunch in Neville's office and thrown the wrapper, or the package, in the trash.

Elsa-May's mouth downturned at the corners. "Carmello wasn't murdered deliberately?"

Silvie shook her head. "They have a suspect in custody and they found the same poison in his car. The same poison that caused Carmello's death."

"Well, that's that then," Emma said. "How's Sabrina coping with the news?"

Silvie fiddled with her apron strings. "She feels no better. Maybe even a little worse that it was all a mistake."

"I'm not satisfied," Maureen said. "Why does the housekeeper have a new car? I don't trust Mrs. Liante one little bit."

"You've never met her though, Maureen," Emma said.

"I've a hunch. I've just a hunch that Mrs. Liante hired someone to kill Neville Banks to cover her tracks after she murdered her husband. Maybe it was true that Neville was a gambler and borrowed money, but what if he was just a decoy to throw the cops off finding the real killer? We know she lied about being unaware of her husband's indiscretions." Maureen said.

"You might be on to something, Maureen," said Elsa-May. "Why don't I pass that scenario by Detective Crowley? I'll suggest he goes to Mrs. Liante and pretend that the hit-man whom they have in custody has given her name as the person who hired him."

"*Nee,* that wouldn't be right. It sounds to me that you all want Mrs. Liante to be the murderer. Why don't you just believe that it was Neville Banks that they were after?" Emma asked.

"Because, dear innocent, Emma, if a hired hit-man wants someone killed, they don't deliver a poisoned lunch to someone's office and risk that someone else might eat it. They are not so hit and miss - pardon the pun. They shoot to kill," Elsa-May said.

"You could be right, Elsa-May, you too, Maureen. I didn't even consider it." Silvie pushed her prayer *kapp* up on her head a little.

"I'll call Crowley first thing in the morning and run what we've said by him. Then we'll all meet back here tomorrow night and have Crowley come and tell us what he's found out," Elsa-May said.

"Don't forget to tell him that Maud, the housekeeper, has a brand spanking new, expensive car. She wouldn't be able to afford that on her wage," Maureen said.

Elsa-May nodded.

CHAPTER FOURTEEN

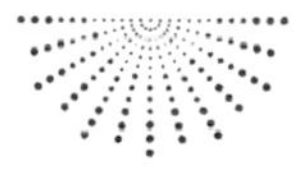

Through faith also Sara herself received strength to conceive seed, and was delivered of a child when she was past age, because she judged him faithful who had promised.
Hebrews 11:11

The very next night Crowley had some news for the ladies when he arrived at Elsa-May and Ettie's house.

"I've quite a lot to tell you ladies. We confiscated all the cell phones and all the computers at the residences of Mrs. Liante, Miss Scotsdale and Miss Tobrill."

"And what did you find out, Detective?" Elsa-May asked.

"As I suspected, Mr. Liante's computer at his residence was automatically logged in and was read from the computer at the house. Mr. Liante was nowhere near his house that day, so the email must have been read by someone at the house."

Silvie gasped. "Did you speak to Mrs. Liante?"

"I called Mrs. Liante into the office and told her that we know that she opened that email and we were able to tell her at what time the email was opened. I also told Mrs. Liante that the man we've got in custody implicated her when he confessed that she hired him to kill Mr. Banks and her husband." The detective chuckled. "It wasn't true of course, we don't have a confession from him yet. She denied it and refused to speak to us any further. We let her leave the station and we had a patrol car standing by ready to bring the housekeeper in before Mrs. Liante had time to communicate with her. We told the housekeeper that Mrs. Liante had confessed. We offered the housekeeper a deal if she testified against Mrs. Liante and she agreed. Now, we have a full statement from the housekeeper."

Everyone was quiet except Elsa-May. "She did it? Mrs. Liante killed him? I knew it, I just knew it."

"You were right about the car. The car was a pay off for her silence." Detective Crowley said.

"Wasn't the lunch labeled for Mr. Banks? How would Mrs. Liante know that Mr. Banks wouldn't be there?" Emma asked.

"It appears Mrs. Liante thought to cover her tracks from the very beginning. We may never find that out, but somehow she found out that Mr. Banks wouldn't be there."

"I'm confused," Emma said to the detective. "Mrs. Liante wasn't trying to kill Neville Banks?"

The detective laughed. "She had to kill Neville in the end to cover her tracks. She knew her husband would eat that meal because she somehow found out that Neville Banks would not be in the office. She knew her husband wouldn't let good food go to waste. In labeling the food for Neville, it made it look as though Neville was the target. The man who cut the brakes to Neville's car was the same man who delivered the lunch full of poison."

Emma nodded.

Detective Crowley continued his explanation. "When we did not make the connection with the meal in the first instance, we started to question Mrs. Liante. She couldn't tell us that we missed the evidence and ruined her little plan so she had to stage that knife attack to cause us to stop looking in her direction. It was only when poor old Banks was killed that we made the connection to the poison in the meal. I guess she thought we'd think that her husband's death was an accident and we very nearly did. Mrs. Liante nearly got away with murder."

"So what was it that gave her away? What was it that led you to believe that she did it?" Emma asked.

"It was the email being opened from the computer in the house when Mr. Liante was nowhere near the house at the time. It was also the fact that the housekeeper was driving an unusually expensive car. Thank you, Maureen for your keen observation." The detective smiled at Maureen.

Maureen smiled back at him and said, "What a wicked woman. She also killed poor Mr. Banks who had nothing to do with anything."

The detective slowly nodded. "Wicked indeed. We're working on getting a statement from the man we're holding, the man who cut the brakes. He'll possibly talk now that we've got the housekeeper's statement."

"Well done, Detective," Ettie said.

"Yes, thank you, Detective. Sabrina will be pleased that justice will be done," Silvie said.

The detective gave a low chuckle. "The quarter that Sabrina's got coming to her will no doubt become a third if Mrs. Liante is convicted."

After Ettie brought the food out, and after the detective ate two pieces of fudge, he got up to leave.

"Detective, why don't you take some fudge home to your wife?"

The detective hung his head and murmured in a low voice, "I'm not married."

"I thought by your age you'd be married," Elsa-May said in her usual candid way.

"In my line of work, it's hard for a woman. I work long hours and don't have much free time. Most women find that difficult."

The widows all stared at him as he tipped his head and walked out the door.

"Imagine, a man of his age not being married," Ettie said. "I might make him a few meals that he can freeze."

"*Jah,* he works long hours. How would he eat without a *fraa* to cook for him?" Maureen asked.

Silvie could not think about Crowley and his stomach; she wanted to go home and be with Sabrina. "I'll go home now and tell Sabrina everything. *Denke* everyone for helping with this."

~

WHEN SILVIE ARRIVED HOME, she sat down with Sabrina and told her everything she'd found out.

"In a way, it makes me feel better that the truth has been told," Sabrina said.

Silvie put her arm around her sister. "I'm sorry that you've been through something so awful at your young age."

"It's my own fault for making bad choices. From now on, I'll not do anything that I could not stand up and tell the congregation of."

Silvie grimaced. "*Jah,* that must have been awful."

"It was, but now I know why the bishop made me do it. Now, I feel clean and can live my life the way that *Gott* would want me to live." Sabrina bounded to her feet. "I forgot to tell you, this arrived today." Sabrina retrieved a letter from the top of the bureau.

Silvie took the letter from her. She knew at once that it was another letter from Bailey. Sabrina walked out of the room while Silvie pulled the letter in toward her heart. Was she at risk of making the same mistake that Sabrina had made? Was *Gott* trying to warn her not to get involved with this *Englischer*? After all, what guarantee did she have that Bailey was ever going to join the community?

She placed the letter on the couch beside her, pulled her knees up under her full dress and hugged them to her chest. She knew she was one step away from falling into something from which there would be no return. Silvie saw what love had done to Sabrina. It had made her lose all sense and control. As Silvie ripped the envelope open, her heart felt just as torn.

Her mood took a turn for the better when she scanned the words of the letter to read:

Just six more months and if I have not closed the case within that time, I will leave my job and come back to you, my dearest Silvie.

And the peace of God, which passeth all understanding, shall keep your hearts and minds through Christ Jesus.
Philippians 4:7

~

AMISH HOUSE OF SECRETS

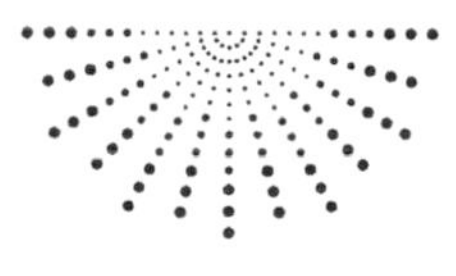

AMISH SECRET WIDOWS' SOCIETY BOOK 5

CHAPTER ONE

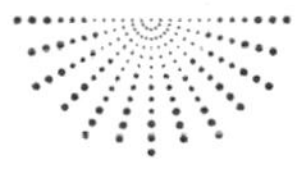

Thy mercy, O Lord, is in the heavens; and thy faithfulness reacheth unto the clouds.
Psalm 36:5

Emma held her head in her hands and wondered if Wil was having another one of his jokes. She looked up to see that he was still smiling at her. It had to be true, she considered, otherwise he surely would have said so by now. "Wil, you can't just go and buy a *haus* without me looking at it too." She stared into his face hoping he'd say that it wasn't the case. Maybe he'd only put some kind of holding deposit on it. They hadn't even had many conversations about buying a *haus.*

His smile quickly turned into a frown. "I thought you'd be pleased. You said that you wanted an old *haus* that we could fix up together." When she made no comment, he continued, "It's just as you said you wanted. It's on the outskirts, on the border of the Amish settlement." Once again, a smile broke out on his handsome face despite Emma's disapproval. "It's got electricity coming into the *haus*, but I can easily have that removed. It does need a lot of work, I'll admit that, but I can fix it in no time flat."

Emma could not contain a heavy sigh as her hands moved from her head to her stomach. She did not want to dampen his enthusiasm, but she was stunned by his impulsiveness. "You were to do the looking and then we were going to buy it together, remember?"

At that moment, Emma thought that maybe they hadn't discussed it as well as they should have, and swiftly added, "Well, that's how I assumed we would do it." That's how Levi, her late husband and she would have done things. Levi would never have bought a *haus* without them both agreeing on it. Wil was different from Levi; Wil's head was in the clouds and he always acted first and thought about things later.

Wil laughed away her anger. He put both hands on her shoulders and looked her in the eyes. "Come and see it before you get angry with me. You'll love it too."

"How did you even get the money to buy it? We haven't spoken about our finances together. Does one of us have to sell?" Emma did not want to sell her farm or her *haus*. Levi had built the *haus* and it was filled with treasured memories, which she was not going to let go of easily. Realistically, Emma knew she might have to sell one day, in order to move on in her new life with Wil.

As Wil was taking his time to answer her question, Emma continued, "You know I live on the lease money that Bob Pluver pays for using my land for his crops. That's the only income I've got." Emma was certain that Wil's adjoining farm, which he also leased out to Bob, was his only source of income as well since he didn't have a regular job.

"We'll figure out the finances later. I've got enough money to cover everything, for now."

It was the 'for now' comment that worried Emma. They were still two months away from being married; she felt that she could not be so bold as to inquire into his personal finances. "I would've thought we might wait to buy a *haus* until after we were married, when we'd talked through and planned our finances together."

He made a dismissive sound from the back of his throat. "Don't worry so much, Emma. It'll be fine; you'll love the *haus*."

Emma raised her eyebrows.

"Have you just baked cookies?" Wil followed his nose to the kitchen leaving Emma standing by herself in her living room.

And that was that. Emma knew that as far as Wil was concerned that was the end of the conversation of purchasing the *haus,* and the end of the conversation of their combined finances.

Dragging her feet, Emma followed Wil into the kitchen. She could not wait to meet the widows tonight to tell them the latest thing that Wil had done. No doubt, they would be as shocked as she.

~

MOSTLY, it was Wednesday nights that the widows gathered in the two elderly *schweschders' haus,* Elsa-May and Ettie. Later that night, everyone was there including the younger widows, Maureen and Silvie.

"How are things going with Sabrina?" Maureen asked Silvie before she bit into a chocolate cookie. Sabrina was Silvie's spoiled younger *schweschder* who had come to live with Silvie from Ohio.

"She's going out a lot now. This time, I make sure I know where she's going. She's got a job at the horse auctions, doing paperwork. She was always *gut* at adding up and the like."

"That should keep her out of trouble," Ettie said.

"For now most likely, not for long," Elsa-May added without looking up from her knitting.

Maureen looked across the room to Emma. "You're quiet tonight, Emma,"

"I'm in shock; that's all." The widows all looked at her. "Well, you remember how I said that Wil's been looking for a *haus* for us?"

The widows nodded.

"He bought one without me even seeing it." Emma looked at them to see what their reaction would be. Maybe she was being too harsh on Wil. The widows were all sensible ladies, and they would know what would be considered rational behavior.

Their mouths fell open. The only one who was not shocked was Silvie.

"You're not happy about it?" Silvie asked.

Emma shook her head. "*Nee,* I'm not happy about it. I'll have to go and live in a *haus* that I had no say in."

"I think it's a lovely thing of Wil to do. You should be pleased that he has taken control like a proper *mann* should," Silvie said with a distinct nod of her head. "I'd be glad if Bailey joined the community and bought a *haus* for me. I wouldn't care that I hadn't seen it."

"I don't mean to seem ungrateful, but we haven't even discussed finances. Where's the money going to come from?" Emma chewed on a fingernail.

Ettie brought her teacup to her lips, took a sip and then said, "Where do you think the money could possibly come from?"

"That's just it; I don't know. One of us might have to sell one of our farms, I guess." Emma could think of no other way to get such a large sum.

"Didn't you ask him about the money side of things?" Maureen asked.

Emma shook her head. "He's so frustrating sometimes. He just dismissed my questions and ate cookies." Emma took a deep breath. "I don't like to talk behind his back…"

"Nonsense," Elsa-May said, "That's what these meetings are for. We all help each other and how can we do that if you keep things to yourself?"

Emma nodded. "It's just that, I don't want to sell my *haus,* the *haus* that Levi built. I mean I would if I had to, but Wil won't even discuss financial matters. It's like he takes no thought for anything and expects things to fall into place with no planning. I get my income from leasing the farm; it's not a great deal, but it's enough to keep me."

Silvie, who was sitting next to Emma, stroked her shoulder. "And you like to plan things ahead?"

"*Jah,* of course. It's a big thing; it's not like buying a spade or a broom."

"Seems as though you two have very different ways of doing things," Ettie said.

"It frustrates me so. I mean, I do love him, but I wish he could be more…" Emma stopped herself just in time. She wished he could be more like Levi.

A hush swept over the room.

Emma looked at each widow in turn. She could see from their faces that they knew what she had been about to say.

The silence was broken by Silvie, "You do love him still, don't you?"

"*Jah,* of course, I love him. I do," Emma said. Maybe she had been so long by herself that she had trouble letting go of things. Why couldn't she be more like dear, kind-hearted and sweet Silvie?

Elsa-May moved uncomfortably in her seat and continued knitting the pale yellow blanket for yet another of her great *grosskinner* which was on the way into the world.

"I mean, the date is set, the bishop has published our wedding and…" Emma's voice trailed away. "…and all that. I've everything done except the dresses and organizing the food."

"I'll help with the dresses, Emma. I can have them done in no time," Maureen said.

"*Denke,* Maureen. I've already made Wil's suit and the suits of his attendants." Emma could feel Ettie's eyes boring into her. She looked up and caught her eye. "What's the matter, Ettie?"

"You're a long time married, Emma. Our other *schweschder,* Virginia, was betrothed to a man and she changed her mind the day before the wedding. Elsa-May and I were teens and the day of the wedding. Elsa-May and I had to stand there, at the front gate, and turn everyone away."

Elsa-May looked up from over her knitting, shook her head

and said to her *schweschder,* "A year later, Virginia married the same man. What's your point, Ettie?"

Ettie glared at Elsa-May and pressed her lips firmly together, tiny little wrinkles appearing deeper around her mouth.

Maureen came to Ettie's rescue. "I think Ettie's trying to make the point that you shouldn't feel obligated, Emma. Just because things have been organized it's no reason to think that you should go through with it if your heart is not in it."

Ettie nodded in agreement with Maureen's explanation "On the other hand," Maureen continued, "A lot of marriages work well when the two hardly know each other to start with and you and Wil genuinely have strong feelings. You just have to iron out a few small differences. I'm sure that's all it is."

Emma felt confronted. She did love Wil. *Every relationship has teething problems,* she reminded herself. Things weren't perfect with Levi from the beginning either. "*Nee,* I do love him." She looked at Ettie and distinctly saw her raise her eyebrows. "Do you think that Wil is not a *gut* match for me, Ettie?"

Before Ettie could speak, Elsa-May said, "Don't listen to others. It's what you think of Wil, Emma. If you are truly in love with him, deep in your heart, it does not matter what others think."

"Marriages work whether people are in love or not," Maureen said, making exactly the same point she'd already made moments before.

"You don't need a *mann,* Emma. I haven't had one for years, and I'm perfectly happy," Ettie said. "When you're married you have to compromise." Ettie shrugged her shoulders. "But, when you aren't married you can do as you please. You can be as free as the wind, as free as a bird soaring in the sky."

"I'm not getting married to Wil because I feel the need to have a *mann,* Ettie."

"Aren't you? Straight after Levi died you and Wil were secretly courting."

Emma's mouth fell open in shock and the other widows gasped at Ettie's words. Emma was not sure in what way she should reply.

"Ettie, everyone needs someone. But sometimes, I think that love is over rated. I've seen many happy marriages where the couple had hardly known each other before they married," Maureen said.

"So you've said before, Maureen," Ettie said. "Are you referring to Bob?"

Maureen gave a surprised laugh. "*Nee,* I'm just saying... I'm not referring to anyone." Maureen looked at her hands in her lap then reached over and took a piece of chocolate fudge off the tray of goodies on the low table in front of her.

Emma realized she was chewing on her nails and put her hand in her lap. "I do love Wil."

"Of course you do," Silvie said. "It must be exciting to have a new *haus*. Have you seen it yet?"

"Tomorrow. Wil is taking me there tomorrow."

As Emma clip-clopped home in her buggy, she was more confused about her feelings than before the widows' meeting. Emma sighed and said aloud, "Everyone had such different views on *menner* and marriage." The cold night air rushed against her face.

CHAPTER TWO

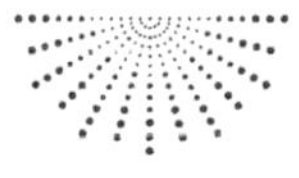

I will sing of the mercies of the Lord for ever:with my mouth will I make known thy faithfulness to all generations.
Psalm 89:1

Wil had talked excitedly so much about the house that Emma was expecting something far grander.

When he stopped the buggy in front of the driveway, the only thing that came out of Emma's mouth was, "This isn't it, is it?"

Wil opened the buggy door and stepped out. "*Jah,* it's stunning, isn't it?"

The word Emma would use to describe the house was 'dilapidated,' rather than 'stunning.' It was built over three levels and it did have a pretty shape. It could look nice with a lot of work, but their plan had been to only change a few things, not to do a full-scale 'rescue' renovation.

"It's big; I'll say that." Then she looked at the small yard. "Where would we put the buggy and keep the horses?"

"It's got land and stables round the back of the *haus*. They look like they haven't been used for a while, but I can soon fix them up."

Emma nodded as she thought sarcastically, *Great, more things to fix*. She climbed down from the buggy.

"Come inside and see," Wil said, linking his arm through hers.

Emma was pleasantly surprised with the interior; it was not as badly rundown on the inside as it was on the outside. "It's quite nice."

"Come and see the kitchen." Wil took Emma's hand and walked to the left, through the large living room, through another room until they came to the big kitchen.

Emma turned around in a circle. "*Ach,* two living rooms, a formal dining room and now this huge kitchen. I didn't expect something so large."

"You wanted a big kitchen, didn't you? I don't think we'll have to do much work in here. We'll have to get rid of the wires and all the electrical things, such as the lighting and the ovens, but that shouldn't take long. Smithy and David are going to help me."

Emma nodded, glad that Wil had some help. She could not help the twinge of a smile that broke out onto her face as she decided that she would be able to live in the *haus.* It had a homey feel to it and once she put personal touches to it, she just might grow to like it.

Wil faced her and put his hands on his hips. "Well, what do you think?"

"It needs a lot more work than you said it would." She was still mad at him for making the decision by himself and not including her. Was this how things would be in their marriage? Even though the man was the head of the house he still had a duty of respect toward the woman; surely that would mean including her in all their major decisions.

"Are you starting to forgive me a little?"

Emma raised her eyebrows. Was it possible that he knew how mad she was? She had not said a portion of how she was truly feeling. "I'm starting to forgive you a little bit now that I've seen inside it. It's certainly a lot better than the outside. I think we could make it nice."

Wil laughed and closed the distance between them and took her in his arms. "I know you're a little cross with me for being impulsive; I know how you like to plan things and organize things to death. I just wanted to surprise you. Everyone needs a little excitement now and again."

As far as Emma was concerned she'd had plenty of excitement over the past months. "I was concerned with the finances. I would have thought that before we made a huge purchase like this, we would have sat down and worked out how much we both had and where the money was going to come from."

Wil threw his head back. "I told you before, Emma, I've got plenty of money."

"Enough for a *haus* like this? Even though it's run down on the outside, it must have cost a lot. Don't you need my contribution, if it's going to be our *haus*?"

"Nope."

Emma breathed out heavily. "Does one of us need to sell?"

Wil shook his head. "Emma, I have a lot of money. Besides inheriting the farm, I inherited quite a bit of money. I've enough that we don't need to be concerned with money."

Emma was a little taken aback. Levi and Wil had been best of friends and Levi had never mentioned that Wil was so wealthy, but then again, why would he have had the need to mention it? She wondered what they would both do with their two vacant houses, once they finally move into this *haus.*

"What are you worrying about now, Emma? I bought this for us because I want you to be happy. I'll get this old place fixed up in no time. Before we're married, okay?"

"That's a lot of work to do in so little time. Are you sure you can do it all?"

"I'll do the essential things first, to make it livable for us and the rest I can do after we move in."

"I insist on giving you money toward the renovations. I've got $20,000 that I've saved; that should make a *gut* start."

"If you insist; now, no more talk of money." He pulled Emma into his hard, muscled chest.

She relaxed in his strong arms, pleased that she liked the place.

"C'mon, I'll show you the rest of it." Wil held her hand and led her through the *haus,* explaining how he would strip the floors back and what he would do with the cornices and the window frames.

He showed her right through the downstairs, through the two living rooms, formal dining room, a large kitchen and a small bathroom at the end of the far living room. The second level was made up of five bedrooms, main with an en-suite bathroom.

Before they made their way up more stairs to the uppermost level, Wil turned to Emma. "We'll have these bedrooms filled up in no time."

"Who with?" Emma frowned, not realizing that he meant that they would have many children. When she caught on to what he meant, she grabbed his arm. "Wil, you know that Levi and I were married for years and didn't have *kinner.* It just didn't happen. What if I'm not able?"

"Emma, I'm sorry. I didn't mean to upset you. It would be nice to have *kinner,* but I'm just as happy if it's always just you and me." He smiled at Emma and the kindness in his eyes made her heart soften. As she followed him up the stairs, she realized that she had started to build walls up in her heart against Wil. She had been looking for reasons why he was not a match with her, instead of looking for reasons why he was a match.

There were two rooms in the uppermost level, and they were both full of cobwebs and dirt.

"Looks like no one has been up here in years," Emma said.

"The realtor said it was owned by an old lady. I guess she couldn't make it up this extra flight of stairs. It's a large place for one lady to clean by herself."

"Wil, what's that over there?"

Wil looked to where Emma was pointing. They both walked closer to the small wooden box, the size of a shoebox.

Will picked it up and brushed off some dust. Elaborate brass hinges covered the edges of the box and the closure on the front side of it was secured with a padlock.

"What do you think's inside it?" Emma asked.

"No idea." He shook it a little. "It's not heavy, but there does seem to be something inside. I'll go and see the realtor tomorrow and see if he has a forwarding address for the old owner. I'll get it to her; must be something of value in there if it's locked. Although it couldn't have been of too much value if she didn't think to take it with her."

"Is it heavy?"

Wil picked it up. "*Nee,* it's fairly light."

"Bring it downstairs and I'll clean it up."

~

WIL WAS anxious to start the renovations, but he had told Emma that he would stop by the realtor, so he kept his word. He did not want to risk Emma getting upset with him again.

He had been warned that women were temperamental sometimes, and Emma had proven that to be true because she did have some mood swings.

Her moods did not bother him; he felt it kept him on his toes, although he hadn't expected her initial lack of joy about the new *haus.*

Maybe she was right; maybe I should have included her in the decision, he thought as he ran a hand through his hair.

Half an hour later, Will sat in front of the realtor waiting for information.

"No, I don't have an address for her," the realtor said as he looked through the file. The realtor looked at Wil and adjusted his neat, blue tie. "Just throw it out, whatever you've found, people are always leaving things behind. Too lazy to do a proper job of things."

Wil was not satisfied with the lack of responsibility the realtor showed. "All the same, I'd feel better getting it back to her and she can make that decision."

"Please yourself. Let's see." The realtor looked through the file again. "I can give you her name. It's Dorothy Welby. I remember that she said she was moving to Florida, to a retirement home."

"How is it that you don't have her address? You'd need it wouldn't you, for contracts and such?"

"She already signed the listing contract, so I didn't need her to sign anything else. I'd say her lawyer would have her address; he'd need to have it for her to sign the final papers." He looked through the file again. "Seems I have a post office box address in Florida." He scrambled through some notes. "I'll write the name and the post office box down for you. I don't think her lawyer would give you her address – privacy reasons. You can write to her, see if she wants her old things." He wrote out her details and handed the piece of paper to Wil.

"I appreciate it." Wil tucked the piece of paper into his pocket. "So, it's still alright that I start work on the property even though things haven't been finalized?" Wil asked.

"Yeah, that's okay. It's all cash isn't it?"

Wil nodded

The realtor continued, "So it'll be finalized as fast as the lawyers can push it through."

Wil left the realtor's office and set off to meet his friends back at the house. They were going to help him assess how much work was needed and where they would start. But first, he would take the address of the old lady to Emma. He knew that once she had one thing on her mind, she thought of little else.

~

EMMA WAS out in her front garden pulling weeds when Wil pulled up in his buggy. He tied up his horse and walked over to her. "Here you go, Emma."

"What is it?"

"The old lady's address. The one who used to own the *haus.* Her name is Dorothy Welby."

"*Denke,* Wil. I'll write to her now then I'll go to the post office and send the letter by overnight mail."

Wil smiled at Emma. He was right about her wanting to do things quickly. "I'm meeting the men at the *haus.* We'll see what we need to do. Don't worry, I won't make plans for the kitchen until you come and look at it again."

"What kinds of things will you be doing?"

"We'll need to strip back the floors, patch the ceiling in a couple of places and Smithy is going to get up into the roof to see if we need to replace it."

Emma gasped. "Didn't you do all that before you bought it?"

"Relax, Emma. It's not much to put a new roof on; I've helped people before, many times. You're not having second thoughts about the *haus,* are you?"

"*Nee,* I do like the *haus.*" Emma was more concerned about the money aspect of things than the physical labor it involved. "It'll be nice once it's had some work done on it."

"I knew you'd love it, I just knew it."

Emma thought back to what Silvie had said the night before.

Silvie would have been pleased for someone to buy her a *haus*. Maybe she was being uncaring. Wil bought the *haus* to be nice; he didn't do it to cause her worry or concern. "*Denke,* Wil for the *haus,* I mean; it was a nice surprise. I'm not much used to surprises, so it took me a little while to get used to the fact that we've got a new *haus,* all of a sudden."

CHAPTER THREE

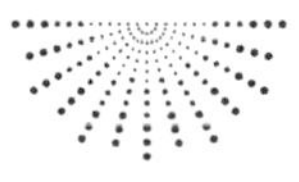

Wherefore, if God so clothe the grass of the field, which to day is, and tomorrow is cast into the oven,
shall he not much more clothe you,
O ye of little faith?
Matthew 6:30

A week and a half went by after Emma had posted the letter to Dorothy Welby, by fast delivery, and they had not heard anything back.

Wil and Emma stood looking at the mysterious locked box, which now took center place on the kitchen table in the new *haus.*

"Stop worrying about the box so much, Emma," Wil said.

Emma ran a finger over the top of the box. "There must be something precious in it if there's a lock on it."

"Perhaps if we open it, we can find out if there's anything in there that someone would be concerned about leaving behind. It could be nothing at all."

Emma swallowed hard trying not to feel guilty at just the thought of opening someone else's box particularly when that box was locked. "Do you think we should open it?"

"Don't see why not. We tried to contact the owner, didn't we?"

"Okay." Emma nodded to Wil.

"I'll get a screwdriver. I should be able to undo these hinges rather than risk destroying the box."

Emma waited for Wil to return with a screwdriver. Minutes later the box was open.

"These are old letters," Emma said as she picked up the letter on top.

"See, nothing valuable in there at all." Wil picked up a letter, held it in the air and turned it over. "Just some musty, old decaying letters."

Emma unfolded one of the pages and read the first few lines of the letter. "*Nee,* Wil. They are valuable, to someone. These are love letters, beautifully written love letters." She looked into Wil's eyes as tingles traveled through her body. "They've been treasured and kept safe in this box."

Wil took a letter and sat in the chair next to Emma and started reading. After they both read some letters, Wil said, "These are letters written to the old lady who used to own the *haus,* Dorothy Welby."

"*Jah,* written to her from someone called Harold." Emma flipped over an envelope to read the return address. "Harold

Fielding, and I can't see from where they've been sent. Can you tell?"

"I think that Harold Fielding was posted overseas in World War Two. I'm sure 'Field post office' means that the letters were sent to a central place then sent home from there. By the yellowing of the paper, it seems to fit with the time frame. "

"And she lived alone. I wonder if he ever came back from the war." Emma pressed the letter to her heart as she thought of the horrible losses that war brought into peoples' lives.

Wil lowered his head. "A terrible thing, war."

"*Jah*," Emma said as she sniffed and wiped away a tear. She had been far more emotional since Levi's death than she'd ever been before.

"Well, what do you want to do, Emma? How badly do you want to find this woman?"

"I think she would like to have these letters back."

"We'll keep trying to track her down then. Sounds like she's changed her post office box. I'll do my best to find the correct address for you tomorrow."

Emma nodded. "*Denke*. Please see what you can do."

~

SOME AFTERNOONS EMMA travelled into town and met Silvie after work. Silvie worked in a bakery/café, and it was there that the two would sit, drink *kaffe* and chat about life.

"Did you like the *haus*?" Silvie asked when she sat down at the table where Emma had been waiting for her.

"*Jah*, it would have been grand in its day. Wil's over there now pulling out all the electrical wires. It needs quite a bit doing to it. You should come past and take a look."

"I will; I'd love to see it."

One of Silvie's colleagues placed their order of two coffees and two doughnuts in front of them.

Emma ran her fingertip around the top of her coffee cup. "I think you were right. I think it was you who said the other night that Wil and I do things differently. I like to plan, and he likes just to go ahead and do things."

"And that doesn't mean that the two of you aren't suited. In fact, it could be a very *gut* match. He can influence you to be a little less cautious, and you can influence him to think more before he does things," Silvie said.

"I guess so." Emma swirled the froth of her cappuccino with her spoon and tried not to think of how her late husband, Levi, would have done things. She looked up to see Silvie biting into a pink iced doughnut. "Have you heard from Bailey?"

Silvie smiled and finished her mouthful. "He said that he would come and join our community in six months."

"*Ach,* Silvie, that's *wunderbaar.*"

Silvie waved a hand in the air. "I'm not believing it though until it happens."

"What about the case he's been working on; is it solved?" Emma asked.

Silvie shook her head and brushed the sugar crumbs away from her mouth. "He said that whether it's solved or not that he'll come back to me and the community."

Emma giggled a little and said, "Maybe we should see if Ettie and Elsa-May will help him solve the case."

"Emma, that's a *gut* idea. I don't know why I didn't think of it before."

"I was joking, Silvie. It wouldn't be a good idea."

"*Jah,* it is; I'll ask him."

"*Nee* don't, Silvie. Bailey's a professional agent with years of experience with access to confidential information; he'd be a lot better at solving crimes than a couple of old Amish ladies who've rarely left Lancaster County."

"It's never been just a couple of old Amish ladies; it's all of us, you, me, Maureen and Detective Crowley. We're a really *gut* team."

Emma's shoulders slouched and she let out a deep breath. Why couldn't she have kept quiet? "Bailey might be offended if you mention it to him; after all, he's been on the case for years."

"What do you mean?" Silvie's clear blue eyes fastened onto Emma.

Emma adjusted her prayer *kapp* and wondered how to phrase what she was trying to say. "I mean if you say that you think that we can solve it he might think that you see him as not a very *gut* detective."

Silvie slumped back in her chair. "Ah, I see what you mean. I will have to be tactful."

Yeah, or not mention it at all, Emma thought, but she could see that Silvie was determined to go ahead with her plan.

"I'll take your advice, Emma. I'll think on things for a while before I mention it to Bailey or the other widows."

Emma nodded, glad that she would not be drawn into something else; she had enough happening with Wil and the new *haus.* Emma filled up the rest of their time together telling

Silvie about the new *haus* and the strange box that they had found.

Later that night, when the widows gathered in Elsa-May and Ettie's home, Emma told them of the box of letters.

"I could find out where she lives, easy as pie. Leave it to me," Ettie said.

"You could, Ettie? That would be *wunderbaar*."

"Don't you have the address, Emma?" Maureen asked.

"*Nee,* I just have a post office box, that's all."

"You said she lives in Florida?" Maureen asked.

"*Jah,*" Emma answered.

Maureen leaned forward, her mouth forming a grin. "Emma, why don't we go to Florida and take the letters with us?"

Emma smiled; she would love to have an adventure and travel somewhere. "I'd like to, but it's so close to the wedding and Wil's working on the *haus*."

"I'll take over the sewing from Maureen," Silvie said.

Maureen turned to Silvie. "*Denke,* Silvie. I've a fair amount already finished."

Elsa-May said, "Leave a list of things that Ettie and I can do for you too."

Emma wondered if she should go. It was all very last minute. It was something that Wil would do, to go somewhere on the spur of the moment. "I've never been to Florida," Emma said, her eyes glazed over, wondering if this was a good idea or not.

"I've been to Pinecraft with my parents when I was young," Maureen said.

"So did I," Silvie said.

"Go on, do it," Ettie said, "Have an adventure before you get married."

Emma chewed a fingernail. "I'll have to see if Wil won't mind."

"He'll be busy with the *haus* fixing up, won't he?" Elsa-May asked.

The ladies were interrupted by a knock on the door. Elsa-May opened the door and Detective Crowley walked in with three large glass bowls in his hands.

"Detective, this is a nice surprise. To what do we owe the pleasure? Has someone been murdered?" Elsa-May asked.

The detective laughed, "Not lately, not that I know of. I was in the area and thought I'd bring back Ettie's empty containers."

Elsa-May took the bowls from him. "Have a cup of tea while you're here and something to eat."

The detective greeted the ladies and said, "Ettie was kind enough to make me some dinners. She thinks I'm going to starve without a wife. Or, should I say a *fraa.* Is that right, a *fraa*?" The detective sat down amidst giggles from the ladies. "Have you all been keeping out of trouble?"

"Emma's found some old wartime love letters," Silvie said with a glint in her eye.

The detective immediately looked at Emma.

Emma's heart raced. Why did Silvie have to say that? Now she would have to speak to him. She cleared her throat. "Yes, I found them in an old house that Wil just bought. Although, we don't have an address to get them to the old owner yet."

"I can find that out for you," he said.

"You can?" Maureen asked.

"Of course; I am a detective." The detective looked away

from Maureen and back to Emma. "You say Wil bought a house?"

Emma nodded and said, "Thank you, Detective it would be good of you to find where the lady lives now. All we've been able to find out is that she lives somewhere in Florida. I've only her post office box number."

"I'll drop her address by your place tomorrow, Emma, since you don't have a phone."

Emma shook her head. "No, I'll go by your office in the afternoon to save you the drive."

"Very well, suit yourself," the detective said.

Silvie said, "Maureen and Emma are going to go to Florida to take the letters to the old lady."

The detective chuckled. "It's a bit of a stretch for the horse isn't it?"

If the detective had not just offered to do her a special favor Emma would have been a little annoyed at his attempt at humor. "We can travel, you know."

"We just can't drive ourselves anywhere. We can go on busses and trains, but our bishop will not let us travel by plane," Ettie said. "Although, my old *daed* used to say that if *Gott* had wanted us to fly He would have given us wings." Ettie giggled.

Elsa-May handed the detective a cup of tea. After he took a sip, he said, "Wil bought a house, you say, Emma? What was wrong with his old one?"

Emma glanced at Silvie hoping she was not going to open her mouth and reveal yet more of her personal information. Emma knew she would have to speak fast to avoid Silvie doing so. "We're due to get married soon and Wil bought us a house for us to live in together." For some reason, Emma felt the awkward need to explain further. "You see, we did not know which house to live in, mine or Wil's, so Wil bought another house."

"Must be made of money," he said in a low voice, his face expressionless.

Emma did not take offence at his sarcasm. She was sure he wanted to get under her skin. "Yes, he's made of money. Money is not a problem to him."

"Emma said that it needs a lot of work," Silvie said.

At that point, Emma gave up. She was a private person and did not want the detective to know all her personal information that Silvie was giving out so freely. Emma knew she should not mind what the detective thought of her, but because of Silvie's prattling, Emma felt the need to add, "It's going to be a nice house when it's finished."

Emma was thankful that Ettie changed the subject by saying to the detective, "I've got some more meals in the cold box for you."

"Ettie, I appreciate it, but it's not necessary. I have learned to cook over the years."

Ettie scrunched up her face at Detective Crowley as if she did not believe that he could cook. "I like having someone to cook for and Elsa-May and I always have so much left over."

"It's true," Elsa-May said.

The detective reached for a chocolate fudge bar and took a bite. While he was chewing, he looked around at the ladies who all had their gaze fastened onto him. "I'm sorry; I'm keeping you ladies from your secret meeting, aren't I? " He raised his half eaten chocolate bar. "One more of these and I'll go."

Ettie rose to her feet. "I'll get those meals ready for you."

Emma tried not to smile. No one had made an effort to be polite and ask the detective to stay. He was right, they could not speak freely while he was there and it was, after all, a widows' meeting.

After Ettie closed the door on the detective, she sat back down on the rickety, wooden chair. "Well, Emma, you can get the address from the detective tomorrow. He'll be able to get it quicker than I could. Let me know if you need my help with anything else."

"*Denke*, Ettie, we might still need your help with something."

Ettie nodded. "No doubt."

Maureen clapped her hands together. "I'm excited to go to Florida."

"Me too," said Emma.

CHAPTER FOUR

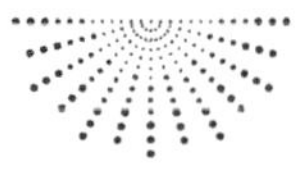

And when he saw their faith,
he said unto him, Man, thy sins are forgiven thee.
Luke 5:20

Going to Crowley's office had not been as bad as Emma had expected since he'd been called out on a case and wasn't there. He had left Dorothy Welby's home address for Emma at the front desk.

Emma saw that the old lady did live in Florida just as the realtor had told them. She went straight to Maureen's *haus.*

Maureen was in her buggy, just about to drive to work. "I can talk for five minutes then I'll have to leave otherwise I'll be late. Did you get the address from Crowley?"

Emma nodded. "I did and she does live in Florida. When do you want to leave?"

"It's up to you, Emma, but if we decide now, I can let them know at work what days I won't be able to work."

"I guess the sooner we go the sooner we get back. I'm just thinking of getting back to all the wedding preparations," Emma said.

"Okay. Shall we go by bus or train?"

"It's a long trip, isn't it?" Emma grimaced.

Maureen nodded. "About a day on the train."

"If it's going to take that long, sounds like a train would be more comfortable than a bus." Emma considered there would be more room to move about on a train rather than sit in a cramped seat for nearly a day, or over a day.

"Let's go the day after tomorrow then, that would be Saturday."

Emma nodded.

"I'll get the tickets organized."

"*Denke,* Maureen. I'm getting excited. I'll go to the new *haus* now to get the box and I'll take it home with me."

"Did you read all the letters?"

"I read some of the letters, but when I realized they were all love letters from the one man, it seemed too private to read further."

Maureen nodded. "*Jah,* I understand. I hope the old lady wants her old letters. It'd be a shame to go all that way to find that she didn't want to take the letters with her."

"Something tells me she will want the letters. They were so touching and so beautiful. Well, I'll let you get to work, Maureen."

~

TWO DAYS LATER, Maureen and Emma were sitting on the train headed for Florida.

"I'm hungry. I've pre-booked us into the dining car so we can have a nice meal." Maureen said.

"Sounds *gut*, let's go."

The ladies stood up, and both adjusted their over aprons and prayer *kapps* before they made their way down the aisle.

"I'll just duck into the ladies' room," Emma said, noticing the sign pointing to the ladies' room to her left. No sooner had she stepped through the doorway, about to shut the door than Maureen pushed her way in.

"Maureen what are you doing? This is a small room. There's only room for one."

Maureen put her hands up and signaled for Emma to keep quiet. "I've just seen an old beau. I would die if he saw me."

"*Nee*, that's awful. Let me open the door a little and have a look at him," Emma said, curious to see what the old beau looked like.

Maureen stood in front of the door. "*Nee*, you mustn't. I can't risk him seeing me."

"A boyfriend after your husband died, or before you were married?"

"Way before, when I was eighteen. I was going to marry him, but changed my mind just two weeks before the wedding. He's left the community now."

"You've never mentioned him."

"I tried to forget him, that's why. He was heading in the direction of the dining car; we can't go there now."

Emma made a face; she was hungry and was looking

forward to a nice meal. "Why not? The price of the meal is included with our tickets. Just say hello and get it over with."

"*Nee,* you don't understand, Emma. I don't know what he's likely to do when he sees me. He's strange, truly weird."

Emma and Maureen were still cramped in the tiny space. Maureen was a large lady, so there was barely room for the two of them.

"I've got to go, Maureen. Peep out the door and see if he's gone. I won't be long."

Maureen snorted and looked out the door. When she saw that no one was there, she moved slowly into the corridor. "Don't be long," she said over her shoulder to Emma.

Once Emma joined Maureen, they knew the only thing they could do was go to the café since the dining car was now out of the question.

Half an hour later, Emma bit into a toasted sandwich while wondering what the food would be like in the dining car. She tried to take her mind off food by finding out more about the man who had struck fear into Maureen's heart. "Tell me about that man you saw just now, Maureen."

Maureen gave an exaggerated tremble of her body. "His name's David Kingsley. He was brought up Amish, but left just after our wedding didn't go ahead."

"What was so awful about him?"

Maureen sucked some chocolate milkshake up through a straw. "I was attracted to him at first because he was different. He was always questioning things, but he went too far with it sometimes. He always questioned the Amish way of doing things and always had questions about *Gott.*"

Emma chased down her toasted sandwich with a mouthful of soda.

Maureen laughed. "One time *mamm* invited the bishop and his *fraa* to dinner, David was there too. David deliberately did disgraceful things. He picked up a whoopie pie from the plate in the center of the table and ate the cream out of the middle and then put the crust back. He knew everyone was watching him, and he did it another three times. No one said anything and everyone just looked at him."

Emma giggled; she could not picture anyone doing what she had just described.

"It wasn't funny at the time, but I can see the funny side of it now. Can you imagine how my *mudder* felt? She was trying to have a lovely dinner with guests."

"I'm sure it wasn't funny while it was happening."

"That's not all he did that night. He picked up a spoon, stared at it, turned it over and over and then he started talking to it."

Emma grimaced. "Sounds like an odd one alright."

"I can't see him. I can't. I mean - I can't let him see me. I especially can't let him know that I'm widowed. If we do happen to bump into him, we must pretend that I'm married."

Emma nodded and tried to keep the smile off her face.

"It's hard to know how he'd react. He might be alright, but he might want to get to know me all over again."

"He must have taken it badly when you didn't go ahead with the marriage," Emma said.

"*Jah,* he left the community. I heard that he married someone and then I heard that he left the poor woman and was living overseas somewhere. I also heard he was doing certain illegal things."

"I had no idea that you were ever involved with someone else; I always assumed that Paul was the only man you had been interested in," Emma said.

"*Nee,* I was dating David before Paul, and before David there was another man, but we only went on a few buggy rides, it was nothing serious."

"So tell me what attracted you to David again?"

Maureen shook her head. "It's too awful to speak about."

"I suppose your parents were relieved when you didn't go through with the wedding?"

"They were delighted, especially my *mudder.* She kept saying to me as the wedding drew closer, 'It's still not too late to change your mind.'"

Emma thought she knew Maureen quite well, but now she was seeing a different side of her. "How did you know that it was right when you met Paul?"

"I didn't know at first. I thought he was handsome; he was very tall and had a solid build." Maureen laughed. "I didn't want a small man. I wanted one bigger than me. We talked one day, after a singing. We liked the same things, and we laughed at the same things. It just felt 'right.'" Maureen squeezed the straw in her drink. "Why do you ask? You must know what it feels like to be in love since you've been in love twice."

"That's just it, Maureen. I'm confused. Wil and Levi are so different. I can't help but compare the two constantly, and I don't want to compare them. Wil scares me a little because he is so vague and forgetful. I fear he might not be as dependable as

Levi was. Then I think that maybe I'm not being fair to Wil expecting him to be like Levi." Emma looked at Maureen hoping Maureen would be able to give her some insight into her feelings about Wil.

"You do love Wil, don't you?"

"*Jah*, I do." Emma rubbed the back of her neck. "Forget I said anything."

Maureen reached her hand across the small table and touched Emma's hand. "Are you having doubts?"

Emma shrugged her shoulders, "I don't know what I'm having."

"Why did you buy a *haus* together and why do you need to marry so soon if you are feeling like this?"

Emma rolled her eyes. "The *haus*. See? He didn't even ask me about the *haus*; he just went out and bought it. What if I didn't like it?"

Maureen tilted her head. "And then you think that Levi wouldn't have done things like that?"

Emma nodded.

"You have to remember that he's not Levi and no one will ever be Levi. Wil is Wil and only you can decide if you want to be with Wil for the rest of your life. Can you stop comparing him to Levi?"

Emma put her elbow on the table and her hand to her forehead. "I don't know; I just don't know."

After they finished their toasted sandwiches, they both ordered chocolate ice-cream sundaes. They looked at each other and smiled.

"I feel a bit naughty, for some reason. I haven't been away

from the community in so long, I can't even remember. I think the change will do us both some *gut,*" Emma said, then tried to steer the conversation away from herself. "How's work going Maureen?"

"*Jah,* it's going well, but I'm thinking of doing something a little different. It's hard work doing the cleaning, and the different shifts are awkward. I'd rather go and do a day's work rather than a few hours here and a few hours there. Often I do a few hours in the morning and have to go back that afternoon to do another few hours."

"What have you been thinking of doing?"

"I'm not sure yet. I've thought about opening a little bakery, but there seems to be so many of them nowadays."

"Perhaps you could specialize in something then. Do something that the others don't do very well."

"That's an idea, but it'd take money."

"Maybe you could take on a partner. Like me." As soon as she said it Emma realized that she no longer had her nest egg; she had given it to Wil to renovate their *haus.*

"Really? You'd be interested in something like that?"

"After I'm married of course. I'd like to do something. Wil always keeps himself busy with things and going from my past history I won't be having *bopplis* anytime soon." Emma wondered how long it would take her to save that same amount of money all over again.

"Let's speak more about it after your wedding. We'll both dream up some ideas."

Emma nodded. "Sounds good, but I won't think about it too much because I'll end up thinking about it more than the wedding." Emma looked at the box on the seat beside her. "I wonder if we should have tried to call her first."

"Did Detective Crowley find a number for her?"

Emma shrugged her shoulders. "I didn't ask him. If he found one, I guess he would've given it to me."

CHAPTER FIVE

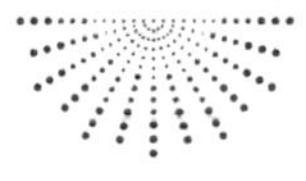

And the light shineth in darkness; and the darkness comprehended it not.
John 1:5

Emma lifted her hand and knocked on the door at the address that Crowley had given her. She hoped that the old lady was at home and more than that she hoped that the old lady still wanted the letters.

The door opened, and an elderly woman stepped toward them. She was small, neatly dressed and her white hair was caught up behind her head. "Hello." She looked from Emma to Maureen and then her eyes fell to the box. She gasped, and her hands flew to her face. "Is that my box?"

Emma smiled. "Yes, it is if you're Dorothy Welby."

"Yes, I am. You found it in my house and brought it all this way?"

Before Emma could speak the lady said, "Please come in."

Once they walked through the door, Emma placed the box on a low side-table then the three of them sat in armchairs. "Thank you for bringing me my box. I was so upset when I realized that I'd left it behind. Tell me, how did you come by it?"

"I bought your house, in Lancaster County. My fiancé and I found the box on the upper level. I must apologize to you for opening it. We wanted to see if there was something of value in it to see if we should keep trying to get in contact with you. We did write to your post office box."

"I never check my post office box." She looked behind her at the box then looked at the ladies in front of her. "Your fiancé bought my house you say?"

Emma nodded.

Dorothy frowned. "Then I've some bad news for you. I got a call from my lawyer this morning, and he said that my house is still not sold. He said that the contract fell through. I'll tell you the name of the buyer; I wrote it down." Dorothy reached for a notepad on the small table beside her. She placed her reading glasses on her nose, lifted the notepad and held it close, in front of her. "The lawyer said that the buyer was William Joseph Jacobson, and the sale did not go through because of no funding."

Emma felt sick to the stomach. "Fell through, why? How did if fall through?"

"You didn't know?" Dorothy looked over the top of her glasses.

"No, we came up by train and left my fiancé back in Lancaster County working on the house."

"Oh dear, I'm sorry to give you bad news my dear. Especially when you've delivered my box back to me. What work is he doing on the house? I hope he hasn't spent too much money on it."

Emma shrugged. "I'll have to call him and see what's happening."

"Stay for morning tea, won't you? Yes, you must." Before they could say another word, Dorothy had disappeared into the kitchen.

Maureen whispered to Emma, "Don't worry, put it out of your mind, and we'll call Wil when we get back to the hotel."

Emma nodded and did her best to push the whole thing out of her mind while they were with Dorothy.

They sat and drank tea with the elderly lady in the tiny living room of her house in the retirement village.

As Dorothy offered a plate of cookies to the ladies, she said, "I can't tell you how much those letters mean to me. I'm so grateful to you both." She looked at Emma. "I do hope I didn't leave the house in too bad a state. It got too hard for me to clean, and the house was far too big for me."

"It was fine. Wil, my fiancé, had planned to do a few things to it." In an effort to drive the whole *haus* situation out of her mind, Emma asked, "If you don't mind me asking, whatever happened to Harold? Did you marry him?" Emma's hand flew to her mouth. "Oh, I'm sorry, I did read one or two letters."

The old lady sat back deeply into her chair. "He just disappeared, missing in action. His name never appeared as dead.

They told me that he was missing presumed dead. Anyway, that's what they said when I pressed them for an answer."

"Have you done any recent checks on him since that time? Electoral roles, driver's license and the like?" Maureen asked.

The old lady did not answer for a while. "No, and I'll tell you why. He knew where to find me. We bought that house together as a promise that he'd come back to me. I waited and waited, and he never came back." Dorothy inhaled deeply and let it out slowly as if trying to calm herself. "Do you know what it does to a person to wait like that?"

Emma and Maureen shook their heads under Dorothy's green-eyed gaze.

"I don't know which would be worse, to know that he was alive and never bothered to come back to me or to find out that he was killed in the war."

"You lived in the same house all those years? The house in Lancaster County?" Maureen asked.

Dorothy shook her head. "We lived in Brooklyn. Our plan was that after the war we would get married and settle in that house in Lancaster. We bought the house and put it in my name in case he didn't make it back from the war. I moved there not long after the war ended and I waited for him there." Dorothy shook her finger at them. "Don't think that we were rich or anything, having a big grand house like that. That old house needed work back then, all those years ago. Even so, I struggled with the upkeep for years, hoping that one day he'd come and find me there."

"I'm sorry to hear that," Emma said.

"All I have of him are the letters. I did have hope, but now I just have the letters."

"Did he have any family?" Maureen asked.

Emma looked at Maureen and knew immediately that Maureen intended to find out what became of Dorothy's love.

"He had a brother who died; that's all."

"Friends?"

"We only had each other. I did have a girlfriend back then, Josephine Cutter, but she disappeared suddenly as soon as the war ended. One day she was here and the next day she wasn't. We were sharing a flat together and then I was left to pay the whole amount. I had to move."

"That seems odd."

"Yes, it was very odd. I called 'round to see her parents and they said she'd moved away. They were always very nice to me, but that day they did not want to speak to me at all. They couldn't wait for me to leave."

"So, you lost your best friend and your fiancé?"

Dorothy nodded and looked up at the ceiling as if she was trying to fight back tears.

"Did you have far to travel to go and see your best friend's parents that day?" Maureen asked

"Only ten minutes by bus."

"Mrs. Welby, do you mind if Emma and I look into things for you to see if we can find your old friend and maybe what happened to Harold?"

"Oh dear, I don't know what you'd find." She looked over at the box. "Is it any trouble for you to look into things?"

"Not at all, we'd love to help," Emma said.

"If he's alive and has not tried to find me then please don't tell me. I could not cope with the pain. Only tell me if you find a death record. I'd like to know how he died and where he died."

Maureen and Emma agreed. Maureen noticed that there was a picture on the mantelpiece of a soldier in uniform.

"Is that him then?" Maureen said, standing to look closer at the photo.

The old lady stood up and walked over to the mantle and handed Maureen the photo. "That's my Harold."

"He looks a very nice man." Maureen turned the photo to show Emma.

"Would you like to hear about him?" Without waiting for a response she said, "I will tell you about him. Sit back down, Maureen."

Maureen obeyed.

Dorothy rubbed her face and looked as though she was deep in thought. "Harold...oh yes. He was lost at war, you know, my poor, poor Harold. I miss him so dearly," she said with a croaky voice. "We met at a dance, before the war started. There were always dances back then, for the wealthy at least. But I got to go because my aunt was wealthy. My aunt's husband, Roy, was a photographer and he got invited to the most fabulous events. I was allowed to go to a lot of them. What a time that was when dances were held every Saturday night."

"How did you two find each other at the dance?" Emma had never been to a dance and wondered how *Englischers* socialized.

"I was standing against the wall while my aunt danced with a man she didn't even know. I was dressed in a full skirt with petticoats, had on my first pair of stilettoes and stockings with the seams down the back." Dorothy laughed. "I don't even know if you can get stockings like that these days."

"I don't know if you can," Emma said.

"Anyway, I thought I looked good and Harold must have thought so too. He was a handsome man and could have asked any girl to dance, but he asked me. I guess he saw me alone and thought I looked nice because he came up, and pulled me onto the dance floor; he didn't even ask." Dorothy's eyes sparkled.

"It sounds romantic," Maureen said.

"He just whisked me off my feet and pulled me to the floor amongst the other couples. I was shocked at first, too shocked to even speak to him. I remember my face was as bright as a beetroot. But when I saw his smile, I couldn't help but feel happy. He had the most beautiful eyes, blue as the sky in the summertime."

"When did you eventually speak to him?" Emma asked.

"We hadn't even talked through the first few dances. But then a slower song came on, so he took my hand and walked me off the dance floor. It was more inappropriate to dance with a stranger to a slow song back then. Today, no one gives a hoot. But, back then, people had manners, and if you were a man, you courted a woman. Not like it is today at all. People jump into things so quickly today."

Dorothy sipped her tea, and then looked at Emma and Maureen. "He would say to me;

Dorothy, Dorothy, Dorothy,

How I love thee Dorothy.

You are a flower, a ray of sun,

and you make my world so much more fun.

You make my world seem new just by standing in my view."

Emma could feel herself about to giggle, and she daren't look at Maureen in case she was about to laugh too.

"That's lovely," Maureen said. "You remembered that after all this time?"

"Yes. He wrote me lots of poetry. He said that he loved me, and I believed him. He meant the world to me for so long. He courted me like a full gentleman, and we did everything together after a time."

Dorothy took a drink of water. "But then the war started and being of age, of course, he was drafted. Not even a second thought, he just left to serve his country. He told me how he loved and adored me, and even how the minute he got back he would carry me straight to the chapel and marry me. But he left. He left me alone to worry, for... who knew how long. Harold was mine, and I could not lose him." The old lady looked across at Emma and Maureen. "War's a terrible thing, isn't it?"

Maureen and Emma nodded in agreement.

"While he was at war, I wrote him every day and nearly every week I got one back. Every day, I worried that he would not come home and when the war ended, he did not come home. I inquired only to be told that he was missing in action. They had to tell me what that meant."

"That's awful for you," Emma said.

"I still love him. If only the war hadn't started, we would still be together." The old lady cleared her throat. "Listen to me prattling on, thinking of only my woes. You've come all this way, all the way from Lancaster County. You ladies are welcome to stay here if you don't mind sharing a room. I've only got one spare bedroom."

"No, thank you. That's very kind of you. We're staying at a

hotel nearby. Before we go, can you tell us all you know about Harold and your friend Josephine Cutter?" Maureen asked.

"Don't try and find Josephine. I'm hurt that she just up and went away like that, and I see no reason to speak to her."

"Tell us some background information about Josephine then, just so we get a broad picture of how things were back then." Maureen smiled at Dorothy.

They stayed for a while longer at Dorothy's house and when they got back to their hotel Maureen headed straight for the telephone in their room. She called Elsa-May and Ettie on their forbidden cell phone. It was only a matter of time before the bishop found out about it. It wasn't right and she'd told them that much. Well, she'd told Ettie. She wasn't brave enough to say it to Elsa-May.

Elsa-May answered.

"Elsa-May, can you have Ettie find out what she can about Harold Fielding and Josephine Cutter? They would've been born in the late or mid twenties. It seems that Harold has never been listed as killed in the war. He was listed as missing in action, but the old lady has not done any recent checks on him. Emma and I are hoping he's surfaced somewhere."

"Will do. Now who's the woman you mentioned?" Elsa-May asked.

"Josephine Cutter. She's an old friend of Dorothy who disappeared not long after the war ended. Josephine just up and disappeared; she was sharing a small apartment with Dorothy, and Dorothy was left to pay for the apartment on her own. That was before Dorothy moved to Lancaster."

"To Emma's new house?" Elsa-May asked.

"Yes. Dorothy and Harold bought it together, but it was in Dorothy's name in case he never made it back from the war."

"He would have come there to find her then if he had survived the war," Elsa-May said.

"Exactly, that's why Mrs. Welby doesn't want to know if he's still alive. She said only tell her if he's dead. She wants to know how and where he died."

"Okay, I'll get Ettie onto things right away and we'll phone you back at the hotel."

As Maureen hung up the phone, she hoped that she would not find out any bad news. The dear old lady deserved some good news, but it seemed as if the only news she would be getting was knowledge of where Harold had died. At least her mind would be put to rest.

It appeared Emma was thinking along the same lines. "I don't see what *gut* can come of this investigation, Maureen. Maybe we should have kept out of the whole thing. It's a far stretch of the imagination to think that he might be alive. He would've come to find her, or she would have heard of him through a friend or relative." Emma sighed. "How long do you think it will take Ettie to find something out?"

Maureen took a deep breath and looked at the digital clock on the bedside table. "It's 12.30 now. I reckon she'd have some information for us later this afternoon."

CHAPTER SIX

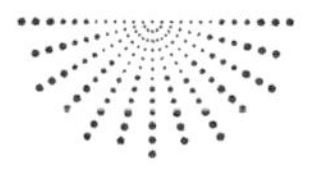

The same came for a witness, to bear witness of the Light, *that all men through him might believe.*
John 1:7

Wil walked into his barn and wiped the frustration from his face. He sorted through his tools wondering which ones he should take with him to the new *haus.* The phone rang, and he hoped it was Emma.

"Hello?" he answered.

"Hello, Mr. Jacobson. I have some troubling news for you. It seems that your bank has declined the transaction. I need to see you. When can you come into the office here?"

The caller had forgotten to say who he was, but Wil recognized him to be the realtor who had sold him the *haus.* "Um, I'm free right now, if you want me to come there now."

"Okay, come straight in."

"Alright, I will see you in just a bit." Wil replaced the receiver on to the hook. His eyes fell to the ground then he shook his head and rubbed his eyes. He had made a mess of things. He had hoped that the money would be through in time, but it was clear that this time things would not work out for him as they had in the past. He'd often gone out on a limb and things had always come right; this time they hadn't.

He looked down at his dusty clothes and knew he would have to change into some clean ones before he went into town. He hurried inside to change, grateful that he already had the buggy hitched and ready to go.

~

ONCE WILL REACHED the realtor's office, the receptionist led him to the realtor's desk. He sat heavily on the chair behind the desk, not waiting to be asked to have a seat.

"Hello, Mr. Jacobson. What's this about the bank not putting the money through?"

"I need a few more days."

"Until you sort it out with your bank, it's best you give me back the keys to the property." The realtor leaned forward and put out his hand.

"But, I've already done so much work to the house. It's already mine; I've done a lot of work on it. And Emma, my fiancé, gave me the money to do renovations while she's on her trip. Why can't I just keep working on the house until I clear things up with the bank?" Wil knew the only way out of this was to buy time.

"Mr. Jacobson, I'm just trying to do my job and I'm not doing my job very well if you have the keys in your possession under these circumstances. I took you at your word that this was a cash transaction, and that's the only reason I let you have the keys early." The realtor whispered, "If the boss knows I've already handed the keys to you, I'll be in all sorts of strife. It's not legal. I did it under the counter—on the side." He lifted his eyebrow. "Know what I mean?"

Wil remained silent, and the realtor continued, "I'll keep it off the market for a while to give you a bit more time – two days. The money is coming, isn't it?"

Wil nodded.

"Are you sure?"

"I'm sure." Wil did his best to sound confident.

"After two days, I'll have to start actively marketing the house again. I won't stop anyone looking through it if they want to, but I will do my best to stall them." The realtor frowned at Wil. "Are you borrowing the money?"

Wil shook his head. "I won't need to."

"But it is coming, from somewhere, isn't it?"

Wil nodded. "I already said it would be there."

The realtor typed something into his computer. Wil leaned over and tried to see what he typed, but he tilted the screen away from him. "Well, that's it, let me know as soon as you've got the money in the bank."

"Thank you. I'll be in touch." Wil said as he stood up. Wil knew he should contact Emma directly. He remembered the name of the hotel where she was staying with Maureen, but he decided to wait until she came back, that way she could have a worry free time away.

As he walked back to his buggy, he felt sick to the stomach about Emma's money that he'd already spent. What if the money didn't come through as he'd planned? There was only one thing for it; he'd have to call the company from where he was expecting the money.

Half an hour later, back in his barn, Wil had finally gotten through to the person with whom he needed to speak. "Mr. Jacobson, sorry that you've been given the run-around. I have your plans in front of me."

"You do? Do you like the concept?" Wil's heart was beating so fast and heavily that he thought he might have a heart attack. So much was riding on the answer that he was about to hear.

"I'm afraid that there would not be enough call for us to manufacture the plough. It would be too costly for us. Maybe you could try a smaller firm; we do things on a large scale. It's not the kind of thing we're interested in; people are using machines now for that kind of thing."

"I know they're using machines, but there's a big movement that's going in the other direction nowadays. People are moving toward organic farming and don't want to use machinery," Wil said.

"That's very true. However, they're still in the minority and it wouldn't be a wise financial move for us to go with your design. As I said, you may try your luck with a smaller company. We'll keep your name and address on file if we may?"

"Certainly, go ahead. And thank you for your time. I appreciate it."

"Thank you, Mr. Jacobson."

Wil hung up the phone. That was that. He had to tell the realtor that he could not go ahead with the purchase of the house. He would also need to find the words to tell Emma that he not only lost their *haus,* but he had spent a portion of the money that she had given him.

~

"Now, to call Wil. I hope he's near his barn," Emma said.

"What are you going to say to him, Emma? Remember, no *gut* comes from anger."

"I'm too numb to be angry Maureen. That was my money he was renovating the house with and now it's all wasted if the sale isn't proceeding."

Emma called the phone in Wil's barn, but there was no answer. She remembered the name of Wil's lawyer, so she called him. The lawyer's secretary was not going to give over any information, but relented when Emma said that she was Wil's fiancé and was away and could not reach Wil.

"Okay, I'll look up that file." A minute later the secretary came back to the phone. "It seems that Wil was expecting money to come through, and it didn't come through in time."

"Is that all you can tell me?" Emma asked. After the secretary had assured Emma that that was all she could tell her, Emma hung up the phone and looked up at Maureen, who was standing over her. "They said that Wil's money didn't come through."

"From what?" Maureen asked.

"I don't know. Wil won't talk about his finances. He's vaguely told me that he has investments and things. I don't know what they were talking about; what money didn't come through in time?"

"Try calling him again," Maureen said.

Emma called Wil's phone in the barn once more, hoping he'd be near his barn and this time he answered.

"Emma, how are you?"

"I'm fine, Wil. I've found the old lady who owned the *haus,* and she said that the sale of her house hasn't gone through. What happened?"

"*Jah,* I'm sorry about that, Emma."

"Well, what happened?" Emma didn't want apologies she wanted answers.

"I thought I was getting money come through, but it hasn't come yet."

It was the same old vague answers that Wil gave her every time regarding money. She had to pin him down. "What money, and where was it coming from?"

Wil blew out a deep breath. "You remember that plough I was working on?"

Emma could not remember, but knew Wil always had several projects that he was working on at the one time. "I vaguely remember."

"Well, I sent the plans off to a company and I was hoping they'd buy the plans from me."

Emma closed her eyes and pushed her fingers into her forehead. "I don't understand. Has the firm ever suggested that they might give you money for it?"

"*Nee,* not in so many words, but you don't understand how these things work. I knew someone who sent in a plan for something similar to that same company, and they gave him three hundred thousand dollars for it."

Emma knew nothing about business, but the story sounded totally unrealistic to her. "Who was that person, Wil?"

"I can't say who, but I distinctly remember someone telling me about it."

Emma shook her head. Was Wil going to be like Maureen's David? At some point in the future, would she tell someone the story of Wil and what he'd done – the man she nearly married? "How much of my money have you already spent on the house?"

"Only twelve thousand."

Emma clutched at her throat. "Only?"

"Well, I could sell some of the timber back. I could see if they'll take the other things back too."

"See what you can do." Emma was doing her best to contain her anger. She had given Wil twenty thousand dollars to renovate the *haus* as her contribution; seeing that she thought that he had bought the *haus* with his money.

"I'm sorry about your money, Emma. You sound angry, but I'm upset about it too."

Emma was too angry to think of comforting him. "We'll talk when I get back."

After she finished her call with Wil, Emma could scarcely hold back the tears as she relayed the entire story to Maureen. "What am I to do, Maureen? What am I to do?"

Maureen put her arm around Emma's shoulder and gave her a tight squeeze. "You'll forget about it while we're here and we'll enjoy ourselves. Now, wipe away those tears and we'll have a walk outside in the sunshine."

Before Emma answered, she sat and looked around the hotel room. The covers on the twin beds were bright pink, the wallpaper was swirls of green and purple and small ceramic sailing ships were dotted along the walls. Emma missed home.

The homes in the community were plain and not fussy at all, and the colors were always muted and pale. She knew if she stayed in that hotel room any longer than she had to she would surely get a headache. "*Jah,* a walk sounds *gut*."

Together, they stepped out of the hotel room and into the bright Florida sunshine.

~

IT WAS five o'clock when they got back to the hotel.

The man on the reception desk of the hotel said, "I've got a message for you, Mrs. Kurtzler."

Emma took the slip of paper. It read, 'Call Ettie Smith back.'

Maureen and Emma walked up one flight of stairs to their room.

"I can't wait to hear what she's found out. I hope it's not something bad," Maureen said as she pressed the buttons on the telephone. She put the phone on loudspeaker so Emma could hear what Ettie said as well.

"I'm sorry to say that it's not *gut* news, Maureen," Ettie said.

"What did you find out? Is he dead?"

"Worse than that, I'm afraid. He's married, or at least he was married. A year after the war ended we have a marriage record for him and one Miss Cutter."

"He's alive?" Maureen asked.

"He's alive, and he married Josephine Cutter," Elsa-May said.

Maureen's mouth fell open as it sunk it that Dorothy's love

had married her best friend, the one who had disappeared. She looked at Emma, who was as shocked as she.

"That's not all," Ettie said. "I've found a death record for a Josephine Fielding and no death record for Harold Fielding."

"Do you have an address for him?" Maureen asked.

"I've got a current address for him, get a pen."

Maureen penned the address and hung up the phone.

Emma looked over her shoulder. "It's not far from where Dorothy lived in Lancaster."

"I wonder how long he's lived there for? Why did he avoid Dorothy and marry her best friend?"

"It doesn't make sense; not if you've read the letters. It's awful. Dorothy won't want to know that. Let's not tell her just yet," Emma said.

"*Nee,* we can't tell her. Let's have Ettie and Elsa-May go visit Harold. He might tell them his side of things," Maureen said.

"*Jah,* Maureen. Quick call them back and see if they'll do it."

CHAPTER SEVEN

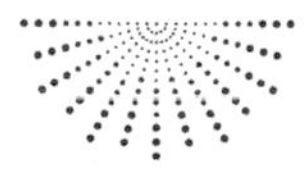

For therefore we both labour and suffer reproach, because we trust in the living God, who is the Saviour of all men, specially of those that believe.
1 Timothy 4:10

Elsa-May and Ettie climbed out of the taxi at the address that Ettie had found for Harold Fielding.

It was a small house and a man was out the front, crouched in the garden and he rose to his feet as the ladies walked through the low gate.

"Would you be Mr. Fielding?" Ettie asked.

He placed his garden fork on the ground and took off his gloves. "Yes."

"Did you once know a Dorothy Welby?"

The man studied the two ladies in turn. "What's this about?"

"We're friends of Dorothy Welby and she believes that you went missing in the war."

"I'm sorry, I think you ladies are mistaken. Dorothy Welby is dead; I'm sorry to say."

The ladies shook their heads. "She's alive and well, two of our friends just visited her yesterday. She's the same Dorothy Welby who you wrote letters to during the war."

Harold sat on the front step of his house. "I was told she died." He looked up at the two ladies and then said, "Give me a minute." After a moment, Harold buried his face in his hands.

Elsa-May and Ettie looked at each other as they wondered what to do.

He took a handkerchief out of his wallet, rubbed his face and then blew his nose. "You ladies better come inside."

They followed him inside and sat at Harold's kitchen table.

"She's really alive?" He studied the two ladies.

They nodded.

"Is she well?" he asked.

They nodded again.

"Who told you she died?" Elsa-May asked, already guessing the answer.

"Josephine."

"The woman you married?" Ettie asked even though they knew that to be the case from the marriage records.

Harold stared at them. "You knew Josephine?"

"Knew of her," Ettie said.

"How can it be that she deceived me? I cannot believe that she could have done anything so cruel to another human being. She knew how I grieved for her. Josephine helped me through my grief. I felt I owed her; I owed her my life. I would have taken my own life if Josephine hadn't stopped me. She suggested we marry, and I agreed. She's gone now; she died just six months ago."

"That's how we traced you, through her death certificate," Ettie said.

"Where is Dorothy now? Does she know where I am?"

"No, she doesn't know anything. She was told that you died, or officially, that you were missing in action."

Harold nodded and said, "I was in a prison camp, but I was freed when the war ended. They didn't release us when they should've, they held on to us longer than they should have. We didn't even know that the war had ended. Thinking about my dear Dorothy was the only thing that got me through."

"She thinks you were lost in the war and then her 'friend,' Josephine Cutter, disappeared suddenly," Elsa-May said.

'It was then that she moved to Lancaster," Ettie added.

"She moved to live into our old house?" Harold asked.

Ettie nodded. "She hoped that you would come and find her there if you ever came back."

"I never had reason to go by that old house. I assumed that since she had died and had no family that the old house would have been auctioned by the state. I put it out of my mind." He looked at the two ladies intently. "This is all true is it? It's not one of those reality television programs or someone playing a cruel trick on me, is it?"

"I can assure you we are telling the truth. Dorothy recently moved to a retirement home in Florida. She's very much alive."

"I must see her. Do you have a phone number for her?" He held his heart. "My old ticker is playing up. I'm not supposed to travel, well not on a plane. They took my driver's license from me as well."

"We've got friends in Florida right now. Our friend, Emma, bought Dorothy's old house and found your old letters. They went to Florida to take them back to Dorothy. She told them the story about you, and that's why we came looking for you."

A smile lit up Harold's face. "She kept my letters?"

Elsa-May nodded and patted the old man's hand. "She kept them all this time, locked in a box."

"Did she marry?"

"No, she never married. I don't think, did she?" Ettie turned to Elsa-May.

Elsa-May shrugged. "I don't know."

"I must see her," Harold said.

Ettie and Elsa-May looked at each other. They weren't sure whether Dorothy would want to see him going by what she said to Maureen.

"Why don't we tell our friends up there that we've found you and let them tell Dorothy?"

The old man nodded. "She doesn't know I'm alive? Please. I'm sorry, ladies. This has all been a shock. I hope I didn't appear rude when you arrived here."

"Not at all," Ettie said. "You weren't to know who we were or what we wanted. Why don't you tell us how you met Dorothy?"

"That'll be a long story; I'll make us some coffee or would you prefer tea?"

"Coffee will be fine," Elsa-May said. "We'll help."

When the coffee was ready they all sat down.

Harold blinked back tears and cleared his throat. "Well,

here's how we met. It was at a dance." Harold relaxed back into the couch. "When I walked into the dance hall that night, I wasn't expecting much. Times were hard, for me at least, and there was talk of war. We were young and had the need for fun and excitement beyond what we were faced with every day."

He paused and the ladies saw a sparkle in his eyes. "Back then, there were plenty of eager women anxious to get their hands on a husband. I wondered if I might be called up if war broke out. I had to do my duty." He slurped his coffee.

Elsa-May asked, "When did you see her?"

"I didn't at first. Music was playing, and people were milling about, each trying to capture the attention of another. Somehow through all of the chatter, I heard the faintest sound of a giggle. Can you believe that? In a noisy dance hall filled with laughter and music, my ears caught a hint of sweet giggle. I looked around, thinking that I was hearing things." He looked up and smiled at Ettie and Elsa-May. He seemed happy to tell them how he met Dorothy.

"It's lovely to have memories," Ettie said.

He continued, "I saw her sitting at a table with a lot of people. She wasn't just any girl. She was the prettiest girl I'd ever seen, bright green eyes shining underneath long lashes; she was as pretty as a movie star. One of those Hollywood starlet beauties, you know? They used to call them pin-up girls. Our eyes met as she continued to giggle with her girlfriend. She blushed and I blushed. My friends teased me and pushed me in her direction. I stammered. I didn't know how to speak to such a pretty woman."

"So, what did you do when your friends pushed you toward her?" Ettie asked, engrossed in his story.

A smile splashed across the old man's face. "I panicked, of course. Now, mind you, I never had trouble talking to women before, but this one...well, she made me nervous. I don't know whether it was her smile or her eyes or her perfectly coiffed blonde hair, but she did something to me. All I could muster was a 'hello.' Then, I stood there looking like a fool with a silly grin on my face." A hearty laugh escaped his lips.

Elsa-May asked, "Then, what happened?"

Shrugging his shoulders, he continued, "She answered me after she laughed at my awkwardness. I didn't care because at least she didn't shoo me away. We spoke for a few minutes. I don't know what we spoke about exactly. All I can remember is her beauty. I couldn't help but stare into her eyes. They were a shade of green I'd never seen before. Just beautiful and honest looking."

Leaning toward the women, he asked, "Do you know what I mean? How you can tell someone's a good person by the look in their eyes? I saw that with her. Everything about her, her alabaster skin and her not-so-done-up face told me she was real – authentic. I mean she wasn't all gussied up or looking like she was trying to impress." Swallowing hard, the old man put his hands to his head.

Elsa-May and Ettie knew that he was lost in the memory of that pretty girl he met at the dance. They sat in silence and waited for him to continue his story.

"Boy, I'll tell you. That woman made my heart sink into the pit of my stomach. I'd heard people use that expression, but I never experienced it before that night. Every word out of her mouth made my knees weak. My hands shook so hard I had to tuck them into my pockets so she wouldn't see. I'm sure she noticed, but she never said a word about them. I'll never forget the smell of her perfume, it hinted of lavender. Yup, even in a smoke filled dance hall, I could smell her sweet perfume. Every time I smell lavender, I think of her."

The two women looked at each other.

"Did you ask her to dance?" Ettie asked.

A broad grin preceded another round of hearty laughter before he answered. "You bet I did, but I wouldn't call it dancing. It was more of me tripping over my own feet while she pretended I wasn't an idiot. It worked out though. She didn't leave me standing on the middle of the dance floor. It gave us something to laugh and talk about later."

He shook his head. "She loved to dance. I loved to try to keep up with her. It gave me an opportunity to take in that sweet lavender scent and hold her tiny frame for a few moments."

Ettie asked, "What happened next?"

"After we danced?"

The two women nodded.

"Well, after I nearly broke my ankle and hers on the dance floor, she invited me to her table. Of course, her friends and my friends tried to be nonchalant about it, but we could hear their snickering. It didn't matter though. All I cared about was getting to know her better. Aside from her looks, she really was the sweetest thing and smart too. That awkward night proved to be one of the best nights of my life. What I wouldn't give to be able to dance with her again."

The old man breathed out heavily. "I can't wait to see her again; I thought I'd have to wait 'til I died. Does she have a phone number?"

"I suppose she might," Elsa-May said as she looked at Ettie who shrugged her shoulders showing that she wasn't sure.

"Can you get me her phone number? I'll give you mine, but I can see that you ladies are Amish and wouldn't have a phone, would you?"

"We can still use a phone," Ettie said, leaving out the information about her secret cell phone.

Elsa-May sucked in her lips and then said, "We haven't told her that you are alive. I'm sorry to say this, but there's a chance she might not want to see you."

The smile left Harold's face. "I'll have to abide by her decision. Please let me know what she decides, as soon as possible? I'd dare say she won't be happy when she hears I married Josephine."

Ettie and Elsa-May left Harold's place with his phone number.

"It must've been a nasty shock for him that Josephine told him that Dorothy had died, and then tricked him into marrying her," Ettie said.

Elsa-May nodded. "A terrible shock. Maybe he found out that she was a deceptive kind of person after they'd been married for a time."

"Maybe."

CHAPTER EIGHT

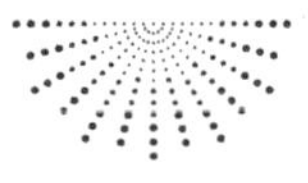

Charge them that are rich in this world, that they be not highminded, *nor trust in uncertain riches, but in the living God, who giveth us richly all things to enjoy;*
1 Timothy 6:17

Maureen hung up the phone after Ettie told her the situation from Harold's point of view. Harold had been deceived by Josephine Cutter into thinking that Dorothy was dead. Then he married Josephine almost out of a sense of gratitude or obligation for her helping him through his grief.

"How are we going to tell her that?" Maureen asked Emma.

"Should we tell her? She'll be devastated. She did tell us not to tell her if he was alive and hadn't bothered to find her. This is worse than him not trying to find her, isn't it?"

Emma and Maureen talked about it for a while longer before they decided that Dorothy should know what happened between her friend, Josephine, and her old beau, Harold.

~

THE VERY NEXT MORNING, Emma and Maureen knocked on Dorothy's door once more.

"Come in, come in," Dorothy said when she opened the door and saw them standing there. "To what do I owe the pleasure of your company again?" Dorothy asked.

"Can we sit down?" Maureen asked.

"Of course, I'll fix us some tea, shall I? I was just about to have some myself."

Maureen and Emma sat in the living room and looked at each other. Emma could scarcely stop her fingers from fiddling with the strings of her prayer *kapp.* She hoped that Dorothy would not be too upset at finding out that her best friend had lied to Harold and then married him.

When Dorothy appeared with a large serving tray, Maureen helped her carry it to the coffee table.

"I'll pour," Maureen said.

"Thank you, it's not often I'm waited on. Now, you two are looking very serious. Do you have bad news for me? I can take it. You don't have to be scared." The old lady brought the teacup to her lips, her eyes flitting between Maureen and Emma.

"We found Harold," Emma said.

Dorothy put the teacup back down on the saucer. "Is he dead?"

Maureen and Emma shook their heads.

"It's a complicated thing," Maureen started. "He is very much alive. He was married, but his wife died recently."

"He married, but where is he? They told me he was missing."

"He's living close to Lancaster County. Two of our friends went to visit him yesterday. He told them that he was in a war prison overseas, but he did come back a little time after the war had ended."

Dorothy pursed her lips. "Why didn't he come and find me?"

"He was told that you had died," Maureen said softly.

The old lady's two hands flew to her open mouth. She stared from Maureen to Emma then placed her hands back in her lap. "Who told him that?" she said, her voice croaky.

"That's the thing where it gets a little complicated." Maureen threw a sideways glance at Emma.

Emma raised her eyebrows and knew that she should be the one to deliver the sad news; after all, she was the one who found the letters and wanted to get them back to their owner. "You see, it was your friend, the one who went missing, it was she who told him that you died. The woman called Josephine Cutter."

Dorothy pushed herself back into the couch and was silent for a while. "How would you know that for sure?"

"Harold said so. I'm afraid that she went on to marry Harold."

Dorothy's mouth fell open, and her eyebrows rose. "Where's Harold now?"

"Lives close to Lancaster County. He's keen to see you if you want to see him," Maureen said.

"He knows I'm alive now?"

Maureen nodded. "He certainly does."

"You said that his wife had died. Does that mean that Josephine is dead?"

Maureen nodded. "I'm afraid Josephine died not too long ago."

Dorothy's eyes looked into the distance. "I always thought that Josephine liked Harold. Harold told me once that she made a play for him. I laughed at him and told him that he must have imagined it. Now, it falls into place, but I never thought she would be capable of doing what she did."

"Do you want to see him?" Emma asked.

"Yes, of course, I do. The past must be as water under the bridge. I've little time left for this world, and I'll not bear a grudge for the rest of it."

Emma and Maureen nodded.

"He's not able to travel; he's got a bad heart. You could come back on the train with us if you'd like to see him," Maureen offered.

"Of course I'd like to see him. When are you going back?"

Emma said, "We planned to go tomorrow, but we could stay a little longer if you won't be ready tomorrow."

"Thank you. I'll be ready for tomorrow. I've waited for this for many years." Dorothy gave a little laugh and clapped her hands together. "I can't believe this is happening." Dorothy leaned forward and took both Emma and Maureen's hand. "You two ladies are angels. God has sent you to make an old lady happy. I thank you from the depths of my heart for bringing my Harold back to me. If I just see his face before I die, that will make me a happy woman."

~

EARLY THE NEXT morning they called for Dorothy in a taxi and took her to the train station.

Once they settled into their train seats, Emma noticed that Maureen was looking around nervously. "Don't worry, it's hardly likely that he'll be on the train this time."

Maureen laughed and looked down into her hands.

"What's the matter, Maureen?" Dorothy asked.

Before Maureen could answer, Emma leaned over toward Dorothy who was sitting opposite. "When we were traveling on the train to see you, Maureen spotted an old beau on the train. We had to hide from him and couldn't even eat our meal that we had already paid for. It was when Maureen was younger; she cancelled her wedding just two weeks before marrying him."

Dorothy looked startled and turned to Maureen who was sitting next to her. "I thought you Amish would have arranged marriages."

Maureen drew her body away from her. "No, never."

Emma giggled. "We have our own choice who we marry."

"Oh, I'm sorry. So, you're not married, Maureen?"

"I was married, but unfortunately he became very ill for quite a few years before he died."

"I'm sorry to hear that Maureen." She looked across at Emma. "What about you, Emma?"

"I was married too and he died about a year ago."

"Emma's engaged to someone now, though," Maureen said with a smile.

"That's lovely," Dorothy said, "Did I tell you that I was once married?"

Emma and Maureen shot each other a look.

"No, we didn't know," Maureen said.

"Yes, it was five years after the war. I knew Harold wasn't coming home, and I met someone I thought was a nice man, but he turned out to be too fond of the whiskey and the women. We only lasted six months together before I filed for a divorce." Dorothy looked out the train window. "I never should've married him; I hoped that by marrying someone else it would take the pain of my Harold away."

Emma joined Dorothy in looking out the window and wondered whether she was trying to block the pain of losing Levi by marrying Wil.

The old lady looked back to Emma. "Tell me about your fiancé, what's he like?"

Emma smiled. "He makes me happy. He's carefree and makes me feel that I'm young again. He's always so full of energy."

"Goodness me, Emma, you are young, compared to me anyway. Is your man handsome?"

Emma nodded. "Yes, he is tall and quite handsome."

Maureen nodded in agreement.

Dorothy turned to Maureen. "Have you found yourself another man?"

"There is someone I like, but he's very quiet; maybe, a little too quiet. Sometimes I don't know what he's thinking, and it unnerves me."

"In what way?" Dorothy asked.

"It's just that I can't work out if we have things in common or if we think the same way on things because he never comments."

Dorothy took hold of Maureen's arm. "Take the advice of

an old lady, don't be in a rush." She looked over to Emma. "You too, Emma. You can't date someone else, or have a relationship with someone else when you are still in love with someone else, even if they are dead, or missing in action, assumed dead."

Emma shot a look at Maureen, and they both smiled at each other. Emma was always willing to listen to her elders. When Emma was younger she thought she knew it all, but as she matured she was grateful to listen to advice. Even though Dorothy was not Amish it did not mean that her advice was of no consequence.

"Were you talking about Bob Pluver just now, Maureen?"

Maureen nodded. Emma did not think that Bob was a suitable match for Maureen, and she hoped that Maureen would listen to Dorothy's advice about not rushing in.

"Tell me, Dorothy," Maureen said with a laugh in her voice, "Did you ever run into that man you married after you divorced?"

Dorothy laughed and put a hand to her mouth. "Heavens, no. I don't know where he's moved. I heard he moved away when I told him to leave the house for the last time. I would cross the other side of the street if I ever saw him walking toward me."

"So you're divorced now?" Emma asked.

Dorothy nodded. "You can't divorce in your religion, can you?"

Both Maureen and Emma shook their heads.

"It always seems that you Amish have an ideal lifestyle. Many of my neighbors were Amish, and they were always so nice and friendly. The children were always so polite. I'd see the children walk by to school as I worked in the garden of a morning."

Emma pictured the small front yard of Dorothy's house. It did have a nice garden, or would've been nice once upon a time before Dorothy moved.

"How do you like living in Florida?" Emma asked.

"I like the weather; it was far too cold in Lancaster County. Now it's warm and sunny all year round. At its coldest, I just need wear a light cardigan, and that's all." After a pause, Dorothy said, "Did I mention I have a son?"

The ladies shook their heads.

"A year after I married, I had a son, I called him Harold. He's still living near my old house, where he grew up."

"It must've been hard to leave him when you moved to Florida," Maureen said.

She shook her head. "He's busy now, with his own family. He'll visit me though. I've got a spare bedroom and the children, my two grandchildren, can sleep in the fold-out in the living room."

"Would you like to stay overnight at my place when we get to Lancaster? We can go and see Harold first thing in the morning," Emma said.

"Thank you, that would be lovely. You ladies have been so kind."

"I have to work tomorrow, so I'll have to leave you in Emma's hands," Maureen said.

~

Ettie and Elsa-May were excited for Harold and Dorothy to meet, so they had invited themselves to Harold's *haus* for the reunion.

Emma helped Dorothy out of the taxi. As they walked toward Harold's front door, Dorothy said, "I feel as though I'm going to burst. I hope he's not disappointed to see how old I've gotten."

Emma laughed. "Nonsense, everyone gets old, he's older too and you look lovely."

When they were nearly two yards away from the front door, it swung open, and Harold stood in the doorway with a huge smile covering his face.

Dorothy walked toward him with outstretched arms. He touched her hands and then they looked into each other's eyes before they hugged.

Emma looked past Harold to see Elsa-May and Ettie just inside the house. Ettie wiped a tear away from her eye, and Elsa-May smiled sweetly.

Once Harold and Dorothy finished their embrace, they looked into each other's eyes once more as their arms locked together.

"I can't believe it; I just can't believe it," Dorothy said.

"I don't know what to say, Dorothy."

Dorothy looked him up and down. "You don't need to say anything, it's so good to see you."

"Come inside," Harold said.

Elsa-May and Ettie disappeared back into the house while Emma and Maureen followed.

Harold briefly introduced Ettie and Elsa-May and Dorothy introduced Harold to Emma and Maureen.

"Thank you, ladies, for doing what you've done. I'm so grateful; you've got no idea what this means to me," Harold said with his arm around Dorothy.

Elsa-May grunted and said, "You two catch up with each other, and we'll make the tea."

Emma helped the three ladies in the kitchen.

"I found out that Dorothy was married briefly and has a son. She called her son Harold and he lives somewhere around these parts. She divorced his father a long time ago," Maureen told Elsa-May and Ettie.

"She most likely never got over Harold," Ettie said.

"I've been thinking that maybe he, the son, can drive her back to Florida when she's ready, or take her back on the train. She's a bit frail to travel by herself," Maureen said.

"I wonder how long she'll stay." Elsa-May put two teacups onto a tray.

"How did she take the news that her friend lied then married Harold herself?" Ettie poured the boiling water into the teapot.

"She seemed shocked, but she got over it quickly. Surprisingly fast," Emma said. "I've told Dorothy that she can stay at my place as long as she wants. I'm guessing she might stay a few days."

Elsa-May made her way to the living room with a tray of tea and teacups. Ettie and Emma followed with a plate of cookies and some of Elsa-May's jam tartlets.

Harold and Dorothy sat on the lounge holding hands. Harold looked up at the ladies when they walked in the room. "Dorothy's agreed to marry me."

"Oh, that's delightful news," Emma said as she placed the plate on the coffee table.

"We're going to live in my new home at the village. There's room for two," Dorothy said.

"Lovely," Elsa-May said.

"We're so happy for you." Emma was going to ask if she was going to see her son while she was here, but she did not know if Dorothy had mentioned her son to Harold yet.

"You ladies have been so good to both of us. I don't know how we can ever repay you for your kindness, but we will find a way, won't we, Harold?"

"Most definitely. We'll find a way," Harold said.

Emma shook her head. "We're happy that you two have found each other again. That's all we need."

"We should leave you two alone to catch up," Elsa-May said.

"Shall I call for you this afternoon, Dorothy? Around five?" Emma asked.

"No, dear. I'll get a taxi to your house. You can't be running around after me; you've done enough."

The widows said goodbye to Dorothy and Harold and they all left the house at the same time.

CHAPTER NINE

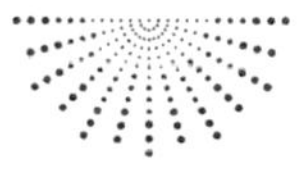

Offer the sacrifices of righteousness,
and put your trust in the Lord.
Psalm 4:5

Later that day, Emma met Silvie at the bakery/café where she worked. Silvie had just finished her shift and was able to sit and talk.

"You should have seen them, Silvie. It was as though they'd never been apart. They just took right back up where they'd left off, and now they're going to get married."

"It's so nice to be in love. It's funny how you can be instantly drawn to another person."

"Did you feel an instant attraction to Bailey?"

Silvie nodded. "I did."

"Harold is going back to live in her retirement home with her," Emma said.

"That was so horrible what her friend did to her. Elsa-May told me what happened." Silvie wrapped her hands around her *kaffe* mug.

Emma nodded and took a sip of her hot drink. "It was awful alright."

"I wonder how things would've turned out if her friend had still been alive when she found Harold, I mean, still married to Harold."

"That's a point. That would've been awkward for everyone involved with the lies that Josephine had told."

"It's odd how those letters sent you on a big adventure. Especially since the purchase of your *haus* didn't go ahead in the end. It was as if *Gott* arranged for you to see the letters and get the two of them back together."

"I didn't think of it like that. I wonder." Emma wondered if more than that *Gott* was teaching her about love. There was Maureen's ex-fiancé as well, which caused Emma to look at her relationship with Wil in a new light. There were also Dorothy's warnings not to rush into marriage with another man when you're in love with another, as Dorothy herself, had done.

"What are you thinking about, Emma?"

"*Ach,* sorry. Just thinking on the journey and how life takes different and unexpected turns." Emma ripped open a sachet of sugar and poured it into her *kaffe.* As she stirred her hot drink, she looked around the café. "Must be nice to get out and meet people like you do."

"You mean when I'm working here?" Silvie asked.

"*Jah*. I've been thinking I should get a part-time job, or do something." Emma had thought of opening a small business, but that was before she gave her nest egg to Wil for the house renovations.

"It is *gut* to get out and meet people. I've made a lot of friends from working here. Did you know many of the people come in every day?"

Emma nodded. "I'm going to think about a job. I've plenty of time on my hands. I could sew quilts like some of the ladies do, but I prefer to do something where I'm amongst people."

Silvie spread butter onto her hot banana bread. "You know that Sabrina's got a job now, don't you?"

"I believe you mentioned it; where's she working again?"

When Silvie finished her mouthful of banana bread, she said, "She's had two jobs, she didn't like either of them, but now she's working at the auction place. She says she likes it."

"That's *gut* that'll keep her out of trouble."

"I'm hoping it will." Silvie laughed.

An hour later, Emma opened the front door of her *haus.* She had no idea what time Dorothy would arrive back and assumed she might be back around dinnertime that night. She looked into the cold box to see what she could make for dinner.

She turned when she heard Growler behind her. "Hello, Kitty. What have you done today?" When she looked closer at Growler, she saw his paw was bleeding. She looked behind him to see blood had trailed all over the kitchen floor. She bent down. "Let me see your paw." Growler would not let her anywhere near his paw.

"You home, Emma?"

"I'm in the kitchen," Emma said recognizing Wil's voice. "Wil, it's Growler, he's hurt his paw."

Wil raced to the kitchen and bent down to take a look. Growler was no more interested in letting Wil pick up his paw than he was to let Emma pick it up. Wil sat on the floor and held Growler against his body and parted the long fur on his leg to see where the bleeding was coming from. "It's not too deep a cut. I'll just put some aloe vera on it, and it'll be fine. Do you still have that aloe vera plant?"

"*Jah,* shall I squeeze out the gel?"

"*Jah,* squeeze out about as much as you can cover on two fingers, make it a *gut* dollop."

Emma rushed out to the garden and pulled some aloe vera leaves and squeezed out the gel and hurried back to Wil.

Wil took the gel with his two fingers, while still holding onto Growler. "Good boy, Growler." Wil talked to Growler in soothing tones while he pasted the gel on his cut.

Growler growled a long, slow growl then leaped away from Wil. "Looks like he's been in a cat fight."

Emma watched Growler walk into the living room. "Are you sure he's okay or should I take him to the vet?"

"*Jah,* he'll be alright."

"I'll have to keep him inside for a while. At least until he heals."

Wil nodded. "I'll wash my hands outside."

Emma was pleased that Wil came just when he had. She was no good in a crisis. She wondered how she would be with *kinner* when they got hurt if she panicked when her cat was bleeding.

Wil came back in the back door wiping his hands on an old towel. "Emma, I came to talk to you about something quite serious."

"What is it?" Emma asked. This was the first time they had come face to face after finding out that the sale of the house Wil tried to buy had not gone through.

"I feel terrible about what happened with the house and you losing money. I will pay it all back to you."

Emma breathed out slowly and nodded, pleased that she would have the money to go ahead with a small business.

"I could still buy the house if I borrow against my farm."

"*Nee,* Wil, don't do that."

"I will if you want me to. If you love the *haus.*"

Emma shook her head. "It's a nice *haus,* but I feel as though we are best to wait until after we're married before we make a final decision. Didn't you say you had inherited money?" Emma did not like to talk about money, but he had mentioned that he had inherited money. Surely he would not have made that up.

Wil looked down. "I've loaned it to people in the community who were in need." He looked back up. "You know I can't ask for it back, don't you?"

"Of course I know. *Nee,* you can't ask for it."

"Will you live at my *haus* though, Emma? Or shall I live here? Or do we live separately once we're married until we have another *haus?*"

Emma was tired, and all his questions required thinking and she was far too weary. "I really don't know. Can we talk about this later? I'm tired from the big trip I've just had and I've got to plan dinner for Dorothy. She's coming back here tonight."

Emma said goodbye to Wil and watched at the door as he walked back to his place.

Remembering Growler's blood all over the kitchen floor,

she headed back to the kitchen. She grabbed a dishrag, wet it with water and wiped the floor.

She had barely finished, when she heard a knock at the door. She hoped it wasn't Dorothy so soon because she hadn't even had a chance to think about dinner. When she opened the door, she was shocked to see Detective Crowley.

He jumped back and stared at her. "Mrs. Kurtzler, who's dead now?"

Emma frowned until she realized she had a rag in her hand filled with blood. She laughed and put the rag behind her back. "Oh, Growler injured himself somehow." She stepped aside. "Come in and have a seat. I'll just get rid of this and wash my hands."

Moments later, Emma sat down in the small couch opposite the detective. "How can I help you?"

"I believe you have one Dorothy Welby staying here?"

Emma narrowed her eyes and nodded. "Yes, she was the one the letters belonged to, the one Maureen and I went to visit in Florida. Anything wrong?"

The detective shook his head. "Why is it Emma that you always land into the middle of things?"

Emma stared at him wondering what he was talking about.

"Mrs. Fielding, who used to go by the name of Josephine Cutter, died in a local hospital. She was there for a simple operation to have her tonsils removed and she died."

"There's a risk with all operations, isn't there?" Emma raised her eyebrows at the detective's silence. "Do you think she was murdered or something?"

The detective ignored her question and continued, "An

autopsy was performed, and it was revealed that she was given a lethal dose of insulin."

Emma's hand flew to her mouth.

The detective continued, "Were you aware that Dorothy Welby was once a nurse?"

"I don't think so, I can't remember whether she mentioned that or not. Surely you can't think that Dorothy had anything to do with it?"

The detective leaned back in his chair. "Mr. Fielding was not happy and claimed hospital negligence. I looked into things and asked around. The woman who was sharing the same hospital room as Mrs. Fielding says she saw an elderly lady around Josephine's bed shortly before she died. Nothing made sense, and there were no suspects until now."

Emma tilted her head to the side. "I'm not following you, Detective. What are you saying?"

"I brought up records of Dorothy Welby and found that she matches the description of the lady who was seen over Josephine's bed."

"Detective, surely all old ladies look the same. There would be thousands upon thousands of women with that same description. An old lady with gray hair of medium build five feet two inches. How many women would fit that description?"

"She has motive from what you ladies told me of Josephine Fielding's deception. At the time of Mrs. Fielding's death, Dorothy Welby did live close by."

Emma said, "You mentioned Mrs. Welby's record, does she have a criminal history?"

The detective shook his head. "No, I was speaking of her driver's license record."

"Detective, Dorothy Welby is a sweet old lady and not capable of doing anything like that. When we told her that Harold was alive, she had no idea, she was truly shocked."

The detective rose to his feet. "Of course, that's what impression she would need to have given you. She could not have turned up out of the blue and gone straight to Harold after she'd killed his wife." He shook his head slowly. "No. If she did kill Josephine Fielding, she would have gone underground and set about planning a legitimate way that she could be reunited with Harold. Such as, innocently leave a box of letters in her house for some 'do-gooder' to read and set about to re-unite them."

Emma thought that maybe the detective had been at the job for far too long if he thought that everyone was a murderer. "Detective, did you just call me a 'do-gooder'?"

"I meant no offence. The old lady needed a cover, a genuine way that she could be reunited with the old man after the wife happened to die. The way I see it, Dorothy knew she'd been seen and figured there would be an autopsy. She had to lay low and have everyone think that Josephine had been mistakenly given insulin by one of the hospital staff. Is it a co-incidence that a few days after Josephine died that Dorothy moved to Florida?"

Emma bit her lip, and wondered whether there might have been someone else who would have wanted Josephine dead. "Detective, are you joking with me? Or is this all true?"

"Emma, I'm not a joking kind of person. I wouldn't joke about something so serious. I went back to question the witness today, but unfortunately she had died." Detective Crowley walked toward the door. "Just thought you might like to know who you're entertaining in your house."

Emma stood in the doorway and watched the detective walk to his car. "Wait." She ran over to him. "Are you going to open up the investigation? I mean are you going to investigate things?"

"The witness is dead. Nothing would stick, and it's not likely she'd confess. Not much point going further, is there?"

Emma studied the detective's hard face. Maybe he'd been in the job far too long and had grown to be too suspicious of people. "Detective, you really should stop seeing a murderer behind every tree."

Detective Crowley looked at Emma for a moment before he got in his car and drove away.

Emma's head started to spin. She had the worry of the sale of the house not going through, and her nest egg gone; the last thing she wanted on her mind was the idea that she might be entertaining a murderer.

CHAPTER TEN

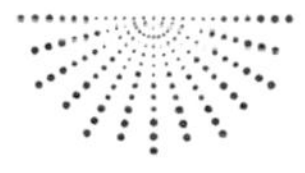

Offer the sacrifices of righteousness,
and put your trust in the Lord.
Psalm 7:1

Emma shelved the ridiculous thing the detective had told her of Dorothy Welby. There was no way that Dorothy would have done what Crowley suggested, besides Dorothy did not even know that Harold was still alive. The main worry on Emma's mind was whether she and Wil were suited to one another.

Silvie might be able to help her sort through her feelings. Emma left a note on her front door for Dorothy telling her to let herself in and that she would be back soon. Emma drove to Silvie's house, which was nearby, and was pleased to find her at home. Once she told Silvie that she had something to speak to her about, Silvie and she sat on the couch.

"Silvie, I don't know what I'm going to do. Did you hear that our new *haus* has fallen through?"

"*Jah,* but I don't know the details. What happened?"

Emma took a deep breath. "I've been trying not to think about it; that's why I didn't mention it to you when we had *kaffe.*"

"I knew you had something on your mind; I could just tell."

Emma nodded and continued with her story. "Wil bought the *haus* without telling me; that was the first thing."

"*Jah,* I know that," Silvie said.

"When Maureen and I were away meeting the old lady, she said that the sale of her house did not proceed and that's the first I learned of it. When I went back to the hotel, I phoned Wil, and he said that he was expecting some money to come through from one of his inventions. What do you think about that?"

Silvie opened her mouth to speak, but Emma continued, "He invented this plough thing and sent plans off to a company and then he expected them to send him a check for hundreds of thousands of dollars. Sometimes I wonder whether he's lost his mind. He signed for the house with no money to back it up."

Silvie covered her mouth with her hands and said nothing.

"It's worse than that. Since I thought that he had paid for the *haus,* only because that's what he told me, I said I'd pay for the renovations. I gave him twenty thousand dollars for the renovations, and he spent a lot of it, so now I've lost money." Emma took a deep breath and stared at Silvie. "I saved hard for that money and now most of it's gone."

"Wow, Emma I don't know what to say. Sounds like you've been through quite a bit."

Emma wiped a tear away from her cheek. "I don't know if I can see myself married to him now. Levi would never have done anything so flighty. I can't be with someone who does silly things and takes risks like that. I'm only a simple woman and just want a simple life. I don't need any grand things. I'm happy how I am."

"Have you told Wil this?"

"*Nee,* I don't know what to say to him. He knows I'm not happy about the whole thing, and we haven't really spoken of it. I don't want to upset him because I know he means well."

"You need to speak to him, Emma. You don't have to marry him; you can change your mind; it's not too late."

Emma stared at Silvie; those were the very words that Maureen's *mudder* had used when she was trying to stop Maureen from marrying the man they were hiding from on the train. Was it a sign from *Gott*? "I know I should speak to him. I just don't know where I would start or what I would say?"

Silvie sucked in her cheeks.

"I don't like talking behind his back like this, but I just need advice. I don't know if I'm thinking clearly. You know I'm not a gossip, don't you?" Emma asked.

"Of course, I do. I'm not thinking that at all. I'm thinking how hard it must be for you since you were so in love with Levi. It'd be hard for someone else to measure up."

"Exactly, that's what I'm struggling with. I know I keep comparing him and it's not fair to him. Every time he does something to upset me, I think to myself that Levi would've done things differently and that's hardly fair to Wil."

"What if it's not about being fair to Wil? What if you're just not ready yet?"

"It seems as if there's not an easy answer. I do love him, but I don't know if deep in my heart, I can go through with marrying him. Then I think, that there will never be anyone for me again, only Levi. I'm so confused."

"Sounds like you need time to think things through. Did the time away with Maureen help clear your head at all?"

"It might have if I hadn't found out as soon as I got to Dorothy's place that we hadn't bought the *haus* at all. I think I've been in shock. I'd better get home. *Denke* for listening to me and my troubles."

"Anytime, I wish I could've been some help to you."

~

WHEN SILVIE CLOSED the door after waving goodbye to Emma, she turned around to see Sabrina. "Sabrina, I thought you were at work today."

"*Nee*, remember I told you I wasn't working today? I worked yesterday."

"I can hardly keep track of the days and times I'm working without keeping track of your hours."

A smirk covered Sabrina's face. "So, Emma doesn't like Wil?"

"Of course she does, they're betrothed."

"Sounds to me like she's having a lot of second thoughts about him."

"It's normal for people to think things like that before they get married. Nothing to worry about." Silvie pushed past Sabrina and made her way into the kitchen.

"When I first came here, you told me to stay away from Wil because he was in love with Emma."

"*Jah,* he is in love with Emma and they don't need you trying to come between them."

"Sounds like she's not too happy about him though, doesn't it?"

"Sabrina, you should not listen in on other people's conversations. None of it concerns you."

"You knew that I liked Wil. You were the one who told me to stay away from him."

"You do have to stay away. Find someone else, Wil and Emma are getting married soon."

Sabrina crossed her arms in front of her chest. "I've a *gut* mind to tell Wil what Emma's running around saying to people about him."

"Sabrina, don't you dare. If you breathe a word, you'll be out of my *haus* in no time flat. Anyway, I thought Carmello Liante was the only man you could ever love."

Sabrina's mouth fell open. "Silvie, how could you? How could you mention his name?" Sabrina's face was red with rage as she stomped into her bedroom.

Silvie knew she was mean to mention Carmello's name, but it was only weeks since his death and Sabrina had sworn that she would never be interested in another man. Silvie had to say something to get Sabrina's mind off telling Wil about how Emma felt about him. Things like that should be left well alone.

~

EMMA OPENED the door of her *haus* and was met by Growler. "Hello, boy. What have you been up to?" Emma was pleased that Growler was finally acknowledging her presence. She looked down at his paw and saw that it was healing over nicely. *He probably knows I'm the one who feeds him, so he's realized he should be nice to me,* Emma thought. Growler followed Emma to the kitchen, and Emma filled up his food and water bowl.

Dorothy had not come home and Emma still had no idea what to have for dinner. There was sure to be something in the cold box she could heat up. Feeling tired and stressed Emma considered it was time to eat some chocolate to cheer herself up. She always kept a supply of milk chocolate, soft centers that she buys from the specialty chocolate shop in town.

She put her head back into the couch, closed her eyes and popped a soft center pineapple chocolate into her mouth and let it melt slowly. Emma felt better now that she had shared how she felt about Wil, but it did nothing to help her figure out what to do.

CHAPTER ELEVEN

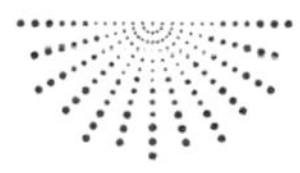

There is one lawgiver, who is able to save and to destroy: who art thou that judgest another?
James 4:12

Wil answered the knock on his front door and was surprised to see young Sabrina standing there.

He looked past her to see if she had come with Emma or her *schweschder,* Silvie. "Sabrina, you're here alone?"

Sabrina nodded, and Wil noticed that something with Sabrina was not right. Sabrina was normally smiling and happy. Knowing that it wouldn't be right to invite a young single woman into his *haus* even if it was very chilly out, he said, "Have a seat on the porch. Would you like some hot tea or something?"

Sabrina sat on the wooden porch seat after shaking her head in reference to the tea.

Wil sat in the chair beside her and rubbed his hands briskly together in an attempt to keep them warm. "What brings you here? Everything's alright, isn't it?"

"I've something to tell you," Sabrina said.

"*Jah*?" Wil asked after she stopped and did not continue.

"It's about Emma."

"What about her? I've only just seen her drive past in her buggy; she's home isn't she?"

"I've overheard something."

Wil frowned. "What is it?"

Sabrina's big blue eyes fastened on to him, and a frown lightly touched her forehead.

"Out with it, you're getting me worried."

Sabrina took a deep breath. "Okay, I'll just say it. Emma was talking to Silvie earlier today, and I heard her say that she's not happy with you."

Wil gave a chuckle. "I know, she's angry with me for making a mistake about a *haus* I tried to buy. Don't worry, she'll be okay when she has had time to calm down."

Sabrina turned her body to face him more directly. "*Nee*, Wil, you don't understand me. I'm saying that she said that she's having second thoughts about marrying you."

Wil shook his head. "Sabrina, what you heard is women's talk and you should not be repeating it. When you grow up you'll realize that when you repeat things you have heard, that you're creating trouble and spreading gossip."

"Wil, I am grown, I'm nearing twenty." Sabrina stood up.

Wil ran a hand through his hair. "Then, you should know better."

"Don't you want to know what she's saying about you?"

Wil shook his head slowly. "*Nee.* It would be best if you go back home."

Sabrina took a step toward him. "What? I'm telling you that the woman that you're so in love with is not in love with you, and you blame me? That's all the thanks I get? I thought you'd want to know." Sabrina put her hands firmly to her hips. "You should thank me."

Wil looked straight at Sabrina's buggy. "See that buggy?"

Sabrina turned, looked at her buggy, and said, "*Jah.*"

"I want you to get in that buggy and go home right now." Wil turned and went into his *haus* and shut the door.

Sabrina leaned close to the door and said in a loud voice, "I also heard Emma say to Silvie that Levi would never do all the stupid things that you do."

He tried not to let Sabrina's words hurt him. He stood leaning against his front door and listened to Sabrina's footsteps as she stomped down the two steps of the porch. Finally, he heard the clip-clop of horse's hooves heading back to the main road. He sank to the floor. He knew it was more than just women's talk; he could feel Emma slipping away from him and that's what prompted him to try and buy the *haus*.

He wasn't stupid; he could see through Sabrina's flirting ways. He could smell the strong rose and vanilla scent she used in an effort to woo him. He knew why she was giving him information about Emma's lack of interest in him. It was clear to him that Sabrina liked him; he knew that from the first day that Sabrina arrived in Lancaster County.

Wil's thoughts turned to the old *haus* he tried to buy. He could still buy the *haus* if he sold his farm, but then he would lose income, which he got from leasing the farm for crops. Alternatively, he could take out a loan against his farm, which is something he did not want to do. All the money he had inherited he'd loaned to people in the community and he could not ask for it back. He might have to take out a loan anyway, to pay Emma back for the money she lost on supplies for the *haus* renovations.

He'd find a way to pay Emma back and now, he'd have to go and speak to her. If she was having second thoughts about marrying him, it's best that he find out sooner rather than later.

He walked to her *haus* and knocked on the door.

"Wil, you don't usually knock." Emma looked into his face. "What's wrong?"

"You tell me," he said.

Emma pulled slightly back away from him. "What?"

"We need to talk."

Emma nodded. "Come to the couch."

As soon as they sat, Wil said, "I feel that things aren't the same between us lately. I have thought that you might be having some hesitations about marrying me. Before you answer, let me just say, I will pay you back every cent that you lost on the *haus*."

"Once you sell all the materials you bought for the *haus*, just pay me back half of what I lost. That way we both lose a little." Emma put her hand to her head and tried to work out whether what she had just said made sense. She realized it didn't, but Wil did not seem to notice so she kept quiet.

Wil lifted his hand. "*Nee*, it was my silly decision and I

dragged you into it. I will pay back every dime. Now, back to us. Tell me in all honesty, how you are feeling about us."

Emma took a deep breath. "I'm feeling confused about whether we should get married."

"When did all this start?" Wil knew deep in his heart that it had started a while ago.

"I'm not sure. I feel in my heart I love you, but I wonder whether we are a *gut* match in a lot of ways."

Wil nodded. "I understand. I don't like it, and I don't agree, but I understand. We can't get married if you feel like this."

Tears started to brim in Emma's eyes. Wil put his arm around her. "I'll still look after you. We'll still be friends."

Emma nodded. "I know. It'll be hard to let go." They were silent for a moment. "Wil, why did you come over here all of a sudden to speak about this?"

Wil pushed some strands of her dark blonde hair back beneath her prayer *kapp.* He knew it would cause a lot of trouble between friends if he spoke of Sabrina's visit. "I just thought it was the right time."

"I'll always love you, Wil."

"And I will always love you." Wil did not want Emma to see him cry. He looked at the low table in front of them and saw Emma's chocolates. "I'll be going now so you can eat your chocolate in peace."

"I'll walk you out."

CHAPTER TWELVE

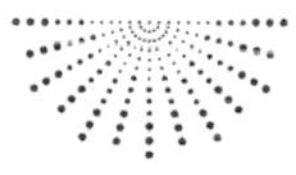

He that covereth a transgression seeketh love; but he that repeateth a matter separateth very friends.
Proverbs 17:9

After Emma closed the door on Wil, she felt sad, but at the same time, she felt a weight had lifted off her. She knew that she had to make a decision one way or the other. It wasn't so bad living alone especially since she had a lot of friends and thanks to Growler, her fat tabby, she was never truly alone.

Emma lifted her face upward. "*Denke, Gott* for helping me through." She hoped that Wil might tell the bishop of the cancellation. She knew people would talk and speculate on why they stopped their wedding, but Emma did not care.

No sooner had Wil left her *haus* than Dorothy came to the door.

"Dorothy, I've cooked dinner for us, but after dinner do you mind if I pop out for a couple of hours tonight? I've got a meeting to go to and I now you like to go to sleep early." Emma had the widows' meeting to go to that night, and she needed their support after everything she'd been through.

"I won't be staying. I've come to tell you that my son, Harold, is going to drive Harold and me all the way back to my home. My son, Harold, has offered me to stay at his place until Harold is ready to go to Florida. My son's picking me up in half an hour."

Emma rushed to hug Dorothy, "I'm so happy for you that you're with Harold finally. Do you need help to pack your things?"

"I'd like it if you come up and talk to me while I pack."

"Of course." Emma followed Dorothy up the stairs. "It might be confusing for you now with two Harolds."

Dorothy laughed a little. "Yes, it's already caused a bit of confusion. I was wondering if you and your friends might come to our wedding?"

"I'd love to and I'm sure that they would too. Thank you."

Dorothy sat on the bed and folded the few clothes that she had brought with her. "I don't know how I can ever repay you and Maureen for what you've done."

Emma sat down on the other side of the double bed and smiled. "It was our pleasure; it was lovely to meet you and Harold and I'm glad you ended up back together." Remembering the detective's words, Emma said, "I bet you were very angry with Josephine for lying to Harold about you being dead."

The old lady looked at Emma. "No, I'm not angry at all; everyone gets what's coming to them eventually. I got my Harold back as I was meant to and Josephine... well, she got hers."

Emma bit hard on her lip, and then asked, "What do you mean?"

Dorothy gave a bit of a chuckle. "Well, she's not here anymore is she? And what's more her thick jet-black hair that she was so proud of turned white and sparse, she was nearly bald."

Emma's blood ran cold. When did she see her last? Could she have been in that hospital room on the day she died? Could she have been the one to inject her with the fatal dose of insulin just as Detective Crowley suspected? *Nee,* she could have simply seen a photo.

Not long after Emma carried Dorothy's two small bags downstairs, her son, Harold, called for her in his car. Emma hugged Dorothy goodbye and waved as she drove away.

Emma sat on the couch and stroked Growler while she thought about what the detective had said. Could Dorothy have discovered Harold's whereabouts and waited for an opportunity for revenge? It did seem odd that she stopped checking for records of him. Did Dorothy deliberately leave the letters in the house so someone would reunite them? If she did cause Josephine's death she would not have gone to Harold straight away. She would have been careful of her next move, particularly if she knew that there was a witness.

If she did do it, Emma thought, *what gut would a life in jail do her? It's not as if she'd kill again. Gott is the one who gives the final judgment on the day of reckoning.* "Well, Growler, we'll probably never know, and sometimes that's the best way – not to know."

Growler looked at her and for the very first time since she had him, he purred.

~

LATER THAT NIGHT, Emma arrived at Elsa-May and Ettie's *haus* for the widows' meeting. After she tied her horse up she waited for Silvie who had just pulled up in her buggy.

"Emma, I'm glad, I can talk to you before you go in?"

"What is it, Silvie?"

"Sabrina overheard you and me speaking. I told her not to mention any of our conversation to anyone. I'm hoping she'll never mention anything to Wil."

Emma held her stomach and wondered whether she might have already repeated it. "Did she hear all of what we said?"

Silvie nodded. "I made her promise she would not say a word to anyone."

Emma relaxed. "That's *gut*. I thought she was at work today."

Silvie rolled her eyes. "My fault, I had the day wrong."

"Wil and I are not going to get married now." Emma felt sick to the stomach at her own words.

Silvie caught Emma by the arm. "What?"

Emma shook her head. "I'll tell everyone tonight. C'mon, they'll be waiting for us."

Emma and Silvie walked through Elsa-May and Ettie's front door.

Emma knew she would be able to think of little else the

whole night, so once everyone was seated she blurted out her news. "Wil and I are not going ahead with the wedding." When the words came from her mouth, she wondered if maybe she had made a huge mistake. She longed to be held in Wil's arms. Then she had to wonder, did she want only what she did not have?

Emma looked at everyone in turn, and no one looked shocked. "Well, isn't anyone going to say anything?"

Elsa-May spoke. "I think we saw it coming."

Emma frowned. "You did? I didn't see it coming."

"I think you did," Ettie said.

Maureen patted Emma on the shoulder. "It's best that you made that decision now. You're a long time married, you know."

Emma smiled and remembered how Maureen and she hid on the train away from Maureen's ex-fiancé. "I won't have to hide from him though," Emma said with a laugh in her voice.

"*Nee,* you won't." Maureen chuckled and then told the other widows in on her ex-fiancé and how they hid from him on the train.

Just as Maureen had finished her story, there was a knock on the door.

Ettie got up to answer the door, and Elsa-May leaned forward and whispered to the others, "That'll be Crowley."

Crowley walked in and nodded to the ladies then sat on the only chair left in the room.

Elsa-May said, "Emma is not getting married now. They've called the wedding off."

Emma felt heat rise to her cheeks under the detective's gaze.

She felt she should say something, but what could she say? She certainly did not owe anyone any explanation. Sadness over the loss of Wil as a future husband tugged at her heart. If love was acceptance, should she have accepted Wil just as he was?

"I'm sorry to hear that, Emma."

The detective's response surprised Emma with its sincerity. More surprising than that was the softness of his words.

Emma pressed her lips together and nodded her head in acknowledgement of his sympathy.

"I hope your grief didn't stop you from baking, did it, Emma?"

A laugh escaped her lips. She laughed at herself for thinking that there might be some softness about the detective, but his question proved he was totally insensitive. "It did, actually. I brought nothing with me today. No chocolate chip cookies and no chocolate sqaures."

"I've got chocolate cake, Detective." Ettie jumped to her feet and headed to the kitchen.

"I'll give you a hand, Ettie." Maureen rushed to help Ettie in the kitchen.

The detective smiled and looked at Emma.

Emma looked away from him and said, "My visitor has left. She's staying at her son's place until Harold is ready, and then they are both going to live in Florida, and they are going to marry."

"That's lovely," Silvie said.

"They were a lovely couple," Emma said.

"They were indeed," the detective said.

Emma wondered whether the detective was being sarcastic going by their earlier conversation regarding Dorothy.

Elsa-May placed a tray of cookies and cake in front of the detective. "So, how exactly did Josephine, Harold's wife, die, if I might ask?"

Emma held her breath and her eyes fastened onto the detective. He had more or less told her that even if Dorothy were guilty that there would not be enough evidence to convict her. Emma nibbled on a fingernail. The detective's theory was too far fetched to be true. Surely, Josephine had been given insulin by one of the hospital staff in error.

The detective reached for a cookie. "Stopped breathing," he said as he bit into the cookie.

Elsa-May gave a disapproving grunt at Detective Crowley's answer, but kept quiet and picked up her knitting.

Emma desperately hoped that no more would be said on the matter.

"Do you think it's odd that Dorothy never kept checking whether Harold had surfaced somewhere after the war? If she was so in love with him, it seems she gave up quite quickly," Elsa-May said.

"Elsa-May, you are seeing a murderer behind every tree. You really should stop being so suspicious of everyone," the detective said.

Elsa-May pursed her lips and her eyes fell to her knitting.

Emma looked up at Detective Crowley and his hard features softened into a smile, and he gave her a wink.

~

As Wil walked back to his *haus* from hearing the news that Emma did not want to marry him, he knew that he could not leave things there. He knew that Emma was the only one for him. *Dear Gott, if it is your will I ask you in desperation to bring my Emma back to me. If there is a way, I ask that you point me to it. Denke, Amen.*

Wil was only at home for five minutes before his friend Smithy knocked on the door.

"Come in. It's not like you to visit."

"David and I heard that the house fell through and we know that with all the money you've loaned people it would've been more than enough for a deposit."

Wil scratched his eyebrow. "I can't ask for it back."

"I've got four men organized to meet you at the bank at ten in the morning tomorrow. Altogether there'll be $42,020. That's your deposit right there."

"Can they afford it, Smithy? Do they still need it?"

"It's all been taken care of. Don't forget, ten tomorrow." Smithy hit Wil on the back of his shoulder and got in his buggy and drove away.

Denke, Gott, I didn't expect such a fast answer. I can get the haus back, and now I have to find a way to win Emma's heart.

Wil closed his door and went inside. He had to come up with a plan. Emma had always told him that he was too quick to jump into things. He would secure the house with a sizeable deposit and then he would tell Emma that they would have a fabulous life together.

The 'old Wil' would have raced to Emma to tell her that they could still buy the *haus* if she would have him back, but the 'new Wil', the 'Wil who thought things through,' would have everything in place before he spoke of it.

~

The next day while Emma was fixing her midday meal, she was deep in thought about Wil. She jumped when she heard a loud knock on her front door.

When she opened the door, she was glad to see Wil. "Wil, you don't normally knock, you usually walk straight in."

Wil ignored her comment. "Emma, will you come somewhere with me?"

"Where?"

"I have a surprise for you."

Emma frowned, and she knew by the look on Wil's face that he was up to something. "I don't know if my heart can take any more surprises."

"I think it will be able to take this one; I'm hoping anyway."

Emma agreed and went with him in his buggy.

After they had been driving for a while, Emma asked, "Is this the way to the *haus* we tried to buy?"

Wil looked over at her, smiled and said, "*Nee*."

When they pulled up outside the old *haus* Emma frowned. "Why did you bring me back here? You said we weren't coming here."

As they sat in the buggy outside the *haus,* Wil was silent for a moment before he spoke. "It's not the *haus* we tried to buy, Emma. It's the *haus* I've just bought. I've been able to put a sizeable deposit on it."

Emma put a fingernail to her mouth. "But how?"

"When he heard I couldn't raise money for the *haus,* without me knowing, Smithy rallied around and found the people I'd loaned money to and most of them had money ready to repay."

Emma opened her mouth to speak, but Wil raised his hand. "Emma, I know I've been unreliable and I know that's not how a provider should be. I should never have taken a risk like I did with the *haus* that first time. I give you my solemn word that I will be more practical, and I will even make plans. I'm asking you again, to leave the past behind us. Emma, will you marry me?"

In that moment Emma realized that she was at fault just as much as he. She was living in the past and expecting Wil to be someone he was not. Wil showed he could change and be more responsible, and if he could do that then she could be less rigid and live in the present.

Emma nodded. "*Jah,* I will marry you."

Wil reached his arm around Emma and pulled her toward him. "I've got enough money to give you back your contribution, too."

"*Nee,* keep that, Wil. Put it toward the *haus* so I will feel a part of it."

Wil shook his head. "You are a part of it, a part of everything I do from now on. And, I give you my word that I will be responsible, I will talk things over with you and we will plan things together. I will be a strong and proper husband for you."

Deep in her heart, Emma felt secure and safe, at last. She sniffed back her tears. "I'm sorry, Wil, that I called things off; I was confused, it wasn't that I didn't love you."

Wil laughed. "I'm glad you called it all off, Emma. It made me realize that I had to think of someone beyond myself. I had to grow up and become a better *mann.*"

Emma was lightheaded and dizzy as Wil pulled her toward him and touched his lips softly on hers.

~

But without faith it is impossible to please him: for he that cometh to God must believe that he is, and that he is a rewarder of them that diligently seek him.

Hebrews 11:6

AMISH SECRET WIDOWS' SOCIETY

Book 1 The Amish Widow
Book 2 Hidden
Book 3 Accused
Book 4 Amish Regrets
Book 5 Amish House of Secrets
Book 6 Amish Undercover
Book 7 Amish Breaking Point
Book 8 Plain Murder
Book 9 Plain Wrong
Book 10 That Which Was Lost